CITY ASCENDANT

C000144435

Christopher Mitchell is the author of the epic fantasy series The Magelands. He studied in Edinburgh before living for several years in the Middle East and Greece, where he taught English. He returned to study classics and Greek tragedy and lives in Fife, Scotland with his wife and their four children.

Brigdomin Books Ltd
First Edition, October 2021
ISBN 978-1-912879-65-6

For Lee

ACKNOWLEDGEMENTS

I would like to thank the following for all their support during the writing of the Magelands Eternal Siege - my wife, Lisa Mitchell, who read every chapter as soon as it was drafted and kept me going in the right direction; my parents for their unstinting support; Vicky Williams for reading the books in their early stages; James Aitken for his encouragement; and Grant and Gordon of the Film Club for their support.

Thanks also to my Advance Reader team, for all your help during the last few weeks before publication.

DRAMATIS PERSONAE

The Aurelians
>**Emily Aurelian,** Queen of the City
>**Daniel Aurelian,** King of the City
>**Elspeth Aurelian,** Princess of the City
>**Lady Aurelian,** Daniel's Mother
>**Lord Aurelian,** Daniel's Father
>**Lady Omertia,** Emily's Mother

The Mortals of the City
>**Quill,** Blade Commander
>**Rosie Jackdaw,** Artificer Blade
>**Inmara,** Reaper Guard, Salve Mine
>**Darvi,** Reaper Guard, Salve Mine
>**Achan,** Hammer Leader

The Former Royal Family
>**Amalia,** Former God-Queen
>**Montieth,** Prince of Dalrig
>**Mona,** Rebel in Jezra
>**Salvor,** Prisoner, Ooste
>**Naxor,** Simon's Lackey
>**Yvona,** Governor of Icehaven
>**Amber,** Elder Daughter of Prince Montieth
>**Jade,** Leader, Salve Mine Expedition
>**Lydia,** Governor of Port Sanders
>**Doria,** Courtier in the Royal Palace

The Lostwell Exiles
>**Kelsey Holdfast,** Blocker of Powers

Van Logos, Commander of the Banner
Lucius Cardova, Officer in the Banner
Flavus, Scout in the Banner
Silva, God; Descendant of Belinda
Felice, God; Governor of the Bulwark
Kagan, Amalia's Consort
Maxwell, Son of Amalia and Kagan
Vadhi, Kelsey's Guard

The Exiled Dragons
Deathfang, Dragon Chief
Burntskull, Deathfang's Advisor
Darksky, Deathfang's Mate
Frostback, Deathfang's Daughter
Halfclaw, Green & Blue Dragon
Dawnflame, Blue & Purple Dragon
Bittersea, Dawnflame's Mother
Firestone, Dawnflame's Son

Ascendants
Simon, The Tenth Ascendant

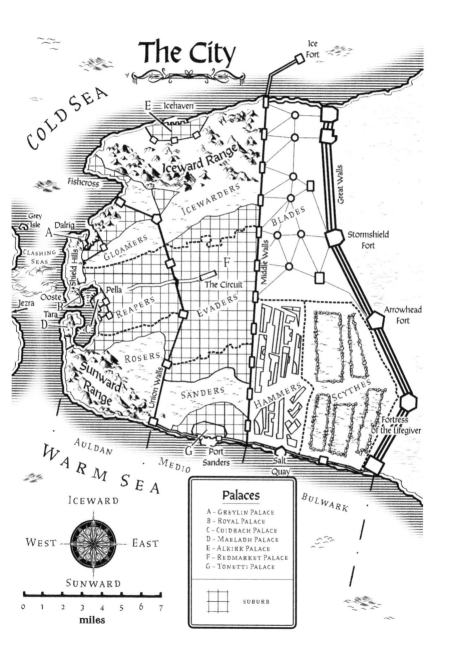

CHAPTER 1

CRITICAL ASSET

Jezra, The Western Bank – 21st Monan 3422

Kelsey Holdfast woke with a start. An oil lamp was flickering in the small, windowless room, providing enough light for her to see four soldiers surrounding her bed. For a moment she almost panicked, her eyes wide as she glimpsed the crossbows, swords and armour.

'Morning, ma'am,' said one of the soldiers, a sergeant.

Kelsey said nothing, her hands pulling the thin blanket closer to her body.

'The major-general wants to speak to you as soon as you're ready,' the sergeant went on.

'Did you come to fetch me?' she said.

'We've been here all night, ma'am.'

'You've been watching me sleep?'

'Orders, ma'am. We're here in case the Ascendant tries to use the Quadrant to assassinate you. You've been designated as a critical asset.'

'Me?'

'Yes, ma'am; you and her Majesty are to have close protection, day and night.'

'Oh. Well, I, uh, need to get washed and dressed. You can leave the room for five minutes, can't you?'

The sergeant nodded to a colleague, who hurried through the doorway. A few seconds later, he returned, escorting a young woman into the room.

'Vadhi?' said Kelsey. 'What are you doing with a crossbow?'

The Brigade Exile smiled nervously. 'I've been assigned to you, ma'am,' she said. 'I'm supposed to follow you round, whenever you need some privacy.'

'Private Vadhi will accompany you on your visits to the washrooms and bathrooms,' said the sergeant. 'She will remain in here while you get changed.'

Kelsey groaned. 'Come on, guys. You're taking it all a bit too far, don't you think?'

'Orders are orders, ma'am,' said the sergeant. 'We'll be waiting outside.'

The sergeant gestured to the other three soldiers, and they walked from the room, leaving Vadhi alone with Kelsey.

'Sorry about this, ma'am,' said the young Exile.

Kelsey frowned at her. 'You're not coming with me to the toilet.'

'Captain Cardova told me I had to go everywhere with you, ma'am,' she said. 'He told me that you would complain about it, but that I was to ignore you. He's really worried that the Ascendant god will try to abduct or kill you.'

'If Simon wants to get me while I'm sitting on the toilet, then good luck to him.' She sighed. 'Bollocks. Look, I need to get dressed.'

Vadhi pointed to a neat pile of clothes sitting on a chair. 'There's a fresh uniform here for you, ma'am.'

'Stop the "ma'am" crap. I'm not a bloody officer; I'm just Kelsey.'

Vadhi's face flushed, but she said nothing. Kelsey pulled the blanket from her and reached for the pile of clothes.

'I might start sleeping fully dressed, if this is how it's going to be,' she said, as she pushed her arms into the sleeves of a tunic. 'I assume there was no attack during the night?'

'Nothing, ma...; I mean, nothing. The defences were on full alert, but there's been no sign of Simon or any of the others overnight. That's because of you. Captain Cardova said that if it weren't for you being here, then we'd all be dead by now.'

Kelsey pulled on a skirt, then laced up her boots. Memories of the previous day rattled round her mind, and a wave of guilt settled in the pit of her stomach. If she had acted differently, then Pella would still be in their hands. She remembered the sight of the hundreds of dead Banner soldiers floating upon the waters of the bay, their ships reducing to burning wreckage.

She stood. 'Have you ever used a crossbow before?'

'In training,' said Vadhi. 'I've never loosed at a real person, but the Banner showed me what to do.'

Kelsey pushed open the door. In truth, she had forgotten exactly where she had been sleeping. She knew it was somewhere within the huge Command Post building close to the harbour of Jezra, but she had been too exhausted to pay much attention to the room where she had been led the night before. The four soldiers were waiting in the corridor outside for her, and the sergeant nodded.

'Why is it so cold?' said Kelsey.

'Heating oil is being rationed, ma'am,' said the sergeant.

'Already?'

'The commanders of the Exiles have been up all night, ma'am, implementing a series of emergency plans. Now, if you would please follow us; we'll take you to see the major-general.'

They moved off along the corridor, and ascended a flight of stairs. Soldiers were everywhere, crowding the hallways, and guarding every landing and doorway. Everyone saluted Kelsey as she passed, and several soldiers gave her a grim smile. They came to a wide hallway, and Kelsey recognised where she was within the building. She was led into Van's private quarters, which were packed with people. Soldiers dominated, but there were also Fordian merchants from the town, and a mass of Brigade staff. Sitting on a couch surrounded by troops were

Queen Emily, Lady Omertia and Silva, with a small cot close by. Emily noticed Kelsey enter, and waved her over.

'I'll inform the major-general that you are here, ma'am,' said the sergeant. 'Sit with the Queen while you wait.'

Kelsey nodded, then squeezed between the armoured soldiers towards Emily. Vadhi stuck close to her all the way over to the couch. Kelsey sat, and exhaled.

'Sleep well?' said Emily.

'Alright. You?'

'I've been awake all night,' said Emily.

'Any news on Daniel and Elspeth?'

Emily nodded. 'Chancellor Mona found them with her vision powers during the early hours of this morning. They're alive. Daniel is being held inside the dungeons under the Royal Palace in Ooste.'

'Ooste?'

'Yes. Simon seems to be basing himself there, along with Naxor and Felice. Doria is looking after Elspeth; they haven't harmed her.'

'Thank Pyre for that,' Kelsey said. 'I wonder why they've chosen Ooste.'

'Cuidrach Palace is still burning,' said Emily. 'My home has been destroyed.'

'Where is Mona now?'

'Sleeping,' said Silva. 'She exhausted herself using her powers. I will alert the Banner if any of the immortals leave their current locations.'

The sergeant returned. He bowed before the Queen, then turned to Kelsey.

'The major-general will see you now, ma'am.'

Kelsey got up, and Vadhi accompanied her to Van's office. Inside, Van was sitting at his desk, while Cardova was standing by the window, half an eye on the harbour below them. The captain looked tired, but Van's eyes were sparkling with energy.

'Let me guess,' Kelsey said; 'you've been awake all night too?'

'I have,' said Van; 'there was too much to organise. To be honest, I fully expected an assault during the night.'

Kelsey sat. 'And you never thought to wake me?'

'We considered that, but felt it better to let you rest. I have a few ordinances that affect you. First, you are not to leave the Command Post, ever. Understand?'

'But...'

'This is not up for debate, Kelsey. You are the only reason that the assault didn't come. You must remain in this building, and you must have guards with you at all times.'

'What if I just walk out of the front doors?'

'The soldiers on duty have been ordered to prevent you from doing so.'

'Am I a prisoner?'

'You are too valuable to risk. Simon ran circles around us yesterday, and he was successful because we divided our forces. That will not happen again. Our priority is to protect the rightful Queen of the City, and you are an essential part of our defences.'

'If it comes to it, would you lock me up?'

'Yes.'

Kelsey shook her head.

'You were close to Simon for a moment yesterday,' Van went on. 'Tell me exactly what happened.'

'Alright. Frostback and I were racing towards Pella. We could see the smoke rising from the palace, and knew that we were too late. Frostback saw a figure up on the roof of the main gatehouse. There are no ballistae on Cuidrach, so we went in for the attack. I could sense the Ascendant's fire powers, so we knew we had the right target, but then we saw the King lying on the ground next to him, and, at the last minute, we also saw that the Ascendant was holding onto a baby. Frostback managed to close her jaws in time, and we sort of hovered over the roof. Simon stared up at us, his face... well, he looked a little surprised, let's put it that way. He pulled out the Quadrant, and whisked them away. I couldn't sense where he went to, so we headed out into the bay.'

Van nodded. 'He's scared of you. Good.'

'We were too late.'

'No. You appeared in time to save the life of the Queen.'

'How many Banner soldiers died?'

'Five hundred and eighty-six soldiers of the third regiment are either missing or dead. Chancellor Mona has confirmed that every Banner soldier who managed to swim back to shore was executed, but a few may have escaped. She has also confirmed that the entire Royal Guard has been slaughtered – all four hundred of them. After that, the Reaper militia formally surrendered to Simon. As of this moment, only the Banner remain loyal to the Crown – Simon holds the rest of the City.'

'Will the Banner stay loyal?'

Van and Cardova exchanged a glance.

'So far,' said Van.

'What's that supposed to mean?'

'There are over twenty thousand Exiles living in Jezra, Kelsey,' he said. 'The Banner forces comprise a tenth of that figure. The rest are made up of eleven thousand Brigade Exiles, and seven thousand civilians from Lostwell. As well as that, we have two thousand on the Grey Isle, split equally between Banner and Brigade, and half that number in Westrig. That's around twenty-four thousand people we are responsible for. If we are to hold out against Simon, we need a majority of those living here to agree.'

'But, you are the commander.'

'I am, but with the King being taken into custody, the clauses of the Banner contracts are under examination. The Combined Council are meeting as we speak, and I am bound to follow their recommendations. If they come to the conclusion that we should surrender, then I will resign from my post.'

'Shit. Does the Queen know this?'

'Yes. She asked if she could speak to the council, but they refused.'

'Can they do that?'

'The Combined Council are elected by the Banner and Brigades,' said Cardova from by the window. 'Without their assent, we have no mandate.'

'The good news is that if they agree,' said Van, 'then we'll all be in it together.'

'I'm not too worried about the Banner representatives on the council,' said Cardova; 'after all, Simon has made his intentions towards the Banner crystal clear – he means to annihilate us, whether we surrender or not. It's the reaction of the Brigades that concerns me.'

'The Brigades will never surrender,' Vadhi blurted out.

Van raised an eyebrow. 'Thank you for that. However, I'd ask you to focus on your job, Private.'

'About that,' said Kelsey; 'does she really have to follow me into the bathroom?'

'Yes. We are facing an Ascendant with a Quadrant, Kelsey. We have to assume that, if he gets a chance to kill you, then he will grasp at it.'

'But, he can't see me with his powers.'

'I know. However, he will have most likely read the minds of a few captured Banner soldiers before killing them, so we must assume that he knows the layout of this building. Do you remember when I snatched you from under the noses of Leksandr and Arete in Yoneath? If I can do that sort of thing, then it's well within Simon's capabilities. If you're not comfortable with Private Vadhi, then I will assign someone else.'

'No. If it has to be someone, then I trust Vadhi. Can I go onto the roof?'

'Yes; as long as you are escorted while there.'

'Can I go and see Frostback, then?'

'She's not on the roof,' said Cardova; 'she's patrolling.'

Kelsey frowned. 'Without me?'

'Don't worry; she's remaining at a safe altitude. Her eyesight can pick out any ships moving towards Jezra while Mona is resting.'

There was a knock at the door and an officer peered into the room.

'Sorry, sirs,' he said, 'but the quartermaster is here to discuss the supply situation.'

'Thank you, Lieutenant,' said Van. He glanced at Kelsey. 'That will be all for now.'

Kelsey stood. 'Where are you living? Have you given the Queen your apartment?'

'I have. I'll be sleeping on the couch. That room where you slept last night is now yours. I can have someone go to your house to pick up your things. That uniform makes you look like a soldier.'

Kelsey stared at him for a moment. From his eyes, she was sure that he had taken salve – he seemed restless and alert; too alert for someone who had been up all night working. She frowned, nodded, then left the room.

Despite the chaos in the Command Post, the next few hours passed slowly for Kelsey. She sat in Van's main living room, on a seat opposite the dozing Queen, while soldiers, Brigade officials and Jezran civilian leaders bustled to and fro. Her escort detail changed after breakfast, and four new guards took up position next to where she was sitting, with Vadhi also close by. The Queen had double the number of guards assigned to her, and had been given a leather cuirass to wear over her dress. Kelsey watched her for a while as she slept on the couch, trying to imagine what it would feel like to know that your husband and daughter had been captured. Maxwell cried, the noise in the apartment too loud for him to rest, and Silva and Lady Omertia took turns in trying to quieten him.

Mona appeared around noon. She went into Van's office, then reappeared a few minutes later, and walked over to sit by Kelsey. She glanced at the form of the sleeping Queen, then bowed her head.

'Lady Lydia has visited Ooste,' she said, 'and has knelt before Simon.'

'Are we surprised?' said Kelsey.

'No. I am disappointed, but not surprised. Lady Doria has also submitted, but I find it hard to blame her. She has no powers beyond long life, and would have had no choice. At least Princess Elspeth has

8

someone like Doria looking after her. The child is safe, for the moment.'

'That's because we have Maxwell,' said Silva. 'What's Amalia doing? I could sense that she was in Ooste last night, but she has returned to Tara.'

'The Roser militia and merchants' guild have submitted to her in Maeladh Palace,' said Mona; 'but I haven't been inside the former God-Queen's mind. She is too powerful for me.'

'What happened to Salvor?' said Kelsey. 'Is he dead, or has he also submitted?'

'Neither,' said Mona. 'He was captured in Cuidrach along with the King, but he refused to kneel before Simon. The Ascendant put him in the dungeons.'

'I should go and get him,' said Kelsey. 'The King and Elspeth too. I could take Frostback, and Simon wouldn't be able to stop us.'

'I'm afraid not,' said Cardova.

They glanced up, and saw the captain join them by the couches.

'Why?' said Kelsey.

'It's simple. The moment that Simon realised that you were in Ooste, then he'd use the Quadrant to come here to kill everyone. You are the eye at the centre of the storm, Kelsey. You are the shield behind which we all huddle.'

Kelsey groaned.

'I had better go,' said Mona. 'There's a room on the far iceward side of the building that lies just outside your blocking range, Kelsey; it's where I've been conducting my vision surveys.'

'I'll walk you down the stairs,' said Cardova. 'Kelsey, do you wish to come? I'm going to check in on the meeting of the Combined Council on the ground floor – they have an announcement for us.'

The Queen opened her eyes. 'Do they?'

'Your Majesty,' said Cardova; 'I thought you were asleep.'

'No; just half-dozing,' Emily said, sitting up. 'It's impossible to sleep with all this noise. I'll come too.'

Cardova turned to face the room. 'Clear a path! Her Majesty is leaving.'

The guards formed up into a large group, and escorted Kelsey and Emily through the busy room. Soldiers went on ahead, to secure the stairs, while more soldiers pushed back the crowds of Brigade Exiles and civilians. Some started shouting out messages, or requests for help, to the Queen as they passed, and Kelsey watched as Emily tried to smile at them. They descended to the ground floor of the Command Post, and through the pandemonium of the hallways. The large chamber where the Combined Council had been meeting was packed out, with more Brigade workers and officials trying to get in. The soldiers cleared them from the entrance, and Kelsey and the Queen were led inside.

At once, the noise in the chamber fell, as every eye turned to the Queen. The members of the council were gathered round a long table by one end of the chamber, and they stood as Emily entered. Soldiers moved the spectators aside, and Emily approached the table, Kelsey at her side.

'Your Majesty,' said one of the council, bowing.

The other members of the council did the same, and then the rest of the crowd followed suit, each bowing low towards Emily.

'The Combined Council has come to a decision, your Majesty,' said the council member who had first spoken, 'and we remain your loyal subjects. The Banner and the Brigade are unanimous – we will follow you in this hour of crisis. Simon is a usurper, and we will stand against him, your Majesty. Command us.'

Emily stared at the council members for a moment, and Kelsey could see her battling to keep all emotion from her features. She turned to face the watching crowds.

'Thank you,' she said. 'I will try to be worthy of your loyalty, though I have nothing to offer except more pain and hardship. We will fight Simon, and we will fight the traitors who have abandoned us; and we will prevail. All that matters is victory, for without victory, there will be no Jezra, only extinction. We have the best soldiers in the City, and the Brigades have been forged in the heat of the struggle against the greenhides.' She gestured to Kelsey. 'We also have the dragon rider; the only person on this world that Simon fears. Thanks to her, we know that if Simon dares to set foot on the Western Bank, we shall kill him; without mercy, and without hesitation. We will turn Jezra into a fortress, an unassailable stronghold; an oasis of safety amid a world of enemies. I understand those of you who are scared. To many in the Brigades, it must seem as though the fate of Lostwell shall also be our fate, but I tell you now that I will never surrender to Simon, even though he holds my husband and my daughter prisoner. The Ascendant has made a mistake coming here; he might not realise it yet, but he soon will; I promise you, he soon will.'

The crowd remained silent, then one of the Banner officers cheered, and the hall erupted in noise; a deafening cacophony of defiant cries and shouts. The cheering grew so loud that Kelsey could barely hear herself think. Emily took Kelsey's hand, and raised it high above their heads, and the volume of noise increased.

Cardova signalled to the guards, and they formed a flanking position around Kelsey and the Queen.

'We should let the major-general know of this, your Majesty,' he said to Emily.

The Queen nodded. The soldiers began to move off through the crowds.

'Did you mean that?' Kelsey whispered, as they left the chamber. 'That bit about your husband and daughter? What if Simon threatens to kill them?'

Emily glanced at her. 'I told them what they needed to hear. But, yes; I meant it. We cannot trust any promises Simon makes.'

'You have nerves of steel, Queenie.'

'I'm glad it looks that way. Trust me; it's not how I'm feeling on the inside.'

They started back up the stairs, when a soldier ran into them.

'I have a message from Chancellor Mona, sir,' he cried, coming to a halt in front of Cardova. 'Dragons are approaching from iceward.'

Lucius nodded. 'Kelsey; you're with me. Lieutenant, escort her Majesty back to the major-general's quarters – we are going to the roof.'

'Yes, sir.'

'I shall follow you up onto the roof, Lucius,' said Emily, 'once I've spoken to Van.'

Cardova bowed his head, and then they set off. Kelsey held her breath as Cardova led her away from the Queen. They raced up another flight of stairs, Vadhi and Kelsey's guards hurrying to keep up, then emerged out into the winter sunshine on the flat roof of the Command Post. Cardova scanned the pink skies, then pointed upwards.

'Frostback is descending,' he said. 'Kelsey, stay close to me.'

She gazed up into the sky towards iceward, and saw two tiny specks against the purple light. A gust of air hit her from above, and she looked up to see Frostback, her silver wings extended as she lowered herself down to the roof.

'Rider,' she said, turning her long neck to gaze at Kelsey. 'My father is on his way, with Halfclaw.'

'Halfclaw?' said Kelsey. She staggered in relief. 'He's alright?'

'It seems so. My beloved rider, my heart is beating like a drum. Yesterday, when I thought that Halfclaw might have fallen, I realised how dear he is to me. We have known each other since we crawled out of our eggs; I love him, Kelsey. If he still wants me, then I shall commit myself to him this day.'

'Of course he wants you,' said Kelsey; 'he's wanted nothing else since we got here.'

They quietened as the two dragons approached. The massive Command Post was large enough for three dragons to fit onto the roof, and they edged back to make space. Deathfang was the first to land, his enormous grey bulk making the building tremble, while Halfclaw alighted a dozen yards from him.

Cardova spread his arms out. 'Greetings, dragons. Halfclaw, might I say how relieved I am to see you? We thought that the Ascendant had cut you down.'

'He did,' said the green dragon. 'I was dead for a few seconds, it seems. Jade revived me.'

'Jade?' said Kelsey. 'Is she alright?'

'Yes,' said Deathfang; 'she returned with Halfclaw, along with some soldiers from the Blades.'

'Including me,' said a voice.

They looked up, and saw two figures clamber down from the harness round Halfclaw's shoulders.

'Adjutant Quill,' said Cardova, grinning. 'And Lieutenant Flavus; welcome.'

The lieutenant saluted Cardova. 'Good afternoon, sir. I thought I'd accompany the dragons back here – we needed to see what was happening in the City. Indeed, we needed to know if the City still stood.'

'Simon is in control of everywhere except Jezra,' said Cardova.

Frostback turned to Halfclaw, her red eyes burning. 'Fly with me.'

Halfclaw tilted his green head, then the two dragons took off. They circled Jezra once, then sped off to sunward.

'Young love,' said Deathfang, gazing up at them.

'I think you might be right, big guy,' said Kelsey.

There was a noise to their left, and Kelsey turned to see the Queen and Van stride towards them across the roof, with soldiers on either flank.

'Greetings, Queen of Jezra,' said the grey dragon.

'And to you,' she said. She smiled at Quill. 'Nice to see you again, Adjutant.'

Quill bowed. 'Lady Jade also survived, your Majesty.'

'Excellent; I am greatly relieved to hear that. How goes it in the mountains, Deathfang?'

'Well enough, for the moment,' said Deathfang. 'Jade and little Jackdaw are at the mine, along with their soldiers. There has been no sign of any Ascendant.' He glanced around at Jezra. 'So, this is all that remains of your realm? What happens next? Will you surrender to the Ascendant, or will you fight?'

'I mean to fight on,' said Emily. 'And you? The Ascendant will learn about the existence of the salve mine in the mountains before too long, if he doesn't already know. Your refuge there might come under pressure.'

'It may,' said the dragon. 'I have killed an Ascendant before; I do not fear them.'

Van smiled. 'You had Kelsey with you then, and she will be staying here. I recommend that you withdraw further sunward. Your colony won't stand a chance if the Ascendant chooses to attack.'

Deathfang stared at him.

'Are there orders I can pass on to Lady Jade, sir?' said Flavus. 'Should we sit tight at the mine?'

'I believe that my husband relayed certain secret orders to Lady Jade,' said the Queen. 'When you return to the mountains, please ask her to act on them.'

Flavus bowed. 'I shall, your Majesty.'

'What secret orders?' said Kelsey.

Emily glanced at everyone present. 'If the Ascendant has read my husband's mind, then he will know about the mine, and he will know what the King ordered Jade to do. Even so, I must ask that you keep this to yourselves.'

Cardova gestured to the closest guards, and they moved back out of earshot.

'Well, Queen?' said Deathfang. 'We are waiting.'

'My husband's orders were simple,' Emily said; 'Jade is to destroy the mine, and all of the salve within it.'

CHAPTER 2

THE DARK BLADE

Jezra, The Western Bank – 23rd Yordian 3422

Mona's eyes snapped open. 'I've located the King, your Majesty. He's still in the Royal Palace, but he has been moved to a cell within the Ascendant's private wing, close to where Lord Salvor is being held.'

Emily nodded, a blanket covering her shoulders in the small, cold room. 'How does he look?'

'He doesn't seem to have been injured in the move, your Majesty, though he remains shackled. Shall I enter his mind?'

'Yes, please. If you don't, he'll worry about us.'

'Very well, your Majesty.'

Mona's eyes glazed over, and Emily waited.

Next to her, Silva frowned, her breath misting in the cold air. 'Simon is probably aware, your Majesty, that you are using Mona to contact the King.'

'I don't care,' said Emily.

'But this is the fourth morning in a row, your Majesty; all at the same time. I'm not suggesting that you cease contacting the King, but perhaps it would be wise to be more unpredictable with the timings?'

'We've been in Jezra for nearly two months, Silva. In that entire time, Simon has made no moves towards an attack; he's too busy ruling the rest of the City.'

Mona blinked again. 'I am inside the King's mind, your Majesty,' she said. 'His Majesty passes on his love and greetings. He doesn't know why he was moved. Lord Naxor was in his cell again yesterday, repeating the same threats, and demanding that the King kneel in front of Simon, but his Majesty thought the attempt seemed a little half-hearted.'

Emily nodded. 'How is he feeling?'

'The same, your Majesty. His spirits are low, and he is in pain from the shackles and the beating he received a few days ago. I could sense his happiness at the vision contact; he misses you immensely.'

'Has he seen Elspeth?'

Mona shook her head. 'No. He hasn't seen your daughter in twenty days.'

'Tell him I love him.'

Mona nodded, then her eyes glazed over again.

Silva shifted in her seat.

Emily frowned at her. 'What's wrong? This is the one time of the day when I get to almost speak to my husband. Would you deny me that?'

'The search for the King has already taken over an hour, your Majesty. Perhaps we should cut it short today? After all, Chancellor Mona is supposed to be scanning the approaches to Jezra.'

Mona coughed, and opened her eyes. 'The King says that he loves you too, your Majesty. He also says that he would rather die than submit to Simon; and he wants you to continue resisting his rule from Jezra. Being able to speak to you through me has given him hope, he says, and...'

The loud peal of a bell echoed through the building, and Mona's eyes widened. Emily glanced at one of the soldiers packed into the small room.

'Find out if that alarm is real or not,' she said.

The sergeant saluted. 'Yes, your Majesty.'

He left the room, and Emily turned back to Mona. 'Tell Daniel that we have to go; tell him we'll be back in contact soon.'

Mona bowed her head.

Silva stood, and glanced out of the narrow window. 'Something's going on, your Majesty. The Brigades are out in the streets, and everyone is running as if a dragon is chasing them.'

'I have closed off the vision connection to the King, your Majesty,' said Mona. 'Should I scan for ships?'

The door to the small room burst open.

'A fleet is approaching, your Majesty,' cried the sergeant; 'they're hugging the coastline due sunward of Jezra. The ships are flying the standard of the Blades.'

The women got to their feet. Silva opened her mouth to say something, then seemed to think better of it.

'Let's go up to the roof,' said Emily. 'Mona, please stay here and carry out a full survey of the enemy fleet, and then send a report up to us.'

'Yes, your Majesty,' said the demigod, sitting again.

Emily, Silva and their guards left the room, and hurried through the Command Post. The hallways and corridors were filling with Banner soldiers and Brigade officials, all rushing around, while the peal of the bell sounded again. They raced up the stairs, passing Van's quarters, then emerged onto the roof.

Van was already there, speaking to Frostback and Halfclaw, while Kelsey and a few others were close by.

The major-general noticed the Queen's approach. 'Your Majesty,' he said; 'have you seen Chancellor Mona? She was supposed to be scanning the Straits, and yet it took a scout down in the harbour to spot the Blade ships.'

'It's my fault,' said the Queen. 'I diverted the chancellor into searching for the King, after he was transferred to a different cell. I'm sorry, Major-General.'

Van nodded. His eyes tightened slightly, but he said nothing. Emily glanced down at the harbour. Banner soldiers were packing the quayside, preparing the shore ballista batteries, while, out in the Straits, at least a dozen large vessels were approaching, each flying the crossed swords insignia of the Blades from their masts.

'Shall we burn this fleet?' said Frostback. 'Are they enemies? Perhaps the Blades are deserting from the City.'

'If that were the case,' said Van, 'then Simon would have destroyed them as soon as they had departed Salt Quay.'

'But, why now?' said Emily.

'Simple wood shortages would explain the delay,' said Van. 'They must have stripped planks from every building in the Bulwark to refit a dozen transport ships. Apart from our own vessels and a few small fishing boats, what we're seeing is probably all that remains on the Warm Sea. Alright; Frostback, Halfclaw, we need you to sink the fleet, but be careful. Without Kelsey, you will be vulnerable if Simon has placed any gods with death powers on board.'

'Shouldn't I go with them?' said Kelsey.

'No. You're staying here, by the Queen's side.'

A soldier barrelled from the stair turret and raced towards them. Emily recognised him as one of the soldiers left with Chancellor Mona.

'Sir!' the soldier cried. 'Report from the chancellor – Simon was up on the ridge in upper Jezra, by the walls.'

'Was?' said Van. 'Has he gone?'

'Yes, sir. The chancellor reports that he was up there for a few moments only. He dropped off a mass of greenhides, then vanished.'

'Shit,' muttered Van. 'Change of plan, dragons – get up onto the ridge before the greenhides breach the walls.'

'What about the ships?' said Halfclaw.

'Simon knows we'll have to send you up there to deal with the greenhides,' said Van. 'We'll confront the attack from the Blades the old fashioned way. Dragons; go. Kill every greenhide up there.'

Frostback tilted her head, then the two dragons ascended into the air. They circled once, then soared up towards the line of cliffs on the western edge of lower Jezra.

Van turned to a Banner lieutenant. 'Get down to the harbour and inform Captain Cardova that there will be no dragon support during the assault. He must repel the invasion with everything he's got – no Blades must land in Jezra. No mercy is to be shown.'

'Yes, sir,' said the officer, then he turned and ran for the stairs.

Emily, Van and Kelsey stared down at the approaching fleet. Due to the ruins of the ancient harbour, the vessels had to negotiate a series of tight turns to reach the main quayside, which was already packed with ships belonging to the Exiles. A dull rumble echoed behind them, and Emily glanced over her shoulder. Smoke was rising from up on the ridge, in thin grey columns that stood out against the pink sky.

'We're at risk up here,' said Van. 'Simon has a plan; the Blades and the greenhides are most likely diversions to keep us busy.' He turned to Kelsey and Emily. 'I need you to get off the roof, your Majesty. Go down to my quarters and barricade yourselves in with your guards.'

'But I need to know what's happening, Major-General,' said Emily. 'I can't do that stuck in a little room.' She glanced down at the harbour. 'The Blades will reach the quayside in a few minutes...'

'And they will be slaughtered, your Majesty,' said Van. 'The Banner and Brigades have trained and prepared for this moment; you don't need to see it. Within a few hours, the harbour will be filled with dead Blades, and their ships will be at the bottom of the sea. Simon is throwing their lives away to distract us; to distract you, your Majesty. Please do as I suggest.'

'I agree, your Majesty,' said Silva. 'You and Kelsey are the targets of this day's assault. Defeating the greenhides and the Blades will be meaningless if you are captured or killed.'

Emily felt her temper rise. She wanted to protest, but knew the wisdom of the advice being offered. She bowed her head.

'So be it,' she said. 'Kelsey?'

The Holdfast woman shrugged. 'I'm getting used to hiding in small rooms.'

'Then go,' said Van. 'Quickly, please.'

At that moment, the lead Blade ship pulled into the narrow channel in front of the quayside, and a tremendous noise rose up as the Banner catapults and ballistae began loosing. Huge ceramic containers filled with oil exploded onto the packed deck of the Blade vessel, then erupted in flames. The sails started to blaze, and Blades fell into the water screaming, their uniforms on fire, as the crossbow units lining the quayside opened up. Ballista bolts tore through the air, ripping through the packed bodies on the deck of the ship.

Emily stared at the carnage, then strode for the stair turret, Kelsey, Silva and their guards following them. The Queen noticed Kelsey and Van share a few words, and then they descended the steps, leaving the major-general on the roof to direct the defences.

'I hate this,' Emily muttered, as they hurried down the stairs. 'People are dying – for me; because of me. And now I have to hide? I don't even have a weapon. I want a weapon. If Simon comes, then I'm not going to be caught defenceless.'

'There are weapons stored close to the major-general's quarters, your Majesty,' said the lieutenant leading her escort. 'If we are quick, we could stop off there first.'

'Thank you, Lieutenant. I'm glad that someone is listening to me.'

They reached the landing, and the lieutenant led them to a door next to the main entrance to Van's apartment. A soldier was outside guarding it, and he unlocked the door at the lieutenant's command. Emily strode into the room, and opened the shutters to provide some light. Crates were stacked up against each wall. Several were lying open, revealing stacks of crossbows and bundles of steel-tipped bolts.

'I don't want a crossbow,' said Emily. 'I want something I can use to hack Simon's head off.'

The lieutenant nodded. 'There are a few crates that were salvaged from Cuidrach Palace in the evacuation; some haven't been opened yet. I think they came from the palace armoury.'

He led her to a pile of crates by the rear wall, and pulled some down for her. He opened one up, and Emily glanced inside. The crate had been filled with gold candlesticks and silver plates. The lieutenant prised another one open, revealing a pile of rolled up flags and standards.

'These were taken from the throne room,' said Emily. 'Why would anyone bother packing them up?'

'The evacuation was rushed, your Majesty; all kinds of things were grabbed at the last moment.'

Emily dug down into the crate, pushing the standards out of the way, and felt something solid at the bottom. She lifted it out, and smiled.

'A sword?' said Kelsey, narrowing her eyes at the weapon in Emily's hands.

'Not any old sword,' said Emily. She pulled the blade from the sheath, and the dark metal glistened in the sunlight. 'My Fated Blade.' She glanced at the lieutenant. 'This will do.'

They pushed the crates back against the wall, and left the room. The lieutenant led them into Van's quarters, and locked the door behind them. Emily glanced around. Her mother was standing next to Maxwell's cot in the corner of the living room, a worried look on her face. As well as her, Kelsey and Silva, they had over a dozen soldiers with them, including young Vadhi, who followed Kelsey around wherever she went. Emily sat on a couch, and the soldiers began dragging furniture against the door.

'Are we in danger?' said Lady Omertia.

'We'll be safe in here, ma'am,' said the lieutenant.

Kelsey sat next to the Queen. 'Could I see that sword again?'

Emily nodded, and handed the sheathed weapon to the Holdfast woman.

Kelsey gripped the hilt and drew the blade from the scabbard. She squinted at it.

'What's it made of?' she said.

'I don't know,' said the Queen. 'The same black metal that is in the Axe of Rand. It used to be a far larger sword, carried by Prince Michael and then Duke Marcus, but it was melted down into two blades for me and Daniel. The original was too heavy to pick up, let alone wield in battle.'

'It reminds me of something; another sword – Belinda's sword. Do you think that Malik and Amalia brought the big sword and the axe to the City?'

'You'd have to ask her that.'

'I know what Kelsey means, your Majesty,' said Silva. 'That sword does look very much like the Weathervane. It's not exactly the same dimensions, but the metal is identical.'

Emily frowned. 'The Weathervane?'

'That's what Belinda called her sword,' said Kelsey. 'It was the key to the Sextant. Without Belinda's sword, the Sextant was just a useless hunk of metal.'

Silva's eyes widened. 'I looked after that sword for a long time, but I had no idea that the Sextant required it. Is that how Queen Belinda managed to get it working?'

'Aye.'

'Why did no one tell me of this?'

'It didn't seem very relevant,' said Kelsey.

'I suppose it isn't,' said Silva. 'Not any more.'

Kelsey handed the sword back to Emily. 'Have you ever used it?'

Emily shook her head. 'I received it after the fighting was over. It's been hung up on the wall of the throne room ever since. I wonder where the other one is.'

A soldier walked through from Van's office. 'The rest of the apartment is clear, sir,' he said to the lieutenant. 'There's also a good view of the harbour from inside the office.'

Emily got to her feet.

'Do you really wish to witness the battle, your Majesty?' said Silva.

'Yes. The Blades are my subjects too.'

She walked through to the office, Kelsey, Vadhi and the lieutenant following her. They went past Van's desk, and gazed out of the window. Emily felt her stomach turn. Several of the Blade ships were burning in the tight confines of the ruined harbour, and the water was filled with bodies. Along the quayside, hundreds of Banner soldiers were loosing ballistae, catapults and crossbows onto the decks of the vessels.

'It's carnage,' muttered Kelsey. 'The Blades are getting pasted.'

'The fires are spreading to our own ships,' said the Queen. 'At this rate, there will soon be nothing capable of sailing on the Warm Sea.'

On the far right of the quayside, a solitary Blade ship was edging closer to the docks. Its central mast had been snapped in two, and the deck was covered in blood and the bodies of the slain, but several hundred Blades were gathering, ready to leap onto the stone quay. Amid the roar of noise, Emily heard Cardova shout out, his stature making his position clear as he rallied the defences. Seconds later, every catapult along the quayside was aiming at the approaching vessel, and it was bombarded with fire bombs and chunks of rubble. A huge fragment of masonry struck the side of the ship, and the wooden boards buckled and shattered. The ship began to list to the side, and Blades tumbled off the deck into the waters of the harbour. Another firebomb exploded onto the deck, and the ship sank in front of them, taking less than a minute to succumb to the dark waters, until only the tip of its forward mast remained visible. Banner soldiers swarmed along the edge of the quayside, loosing their crossbows down into the Blades trying to swim to shore.

Emily turned away, feeling sickened by what she had witnessed. She wondered how many Blades had been willing accomplices of the Ascendant, and how many had been forced to take part in the invasion. Either way, their fate was the same.

'The Banner are killing them all,' Kelsey said; 'even without the dragons.'

'The Brigades are playing their part also, ma'am,' said Vadhi; 'supplying munitions and operating some of the catapults. Everyone is doing their bit.'

Emily walked back into the living room and sat down, the noise from the harbour dimming but still loud enough for her to pick out individual screams of agony. Her mother glanced at her. She had Maxwell in her arms, and the infant was crying.

'Are we winning?' she said.

Emily nodded. 'So far. All those poor Blades.'

'They are the enemy, your Majesty,' said Silva. 'They would do the same to us if they could.'

'I know, but only because Simon is making them do it. Why couldn't he just leave us alone? We aren't any threat to his rule out here on the Western Bank.'

'You are a threat to him as long as you are alive and refuse to submit, your Majesty. It will have taken him this long to attack only because he lacked a sufficient number of sea-worthy vessels. If we defeat him today, then he might rethink his plans.'

A thunderous roar came from the doorway, and the barricade was flung backwards into the room. Chairs, tables, and a couch were thrown aside and the door was smashed in. Standing in the entranceway was an enormous figure, decked out from head to toe in thick steel armour, a massive sword in his right hand.

'He has no powers!' cried the lieutenant. 'Loose!'

The Banner soldiers levelled their crossbows as they formed into lines, but Simon was faster.

'I still have battle-vision, you fools,' he laughed, as crossbow bolts ricocheted off his breastplate.

He swung his sword, and the long blade ripped through the two closest Banner soldiers, cleaving them apart. With his free hand, Simon reached out and picked up the lieutenant by the throat. He squeezed, and snapped the officer's neck, then Simon threw him to the ground. Some of the soldiers drew their swords, and one managed to land a blow on Simon, but his armour was too thick. The Ascendant moved quickly, his sword flashing, and more soldiers fell.

Simon dispatched the last soldier, flinging him to the floor and stamping on his head with an armoured boot. Vadhi pushed Kelsey behind her, her hands shaking as she held the crossbow. To their right, Emily, Lady Omertia and Silva backed away from Simon.

The Ascendant laughed. 'Five feeble women, and a baby, huddling in terror before me. Holdfast witch, you will be coming with me. Queen; prepare to die.'

Emily drew the Fated Blade, dropping the scabbard to the floor.

'Do you think a little sword will hurt me, Queen? Imagine your husband's cries of grief, when I bring him your head. Before you die, I want you to know my plans for the pretend king, and for your daughter. Elspeth will be brought up as mine, and I will teach her that you were nothing but a vile traitor. Your husband will be my personal slave. The humiliations and degradations I will put him through will break him soon.'

Silva pulled a knife from her robes and held it to Maxwell's throat. 'Stay back, Ascendant, or Amalia's child dies.'

Simon laughed again. 'I have read your mind thoroughly, demigod. You do not possess the ruthlessness required to slaughter an innocent child. I also read the mind of Mona, before I removed her head from her shoulders. Did you think that I wouldn't be able to see her spying on me? She wept on her knees, begging for mercy; I showed her none.'

'You killed Mona?' said Kelsey.

'I did. You, however, I shall not slay. I have a far better idea of what to do with you. You are a freak of nature, Holdfast witch; an abomination that should never have been allowed to live. Your mother should have throttled you in your crib.'

'Eat shit, Simon,' said Kelsey. 'If you want me, come and get me.'

'Are all the Holdfasts like you, little witch?'

'If my sister was here, she'd kick your sorry arse for you. My family has already killed Nathaniel; one more Ascendant would be no problem.'

Simon's eyes darkened. 'You were responsible for Nathaniel's death? You're lying.'

'Nope. My world is the graveyard of gods. I hope Edmond finds it, so we can kill him too.'

'Wait; you are an enemy of Edmond?'

'Aye; what's it to you?'

'We should not be fighting, Holdfast witch, for I too hold the Second Ascendant in contempt. Join me, and we will strike at Implacatus. With your powers, we could overthrow the evil that rules that world, and bring in a new order.'

Kelsey started to laugh, and Emily glanced at her.

'Are you mocking me, witch?' cried Simon.

'Aye, bawbag,' said Kelsey. 'I'll never work for you. As far as I'm concerned, all you gods are for the chop. One day, a Holdfast will stand upon the grave of the last Ascendant. If it's me, I might do a little dance.'

Simon took a step forward. 'You will watch as I kill the Queen in front of you, witch, and the other women here. You will weep as I rip the life from them.'

He bounded forward, his huge sword swinging above his head. Lady Omertia screamed as Emily pushed her to the side, the edge of the blade missing her head by an inch. Maxwell fell to the floor, howling and crying. Simon raised his sword to hack down at Lady Omertia, and Emily lunged forward, the Fated Blade gripped in both hands. Her mind staggered at the futility, but if she was going to die, she would go down fighting. She stabbed with the sword, aiming for his breastplate, and the dark blade pierced the god's armour as if it weren't there. Emily fell forwards, off balance as Simon screamed in pain, the Fated Blade lodged in his chest. Silva leapt up, and rammed her knife into Simon's face, striking his left eye socket. He swung his free arm, swiping Silva aside, and sending the demigod flying through the air. Emily pulled the Fated Blade from his chest and lashed out with it, catching Simon's sword arm and slicing his right hand off at the wrist. The huge blade fell to the floor, and Simon fell backwards, howling in agony. Emily raised her sword, and the Ascendant vanished.

'Holy shit,' gasped Kelsey, her eyes wide with terror.

Emily glanced down at the empty space on the floor. Lying a foot away was Simon's sword, his right hand still attached to the hilt. Lady Omertia scrabbled on the floor, and clutched Maxwell to her chest, her face wet with tears, while Vadhi collapsed onto a couch, her crossbow unused.

Kelsey stared at Emily. 'How... how did you do that? You beat him.'

Emily glanced at Silva. 'Are you alright?'

The demigod pulled herself to her feet by the corner of the room. 'Just a few broken bones, your Majesty. I'm fine; you saved us.'

'We beat him together,' she said.

'I didn't do anything,' sobbed Vadhi.

Kelsey shrugged. 'Neither did I, Vadhi. We survived; that's all that matters.'

Soldiers burst into the room, crossbows levelled. Van pushed his way to the front. His eyes scanned the room, taking in the sight of the dozen dead Banner soldiers, and then the huge sword on the floor.

'He's gone,' said Emily.

'I should have been here sooner, your Majesty,' Van said. 'Chancellor Mona is dead. I was down there when I heard that Simon had moved up here.' He crouched down by the huge sword, as the other soldiers began picking up the bodies of their fallen comrades. 'He's missing a hand.'

'The Queen did that,' said Kelsey; 'and Silva got him in the eye with a knife. They were amazing, both of them.'

Van glanced at Kelsey, his eyes unable to hide his feelings for her. She stared back.

'We've lost Mona,' said Emily. 'She was more than just our eyes in the City; she was a friend.'

Van tore his gaze from Kelsey. 'Yes, your Majesty, but the day is ours. The Blade fleet has been shattered; only two ships were able to retreat, and both of them were ablaze. And, the dragons have returned. Frostback and Halfclaw dealt with the greenhides up on the ridge, but not before over a hundred Brigade workers were torn to shreds. A bitter day, but the victory is ours.'

Emily nodded. 'Did any Blades make it onto the quayside?'

'No, your Majesty; the defences were sufficient to slaughter them on their vessels; the entire harbour is blocked with burning ships. There will be no more assaults from the Warm Sea.'

'How many dead?'

'No Banner forces were killed on the quayside, your Majesty.'

'I meant, how many Blades?'

'Perhaps three thousand, your Majesty.'

Emily put a hand to her face, the other still clutching the Fated Blade, its dark metal stained with the blood of the Ascendant.

'It seems wrong to call it a victory,' she said.

'It is the greatest of victories, your Majesty,' said Silva. 'You defeated an Ascendant, and made him turn and flee. You have weakened his rule. Imagine the faces of the traitor gods and demigods, when Simon returns to the Royal Palace in disgrace. You have given everyone in the City hope.'

'But the cost, Silva. The soldiers who died to defend us; the Brigade workers up on the ridge. Mona. How am I to deal with this loss? Every death strikes at my heart.'

Kelsey put an arm round her shoulder. 'That's why you're the Queen.'

'What if Simon kills Daniel and Elspeth in revenge?'

'You mustn't think of that, your Majesty,' said Silva. 'Simon failed to rescue Maxwell. Amalia will never allow him to kill your child, not while we have hers.'

Van nodded. 'I would be obliged, your Majesty, if you would greet the crowds gathered by the entrance to the Command Post.'

'People have gathered there?' she said. 'Why?'

'To celebrate, your Majesty. If you were to speak to them, even for a minute or two, it would mean a lot to them. They have bled and killed for you, and now they need to see that you are unharmed and still in control. And Kelsey, you too; they should also see your face.'

'Alright,' said Kelsey. 'Queenie?'

Emily cast her gaze down at the bloodstains on the carpet. Simon's huge sword was still lying there, next to the remains of the Banner soldiers who had fallen.

Her mother placed a hand on her arm. 'The major-general is right, my dearest daughter. There will be time to weep for Mona and the soldiers; go and see your people.'

Emily picked up the scabbard, and slid the dark blade into its leather sheath. It had been the Fated Blade that had made the difference, its edge shearing Simon's armour as if it had been made of paper. She decided there and then that it would never leave her side again.

She glanced up, drawing on all her strength of will. 'I'm ready.'

CHAPTER 3

HOUSE GUESTS

Tara, Auldan, The City – 25th Yordian 3422

Kagan was lost. He had been living within the walls of Maeladh Palace for almost two months, but its wings and hidden hallways, tunnels and galleries, were like a maze designed to confuse the unsuspecting. He had tried drawing out a rough plan of the wing where he was living with Amalia, but kept finding other routes to get to the same destination, and the scrap of paper he had been using was covered in alterations and scribbles.

He glanced around. Sunlight was filtering through the slats of a closed set of shutters, so he knew that he was above ground, but the dark marble-lined corridor looked similar to a dozen others he had walked through. It was also deathly quiet. Following the submission of the Rosers, the town's leaders had assigned two dozen staff to go along with a detachment of militia to guard the palace; but Amalia had them cleaning and redecorating the small number of rooms where she had based herself, and Kagan could roam the palace for hours without bumping into anyone. The basements and tunnels were the eeriest part of the huge, sprawling complex. Down there, most of the doorways were locked and barred, though Kagan had seen a dark hall, with small stone cells along three walls. The fourth wall housed a guardroom, and another chamber, which was filled with what looked to Kagan to be interrogation equipment; elaborate torture devices, and piles of rusty shackles and chains.

The entire iceward wing, where the government of the Rosers had once sat, was completely sealed off, but Kagan had wandered close to the locked offices and meeting halls. From that side of the palace, there was a great view down Princeps Row, where the grand mansions of the Taran aristocracy lined a tree-filled avenue. They reminded Kagan of the palaces of the gods upon Old Alea. Several of the leading men and women of Tara had made the short journey from there to the palace over the last month, to kneel before Amalia and pledge their undying loyalty. One of those had been a certain Lord Chamberlain, a nephew of the previous holder of that title, who struck Kagan as the worst type of duplicitous sycophant. He had given a two-hour long speech on the divine magnificence of the God-Queen, heaping praise and flattery upon her. They called Kagan a lord – Lord Kagan of Alea Tanton; and a consort to the God-Queen. The aristocrats had knelt before him, just as they had knelt before Amalia, and he wondered what his mother, or Dizzler, would have made of it all.

He stopped by one of the shutters, and forced it open, its catches stiff from lack of use. The hinges squeaked in protest as he pushed the wooden slats free, letting the bright morning sunshine enter the corridor. He blinked in the light, then shielded his eyes. Outside, on what must be the sunward flank of the palace, he could see the old gardens. Almost three years of neglect had resulted in the neat flowerbeds and tidy patches of grass becoming overgrown, and Kagan saw one of their new servants on her knees by a stretch of soil, pulling the weeds out. She turned, hearing the shutters opening, and bowed her head to Kagan as he watched her.

He nodded back, feeling embarrassed. He was a fraud. He had gone from being a slum-dwelling gang member to the consort of a mighty god in a couple of years. In many ways, he could be considered to be the most successful of the Exiles. While the majority of those who had fled from Lostwell were shivering in the cold Brigade barracks of rebel Jezra, he was living in luxury. However, that wasn't how he felt. Isolation was the strongest emotion; isolation, and fear over the fate of his son. If he had gone to Jezra with the others, then he might be cold and hungry, but he would be among his own people, and he wouldn't be living with the horrible knowledge that Maxwell was in the hands of the enemy. For that was what the rest of the Lostwell Exiles had become under Simon's rule – enemies.

He left the shutters open and carried on down the corridor. As soon as he came to a door on the right, he pushed against it, and it opened. He walked outside into the unruly gardens, and breathed in the fresh air. An arched trellis led into the main part of the gardens, and he followed the path, his breath misting in the chill breeze.

Below him on the left, the cliffs fell away, and the town of Tara spread out along the eastern side of the narrow peninsula. Kagan had yet to walk round the town, but it looked inviting from the heights of Maeladh Palace. At night, the sounds of the many taverns would float up to the terraced ridge where the palace sat, and Kagan missed the feeling of being around other people, especially people who didn't bow and flatter him. Beyond the town was the bay, its waters sparkling in the sunshine, and the suburbs of Outer Pella began at the edge of the shoreline.

He turned his eyes from the view and scanned the gardens. Down to his right, on a terrace one level below him, he could see a figure sitting on a wooden bench, her gaze on the same view that he had been looking at. He descended a set of stone steps and approached the bench.

'Good morning,' he said, as he reached where the woman was sitting.

Amalia glanced up at him.

He sat. 'It's so beautiful here.'

'To me, it's ugly,' she said. 'Everything is ugly. I never knew that I was capable of hating the City with such unheeded passion.'

Kagan tried to smile. 'We'll get Maxwell back.'

She glared at him. 'Will we? For two months, Simon told us to be patient, that he had a plan, a grand plan that would destroy the Queen's grip on Jezra, and return our son to us.' She turned back to the view, her eyes smouldering. 'He lied.'

'He failed,' said Kagan. 'He underestimated the Holdfast girl, just as you said he would. Three thousand Blades were killed trying to assault Jezra.'

'I know that. And now what? With the merchant and Blade fleets both destroyed, how is he supposed to take Jezra now? With fishing boats? Greenhides? Simon has made a mess of everything; he's been too busy filling his harem with Reaper girls and holding parties in the Royal Palace to pay attention to the running of the City; leaving Naxor to swan around as if he were the new God-King. While here I sit, the actual God-Queen, sidelined and ignored.'

Kagan nodded. 'But, Amalia, I thought you didn't want to rule?'

'I don't, but if the alternative is to sit and watch while the City is ruined beyond repair, then perhaps I should rule.' She gave a grim laugh. 'Not that Simon would allow me to, not while he has Naxor, Felice and the others grovelling before him. And, what do we have? An empty palace and no son.'

'I...' Kagan began, then his words faltered.

She turned to him. 'Yes?'

He took a breath. 'I could go to Jezra. I could disguise myself as a member of the Brigades and sneak into their headquarters without causing too much suspicion. I could find Maxwell and bring him back.'

She took his hand. 'Thank you for the offer, Kagan. I know that you would do it; you're brave enough, but all that would result is that I would lose you too. The Banner would catch you in ten minutes, and I would have two hostages to worry about. Elspeth is the key. If we could only somehow arrange a swap. Emily must be feeling as desperate as we are; surely she would do anything to have her daughter returned to her, and her husband; but Simon, in his wisdom, has forbidden any negotiations with the Exiles in Jezra. He killed my granddaughter, Lady Mona – he would do the same to us if we went behind his back.'

'When we agreed to follow Simon,' he said, 'you suggested that I stay quiet, and not complain.'

She glared at him. 'So I did. And your point is?'

'He could be listening to us, right now.'

'I don't know if I care any more. Simon knows fine well that I have my doubts, which is one of the reasons he's been ignoring us here in Maeladh. I'm not like Naxor, or Lydia; I am used to ruling this City, not prostrating myself in front of others. I have never been happy taking orders, especially from people who know nothing about the City and its tribes. Simon skims through our minds, and thinks he understands the intricacies of balancing all of the different factions that exist within the City, but then he murders Mona, who probably knew more about the City than anyone else alive. One and a half millennia of knowledge and learning, gone with the stroke of a sword. Don't get me wrong; I had my differences with the Chancellor of the Royal Academy – she conspired against me in the dying days of my rule, but, then again, so did everyone else. If I had a Quadrant, I think I'd leave, once I had rescued Maxwell, of course.'

She quietened as a group of nobles appeared at the bottom of the garden. Roser militia were guarding the perimeter of the palace, and they had opened one of the many gates that ran along the lower terrace facing Tara.

'What do they want now?' Amalia muttered.

Lord Chamberlain was leading the small group of aristocrats, and Kagan suppressed a frown, trying to keep his features even.

Chamberlain bowed deeply before Amalia as they reached the bench.

'Your Excellency,' he said, 'your beauty and majesty light up this wonderful morning, and the sight of your glory fills my heart to over-flowing; truly your radiance rivals that of the life-giving sun.'

Amalia fixed a smile onto her face. 'How can I help you, Lord Chamberlain?'

The nobleman bowed his head low, his face anguished. 'Unfortunately, your Excellency, we bear grim tidings.'

'Really?'

'Yes, your Excellency. Due to the terrible shortages of wood afflicting the City, your order of new furniture for the palace will be unavoidably delayed.'

'You came up here to tell me this?'

'We are doing all we can, your Excellency. Teams of Roser militia are stripping the wood-panelling from the public buildings of Tara, but all of it has been requisitioned by the Royal Palace in Ooste; there isn't enough to even repair the broken window shutters.'

'I'm sure we'll survive.'

'Your courage in the face of such news is inspiring, your Excellency. I have one suggestion that might alleviate some of these problems. If you would give your permission, then we shall order the militia into the mansion of the traitor Aurelians, and strip it bare. It seems only right and proper that those treacherous creatures should pay the price of their folly. Their mansion on Princeps Row has, thus far, been left alone. I would consider it just to transfer their belongings here, to the palace.'

'And, this has nothing to do with the fact that your family has hated the Aurelians for centuries?'

Lord Chamberlain smiled. 'Nothing whatsoever, your Excellency. It does seem a little strange that the dismemberment of the Aurelians' property has not yet taken place. Their enormous wealth would ease the cash flow problems currently being experienced by the Roser leadership.'

'What about due process? The Aurelians have appeared in front of no court, and none of them have been charged with any crime.'

'That situation could be remedied very easily, your Excellency. Give me permission, I beg you, to pursue the traitors in court. The verdict is all but assured.'

Amalia frowned. 'You know, your uncle was a lot more subtle; but then, he knew my ways better than you do. The old Lord Chamberlain would have cooked up some evidence beforehand, whereas your greed and ambition are a little too brash for my tastes. Leave the Aurelians alone for now. Four of them are in the dungeons of the Royal Palace, while the other is still at large in Jezra. They are Simon's to deal with; I shall not interfere.'

Lord Chamberlain bowed low. 'Your munificence humbles me, your Excellency.'

'You are dismissed.'

The aristocrats bowed again, then began to stride away, back down to the gate.

'Gods, I hate them,' said Amalia, her eyes narrow as she watched the nobles leave the palace grounds. 'They're like flies buzzing over a warm corpse. They annoyed me so much that I actually defended the damned Aurelians.' She shook her head. 'This is not what I wanted.'

'Maybe Simon will decide to leave,' said Kagan, 'now that his assault on Jezra has failed. From everything he's said, I think he wants to go off to Implacatus to fight the Second Ascendant. Maybe he'll get bored here.'

'One can hope, but after four thousand years stuck on Yocasta, I sense he wishes to relax for a while first. Unfortunately for us, his relaxation means the subjugation of the City.'

She got to her feet and Kagan joined her. They walked in silence among the untidy gardens, passing another servant, who was pruning back a row of overgrown bushes, the sound of his shears the only noise except for the crunch of their feet on the gravel paths. They entered the palace, and walked to the large apartment in the sunward wing. It was in a different part of the palace from where Amalia had previously lived, but, after two months of work by the servants, it was bright and airy, and had been repainted. Amalia had chosen the apartment because it had a sitting room with huge bay windows that overlooked the bay, and that room had become the place where they spent most of their time.

Servants bowed low as they walked into the sitting room. It was sparsely furnished, the couches, tables and cupboards having been moved from other wings of the palace, and Kagan was yet to feel at home there. He sat on a couch, while Amalia walked straight to the drinks cabinet and poured out two brandies. She downed a large measure in one go, then turned, and with a cry of rage flung the glass against the wall, shattering it into a hundred pieces.

'Those fools!' she yelled. 'My son is a prisoner, and they come up here to tell me about damn furniture. Curse them all. I should kill every sycophant in this City, starting with the odious Lord Chamberlain.'

Kagan watched her in silence, his heart breaking to see the pain she was in. Amalia put a hand to her face, then her eyes widened as the air shimmered in the corner of the room.

Simon appeared, wearing long white robes rather than his usual suit of battle armour. Kagan's eyes darted to the end of the Ascendant's right arm. He had heard the rumours, and they were true. His hand was missing. His left eye was also bloodshot, and a clear fluid was leaking down his cheek.

Amalia bowed her head. 'Your Grace; this is a surprise.'

Simon smiled, but it came out crooked. 'Pour me a drink. I'm getting a taste for Taran brandy, and I do believe that you own the best distillery in the City.' He glanced at Kagan. 'Greetings, feeble mortal.' He walked up to the bay windows while Amalia prepared two more drinks. 'So, this is the fabled Maeladh Palace, eh? It certainly has a better view than the Royal Palace.' He eyed Amalia. 'Not that I've been gazing at the view; the young women of Pella have been keeping me busy. You should get yourself a harem, young Kagan. You get all the pleasures, without any of the tedious pandering and pampering that women usually require.'

Amalia handed him a glass. 'Is this what you came here to discuss, your Grace? Your harem?'

Simon gave her a look that bordered upon contempt. 'No. I came here because I'm sick of listening to your complaints. Every time I cast my vision towards Tara, all I hear is your whining about that child of yours.' He raised the stump on his right arm. 'Look! Do you see how I have paid for trying to rescue your son? Where is the gratitude that you owe me? Even with the salve I took from Naxor, it will take the entirety of Freshmist to re-grow my hand. That nest of Jezran bitches almost killed me; do you understand?'

Amalia kept her face steady. 'Thank you for trying to rescue Maxwell, your Grace. I am very sorry that you failed.'

Simon sat on a couch. 'Not as sorry as I am. You know, I was tempted to abandon this awful world of red skies, greenhides and ungrateful allies. I have done what I said I would do – the City is back under our control, and the false Crown has been removed from power. What else is there for me here?'

'I don't know, your Grace.'

Simon stared at her. 'You would love me to leave, wouldn't you? I can sense it at the forefront of your thoughts.' He paused for a moment. 'The false Queen had a sword; what do you know about it?'

Amalia sat on the couch next to Kagan. 'A sword, your Grace? I'm not sure I understand the question.'

'It was simple enough. She was wielding a sword that cut through my armour like a knife through butter. Where did she obtain such a weapon?'

'I don't know what you mean, your Grace.'

'Its blade was black.'

Amalia raised an eyebrow. 'Black? I see. Or rather, I don't, your Grace. Queen Emily does not possess the strength to wield the Just. How large was this sword?'

'A little on the short side; perhaps a two-foot blade? What is the Just?'

'The Just was Malik's old sword, your Grace. It had a blade in excess of five foot, and only those with battle-vision could pick it up. He brought it with him to the City when we arrived, and used it to slay greenhides by my side. He had another weapon, also with black metal, which is now known as the Axe of Rand, after Malik gifted it to a grand-son. Yendra was the last to wield it, and after her death it was given back to Yvona in Icehaven. The metal that went into these weapons differs from normal steel; it is far more durable, and much sharper.'

'Where is the Just now?'

'I don't know, your Grace. My grandson Marcus was the last to hold it, as far as I know. I suppose it is possible that it was melted down, to make new weapons that ordinary mortals could carry.'

'Where did Malik get these weapons? He wasn't in possession of a black blade when I knew him.'

'He never told me their origin, your Grace. Presumably it was on one of the many worlds that he visited before I met him.'

'I might have to pay a visit to Icehaven, if there is an axe of similar quality in that town. Lady Yvona has yet to kneel before me. If she refuses, then I will use her own axe to end her life.'

'You could ask Naxor about the sword that Emily had, your Grace. He was present for her coronation, whereas I was on the run by that point.'

Simon frowned. 'Naxor? A more treacherous rat I have yet to meet. He is remarkably skilled in hiding his thoughts and memories – he buries them so deeply within his mind that I have already wasted countless hours trying to unravel his secrets. His greatest secret, however, is now mine. I had to wrench it from his mind with such brutality that I almost killed him.' He smiled. 'Were it not for that secret, I would be tempted to depart this world today.'

'I dread to ask what Naxor was keeping hidden in his mind, your Grace.'

Simon stared at her. 'Salve, Amalia. The mines are exhausted, yes?'

'Yes, your Grace.'

'Therefore, this world is of no more interest to Edmond and the others, correct?'

'That would seem to be the case, your Grace.'

He laughed. 'Wrong. Very, very wrong. Still, at least I know that you weren't also hiding it from me. The truth is that Naxor has seen a mountain, two hundred miles east of here, that has salve deposits beyond anything that the City ever held.'

Amalia gasped. 'What? There's salve in the Eastern Mountains? And Naxor knew?'

'Yes. It turns out that Salvor also knew, but I scrubbed his mind too harshly, and missed it. I was too hasty, in my anger at his refusal to bow before me. There is a lesson there.'

'Naxor told his brother about it?'

'No. Salvor knew, because the false Queen also knows. She sent an expedition there to survey the new mine, under the command of Montieth's younger daughter, who was killed by dragon fire in the Fortress of the Lifegiver.' He drummed his fingers on the table. 'And now I must find a new plan; one that allows me to gather all of the salve left in existence. The gods of Implacatus will have to bow before me then, if I control the supply of salve. Edmond's allies will desert him, and flock to my banner. I will have to deal with the dragon colony first, naturally, but that shouldn't be too difficult. After all, I created Dragon Eyre, and I know their weaknesses.'

'You created dragons, your Grace?' said Kagan.

'Not exactly, but I created the conditions for them to exist. Modified winged gaien, suitable to host the mind of a god. I needed help from Theodora, but she was the master of creation, and she guided my steps. Once the world was fully formed, a legion of gods departed Implacatus, to take up residence within the minds of the new beasts, and dragons came into being. The first dragons had a far wider range of powers than the current generation; now all they can do is breathe fire, and a few have various vision tricks; but they are a pale imitation of the first dragons. Do I awe you, mortal man?'

'Yes, your Grace,' said Kagan, feeling shamed by his words.

'Good. Of course, while on Yocasta, I knew nothing of the conflicts that have recently raged across Dragon Eyre. It seems my creation has been causing Edmond all manner of problems.' He sipped his brandy. 'I have a task for you both; something to keep you two rascals busy and out of mischief.'

Amalia leaned forward. 'Does it involve getting our son back, your Grace?'

'No. You're going to have to wait until summer for that, young Amalia, because even someone as magnificent as me needs two hands to defeat the rebels. Fret not, though; I saw your son in Jezra – he was well. The rebels are caring for him, just as we have been caring for the false Queen's child. That will come to an end when we capture the false Queen, for then I intend to have the entire Aurelian family publically executed in Prince's Square in Tara, for all to see. Until that moment, however, I wish the false Queen to retain some hope that she will be reunited with her daughter; her compassion will force her to make mistakes.'

'What do you want us to do, your Grace?' said Kagan.

Simon grinned. 'Wait here; I'll be back in a moment.'

The air shimmered, and Simon vanished. Amalia and Kagan glanced at each other.

'So, the rumours are true,' said Amalia. 'Kelsey Holdfast and Emily Aurelian almost killed Simon, an Ascendant. By all the gods, I...'

She fell silent as the air shimmered again. A small group of people appeared, with Simon in their midst. Kagan narrowed his eyes as he saw who was with him.

'I bear a gift for you, young Amalia,' Simon said; 'the Aurelian family. It is true that two months in prison hasn't done much for their health, or their appearance, but they are all still in one piece – Lord and Lady Aurelian, the false King, and his daughter.'

Amalia stood, her eyes wide, while Kagan stared at the three adults and child. The King and his parents were shackled and dressed in rags, and were covered in bruises and cuts. The King was clutching his daughter in his arms, but he looked broken and exhausted.

'What am I supposed to do with them, your Grace?' cried Amalia.

Simon shrugged. 'I don't care, as long as you keep them alive for the grand executions I am planning. Presumably, you will have to feed them occasionally.'

'But, why, your Grace?'

'I intend to spend Freshmist in one long, continuous orgy, and I'll have no time to look after pathetic mortals. Lady Doria was caring for the child, but she's better suited to my harem, rather than as a nurse-maid, and Naxor simply cannot be trusted. I'd ask Felice, but she has her hands full running the Bulwark. Would you rather I let Montieth look after them?'

'Not if you want them to survive long enough to be executed, your Grace.'

'Precisely.' He beamed. 'Have fun!'

Simon vanished, leaving the four Aurelians in the middle of the room.

Lady Aurelian spat on the floor in front of Amalia. 'If I wasn't cowed by Simon, what makes you think I'll be cowed by you, Amalia?'

'I wasn't thinking anything of the sort, Lady Aurelian,' said Amalia. 'Believe me, you are the last house guest I would possibly want in Maeladh.' She signalled to a servant by the door. 'Summon a squad of Roser militia from the gates, and have someone prepare some cells in the dungeon.'

'Are we putting them in the dungeon?' said Kagan, as the servant hurried away.

Amalia shrugged. 'Where else can we put them?'

Lord Aurelian shook his head slowly. 'Kagan? And I thought you seemed like a nice chap when we visited; how did you stoop so low? My wife is ill from her imprisonment, and my son has been beaten by Simon's thugs. My granddaughter hasn't even reached the age of one, and you're putting her into a dungeon. Shame on you; shame on you both.'

Daniel raised a hand. 'Give them nothing, father. They can't be reasoned with; they have sold the City to Simon.'

Amalia frowned. 'I see that a spell in prison hasn't stopped any of you from talking. You will be going to the dungeons, because that is the only place in the palace that is secure enough to hold you. But, I am not a savage...'

Lady Aurelian gave a bitter laugh.

'As I said,' Amalia went on; 'I am not a savage. We shall have a small basement apartment converted for you, with guards and locked doors and suchlike; somewhere I don't have to see you.'

Kagan walked forward, and the King pulled back, his hand raised to shield Elspeth.

'I only wanted to look at her,' Kagan said. 'Your wife has my son.'

'I have been in contact with the Queen,' Daniel said; 'Maxwell is being well looked after. My wife ordered that he be cared for as if he were her own flesh and blood. That's the difference between us; don't try to pretend that our situations are the same.'

'Your wife has my gratitude,' said Amalia, 'whether you believe it or not. I swear to you now that I shall not see any harm done to Elspeth while you are in Maeladh.'

'And after that?' said Daniel. 'You heard Simon – he means to execute us all.'

The servant returned, leading a squad of a dozen Roser militia.

Amalia clicked her fingers. 'Take the Aurelians to the dungeons, lock them in, and post a guard. They are not to be harmed without my permission, and they are not to escape.'

'Yes, ma'am,' said their officer, saluting.

The militia gathered round the Aurelian family, and escorted them from the room. As soon as they had gone, Amalia collapsed into a chair.

She shook her head. 'Lady Aurelian's dream has finally come true – she's living in Maeladh Palace with her family. Somehow, I doubt she'll appreciate the irony.'

CHAPTER 4

THE GATHERING CLOUDS

The Eastern Mountains – 3rd Malikon 3423

Jade stared up at the red sky, searching for clouds, as a chill wind swept across the valley. The dawn had been clear but she knew, they all knew, that Freshmist could begin at any time. Often, there was only an hour or two's notice – the clouds would rush in from iceward, and the rains would begin, signalling the end of winter. New Year's Day had passed, and yet winter had continued, and the extra two days had given them a chance to increase the reserves of supplies that they would need to see them through to summer.

'We might get another clear day,' said Rosie, her clothes reeking of smoke.

'We might,' said Jade, keeping her eyes on the horizon.

'That's the last of the goat meat smoked,' said Rosie. 'We're all going to be very sick of eating goat by the end of Freshmist, but we can alternate – smoked one day, salted the next. There are enough apples and berries for each of us to have a handful every three days, and that's it; that's our diet for the next two months.'

Jade nodded, barely listening to the young Jackdaw.

'Worst of all,' Rosie went on, 'we'll run out of wine in about five or six days, and the gin's long gone. I should have learned how to distil while I was in the City, or at least make ale, but I was too busy designing and building ballistae. Next time, I'll be better prepared.'

Jade frowned. 'Next time?'

'Yeah. Who knows how long we'll be here? I have a plan – I'll keep stuff by throughout summer, so if we're still here for Sweetmist, we'll have a greater selection of food to eat. I feel a bit bad; I'm in charge of food, and all we have is goat.'

'You've cooked the food for us every day since we got here, Rosie,' Jade said, 'and you've managed to put aside enough for Freshmist. I'd say that you've done a decent job.'

She turned from the sky and glanced around. The two sergeants, Inmara and Darvi, were chopping wood down by the pool. They had felled a few trees, though Jade had insisted that none of those in the little valley had been cut down, as she wanted to preserve their home; it was her garden now, and it was perfect just as it was. The tents had been taken down, as they would be useless in the storms of Freshmist, and the sheeting had been re-used to build a canopy over the mouth of the cave. They had also constructed a rudimentary door to seal up the entrance from the wind and rain that was coming, and had moved everything else into the interior of the cavern.

'I've spent every Freshmist in a warm barracks,' said Rosie, 'or at my parents' old house. We used to play games every evening, then Maddie would go off in a huff because she kept losing. This cave is certainly going to be different. What did you used to do?'

Jade shrugged. 'Sometimes, I would go for so long without looking outside, that Freshmist would come and go, and I wouldn't even know. The walls of Greylin are so thick, that you couldn't hear the rain or the wind, and when there are no windows, every day feels the same. That's why I started the garden on the roof. Looking back, I think it was my first act of rebellion against my father. He stayed in the basement most of the time, experimenting on mortals, and the roof was the furthest away from him that I was allowed to go.'

'Until Aila arrived?'

'Yes. She was the first cousin that I had spoken to in a long time. I didn't like her much, but she made me realise that I had to get out of Greylin. And then she abandoned me in Port Sanders, and I was so angry; that's when... never mind. You know what I did after that. It's the power, the power I have over mortals. With a click of my fingers I could kill them, and with another click bring them back. They were only mortals; what did it matter? I preferred cats to mortals; I still do. Cats only live for a few years, so do mortals, but at least cats don't tell me that I'm stupid or crazy, or run away from me in terror.'

'Do you miss your cats?'

Jade frowned at her. 'More than anything. I should have brought them here; I wish I had. I was in such a rush to get to the Fortress of the Lifegiver on time for Halfclaw, that I left them in the cottage next to Cuidrach Palace, and now the palace has been burnt down, and Simon is in charge of Pella. If he's harmed my babies, then I will rip his head off with my bare hands.'

'From what Quill and Flavus told us, Simon probably thinks that you're dead. Frostback torched the Duke's Tower while you were supposed to be inside. If Simon comes here, you should hide; he won't be looking for you.'

'When he comes. You said "if." He'll come, for the salve.'

'If he knows about it.'

'Don't be naïve, Rosie. He can read the mind of anyone in the City, apart from the Holdfast witch. He'll know.'

'Then, why hasn't he been here?'

Jade shrugged. 'You're thinking like a mortal – Simon is a god who isn't in a hurry. Time moves differently for us. Mortals are always rushing about, because they have so little time. Gods can always put things off.'

'Well, if he comes, we might have a few surprises for him. I plan on building a few defences over Freshmist.' Her eyes gleamed. 'I almost hope that Simon comes. Did I ever tell you that I constructed a ballista on the roof of my parents' house when I was only fifteen?'

'Yes; a few times.'

'Oh.'

Jade pointed upwards. 'Halfclaw.'

The two sergeants took a break from chopping to lean on their axes and watch as the green dragon descended into the valley. On his shoulders was Flavus, wrapped up in a blanket to protect him from the searing cold. The dragon landed by the pool, and lowered his head towards the group of humans.

'Greetings,' he said, as Flavus began scrambling down from the harness.

'Hello, Halfclaw. We were talking about where to spend Freshmist,' said Rosie; 'what are you going to do?'

'I intend to fly back to Jezra before the rains start,' said the dragon. 'I want to be with Frostback. The Brigades have excavated a cavern large enough in the cliffside for both of us to shelter from Freshmist.'

Rosie smiled. 'Two months in a cavern with your betrothed? Should we be expecting any tiny dragons to appear soon?'

Halfclaw glanced away, looking almost embarrassed. 'That is not something I am prepared to discuss.'

'Will you be safe in Jezra?' said Jade.

'Yes, demigod. I was there a short time ago, when Simon assaulted the town. He sent ships full of Blades, and set down greenhides inside the walls. He also came in person.'

Rosie gasped. 'What happened?'

'Simon was defeated by Kelsey and the Queen, while the Banner sank the ships, and Frostback and I destroyed the greenhides. Simon fled back in shame to his palace in Ooste, maimed and half-blinded. I do not think he will venture towards Jezra again in the near future. He was taught a lesson he will not forget.'

Rosie cheered.

'It is not all good news, little Jackdaw. One of the vision demigods, by the name of Mona, was killed by the Ascendant, and Jezra now has no far-seeing eye to watch over affairs.'

'Mona's dead?' said Jade.

'Yes. I am sorry for the loss of your cousin, demigod.'

Jade said nothing. She barely knew Mona.

Flavus unbuckled a pack from the harness, and slung it over his shoulder.

'Did you find anything?' said Jade.

'No, ma'am; another fruitless survey, I'm afraid. There's no time for another survey before the rains begin; in fact, we were fortunate to escape the weather this time.'

'Maybe we're next to the only salve deposit in the mountains, sir,' said Rosie.

'That's what I'm starting to believe, Private,' said Flavus, 'though the mountain range is over a hundred miles long, and my little surveys have barely scratched the surface. I did find a few caves with evidence of human occupation, but from a very long time ago. Still, it seems like too much of a coincidence that Blackrose happened to find a valley with the only salve in the mountains. If I had to guess, then I think that there will be other mountain ranges upon this world, with more salve, but they are beyond our reach.' He glanced at Jade. 'Perhaps it is time to put the King's orders into effect, ma'am.'

'Are you joking?' said Rosie. 'Sorry, I mean, sir.'

Flavus frowned at her. 'The King's orders were clear, Private.'

'Yes, but if the salve mine is burned by the dragons, then where are we going to stay over Freshmist, sir? The rains are due to start any moment, and the tents have been dismantled, and all our food and supplies are in the cave.'

'We could travel to the dragon colony,' said Flavus.

'We were also ordered to stay here,' said Jade, 'and the colony is full of humans now. How many are there, Halfclaw?'

'Around thirty Blades are in the colony's caverns,' said the dragon. 'You would fit, but it would be a squeeze, as Darksky is insisting that they all stay in Frostback's old cavern. Wait until summer, and then destroy the mine; that's my advice.'

'Agreed,' said Rosie.

They glanced at Jade, waiting for a decision. She turned away from their expectant eyes, and tried to think. The King had told her to destroy the mine, if it were proved that it was the only one. Was it the only one? It was impossible to judge, not without a dozen more survey missions, and they had no time before Freshmist to carry out any further expeditions.

'The King told me that the decision would be mine to make,' she said, 'and I have doubts that dragon fire would be able to destroy all of the salve within the mine, for the simple reason that their necks aren't long enough to get very far down the tunnel. If we try to destroy it now, the attempt would probably fail, and we'd have nowhere to stay.' She nodded. 'We'll wait.'

'Very good, ma'am,' said Flavus. 'I defer to your authority.'

Rosie sighed in relief.

'If that is the decision,' said Halfclaw, 'then I shall depart now. Take care over Freshmist, humans; I will return as soon as summer begins.'

'Enjoy yourself!' cried Rosie, as the green dragon spread out his wings and took to the air. They stood and watched as he circled once over the valley, then soared off to the east.

Flavus frowned. 'The dragon will inform Queen Emily of our decision, ma'am.'

'She can come here herself if she feels differently.' She scanned the sky to iceward, but there was no sign of any clouds. She nodded. 'Back to work.'

Flavus had returned to the valley with more than maps. He had collected seeds and cuttings from the places he had searched in the mountains, and spent the rest of the morning sorting them, and explaining to Rosie the best ways to plant them once Freshmist had passed. Jade had taken an interest at first, but had become bored when she had realised that the seeds were all for fruits, cereals and vegetables, rather than flowers. Flavus told her his plans for cultivating the lower side of the valley, but Jade didn't want her garden to become a vegetable plot, although Rosie seemed enthusiastic about the idea. The two sergeants finished dismembering the last of the trees they had cut down, and stacked the firewood carefully within the cave. They were debating if they had enough time to cross the ridge to fell another tree, when two more dragons were spotted in the skies above them.

'Who's that with Deathfang?' said Rosie, a hand up to shield her eyes from the noon sun. She gasped. 'Malik's ass; it's Dawnflame.'

Sergeant Darvi dropped his axe, a look of terror on his face.

'Stay calm,' said Jade. 'I've already hit Dawnflame with death powers once; I'll do it again if I have to.'

They watched as the pair of dragons glided in wide circles over the valley. They were getting lower with every revolution, and Dawnflame's distinctive purple and blue markings contrasted with the metal-grey of the enormous Deathfang. Jade flexed her fingers, feeling for her powers. The last time she had used them had been out on the desolate, blood-soaked plains in front of the Fortress of the Lifegiver, where she had employed them to save a dragon. If Dawnflame attacked, then she would give her everything she had, though she doubted that she possessed enough power to take down both dragons.

Deathfang landed, then moved aside to allow the more slender Dawnflame to alight by the pool. The humans edged closer to each other, Sergeant Darvi moving slightly behind Jade.

'Welcome back to the valley, dragons,' said Jade. 'What brings you here?'

'Demigod,' said Deathfang, 'you have only a few hours until the rains commence.'

'Are you guessing?' said Jade.

'No. I can feel it. I sensed it last year, and the year before that; a tightening of the air, far too subtle for humans to detect. Has Halfclaw been?'

'Yes, though he left a couple of hours ago, after dropping off Flavus. He's gone back to Jezra for Freshmist.'

'He should be safe there with my daughter. Did you hear that the Ascendant was defeated by the Queen?'

'Yes,' said Jade; 'Halfclaw told us.'

'It was a noble victory,' Deathfang went on. 'However, the Ascendant will not give up so easily. He will be back. When he does, we can help each other.'

'Do you want an alliance?' said Jade.

'An understanding, let's say,' said the grey dragon. 'If Simon comes to the salve mine, then he will not ignore my colony, and the four infant dragons will be at risk. Your death powers could help protect them, and in return, we could help to protect you, here in this valley. We could destroy the mine, or evacuate you, or stand and fight, if it comes to it. What do you say?'

Jade considered for a moment. 'Have you spoken to the Queen?'

'I have. I visited Jezra a few days ago, which is how I know about Simon's failed attack. She asked me to enquire if you had destroyed the mine yet. I see that you have not.'

'We're waiting until Freshmist is over,' said Jade.

'Is that wise, demigod?'

'I don't know. It is, however, the decision that I have made. I was also ordered to remain here, at the mine, and we will have to use the cave to shelter in over Freshmist. And I was thinking about what will happen if Simon gets here. If the mine is a smoking heap of rubble, then he might go wild, and try to kill us all, but if the mine is open, then we might be able to trap him inside.'

'In which case, you will certainly need our assistance. We shall fly here as soon as the rains stop, demigod, and then one of us will remain here. Dawnflame has volunteered to be the first to act as your guard and protector, which is one of the reasons she has come here today – she felt it wise to scout out the location.'

Jade nodded, keeping half an eye on the blue and purple dragon by Deathfang's side.

'What was the other reason?' said Rosie.

Deathfang glanced at her. 'I will let Dawnflame herself tell you that.'

The other dragon lowered her head, her eyes burning.

'Well?' said Jade.

'Do not shame me, demigod,' said Dawnflame; 'it has taken me months to summon the will to do what I have come here to do.' The dragon paused, as several emotions passed over her features. 'I... I was wrong about you. You saved my son, and I tried to kill you. Firestone is the most precious thing in the world to me, and I will never forget the wounds the greenhides inflicted upon him; wounds that you healed. I have perhaps not shown the necessary gratitude that I owe you for what you did, and for that you also have my apology.'

Jade stared at the dragon.

'Wow,' said Rosie; 'that's great. Jade, do you have something to say also?'

'I don't think so.'

Rosie nudged her with an elbow. 'I think you do.'

'Fine. Dawnflame, I accept your thanks, and your apology. I know how much you hate us, so this must have been hard.'

'I do not hate you, demigod. It is true that I loathe the insects of the City, but how could I hate the one who saved the life of my son? It rankles with me that you acted without any thought of reward, and I swear that I will repay the debt I owe you.'

Deathfang tilted his head. 'Well said, Dawnflame. So, are we agreed – we shall help each other if Simon comes?'

'Yes,' said Jade. 'How are Quill and the other Blades?'

'They are well,' said the grey dragon. 'Darksky has been supervising their work and keeping them busy. They have sealed up the leaks in the cavern ceilings, so we should have a dry Freshmist, at last. They have also widened a tunnel connecting my cavern to the one where Burntskull and the humans are living, so Darksky can pass on her instructions without having to go outside. The rains won't stop them from working, so we shall have them carry out all manner of other improvements during Freshmist.'

'Does Burntskull agree with our new deal?'

'No, but he was out-voted four to one. I fear that you will have to save his life before he drops his hatred of you, demigod.' He lifted his head and sniffed the air. 'The rains are close; farewell.'

Dawnflame stared down at Jade. 'I will return, friend.'

The two dragons ascended into the pink sky, and flew off to sunward.

Rosie started to laugh. 'Can you believe that? Dawnflame called you a friend. I bet it pained her to say that.'

'She will have meant it,' said Flavus. 'Dragons never say anything they don't mean, which is why we should never be sarcastic with them – they take things too literally. And let's remember that she still hates the rest of us; she won't ever forget what happened to Tarsnow. She remains an exceedingly dangerous wild beast.'

'Deathfang said four to one,' said Jade. 'That means that Darksky and Bittersea are also in favour of helping us.'

'Bittersea is Firestone's grandmother,' said Rosie, 'so that's understandable, and I guess Darksky has been won over by all the work the Blades have done in the caverns. There's nothing like fixing the leaks in your roof to warm your heart towards someone.'

'I'm going for a last walk,' said Jade. 'I want to clear my head before the rain starts.'

She turned and walked away from the others, feeling a longing to be on her own. She would be shut up inside a cave with Rosie, Flavus and the Reaper sergeants for two months, something she wasn't looking forward to, and craved a bit of solitude. Her steps took her up paths that would soon be overflowing with water, until she reached the ridge that looked out towards iceward. The mountains were capped in the last of the winter's snow, and a fierce wind was gusting sunward. In the distance, she saw a dark front of cloud approaching, and she shook her head. Deathfang had been right; Freshmist was on its way.

She sifted through her thoughts, trying to work out how she felt about the words the dragon had said. She had no feelings for Dawnflame; no love, but no hate either, but the dragon now considered her a friend. Rosie did also, and Jade was starting to feel a little suffocated. Without any attachments, she had been free to act as she pleased, but now she had people depending on her, people who actually seemed to like her. She remembered a time when she had assumed that all mortals loved, envied and worshipped her, after all, her father had taught her that it was true. Mortals were like dogs – they lived briefly, were born to serve their masters, and could be quite loyal if domesticated properly. Rosie behaved more like a cat, with her refusal to bow slavishly before authority, and her tendency to say whatever popped into her mind. And, just like a cat, she would be gone in the blink of an eye. While Jade might end up being a dominant figure throughout Rosie's life, to Jade, Rosie's life was too short for any meaningful relationship to develop. She thought about her cousin Aila; she had foolishly run off with a mortal, and in a few brief decades she would be weeping and mourning his loss. Jade tried to harden her heart. It was better to never love at all, than to love a mortal.

She glanced up again, and realised that the clouds had moved a lot closer to the valley. Grey, hazy sheets of rain were hanging in the sky, and a flash of lightning streaked down from the heavy black clouds. A moment later, thunder rumbled, and Jade got to her feet. The wind was picking up as she ran back down to the valley, and she felt the first drops of rain on her shoulders as she reached the path by the stream. She picked up her pace, sprinting along the grassy bank. She could see the others already sheltering under the canopy at the entrance to the cave, and run under its cover just as the heavens opened. The rain crashed down upon the valley, and lightning followed – great forks of bright light mingling with the torrential downpour.

'I'm not sure I'll ever get used to the weather here,' said Flavus, as he gazed out from under the canopy.

Rosie gave him a look. 'Does it never rain on Implacatus?'

'Of course it does, Private, but for an hour here and there, not for two solid months without a break.'

Rosie nodded. 'Well, that's the five of us stuck in a cave until summer. What shall we do first? Anyone want some smoked goat?'

CHAPTER 5
PROGRESS

Jezra, The Western Bank – 28th Malikon 3423

The rain battered off the closed shutters, providing the never-ending background noise of Freshmist, along with the low rumble of thunder.

'I prayed for Freshmist to begin,' said Emily, shivering despite the blanket over her shoulders, 'and now I can't wait for it to end.'

Silva seemed unaffected by the cold. 'The storms are protecting us from invasion, your Majesty. I fear that Simon will make another attempt once summer starts.'

'Part of me wants him to,' she said, 'that way, no matter what happens, it will be over. It was bearable when Mona was here – at least then I could communicate with Daniel; now I don't know where he is, or even if he's still alive. It was Elspeth's first birthday seven days ago, and I have no idea if she is alive or dead. Simon could have killed them both when he returned to Ooste in Yordian, and we'd have no way of knowing.'

'You cannot assume the worst, your Majesty, regardless of how bleak things seem. We are alone, it is true, but we are not beaten.'

The oil lamp flickered, then went out, plunging the little room into semi-darkness, the only light filtering in from the cloud-covered skies through the slats in the shutters. Emily made no move to re-light the lamp; the supplies of oil were so low that it was being conserved for night time emergency meetings, and she was getting used to the gloom.

'Should we go back upstairs to your quarters, your Majesty?' said Silva. 'Sitting in the dark, especially inside this particular room, is not going to help anyone's mood.'

Emily nodded. She glanced at the floor, where the decapitated body of Mona had been found following Simon's attack. It was the only area in the Command Post that was out of the blocking range of Kelsey's powers, as long as the Holdfast woman remained within her own rooms, and Emily had taken to going there every few days. She knew it was risky; after all, Simon had himself, Naxor and Felice, who were all capable of using their vision powers to reach the room, but she had never sensed their presence inside her mind.

She nodded to the two soldiers by the entrance, and they opened the door as she and Silva got to their feet. The soldiers flanked them as they made their way along the claustrophobic passageways of the Command Post. The Banner were keeping busy over Freshmist, organising training sessions with the Brigades, and coming up with plans for every possible contingency. The morale of the Brigades and civilians had been slowly eroding over the rainy season, but the Banner soldiers seemed to take the weather in their stride. 'It's not as bad as Dragon Eyre,' – that was a refrain she heard often from the soldiers' lips, as if even the worst situation was nothing compared to the nightmare of that troubled world.

Several soldiers and officials bowed or saluted as they passed, but Emily was finding it harder to smile. She and Silva ascended the long flights of narrow stairs to the upper storey, where more soldiers let them enter Van's old apartment, where the Queen now lived. The major-general was still using his old office to run the Western Bank and the Grey Isle, but had given up his personal rooms to Emily.

The wind was making the shutters rattle, and a long rumble of thunder seemed to shake the building. Emily sat on a couch, then the door to the office opened.

'Your Majesty,' said Van, his eyes piercing her with intensity; 'I thought I heard you come in. I have a few updates for you – as you already know, the Brigades are working through Freshmist, and I have an entire detachment up on the ridge, replacing the old wooden palisades with brick and stone walls. This morning, a lookout reported seeing one of the young greenhide queens. The fact that it was spotted outside during Freshmist means that it was probably fleeing another queen. The Banner responded with a few ballista bolts, and that seems to have scared it off for now. Due to this, I am going to send more Brigade workers up there from tomorrow, to speed up the work. An angry queen could probably tear its way through the palisades, and the sooner we replace them with proper walls the better.'

Emily kept her eyes on him. His words had emerged in one long stream, and she noticed that his left hand was trembling. The salve was starting to take its toll on the major-general – she knew it, and so did Captain Cardova, if the frown on his face was anything to go by.

'You seem to have the situation under control, Van,' she said.

'Thank you, your Majesty. I have also ordered the Brigades to continue lifting the wrecked Blade ships from the bottom of the harbour...'

'In this weather?' she said.

'Yes, your Majesty. If we wait until summer, it will be too late. We are anticipating a strike from Simon as soon as the rains clear.'

'As long as you aren't pushing the Brigades too hard.'

'We have no choice, your Majesty. Our survival depends upon everyone in Jezra working as hard as possible over Freshmist. Our navy, small though it is, will control the Warm Sea and the approaches to Jezra. It's the Cold Sea where I fear the next attack will come. I have compiled a number of plans regarding the defence of the Grey Isle and Westrig; would you like to take a look at them?'

'Maybe later, Major-General. I'm tired just now.'

Van looked at her as if her words had confused him.

Cardova stepped forward. 'Sir, the leadership of the Fordian Exiles is downstairs, waiting to discuss the new rationing quotas.'

'Excellent,' said Van. 'I shall attend immediately.'

He bowed in front of Emily, then strode from the living room, a group of soldiers flanking him as he went.

Cardova sat down next to Emily.

'How long can he keep going at this pace, Captain?' she said.

'I don't know, your Majesty.'

'When did he last get a good night's sleep?'

Cardova laughed. 'Not since Simon's assault. I think he feels that he was caught out then, and so is determined not to let it happen again. He's working twenty hours a day.'

'Fuelled by salve?'

'Unfortunately, your Majesty.'

A side door opened, and Kelsey peered through. 'Has he gone?'

Cardova nodded.

'Thank Pyre for that,' she said, entering the room, Vadhi trailing by her side. 'He's too intense for me to handle right now.'

Emily frowned. 'Could you not speak to him about it, Kelsey?'

'What? Do you think I haven't tried? He doesn't listen to anything I say any more.' She sat, a heavy folder clutched to her chest. 'He's made his decision, and he's picked salve over me.'

The Queen turned to Cardova. 'Can we not intervene? What if we forcibly took the salve from him and locked him in a room?'

'I don't have the authority to do that, your Majesty.'

'I am the Queen – surely I have the authority?'

'You do, but the members of the Combined Council are unaware of the major-general's addiction. If we removed him from power, even for a few days, they would notice, and there would be all manner of messy consequences.'

'Then, what can we do?'

Cardova shrugged. 'Nothing, your Majesty. The major-general is a hero to the ordinary soldiers and to the Brigades, and his work rate is currently phenomenal. They all think he's working hard to save everyone; morale would collapse if they discovered it was down to salve.'

'Can we change the subject?' said Kelsey. 'I don't want to talk about this again.' She laid the heavy folder down onto the low table in front of them.

'What's in there?' said Emily.

'Mona's research notes. I've been reading them.'

'I thought I hadn't seen much of you recently,' said Cardova. 'Is that what you've been doing?'

'Aye,' Kelsey said. 'It's Mona's legacy; her last research.'

'Did you find anything useful?' said Emily.

'Useful? I don't know. I started off trying to discover more about the history of that sword – the Just, to see if I could find out where it came from. Malik brought it here, to the City, along with the Axe of Rand, so neither weapon belongs on this world. The Just ended up becoming a symbol of the sovereignty of the City; that's why Prince Aurelian had it in his possession. After his arrest, Malik took it back, then gave it to Prince Michael.'

Emily's eyes widened. 'My Fated Blade is from another world?'

'But where?' said Silva.

'I was hoping you'd know,' said Kelsey. 'Mona's notes don't mention any origin. Where did the Weathervane come from?'

'I don't know. Queen Belinda had it long before I was born, and she never told me how it came into her possession.'

'I've searched through every crate that was brought from Cuidrach Palace,' said Emily. 'None of them contained the other Fated Blade.'

They paused as a loud roar of thunder shook the building.

'Most likely, your Majesty,' said Cardova; 'it's still in the ruins of the palace.'

Emily nodded. 'I had no idea it could penetrate steel armour, and I've read every book in the City on Prince Michael. I don't think he actually used the Just much as a weapon, except perhaps in the Civil War, when he fought Yendra in the Circuit.'

'Prince Aurelian couldn't even pick it up on his own,' said Kelsey. 'It remained on the wall of Maeladh Palace when he was sitting on the throne. Anyway, that's all I learned about the Just. Mona's notes only had a few lines about it; she was much more interested in what the scrolls contained. She dampened them slowly over months, softening them until she could unroll the material without it breaking or crumbling. Some of it was the boring old lists that the Banner guys predicted – inventories of supplies and stuff like that, but some scrolls contained drawings and designs of machines.'

'What kind of machines?' said Emily.

Kelsey shrugged. 'I didn't really understand them. Wheels and gears turned by steam. But, that's not the point. In Mona's notes, she had written about how backward the people of the City were until Malik and Amalia arrived. The God-King and God-Queen gifted them loads of new inventions, from plumbing to the printing press, and better forms of farming, which makes sense, as Lostwell had all of those things. However, this seemed to set off a great expansion in knowledge within the City, especially in the new Royal Academy that Malik and Amalia established. For a while, the students were encouraged to research whatever they wanted, but then, something changed. Almost overnight, the Academy was ordered to cease all research, and told to concentrate solely on art and poetry. Thousands of books were burned in Ooste, and whole branches of knowledge became forbidden.'

'Why?' said the Queen.

'Apologies, your Majesty,' said Cardova, 'but it seems obvious to me, as the same thing happened on Implacatus. The gods don't want mortals to get too clever. If mortals could invent a machine that could kill a god, then we would be on the same level as them, and they would be in danger of losing their power over us.'

'That's the conclusion Mona came to,' said Kelsey. 'She reckoned that Malik and Amalia started to worry where all of the research at the Academy was leading, and that they acted before the mortals could learn too much. Prince Aurelian realised this, and rebelled against them. He controlled Jezra from Tara at the time, and when he was overthrown and arrested, some of the knowledge was kept safe here, hidden under the ancient library. Then the greenhides came, and Jezra fell; and the knowledge was lost.'

Emily frowned. 'Until now?'

'If you're hoping I'll discover some amazing new weapon to kill Simon, then don't get too excited, Queenie. Mona left a mountain of notes, and I've barely scratched the surface; and, there was still a ton of scrolls that she hadn't even touched. Worse, the scrolls were written in an ancient alphabet that I can't decipher, probably one native to the City that went out of use millennia ago. If I had access to the professors of the Imperial University in Plateau City it would be a different story, but out here in Jezra? Vadhi's been helping me transcribe some of the documents, but it would take decades of work to get through everything on our own.'

Emily turned to Cardova. 'Captain, how do the Ascendants stop mortals from learning new knowledge on Implacatus?'

'By branding certain fields of knowledge as heretical, your Majesty. The very first Banners were formed by the gods to hunt down those guilty of heresy. The condemned would be burned at the stake, and their forbidden books thrown onto the pyres. That's the legend; I don't know how true it is. If I had to guess, then I would say that the Ascendants will have had to enforce this rule countless times over history. They have been alive for over thirty thousand years, according to them; thirty millennia of keeping mortals in their place.'

Emily remembered that Silva was sitting with them. She turned to the demigod. 'Do you have anything to say about this?'

'None of this comes as a surprise to me, your Majesty,' said Silva. 'Most gods are of the opinion that mortals cannot be trusted with too much knowledge. Under the rule of Queen Belinda and King Nathaniel on Lostwell, mortals were forbidden from learning many things, and new inventions would routinely be destroyed, if discovered. Farming practices remained unchanged for thousands of years, and the study of medicines was discouraged, to prevent the mortal population from expanding too quickly. Does it surprise you, your Majesty, to learn that Amalia and Malik would have done the same?'

'The histories of the City have no mention of it,' said Emily, 'nor do the many works regarding the governance of Prince Michael, who must have carried on his parents' work. In some ways it seems obvious, and yet I have never thought of it in that way before. What's it like on your world, Kelsey?'

'Well, there are no gods ruling us, for a start, but most of us have only had a few hundred years of relative civilisation, roughly from when the earthquakes stopped. The Holdings calendar is on the year five-three-three. Half a millennium. Except for one of the five nations – Rahain. They had a civilisation that went back thousands of years, but unfortunately most of it was destroyed in a series of wars. The important thing is that there are no gods to stop us.'

Emily frowned. Could it be true? Had the gods been deliberately holding the mortals back? Her thoughts went to the unchanging ways of the Hammers and Scythes, where a millennium of oppression and servitude had seen them perform the same roles year after year. She had always imagined that it was due to tradition that nothing had changed in that time. On the other hand, she could hardly believe that Yendra had conspired against the mortals; was her willingness to help them another reason she had been loathed by most of her family?

She glanced at Silva again. 'Do you think this is right?'

'By "right," your Majesty, do you mean "morally correct?"'

'Yes.'

'I don't have an answer to that, your Majesty. If I condemned it, then I would be condemning the policy of Queen Belinda, and that I will not do.'

'Would the new Belinda feel the same?' said Kelsey. 'She's not the same person you used to know, Silva. I think her opinion on this might have changed.'

Silva said nothing.

'We must win this struggle,' said Emily. 'If we don't, then Simon will keep us under his heel forever; we shall all become his slaves. If we win, then I want you, Kelsey, to open one of those universities you keep talking about. No field of study will be forbidden; you have my word on that. For now, the most important thing is to keep the scrolls and all of Mona's work safe, so we can examine it properly without the threat of invasion hanging over our heads.'

Cardova glanced at Kelsey. 'Are there truly no gods on your world?'

'Well, I guess there's one now – Aila. She was going to go there with my brother. If they made it, then she'll be the only one.'

Emily smiled. 'I hardly think that Lady Aila would try to take control of your world.'

'My mother wouldn't let her, even if she wanted to. My sister would also stop her; my powers are nothing compared to hers. The Holdfasts prevented the gods from taking over the last time they invaded, and that was before Corthie became the greatest mortal warrior ever.'

'Then,' said Emily, 'I'm very glad we have our own Holdfast, right here.'

'I think I'd like to see this world one day,' said Cardova.

Kelsey narrowed her eyes and squinted at him.

He shrugged. 'A world where no gods are in charge sounds appealing, to say the least. No offence intended, Silva.'

The demigod frowned. 'I think perhaps that everyone is forgetting all of the benefits that the gods have brought to mortals. Queen Belinda worked tirelessly to protect her subjects.'

'Aye, from other gods,' said Kelsey.

'Tell me, Kelsey,' she said; 'your perfect world, where there are no gods; is it peaceful; is it a paradise? Do mortals live side by side without fighting each other?'

'No, we've had our fair share of wars that have had nothing to do with gods. No one's saying that mortals are perfect. Left to our own devices, we're as liable to screw things up as anyone else. But, the gods have definitely made things worse; the most terrible wars have been because of them.'

'You're generalising, Kelsey. What if Princess Yendra had been on your world?'

'Look, I get that some gods are better than others, Silva. But why take the risk? For every Yendra, there are a dozen Amalias or Simons or Edmonds who want nothing more than to treat us like slaves. Being in possession of self-healing powers does not make you a better person.'

'But only immortals have a proper sense of perspective. We can look forward, and backward, with greater clarity than someone who only lives for a few short decades. All of that accumulated knowledge and experience would be lost if there were no gods.'

'And what has that wisdom done for us? Kept us in chains, while they live in palaces; that's what.'

'Amalia kept the greenhides out of the City for thousands of years,' said Silva; 'without her, there would be no City.'

Kelsey laughed. 'You're defending the woman who opened the gates in the Middle Walls?'

'Let's not argue,' said Emily.

Kelsey and Silva glared at each other, but fell silent.

'Thank you,' said Emily. 'These debates can get heated, especially in Freshmist when there's nothing to do but stay inside. This conflict has already seen four demigods lose their lives – along with thousands of mortals, but a middle ground exists, one that Daniel and I were trying to achieve – a City where mortals and immortals can live together peacefully; a City where loyalty and merit are rewarded, and immortals aren't in positions of power based solely on the fact that they live longer. Lady Silva, your help in recent years has been invaluable. Kelsey, your help has also proved vital; the City needs you both. I need you both.'

Silva bowed her head. 'Thank you, your Majesty.'

Emily stood. 'I think I shall visit my mother, to see how little Maxwell is doing today.' Her eyes fell on Vadhi, who had been sitting quietly while the others had talked. 'Vadhi, you have said nothing on this; do you have an opinion?'

'Me?' said the young Brigade worker.

Emily smiled. 'Yes, Vadhi; you.'

She glanced around at the others. 'The gods destroyed my home, your Majesty. I've lived my entire life in fear of them, and I don't want to live like that any more.'

'Thank you, Vadhi.'

Emily went to a side door and opened it. Inside, her mother was sitting on an armchair, while Maxwell was crawling on the rug. Emily closed the door behind her and sat down next to her mother.

'I heard raised voices, dear,' said Lady Omertia. 'Is everything alright?'

'Yes, mother. It's just Freshmist, making everyone irritable. How is Maxwell?'

'Fine. I think he'll be walking soon, and then I'll have my hands full.'

Emily nodded. 'He has self-healing, doesn't he?'

'Yes, dear. He hasn't been remotely ill since we've been looking after him, and he never bruises, even if he falls over. Elspeth was so delicate in comparison.'

Emily stared at the child as he gripped the side of a chair and tried to stand. She was missing Elspeth doing the same things, just as she had missed her daughter's first birthday. She felt a dark cloud hover over her thoughts as she pictured Elspeth in the hands of her enemies. Despair swirled through her mind, and she tried to suppress it.

'It will be fine, dear,' said her mother. 'You'll get your daughter back.'

'Will I? Sometimes, mother, I think that she's already dead, and then I wonder why I'm still doing this. It's wrong of me to think this way, but I'd give up everything to have her back; everything.'

She started to cry, and her mother pulled her close, saying nothing.

When Emily returned to the living room, Kelsey and Vadhi had gone, along with the heavy folder containing Mona's research notes. Silva was sitting in the same place, a sullen expression on her face, while Captain Cardova was signing off a large pile of papers while he reclined on a couch. His eyes glanced up as Emily entered.

'Do you have five minutes, your Majesty?' he said, swinging his feet back onto the floor.

'For you, Lucius? Of course. What is it?'

'A lieutenant was here while you were speaking to your mother, your Majesty. Apparently, we have captured our first spy. A Torduan, disguised as a Brigade worker, was apprehended while attempting to get into the Command Post. When confronted by Banner forces, he tried to run for it.'

'A Torduan? He's an Exile?'

'Yes, your Majesty. He made his way here via Icehaven and Westrig, in the last days of winter. Do you want to speak to him?'

'I don't know. Should I?'

'He claims to have a message for you, your Majesty.'

'Concerning what?'

'He refuses to say, your Majesty. We could use interrogation techniques on him, but I thought I'd speak to you first, before authorising that course of action.'

'You mean torture him?'

'Yes, your Majesty. I know how much you dislike that.'

Emily nodded. 'Take me to him.'

Cardova stood, and led Emily out of the apartment. A squad of Banner soldiers was waiting to escort them, and they descended two floors to where a corridor of cells was located. Banner soldiers were there in numbers, and Cardova spoke to a few officers, who took them to a locked cell. Emily peered through the bars as an officer found the correct key. A man was sitting inside the cell, his face bruised.

The officer unlocked the door, and Emily entered the cell, accompanied by Cardova and two soldiers, who kept their crossbows aimed at the prisoner. The man looked up, his eyes wary.

'I am Queen Emily,' she said. 'Do you have something you wish to say to me?'

The man stared at her. 'Will I be executed?'

'You certainly have a Torduan accent. Why are you here? Why didn't you join the Brigades two years ago?'

'I escaped the camps in Scythe territory,' he said. 'I've been living in the Circuit.'

'Who recruited you to come here?'

'Are you really the Queen?'

Emily slipped her hand into a deep pocket and withdrew her slender crown. 'I could wear this, if you like.'

The man smiled for a second, then his face dropped again. 'I was told to pass on a message to you if I was captured.'

'What were you trying to achieve?'

'I was asked to kidnap the child. Failing that, I was asked to monitor the child's condition, to see if he was healthy and well.'

'By child, do you mean Maxwell?'

'Yes, but I couldn't even get into the Command Post. I've been trying to get inside this building for days, ever since I walked here from Westrig.'

Emily crouched down next to him. 'Who sent you?'

'Lady Amalia.'

Emily glanced up at Cardova, then turned back to the prisoner. 'Is Simon aware that she sent you here?'

The man shrugged. 'I don't know.'

'What did Amalia promise you?'

'Enough gold to buy half of the Circuit. It sounded easy, and it was, until I tried to get inside the Command Post. Are you going to have me killed?'

'That depends. What was the message?'

'She made me memorise it. She said that your husband and daughter are now in her custody, in Tara, along with the King's parents. She said that Simon means to execute all of them, once you are captured or killed. She asked me to appeal to you as a mother, and begs you not to harm Maxwell. She will keep Elspeth safe, if you keep Maxwell safe, but she won't be able to stop Simon from killing them. She wants to meet you, to discuss the children; she is willing to hand over Elspeth, if you are willing to hand over Maxwell.'

'But, she sent you here to kidnap Maxwell?'

'Yes. My message was for if I failed.'

'That sounds like Amalia. How did she recruit you?'

'A man called Albeck approached me. He works for the Refugee Council in the Circuit, and he said that there was a lucrative job on offer. I only met Lady Amalia once, when she interviewed me in Tara, then I was put on a wagon going to Icehaven, where Albeck had arranged for a boat to pick me up. He gave me a Brigade uniform, and saw me off at the quayside. Look, I've told you everything. I was trying to return the child to his mother – are you going to kill me for that?'

'No,' said Emily, 'but you'll be staying here in prison for the time being.' She stood and gestured to Cardova.

They left the cell, and the Banner officer locked the door.

'We have no way of knowing if he's lying, your Majesty,' Cardova said, as they began to walk back to the apartment. 'Frankly, it sounds like a trap.'

'Do you believe that Amalia sent him?'

'That part I do believe, your Majesty. She sent him here to kidnap Maxwell, but she underestimated the security measures that we have put in place.'

'Maybe. Perhaps she expected his mission to fail. Perhaps the real reason he's here is to pass on the message.'

Cardova glanced at her. 'That seems unlikely, your Majesty.'

'But what if it's genuine? What if Amalia is just as scared of Simon as we are? We would be negligent if we passed over an opportunity to find an ally among the gods of the City.'

Cardova halted in the passageway. 'Forgive me, your Majesty, but Amalia is trying to play on your desire to have Elspeth returned to you. She knows that your daughter is your vulnerability, and she's trying to trick you into making a mistake.' He looked her in the eye. 'She cannot be trusted.'

Emily held his gaze. The Banner captain was probably correct; it was most likely a trick. All the same, a small seed of hope had been planted within her; a foolish hope, perhaps, but hadn't she sworn earlier that day that she would do anything to get Elspeth back?

'I'm sure you're right, Lucius,' said Emily. 'Let's say no more about it.'

Cardova narrowed his eyes a little, but said nothing. They began walking again, passing through the cold hallways of the Command Post, the beginnings of a plan forming in Emily's mind.

CHAPTER 6

TROUBLES OF THE HEART

Jezra, The Western Bank – 27th Amalan 3423

Kelsey ran up the stairs, her heart racing with excitement. Vadhi was following her, trying to keep up, as they passed a multitude of Banner soldiers and Brigade workers on the staircase. Kelsey burst out onto the roof and grinned, the sunlight warming her skin. She closed her eyes and took a long breath. After two months of nothing but rain and storms, Freshmist was over. Even better, the end of the season had arrived a few days early, with four days of Amalan still remaining.

'I can't see anything,' said Vadhi; 'it's too misty.'

Kelsey smiled. 'It'll burn off soon.' She gazed around at Jezra. Vadhi was right – sheets of mist were rising from the waterlogged town as it began to dry out, and the cliffs to the west were invisible, shrouded behind a thick wall of fog. She pulled off her long coat. 'Summer, at last. Four months of sunshine and warmth are ahead of us, Vadhi.'

The young woman frowned. 'And we'll be spending it inside the Command Post.'

'Sorry about that, Vadhi. You know, it's too late to have you replaced – you know too much from sitting with the Queen, and the Banner commanders. You're stuck with me now.'

'It will be worth it, if we win. Maybe Simon will decide to leave us alone?'

'That's the spirit, Vadhi – blind optimism.'

'I thought that sharing the same rooms as Captain Cardova for months on end might have given me a chance with him – that was blind optimism.'

'Ah, so that's why you volunteered?'

Vadhi's face flushed. 'No. Well, it wasn't entirely my reason. I was wasting my time, though – he's not interested in me.'

'He's in love with the Banner.'

Vadhi shrugged. 'I've officially given up. There are plenty of other good-looking Banner officers around.'

A pair of shadows flitted overhead, and Kelsey's smile increased. She glanced up, and saw Frostback and Halfclaw above them, circling the town. The silver dragon saw her on the roof, and descended. The moment she landed, Kelsey took off, running towards her. She flung her arms round the dragon's long neck.

'Pyre's arse, Frostback,' she said; 'I missed you.'

'I missed you too, rider.'

'Really? Even though you had Halfclaw all to yourself?'

'Halfclaw is my betrothed; you are my beloved rider. I feel incomplete without you.'

A tear rolled down Kelsey's cheek. 'I feel the same. How I wish we could go flying together; just you and me, but Van would go berserk if I left the Command Post.'

'How are you and the major-general getting along? I sense there has been no reconciliation between you?'

'No. He's so deeply into his work that he barely glances at me. And, when he speaks to me, it's usually to give me a telling off for something. The salve is rotting his mind; he's like a machine, with no emotions. Except anger; he has lots of anger.'

Frostback glanced at Vadhi. 'Some privacy, human; I am talking to my rider.'

Vadhi's face flushed again.

'It's not her fault,' said Kelsey. 'Van once shouted at her because she went to the bathroom on her own, without me. She's not supposed to leave my side, even for a moment.'

'Sorry,' mumbled Vadhi, as the silver dragon stared at her.

'Tell me about you and Halfclaw,' Kelsey said, changing the subject.

'What I have to say is for your ears only, rider. My personal life is of no concern to this girl.'

'I'll walk to the other end of the roof,' said Vadhi. 'No one will know.'

'You do that,' said Frostback.

Vadhi nodded, then retreated out of earshot, taking a seat on the low wall that ringed the roof.

'That's better,' said the silver dragon. She turned back to Kelsey. 'Halfclaw and I are in love. I won't go so far as to say that I was wrong to wait, but many of my fears were without foundation. Halfclaw is devoted to me, and we have pledged ourselves to each other.'

'That makes me very happy,' said Kelsey. 'Do dragons get married?'

'Not as humans do. After our pledge to each other, I suppose you could say that we are married. While Halfclaw lives, and remains true, I will never betray his love for me.'

Kelsey glanced over her shoulder to make sure that Vadhi was still out of hearing range.

'I have something to tell you as well,' she said.

'About Van?'

'No. Something that I didn't want to tell anyone else. I had another vision, back in winter.'

'In winter? Why did you not tell me before now?'

'Too much was happening. Do you want to hear it?'

'As long as it doesn't affect my future. Does it?'

'No. I mean, you're not in it. Neither am I, for that matter.'

'Very well. What did you see?'

'I was drinking with the Queen and Cardova one night, just after I split up with Van. I was a bit drunk, but the vision was clear; well, as clear as they ever are. I looked into Cardova's eyes, and saw it.'

'Does that mean the vision is of the captain's future?'

'Aye. It's something that he will see. That's the strange part, because he's somewhere he shouldn't be. He's up on a roof, just as we are now, and I recognised the view. He's on my world, in a place called Colsbury, and standing next to him is my sister.'

'Karalyn?'

'Aye.'

'What are they doing?'

'Just standing there, talking. It was only a flash; I have no idea what they were discussing.'

Frostback tilted her head. 'I don't mean to sound disappointed, but your vision seems a little inconsequential, when weighed against our present troubles.'

'Maybe, but it's made me think. First, how does he get to my world? And, more importantly, it means that Lucius isn't about to die on us.'

'I'm not sure what I should do with such knowledge.'

Kelsey raised an eyebrow. 'Now you know how I feel.'

'Have you told him?'

'No. I'm not sure what effect it would have on him. And what would I say? "You can't die until you've met my sister?"'

'What if I were to strike him down?'

'You wouldn't be able to. Nothing can prevent my visions from coming true.'

'That seems impossible.'

'I know, but trust me on this. I've tried countless times to stop my visions from taking place, and have failed with each attempt. It's better just to let them happen.'

'Private Vadhi,' cried a voice; 'why are you not at your post?'

Kelsey turned, and saw Van stride towards the dragon, fury written on his features.

'Sorry, sir,' said Vadhi, running across the roof.

Van glared at her. 'What have I told you before, Private? Are you too stupid to understand simple instructions?'

'No, sir.'

'Then why do I find myself having to speak to you like this again?'

'I don't know, sir. Sorry, sir.'

'Leave her alone,' said Kelsey. 'We asked her to step back a little so that I could talk to Frostback.'

Van stared at her, his eyes burning. 'You know the rules, Miss Hold-fast. If Simon reaches you, then our resistance is over, and everything we've built will be destroyed. Do you understand?'

'I understand that you're shouting at me like an arsehole.'

Van clenched his fists.

'Major-General,' said Frostback; 'I would be exceedingly careful with your next words or deeds, if I were you.'

'This is none of your business, dragon. I need you and Halfclaw to fly with all speed to the Grey Isle. Scouts have just returned from the island, reporting that Gloamer ships have been seen approaching. I need you both out there, to observe, and to retaliate, if an attack is underway.'

Frostback kept her gaze steady. 'Halfclaw is due to fly to the Eastern Mountains. He promised Jade that he would visit as soon as summer began.'

'This operation is of a far higher priority,' said Van. 'We cannot afford to lose the Grey Isle. Go, now.'

'Your tone is objectionable, Major-General. Halfclaw and I are not your possessions, to be ordered around as if we were children.'

'Then go to the Eastern Mountains,' said Van, the veins on his fore-head bulging, 'and then never come back. If you are not with us, then you might as well be enemies.'

Sparks rippled across Frostback's jaws. 'Are you threatening me?'

Van didn't move. 'Are you disobeying an order?'

Kelsey raised her hands. 'This is pointless. Van, calm down, for Pyre's sake. Frostback, imagine for a moment that Van asked you politely; imagine that I'm asking you politely. A quick trip to the Grey Isle and back will only take a couple of hours; let's not fall out over it.'

'Are you siding with him, rider?'

'No; I'm trying to forge a future where we don't all hate each other. Please, do it for me.'

'Very well, rider. I will go; for you, not for Van. How you were ever attracted to him is beyond my understanding.'

The silver dragon turned from Van, as if pretending he wasn't there, then extended her wings and ascended into the pink sky. Kelsey waited until she had joined Halfclaw above the town, then turned on Van.

'You utter dipshit; what are you trying to do? Frostback has saved us all; without her, Montieth would be ruling the City; have you forgotten?' She pointed a finger in his face. 'Never speak to my dragon like that again.'

'Get your finger out of my face, Miss Holdfast. I only need your presence in the Command Post; I don't have to listen to your endless complaints. One more word from you, and I'll make good on my promise to have you locked up.'

They stared at each other for a moment, then Van wheeled away, and strode back towards the stair turret.

'Arsehole,' Kelsey muttered.

'It was my fault,' said Vadhi.

'No, it wasn't. He's just being a prick, and you know why, don't you? You've sat in on enough conversations with me and the Queen.'

'Salve?'

'At least I know I was right to break up with him. I can't believe I actually thought I loved him.'

'Are you alright?'

'No, Vadhi. If he tries to come between me and Frostback again, I'll give her permission to burn his bollocks off.'

Captain Cardova appeared on the roof, and walked over to where Kelsey and Vadhi were standing.

'The Queen wants you,' he said.

'Did you bump into Van on the way up?' said Kelsey.

Cardova pursed his lips. 'I did, though he was too angry to speak to me.' He raised a hand. 'I'm not going to ask why. Has Frostback been sent to the Grey Isle?'

'Aye. She's on her way.'

'Come on, then. The Queen is waiting.'

They began to walk back to the stair turret.

'How do you cope with him?' said Kelsey. 'He must be driving you mad.'

'I'm not going to bitch about Van, Kelsey. It is what it is. We just have to keep going.'

'Aye? Well, I've had just about enough of him. He threatened to lock me up.'

'What did I just say? I don't want to know.'

'You're never usually this tetchy, Lucius; I know he's getting to you.'

Cardova said nothing as they descended the stairs, and Kelsey fell into an angry silence. They went to a guarded meeting room, which had all of its windows lying open to let in the light and the warm summer breeze. Around a table was sitting the Queen, Van, Silva, and a few other Banner officers.

Emily smiled at Kelsey. 'Thank you for coming.'

'Aye?' said Kelsey, taking a seat next to Cardova. 'Why am I here?'

'I value your opinion and advice,' said Emily.

'Really? Perhaps you should mention that to Van. He thinks I'm good for nothing except locking up.'

A few officers glanced at each other, while Van stared, his eyes boring into her.

'Let's not bicker, please,' said Emily. 'We are here to discuss the Grey Isle, while we await news from the two dragons that have been sent to see what's happening. With luck, it will be a false alarm. However, now that summer has arrived, we have to accept that the Grey Isle is at risk from an attack from Dalrig. The question before us is – should we evacuate?'

'It might already be too late for that, your Majesty,' said Van. 'The time to evacuate the Grey Isle was in winter.'

'What exactly did the scout see?' said Silva.

'Ships,' said Van. 'The entire Gloamer fleet, heading out to sea. If

Simon is with them, then the garrison on the Grey Isle will be massacred.'

'The entire second regiment is there, along with a thousand from the Brigades,' said Cardova. 'If the Gloamer fleet blockades the harbour entrance, then there will be no way to get our people off the island.'

'It could be another diversionary attack,' said a Banner major. 'We cannot risk sending Miss Holdfast to counter the Ascendant if he is there.'

'I know that,' said Van. 'Miss Holdfast will be going nowhere. She stays by the Queen; that is her role.'

'If it turns out to be a false alarm,' said the Queen, 'then what is our next step?"

'I recommend an immediate withdrawal from the Grey Isle, your Majesty,' said Cardova.

'No,' said Van. 'The time for that has passed. We need access to the Cold Sea to feed the population of Jezra, and to get our hands on oil for heating and lighting. If we're cut off from both seas, then Jezra will start to starve.'

'Could we not sail from Westrig, sir?' said the major.

'Not with the Gloamer fleet based upon the Grey Isle,' said Van. 'They'd sink our vessels with ease. The Banner and Brigades lack the seamanship to compete with the veteran sailors of Dalrig.'

'I disagree, sir,' said Cardova. 'We can hold our own.'

'You're delusional, Captain. Our best crews have had two years of practice, compared to the Gloamers' centuries of sailing the Cold Sea.'

'What about Icehaven, sir?' said Cardova. 'Lady Yvona has profited immensely from the Gloamers being forced off the Cold Sea for the last two years. She won't be happy about them taking control of the Grey Isle.'

'Lady Yvona is a coward,' said Van. 'She only fights when assured of victory. If Simon goes to Icehaven, then she will bow before him, just like the other traitors. We will get no help from her.'

Emily frowned. 'Then, Major-General, what are you recommending?'

'There is no course of action that we can take at the moment, your Majesty; none that will do us any good. We should prepare for the worst.'

'Let us not fall into despair,' said Emily. 'At the very least, perhaps we should ask Lady Silva to use her powers to sense Simon's current location.'

'I am more than happy to do that, your Majesty,' said the demigod. 'Should I go downstairs to Chancellor Mona's old chamber, where she conducted her vision surveys?'

'No need,' said Kelsey, standing. 'I'll leave. You can wait here, Silva, so that you can tell the others right away.'

'Thank you, Kelsey,' said the Queen; 'most considerate of you. Please come back in ten minutes or so.'

Kelsey walked from the room, Vadhi hurrying after her. They went down to the ground floor, squeezing past the bustling soldiers, then strode to the other end of the large building. They entered the small chamber tacked onto the end of the Command Post, and Kelsey opened the shutters to let in the sunlight.

'I'm worried,' said Vadhi, as Kelsey paced the floor of the room.

'Aye?'

'I've never seen the major-general disagree with Captain Cardova before, at least not in front of the Queen and the other officers. Have they fallen out?'

'You know as much as me. Do you realise that, even if we win, you won't be allowed to go back to your normal Brigade? You know too much. You've seen the Queen upset and depressed, and listened to her woes, and you've heard every secret that Van and Cardova share.'

'I know. I realised that a while ago.'

'Doesn't it bother you?'

'No. I like hearing what's going on. Most people in Jezra see the Queen and Van as being rock-solid, immovable and emotionless, but I've seen them at their best and worst. It makes them seem more human.'

'Even when Van's being an arsehole?'

'It's the salve that's doing that to him. That's one secret I'd never reveal; the Brigades would not be pleased to know that the major-general is a slave to salve. It makes him seem weak.'

'He's not weak. He only got addicted because he was poisoned with concentrated salve. If that hadn't happened, then we'd probably still be together.'

'Maybe if you'd stayed with him, then you could have helped him to give up.'

'Is that what you think? I tried to make him give up.'

'Did you? How hard?'

Kelsey glared at her.

'I'm only saying,' said Vadhi; 'you know, perhaps you could have stuck it out a bit longer. It's like you gave up at the first problem you encountered. Now look at the state he's in; shouting at everybody, and angry all the time. He's not the same guy any more.'

'Are you blaming me for this?'

'No, but what you did hardly helped.'

For a moment, Kelsey almost told Vadhi to mind her place, but how could she, after she had ordered the young woman to always be informal with her? All the same, she felt like slapping Vadhi. How dare she blame her for Van's stupidity?

'That's ten minutes,' said Vadhi. 'Should we go back?'

Kelsey realised her heart was pounding. She took a breath, then strode from the room, not waiting for Vadhi. The soldiers escorted them back up the stairs, and she went back into the meeting room, trailed by the young Brigade woman. Kelsey frowned at the downcast expressions on everyone's faces.

'Bad news?' she said.

The Queen glanced up at her. 'Simon is on the Grey Isle.'

Kelsey fell into her seat. 'Shit.'

'We don't need the dragons to know what's happening right now,' said Van. 'We must assume that the second regiment of the Banner has ceased to exist.' He glanced round the room. 'I need to speak to the Queen alone. Captain Cardova and Miss Holdfast, please also remain.'

Silva and the remaining Banner officers got to their feet in silence, and filed out of the room. Vadhi lingered, as usual, but Van gestured for her to leave, and she followed the others out.

Van stared at the surface of the table, then got to his feet and walked to a window, gazing out at Jezra.

'This is a disaster,' he said. 'I take full responsibility; I should have foreseen this before Freshmist got underway, and evacuated the Grey Isle back then. I should have guessed that Simon would act as soon as the rains stopped. I missed it, because I was too concerned with making sure we entered Freshmist safely. I was stupid.'

Kelsey, the Queen and Cardova glanced at each other, then the Queen opened her mouth to speak.

'I was stupid,' cried Van, raising his voice, 'and because of me, two thousand Exiles are being slaughtered by that bastard.' He clenched his fists. 'A thousand Banner soldiers, and a thousand young Brigade workers, practically children, and I as good as abandoned them.'

'Van,' said the Queen, her eyes full of pity; 'it's not your fault alone. We all...'

'Of course it's my fault!' he shouted. 'The garrison on the Grey Isle trusted me, and right now Simon is killing them all, while we sit here and do nothing!' He drew back his right fist and punched the thick wooden window frame. 'I am going to kill Simon!' he cried. 'And Amalia,' he yelled, punching the window frame again; 'and Montieth. I'm going to kill all of those bastards...'

His face seemed to freeze, and he raised his left hand to his chest. A strange choking sound escaped from his lips, then he collapsed, toppling over and striking his head on the floor. His bloody right fist trembled, and another choke emerged from his throat, then he went quiet. Cardova jumped to his feet and raced over, kneeling by Van's body. He felt for a pulse, then lowered his head to Van's mouth, listening.

'He's not breathing,' the captain said, his voice low.

Kelsey and the Queen stood staring, as Cardova joined his hands together and began pushing down on Van's chest.

'How can we help?' said Emily. 'What should we do?'

'Take over from me,' Cardova said.

Emily rushed over, crouched down, and began pushing on Van's chest, while the captain moved up to Van's face. He breathed into his mouth, as Kelsey stood, frozen to the floor, staring, the sight of Van lying on the ground paralysing her to the spot. Was he dead? She couldn't bring herself to imagine the worst, despite the warnings Cardova had repeated over the previous few months. She tried to take a step forward, but her feet refused to move. Emily was pounding on Van's chest with her fists, as Cardova continued to breathe into the major-general's mouth.

Van gasped for air.

'He's breathing,' said Cardova, the relief in his voice obvious. He placed a hand onto Van's neck. 'And I can feel a pulse again.' The captain rubbed his face, then he and the Queen shared a glance.

'Is he alright?' said Kelsey.

Cardova looked up at her. 'He's alive, but unconscious. We need to get him into bed.'

'Perhaps we should be discreet,' said Emily. 'No one knows what happened just now, except the three of us in this room. Do the other commanders need to know? We could tell them that he was feeling sick, but not go into any details.'

Cardova glanced down at Van. The major-general's face was pale, but his chest was rising and falling.

'That's an order,' said the Queen. 'The last thing we need right now is panic.'

'Yes, your Majesty,' said Cardova. He pulled himself to his feet, then walked to the door. 'I'll clear the hallway.'

'Thank you, Captain,' said the Queen.

Cardova slipped out of the room, and closed the door. Kelsey walked over to where Van was lying, unable to take her eyes off him.

'I thought he was dead,' she said.

'So did I, for a moment,' said Emily. She reached out with her hands, and began rifling through Van's pockets.

'What are you doing?' said Kelsey.

'Looking for his salve,' the Queen said. 'If I find it, I'm confiscating it.' She looked through a few more pockets, then glanced up at Kelsey. 'It's not here. Go to his bedroom, and look there. Get his bed ready at the same time, and we'll bring him to you.'

Kelsey nodded.

'Now, please?' said the Queen.

Kelsey blinked, as if awakening from a nightmare. She nodded again, then ran for the door. Outside, only Vadhi was waiting, standing by the stairwell.

'Captain Cardova told me to leave,' the young woman said, 'but I didn't want to get in trouble again.'

'Come with me,' said Kelsey.

They hurried along the deserted corridor, then entered the apartment. The living room was empty, but the soft sounds of Maxwell gurgling and playing were filtering through from a side room. They went into the small room where Van slept, and Kelsey opened the shutters to let in some light.

'Stand by the door,' Kelsey said; 'keep it shut to everyone except the Queen and Lucius.'

Vadhi walked back to the doorway. 'Is something wrong?'

Kelsey ignored her. She spent less than a minute preparing the bed, then got down onto her hands and knees and starting looking around. She hauled out a trunk from under the bed, opened it, and delved inside, her hands feeling through the piles of clothes.

'That's the major-general's personal stuff,' said Vadhi, watching from the doorway.

'I know,' said Kelsey.

Her hands found something solid, and she pulled a metal hip flask from the trunk. She twisted the stopper open, and took a sniff, then recoiled as her head span. She closed her eyes, fighting the dizziness.

'Pyre's arsehole,' she muttered.

Her hands were trembling, but she managed to secure the stopper onto the hip flask without dropping either.

'Is that his salve?' said Vadhi. 'What are you going to do with it?'

'You never saw this, alright?' said Kelsey. 'If Van asks, you didn't see anything.' She tried to stand, but her legs were too unsteady. 'My head is spinning. If I was a demigod, I reckon I'd be looking a bit younger by now.'

The door handle turned, and Cardova peered into the room. His eyes went to Kelsey, then he pushed the door open. Behind him, two Banner sergeants were carrying the unconscious body of the major-general, while the Queen was standing behind them. Cardova guided the sergeants into the room, and watched as they placed Van onto the bed.

'Remember what I told you,' said Cardova. 'Not a word of this to anyone.'

The two sergeants saluted. 'Yes, sir.'

'Off with you; and thank you, Sergeants.'

The two sergeants left the apartment. Cardova extended a hand towards Kelsey and pulled her to her feet.

She staggered, and Cardova gripped her elbow.

'I might have taken a little sniff,' said Kelsey, 'to check it was salve. It is.'

She held out the hip flask, and the Queen took it. She glanced at Vadhi, but said nothing.

'What are you going to do with it?' said Kelsey.

'I'm going to put it to use,' said the Queen. 'There's probably enough salve in this to heal wounds for the next six months.'

Cardova nodded. 'It's not going to be pleasant when he wakes up,' he said. 'He'll be desperate for some salve from the moment he opens his eyes.'

'Tough shit,' said Kelsey. 'Are we all agreed that we don't give him any?'

'Yes,' said the Queen. 'We can't go on like this. If he takes salve again, then the next time might kill him.'

'If Van orders me to tell him where the salve is,' said Cardova, 'then I might have a problem, your Majesty.'

'I'm appointing you as temporary commander of the Banner,' said Emily. 'Until Van recovers, you are not bound by his orders.'

'What about the Combined Council, your Majesty? They might have some difficulty understanding this decision, if they don't know the reasons.'

'Leave them to me. We'll tell everyone that Van took ill after receiving the news about the Grey Isle, and that he'll need a few days of bed rest to recover. That's it. We allow no one into the apartment who doesn't know the truth. Captain, how long will his recovery take?'

'I don't know, your Majesty. I can't imagine it would be less that ten days or so; maybe a lot longer.'

'Summon the officers and reconvene the meeting,' said Emily. 'I'll join you, and we'll explain the situation. Kelsey, you stay here and guard this room. We'll post a few extra soldiers on the main entrance. We'll have to tell my mother the truth, and Silva too, as they both live here; tell them if you see them.'

She slipped the hip flask into an inner pocket of her robes, then placed a hand on Kelsey's shoulder.

'Everything is going to be alright.'

Kelsey nodded, but said nothing, then Cardova and the Queen left the room. Dizziness clouded her mind, and Kelsey sat on the edge of the bed.

Vadhi walked over.

'Here I am again,' said Kelsey, 'by Van's bedside, watching him almost die. This time will be different.'

'How?' said Vadhi.

'I'm not letting him out of my sight,' she said. 'If he wants any salve, he'll have to go through me first.' She took one of his hands in hers. 'Do you hear me, you stupid numpty? You're not getting rid of me that easily.'

CHAPTER 7

FAMILY PORTRAIT

Tara, Auldan, The City – 27th Amalan 3423

Kagan glanced down the empty marble-floored corridor. Despite having lived within the walls of Maeladh Palace for months, he still enjoyed finding new hallways and wings to explore. So far that morning, he had wandered through four different throne rooms, their furniture covered in white dust-sheets. The largest was able to fit several hundred people, while the smallest was in front of a long curving window that looked out directly over Tara and the bay below the ridge, though the tall shutters remained firmly closed. He had also found at least a dozen apartments; some empty, while others looked as if their occupants had left in a hurry. One luxurious apartment still had a name tag on the entranceway, stating that it had been lived in by a Lady Yordi, another dead grandchild of Amalia. One evening, she had listed every one of her grandchildren for him, and out of thirty, a mere seven were still alive and in the City, while one had fled to another world.

He heard voices and footsteps up ahead, so Kagan strode to the end of the corridor, and saw a group of servants. They had opened a store-room, and were removing tools and equipment. They stopped what they were doing and lowered their heads as soon as Kagan appeared.

'What's going on?' he said.

'My lord,' said one, bowing low; 'the rains have stopped, and we are preparing to begin work in the gardens.'

'The rains have stopped?' Kagan said. 'Freshmist is over?'

'Yes, my lord. The sun is out again and the clouds have disappeared.'

Kagan grinned. 'Well, carry on.'

'Yes, my lord,' said the servant, and they all bowed again.

Kagan changed direction, and hurried back down the corridor. He ascended a flight of stairs, and entered the rooms he shared with Amalia. He walked into their living room. It was thick with shadows, and he went to the far left of the enormous window, and began sliding the tall shutters open. Light flooded the room, and he blinked. He marvelled at the difference the sunshine made to the view. After two long months of grey, the water in the bay was glistening pink, reflecting the light of the sun to his right. Upon the far shore, Pella looked resplendent, its red roofs shining. Gulls were circling a small flotilla of fishing boats that were pulling out of the harbour of Tara, off to bring home their first catch of summer.

He opened the left hand window to let in some fresh air, and took a deep breath. He turned, then jumped in surprise. Amalia was sitting on a couch in silence, her head bowed. Kagan left the rest of the shutters and walked over.

'Were you sitting in the dark?' he said.

'It mirrors my mood.'

'Freshmist is over.'

'So I see.'

He sat down next to her. 'Has something happened? Is there news?'

'Naxor was in my head an hour ago,' she said. 'He told me that Simon was on the move, and I thought for a split second that he was going to Jezra to get Maxwell.'

Kagan nodded. 'I assume that he isn't?'

'You assume correctly. Simon, in his infinite wisdom, has decided to slaughter a few thousand people on the Grey Isle instead. I imagine he's ankle-deep in blood by now.'

'Why was Naxor telling you this?'

'Simon ordered him to inform the other gods in the City. He's taken the entire Gloamer fleet with him; they set off from Dalrig this morning at dawn. He wants us all to know that his hand has healed, and that he's taking the fight back to the rebels.'

'That's good news, isn't it?'

Amalia turned to glance at him. 'No, Kagan, it is not. The next part of his master plan involves cutting off the rebels' access to the Cold Sea, in order to starve them out. All ships belonging to the Exiles are to be sunk, and Jezra will effectively be under siege. Maxwell will be stranded amid a mob of desperate and starving rebels.'

'I can go to Jezra,' he said. 'Now that the weather's cleared up, I could get myself onto a fishing boat and infiltrate the town, pretending to be from the Brigades. You have to let me try.'

Amalia gave him a smile. 'I appreciate the offer, but I've already attempted that approach.'

Kagan narrowed his eyes. 'What?'

'You suggested the same course before Freshmist, and I took your words to heart. I couldn't risk sending you, so I used Dizzler's old contact in the Circuit to recruit a Torduan Exile, and sent him to Jezra.'

'You should have told me this.'

'And risk Simon reading it from your mind? I can tell you now, as my approach has clearly failed, and it no longer matters if Simon finds out. There's a small possibility that my message made its way to Queen Emily, but it's more likely that the Banner killed him as soon as they discovered who sent him.'

'You sent a message?'

'Yes. I wanted to see if Emily Aurelian was open to discussing the children with me. She hates me, obviously, but she must want her daughter back, not to mention her husband.'

'If I were her, I think I'd assume that you were trying to trick her; or set a trap.'

'I realise that, but I had to try. Kagan, I have killed thousands of people without mercy; I have watched as my orders have led to the massacre of innocent mortals. I shed not a single tear for the third of the City who perished at the teeth and claws of the greenhides; and yet, I am filled with shame and disgust at the thought of Simon killing Elspeth. Is something wrong with me?'

'No. It's how I feel about it too.'

'The Aurelians are my bitter enemies, and have been for a very long time. At many points in history, I was tempted to wipe out their entire line; I came close, destroying several branches of their family about three hundred years ago, but I always left some of them alive. They are the oldest royal house in the City, and had been ruling Tara for centuries before Malik and I arrived. Maybe I got sentimental about that, and spared them for romantic reasons, never imagining for a moment that one day they would be in a position to retake power. And now I have Daniel and Elspeth in my hands. Daniel is the last heir, and Elspeth is his only child; with their deaths, the family line would be extinguished forever. One would think that I'd be delighted, so why do I feel sick?'

'Because you do have a conscience.'

Amalia snorted. 'Please. Did you not hear what I said? I have the blood of countless thousands on my hands, and it has never once caused me a sleepless night. For all the vile things that Montieth and Naxor have done, they are mere amateurs compared to me, pretenders to the throne of suffering. One young man and an infant girl should be no problem.'

'Listen; I'm going downstairs later to visit the Aurelians. Maybe you should come with me.'

'Don't be ridiculous, Kagan. I can't bear to look at them.' She narrowed her eyes. 'And just why do you insist on visiting them every few days? It's not healthy, and Simon might get suspicious.'

He shrugged. 'I like seeing Elspeth. We can't see Maxwell, but somehow, when I see that little girl, it makes me feel that we'll get Maxwell back. It sounds stupid, I know.'

'No more stupid than I'm feeling. But, be careful. Lady Aurelian's words are filled with spite and poison, and she might try to turn you against me.'

He gave a wry smile. 'She's already tried that. I pay her no attention. She thinks that you are the most wicked person to have ever lived, but I realised a while ago that she knows nothing about you. She has an image of you that doesn't match the reality.'

'I don't know about that; it's probably a quite accurate depiction.'

'It's not. Amalia, you are not as evil as you think you are.'

'That sounds a little like an insult. Kagan, do you love me?'

'You know I do.'

'Do you think that your love may have blinded you to my real character?'

'I think it did, for a while. Visiting Amber in Dalrig changed things; that's when I found out about you opening the gates in the walls. If I was going to leave you, that would have been the time. I struggled with the knowledge of what you'd done; I still do, but that was the God-Queen, not the woman I fell in love with.'

'Our time in Port Sanders seems like a dream to me now,' she said. 'For two short years I felt happier than I've been in centuries. Everything seemed possible, and the joy I got from being with you and Maxwell outshone much of my earlier achievements. I should have killed Naxor when he visited; not doing so was my biggest mistake. I should have delivered his head to Emily Aurelian as a peace offering. She might have appreciated that.'

'She still would.'

'Yes; that would make her day. Thank you for listening to me go on, Kagan. Some days, I feel so low that I wonder why I keep going; today is one of those days.'

He put his arm over her shoulder and pulled her close.

'One day,' she whispered, 'Simon will come, and he'll take Elspeth and the others away, and then butcher them like animals in Prince's Square. He might decide to make us watch. Some Rosers will cheer, while others will look away, but no one will lift a finger to help the

Aurelians. You and I will stand there, and silently play our roles, and the world will not stop. The day after, things will carry on. We must harden our hearts, Kagan; otherwise we might as well give up now.'

Kagan held onto Amalia, but said nothing.

A few hours later, Kagan stopped by the vast kitchens that lay in a basement level under the sunward wing. Most of the space was lying unused, but two servants were occupying one corner, chopping vegetables in preparation for the evening meal. They bowed to Kagan as he entered, then went back to work. Kagan walked over to the drinks cupboard, and opened it, revealing tall racks of wine and brandy. He took down an opened bottle of vintage brandy, and filled a small flask with the dark, golden liquid, then stoppered the flask and slipped it into his pocket. He closed the cupboard door, then retreated from the kitchens, making his way to a lower basement level that ran under the boilers that heated the palace in winter. There were no windows at that level, and Kagan's eyes adjusted to the low gloom given off by the small number of lit oil lamps. He passed a guard post, but the militia soldiers were used to him coming and going, and moved aside to let him pass. At the end of the corridor were more guards, who saw him approaching. One took a set of keys from a pocket, and unlocked a door.

'Three quick knocks, then two slow today, sir,' said a soldier.

Kagan nodded. 'Thank you. I shouldn't be too long.'

He pushed the door open and went through into a small, dark hallway, hearing the soldier lock the door behind him. There was only one other door, and Kagan eased it open. He walked into a compact living space, lit by a couple of feeble oil lamps and a few candles.

'Hello,' he said.

The three adults in the room turned to him. Lord Aurelian and King Daniel were both sporting beards, as no blades or knives were allowed within the prisoners' small apartment.

'Our visitor returns,' said Lady Aurelian. 'One might almost feel that you prefer our company to that of your wicked mistress. Is that so, young Kagan?'

He ignored her, and walked over to the low bench where the two men were sitting. He reached into a pocket, and passed the flask to Daniel's father.

'What's this?'

'Brandy,' said Kagan.

Lord Aurelian shook his head. 'Are you trying to buy us, young man? Do you think a gift of brandy will make me any better disposed towards you?'

'No.'

'Good.'

'He did it because his conscience is bothering him, dear,' said Lady Aurelian.

Kagan sat on a stool. 'How are you all?'

Daniel had Elspeth on his knee. He glanced at Kagan, saying nothing.

'Summer started today,' Kagan went on. 'The rains are over.'

'Elspeth needs some fresh air and sunshine,' said Daniel. 'It's not healthy for her down here.'

'I could take her upstairs for a while.'

'That's not what I meant,' said Daniel. 'I'm her father; I'll never willingly hand her over to you.'

'I have other news,' said Kagan.

'Does it involve the death of our enemies?' said Lady Aurelian. 'If not, then I'm indifferent.'

'Simon is attacking the Grey Isle. The Gloamer fleet sailed at dawn. The Ascendant is planning on blockading Jezra from both the Warm and Cold Seas, to starve them into submission. Will it work?'

'Why are you asking us this question?' said Lord Aurelian.

'Because my son is there.'

'We are aware of that.'

'You also know a lot more about Jezra than I do.'

'Only because you shirked your duty,' said Lady Aurelian. 'You should be in Jezra, wearing the uniform of the Brigades, along with all of the other Exiles from Lostwell. That's what the brave ones did; you, on the other hand, fled into the arms of the greatest mass murderer in the history of the City. Do you lack courage, Kagan?'

'Maybe I do.'

'You must. How else could your behaviour be explained?'

'Jezra could hold out for a very long time,' said Daniel, his arms round Elspeth. 'Countless shiploads of supplies were sent there; enough to last the people for months, maybe years.'

Kagan stared at the King, wondering if he was lying.

'I have a question,' said Lord Aurelian.

'Yes?'

'When my wife and I visited your little estate in the Sunward Range; you do recall it, yes?'

'Yes; I remember.'

'Good chap. What I wanted to ask was this – when we visited, were you aware of Lady Sofia's real identity?'

'I knew who she was.'

The older man shook his head and sighed.

'What did I tell you, dear?' said Lady Aurelian. 'Of course he knew.'

'The God-Queen was just a name to me then,' Kagan went on. 'I knew next to nothing about the history of the City, and absolutely nothing about its politics.'

'But, you know now; yes?' said Lord Aurelian. 'And with this new knowledge, has your opinion changed?'

'My opinion about what?'

Lady Aurelian glared at him. 'About that monster you worship. The monster who sold the entire City to Simon.'

Kagan shook his head. 'That was Naxor, not Amalia.'

'But, you do not deny that Amalia is a monster?'

'You don't know her, Lady Aurelian.'

'Oh, I know her well enough. This is not the first time my husband and I have been prisoners within Maeladh Palace. The last time, the God-Queen had every Roser aristocrat summoned so they could watch the greenhides destroy Medio. She is a vile woman, who would rather watch the City burn than help a single mortal.'

The door to the hallway opened and Amalia walked into the small apartment. The room fell silent.

Amalia smiled as she glanced at the occupants of the room. 'What were you all talking about? Me, by any chance?'

Kagan frowned. 'I didn't think you wanted to see the Aurelians.'

'I don't. They mean nothing to me. I have received some news, and wanted to tell you. I knew you'd be down here, though why you bother wasting your time with the condemned is beyond me.'

'We have nothing to say to you, God-Queen,' said Lord Aurelian.

'Excellent,' she said, 'because conversing with you is not my idea of fun. In fact, your presence here is somewhat like having an irritating boil that requires a good lancing. Simon means to execute each one of you down in Prince's Square, in front of a crowd of cheering Rosers. Fitting, I think.'

'You shame only yourself with your words,' said Lord Aurelian. 'I almost feel sorry for you.'

'It is little Elspeth you should be feeling sorry for. After all, it will be her swinging from the gallows, not I.'

'You disgust me,' said Lady Aurelian, 'but you already knew that, didn't you? Deep down inside, you understand how low you've sunk. You used to be the almighty ruler of the City, and now you are nothing but Simon's willing slave. Do you enjoy bowing before him? It's quite a step down, isn't it? How your pride must be suffering, knowing that you have to ask his permission before you can do anything. Did you beg him to be allowed to live in your old palace? Do you sit on your throne, alone, and wonder how it came to this? It must hurt you deeply, if you feel the need to come down here to mock us over the execution of a child.'

Amalia's eyes tightened. 'It hurts less than the pain you will soon be feeling, when you are hanging by a noose, watching your family suffer next to you. I will enjoy watching you die.'

Lady Aurelian turned to Kagan, and smiled. 'You were saying something earlier about Amalia not being a monster. Would you care to revise that opinion, based upon her own words?'

Kagan said nothing.

'Did you come here to gloat about the Grey Isle?' said Daniel. 'We already know.'

'The capture of the island means that your execution day grows ever closer,' Amalia said. 'Your wife's remaining subjects will soon be getting hungry, and then they'll have no choice but to surrender. To encourage her, Simon decided not to slaughter the entire garrison of the Grey Isle. Instead, he is transporting the survivors back to Pella, where ten will be executed at dawn each day, outside the ruins of Cuidrach Palace. There are enough prisoners to last the whole summer, should Emily decide not to surrender.'

'The Queen will never surrender,' said Daniel. 'You have no idea how strong willed she is. She'd fight on, even if she were the last person alive.'

Amalia glanced at the child in Daniel's arms. 'Oh, I think she might have her weak spot.'

'It's not too late, Amalia,' said Daniel.

'To do what?'

'The right thing. Kagan has been visiting us, as you know. He is misguided, but he doesn't seem like an evil man. If he can see something in you that we can't, then perhaps you aren't evil either.'

'Really, son?' said Lady Aurelian. 'Do you honestly believe that this vile creature has some redeeming qualities?'

'No, mother; but Kagan clearly does. For all our sakes, let us hope that he is right.'

'A fool's hope, son.'

'Then I am a fool, mother. I cannot accept that Amalia has given up on Maxwell. Recall her devotion to Prince Michael, and to Duke Marcus. She may be many things, but she has always loved her children.'

'She had Khora murdered, son; her own daughter. And, do you

think she shed a tear over Yendra's death? Or Isra's? Her family have been slaughtering each other for centuries; do not be naïve.'

'Well, this has been lovely,' said Amalia, 'but if you've quite finished dissecting my personality, then I think I shall take my leave. There's only so much gloating one can endure. Remember, the moment that Emily is captured, you will all be taking one last trip down the ridge into Tara, and then the City shall finally be rid of the Aurelians. Come, Kagan; let us go.'

Kagan glanced at Elspeth for a moment, then got to his feet. The Aurelians stared in silence as Amalia and Kagan made their way back to the main entrance. They gave the required knock, and the soldiers let them out, and relocked the door behind them.

'That was interesting,' said Amalia, as they walked back along the deserted corridors of the basement. 'Lady Aurelian was charming, as always.'

Kagan kept silent. Daniel's words were echoing through his mind, about having hope because Kagan could see something in Amalia that they couldn't. They reached the living room with the tall windows, and Amalia walked over to gaze out at the view, while Kagan sat, feeling like he was about to explode.

'Such a beautiful day,' Amalia said. 'I have plans for the gardens on the sunward side of the palace. I was thinking of...'

'You just can't help yourself, can you?' Kagan cried.

Amalia frowned at him. 'Excuse me?'

'When you're alone with me, you're almost in tears about the prospect of Simon murdering Elspeth, but in front of the Aurelians, you can't help but be a bitch. You mocked them with the image of Elspeth swinging from a noose. Why? What's wrong with you?'

'It's part of the game, Kagan.'

'A game? Executing a one-year-old girl is a game? I've had it. I love you, but I cannot bear to see you do this to yourself. What are you scared of? Do you fear the Aurelians knowing that you care? They're staring death in the face, but at least they're keeping their dignity.'

'And, by implication, I am not? Are these your true feelings, Kagan? You care more for our prisoners than you do for me or Maxwell?'

'Don't twist my words; did I mention Maxwell? This is about you. Who are you, Amalia?'

'I don't think I like your tone.'

'Yeah? And what do you think was going round my head, while you were gloating in front of the Aurelians? I was embarrassed for you.'

Amalia turned back to the window. 'This conversation is over. Leave.'

Kagan got to his feet. 'I might just do that.'

He strode from the room, unintentionally slamming the door behind him. He stopped, staring at it for a moment, then carried on, his anger fuelling his steps. Without realising where he was going, he came to a side entrance to the palace and stepped outside into the afternoon sunlight. He closed his eyes and took a long breath, feeling the warmth on his face.

Sometimes, he hated Amalia. No. He hated what she had become; that was it. But, maybe she was reverting to her true character, and the aberration was the short time they had spent together before Naxor had made his appearance. Which was the real Amalia? If he knew the answer to that question, then his choices would be clearer. He had dreamed that he would be the one that could change her; had he been delusional to believe that she was capable of change? And yet.

He walked down the steps to a lower terrace, and wandered along the path. Below him was a gate that led to a road that went down the slope to Tara. Would the soldiers let him pass without any questions, or had Amalia or Simon told them to prevent him from leaving the palace grounds? Where would he go if they did let him pass? As consort to Amalia, he was probably one of the most hated mortals in the City; would the citizens recognise him? Too many questions, and no answers. He sat on a bench, then stood again, and walked down to the gate.

Half a dozen members of the Roser militia were guarding the barred entrance to the palace grounds. They glanced at him as he approached.

'Good afternoon, my lord,' said one. 'Can we assist you?'

'I'm going for a walk around Tara.'

'Right you are, my lord. How many escorts do you require?'

'None; I want to go alone.'

The guards shifted uncomfortably.

'We would recommend at least four guards accompany you, my lord, preferably six or eight.'

'Why? Am I liable to be attacked? How would anyone know my face?'

'There is a large portrait of you and Lady Amalia hanging in Prince's Square, my lord. It's a decent enough likeness.'

'There's a portrait of me?'

'Lord Chamberlain commissioned it before Freshmist, my lord.'

'And it's in Prince's Square?'

'That's right, my lord; right next to the gallows that are being constructed for the Aurelians. I would guess that everyone in Tara knows your face by now.'

Kagan nodded, his glance falling. 'Perhaps another time.'

'That might be a good idea, my lord.'

Kagan turned, sensing the looks he was getting from the six soldiers. He glanced up at the great, sprawling bulk of Maeladh Palace – his home, but also his prison, and began climbing the steps.

It was too late to run. He had made his choice, and he would have to live, or die, by the decisions he had taken. As he ascended the steps of the terrace, his eyes went to the tall windows of their living room. Amalia was standing there, watching him. She would have seen him attempting to leave the palace grounds, and had then witnessed his retreat from the gate. She knew that he was as trapped as she was; trapped by Simon, trapped by the City. Pity for her streaked through him, and he knew that he still loved her.

He went back into the palace, and walked to their apartment.

'I'm back,' he said, as he entered the living room.

She smiled at him, though her cheeks were wet with tears. 'I know.'

CHAPTER 8

DURESS

The Eastern Mountains – 3rd Mikalis 3423

Flames licked the sides of the dragon's jaws. 'If you touch me again, insect, I will render you to charred bone and ash.'

Sergeant Darvi trembled. 'Sorry, Dawnflame.'

The sleek dragon turned away, and rested her head on the ground, her eyes closing.

Rosie nudged Jade with an elbow. 'You should speak to Dawnflame; she can't go around threatening to kill everyone.'

'Darvi shouldn't have touched her.'

'It was an accident; he brushed past her trying to get to the waterfall.'

Jade shrugged. 'He should have been more careful. If I were a dragon, I wouldn't want humans touching me either.'

'Oh yeah? How many times have you ridden on Halfclaw's back?'

'That's different. Halfclaw consented. Yendra taught me all about consent, though her lessons were mostly aimed at me. It was because of her that I had to abandon my plans to have a harem. I had a little list of all the Blades that were due to be enrolled as well. Such a pity.'

'That's just plain wrong, Jade.'

'That's exactly what Yendra said. It's double standards. Malik had a harem, and so did Michael, Isra and Marcus. But I'm not allowed one? It's because I'm a girl.'

'I'm sure Amalia could have had her own harem, if she'd wanted one.' She shook her head. 'So, eh, what kind of guys were on your list?'

'They were all aged between twenty and twenty-six, with just the right amount of muscles. And each of them was over six foot tall, but under six foot four; I didn't want to strain my neck. And, they had to like cats, and not be drunkards. I spent a lot of time compiling that list, then Yendra tore it up.'

Flavus emerged from the cavern, and walked across the grass towards them.

'Good morning, ma'am, Private.'

'Hello, Flavus,' said Jade; 'we were just discussing the criteria for joining my imaginary harem. You're too old.'

'I see, ma'am. Should I be insulted?'

Jade narrowed her eyes.

'Apologies, ma'am; I was joking. My humour can be a little dry at times.'

'Do female gods on Implacatus have harems?'

Flavus raised an eyebrow. 'I couldn't answer that, ma'am. The palaces of the gods are off-limits to the vast majority of mortals, and I personally have never been inside one. I do know, however, that several Banner officers have found themselves in the beds of some of the more powerful goddesses, whether willingly or not. Thankfully, I was never called upon to provide that particular service.'

'Wait a minute, sir,' said Rosie. 'All those nights when we were stuck in the cave over Freshmist, and you told us loads of boring stories about the campaigns you've been on, you could have been telling us stuff like this?'

'I'm sorry my stories bored you, Private.'

'Well, they weren't that bad, sir. But, we could have done with some on the sex-lives of the gods.'

'I'll try to remember that if we are still here for Sweetmist, Private.

Now, I do believe that we are due to sow more cereal crops this morning for our experimental farm. Do you have the bag of seeds?'

'Oops. Sorry, sir; I forgot. Hang on a moment.'

Jade and Flavus watched as Rosie sprinted towards the cavern.

'For someone so skilled with her hands,' Flavus said, 'Private Jackdaw can be remarkably forgetful.'

He gazed up at the sky.

'What are you looking for?' said Jade. 'Halfclaw isn't coming back; he told us that five days ago, when he visited.'

'I know, ma'am, but I still hope. Without Halfclaw, there will be no more surveys of the neighbouring mountains, and we'll never get to the bottom of whether or not other salve deposits exist.'

'I don't think Halfclaw cares about that any more. He's got Frostback.' She glanced at the blue and purple dragon lying by the pool. 'You could always ask Dawnflame.'

'No, ma'am; I won't be doing that. She has made it quite clear what she thinks of me.'

The dragon cracked open an eye. 'That is correct, soldier-insect. I am here to pay off my debt to Jade, not to ferry insects around on my shoulders. I will tell you now; if you ask me if you can ride on my back, I shall pick you up, fly out over the plains, and drop you among the greenhides.'

'I thought you were sleeping,' said Jade.

'I am resting,' the dragon said, 'but my ears are alert, and I can pick up every word and movement in this valley. For instance, little Jackdaw is searching through crates in the cavern, presumably looking for your seeds, soldier-insect; while the other male insect is pretending to chop wood – he only swings his axe whenever the female soldier-insect is watching.'

'Why does Rosie get a name, while the others in my team are just insects?' said Jade.

'Little Jackdaw has earned that right, due to the respect in which her sister is held by Deathfang. Although, personally, I admit that I didn't care for Maddie. She talked too much.'

'Who talks too much?' said Rosie, coming out of the cavern with a bag clutched in her hand.

'Your sister,' said Jade.

'I won't argue with that,' said Rosie. She held out the bag. 'Here are your seeds, sir.'

'You keep a hold of them, Private,' said Flavus. 'I'll hoe; you sow.'

'That sounds like you're singing, sir.'

'Excuse me, Private?'

'Never mind, sir.'

Flavus frowned. 'You are a peculiar young lady, Private.'

Dawnflame raised her head. 'A dragon approaches.'

Jade and the others turned to gaze up at the sky.

'I can't see anything,' said Rosie.

'I can hear the air moving across their wings,' said Dawnflame, extending her neck upwards. 'No one is due to visit today.'

'Perhaps Halfclaw has come back to the mountains to see us,' said Flavus.

The dragon ignored him. Jade waved to Sergeant Inmara and Sergeant Darvi, and they walked across the grass towards them, axes over their shoulders.

'It's Darksky,' said Dawnflame, in a low voice. 'I can see her.'

Jade squinted into the distance, a hand up to shield her eyes from the sun. She spotted the approaching dragon, a small speck in the sky. To Jade, it could have been any dragon, apart from Deathfang – his wide bulk was easily recognisable. Dawnflame shifted position, and pushed herself up by her forelimbs, which shimmered like lavender in the sunlight. Darksky drew nearer, then soared down, without circling, and landed by the stream.

'Dawnflame!' she cried. 'A calamity has occurred; a fearful thing. My babies, and Firestone – he took them; and my mate is dying...' She turned to Jade, lowering her head swiftly in front of the demigod. 'You. You must return with me to the colony immediately. Deathfang is dying.'

'Speak slowly and clearly,' said Dawnflame. 'What has happened to my son?'

'The Ascendant, he came to the colony, alone and unarmed. He killed many of the worker insects first, then struck down Deathfang when he tried to protect my babies. He struck him down; do you hear me? My beloved Deathfang. The god took my babies away, and Firestone too; he vanished, and they vanished also, leaving Deathfang dying on the cavern floor. I flew straight here; I didn't know what else to do.'

Rosie took a step forward. 'Simon has taken the four young dragons?'

'We are wasting time!' bellowed Darksky. 'No more questions.' She lunged out with a forelimb, and grasped Jade round the midriff.

'If you leave the ground, you die, dragon,' came a voice from across the pool.

Jade turned her head. Simon was standing on the banks of the pool, at least a hundred armed Blades with him, all armoured and holding crossbows and packs. The Ascendant was also wearing his armour, and had a long sword in his right hand, its end trailing on the grass.

'Where are our children?' cried Darksky.

She and Dawnflame turned to face the Ascendant, like cats stalking prey. Flames leapt across their jaws as they slowly approached.

Simon laughed. 'Dragons, go to sleep.'

The effect was immediate. Both dragons let out a cry, then they collapsed to the ground, the earth trembling from the impact. Jade was flung clear from Darksky's forelimb, and she rolled down to the edge of the pool. She glanced up, to see Simon pointing a finger at her.

'Do not move, demigod,' he said. 'I am pleased to see that you survived the fire in the Duke's Tower; you must be more cunning than I had given you credit for. However, you will not escape this time.'

He narrowed his eyes, and a wave of pain struck Jade, rippling through her body as she lay on the grass. Jade closed her eyes, the agony reminding her of Greylin Palace. Her father and sister had often sent their death powers into her, and, over a long period of time, she had learned to detach her thoughts from the pain. It didn't always work, but Jade relaxed her body, letting her self-healing battle Simon's powers. He wasn't trying to kill her, she told herself, as her flesh rotted; if he were, then she would already be dead.

The wave of power coming from Simon ceased.

'You bastard!' cried Rosie. 'You killed her.'

'No, mortal; I did not,' said Simon; 'I merely slowed her down for a while. Her sister has turned out to be one of my more reliable allies in the City, and after Jade's escape from the Bulwark, I want to give her one last chance to see sense. She could be very useful to me. As might you, girl,' he went on, 'and you also, Banner soldier. You two, on the other hand, are of absolutely no use to me.'

Jade tried to open her eyes, but they weren't working, and she could only hear the screams coming from the two sergeants as Simon unleashed his powers at them. Rosie cried out in anguish, her voice echoing off the side of the valley as she lamented the Reaper sergeants.

'Captain,' said Simon; 'have your soldiers secure the valley, the two mortal prisoners, and the mine. I want the excavation of the salve to commence within an hour. Naxor, you will supervise the operation, while I have a little word with Lady Jade.'

'Yes, your Grace,' said Naxor.

Jade heard footsteps approaching, then a strong hand grabbed her hair, and began dragging her across the grass. She felt a fingertip on her forehead, and her vision cleared as her health was partly restored. She looked up, and saw Simon's face just inches from hers, his left hand still gripping the back of her head.

'Ah, Lady Jade; whatever shall I do with you?'

Jade spat in his face.

Simon raised an eyebrow, wiped his cheek, then plunged Jade's head into the pool, submerging her face. Jade struggled, lashing out with her fists, but Simon's strength was immense, and he held her head under the water. Jade choked, trying to hold her breath, but failing. Agony and panic exploded within her, then Simon pulled her head back out into the air. She half-vomited, half-choked, as water streamed from her mouth. She powered her self-healing, but it had already taken a battering from Simon's death powers.

'Silly little demigod,' he said. 'I'll ask you again – will you work for me, or do I have to kill you?'

She tried to speak, to tell him that she would never work for him, but no words came out, then she slipped into unconsciousness.

Jade opened her eyes. She was lying down, with her hands tied behind her back, and she could see the interior of a low-ceilinged cave. There was a small opening in the wall that led outside, and daylight was filtering into the interior. Footsteps and voices echoed through to her, and several soldiers were blocking the entrance to the cavern, with their backs to Jade.

'How are you feeling?' whispered Rosie.

Jade turned her head, and saw the Jackdaw woman sitting close by. Her hands were also tied behind her back, but she didn't appear to have been injured.

'I'm fine,' Jade said. 'Where's Simon?'

'I'm not sure; I haven't seen him since we were put into this cave. Flavus is still outside, I think. Simon ordered him to begin training the Blades in excavating and refining salve. Do you remember what happened? Simon killed Inmara and Darvi, for nothing. Their heads... He...'

'Try not to think about it,' said Jade.

'Any ideas on how to do that? I see them every time I close my eyes; it was horrible. I still have their blood on my clothes. Why did he do that? Why? They would have surrendered without fighting; he didn't need to murder them.'

Jade said nothing. She managed to get herself into a sitting position, and leaned her back against the cavern wall. Her fingers felt strange, and she peered behind her back, to see that thick leather gloves had been bound to each hand. She felt for her self-healing, and found it.

'How long was I unconscious?'

'A couple of hours, maybe?' said Rosie. 'Not very long.'

'The dragons?'

'They were still sleeping, last I saw. We're screwed, aren't we? I mean, we have nothing to compete with Simon's powers. He could kill each of us with a glance. He said that he thinks you would be a useful ally; so I think he's going to give you another chance to surrender. You have to do it, Jade; otherwise he'll kill you.'

Jade frowned. 'Is that a serious suggestion? You think I should bow before him?'

'If you want to live through this, you'll have to.'

'Yendra would never have done that.'

'Yendra's dead, Jade. She stood up to Montieth, and he killed her. Simon will do the same to you.'

'Wise words, girl.'

Jade and Rosie looked up. Naxor was standing by the entrance to the cave, a light smirk on his lips.

'I thought I'd pop by,' he said, 'to check how our two prisoners are doing. I'm glad to see you have recovered, cousin, and my heart is warmed by the sage advice from young Miss Jackdaw. You would do well to listen to her. Simon doesn't want to kill you; he's short of reliable, loyal servants. And your sister submitted, so perhaps...'

'Shut up, you pig,' said Jade. 'You disgusting little traitor.'

Naxor laughed. 'That attitude will kill you, cousin. Can't you just accept that you've been beaten? The entire City belongs to Simon now, and we either adjust to the new reality, or we perish. It's simple. Do you really want to throw your life away due to some misplaced loyalty to the mortals who used to sit on the throne? The second Aurelian rebellion is officially over, and, guess what – they lost again.'

'Has Jezra fallen?' said Rosie.

'No, Miss Jackdaw; Jezra remains occupied by the Exiles, but the noose is tightening. A few days ago, Simon retook the Grey Isle, cutting off the rebels' access to the Cold Sea. Their food supplies will be running low around now; their surrender is only days away. And when that happens, Simon has decided to be merciful – the Brigade workers will be spared, and allowed to continue living in Jezra. Only the Banner forces and the rebel leadership will be executed. You, Miss Jackdaw, also have a fair chance of survival, if you prove willing to assist Simon and the Blades in the excavation of the salve mine, just as Lieutenant Flavus is doing. I recommended that he keep you alive, so you have me to thank that you weren't summarily executed like the two sergeants.'

Naxor paused, as if expecting Rosie to thank him, but the Jackdaw woman said nothing.

'Oh well,' he said after a while; 'I suppose gratitude was a little too much to expect. Can I tell Simon that you are both ready to profess your loyalty to him?'

Jade shook her head. 'I do not consent to that.'

'Really? Do you have any idea of how foolish you sound, cousin? Simon is very forgiving to those who admit the error of their ways. If you submit to him, willingly, then he will likely appoint you into a position of authority. Jezra will soon need a loyal governor, for example, and so will Pella. Simon only trusts immortals to rule by his side, and, as you are no doubt aware, our numbers have been thinned of late. Submit, and you will instantly be promoted, and handed all the power and riches that you could ever require.' His face darkened. 'However, if you refuse, then things will not go so well. Simon is aware of the love you have for your four cats in Pella, cousin; he read your thoughts while you were unconscious, looking for your weaknesses. The only things you seem to care about are those damn animals, and Rosie. I won't be able to stop Simon from inflicting great pain and suffering upon those you love, cousin. As I said, he can be forgiving, but if you continue to defy him, then his wrath knows no bounds.'

'He would kill my cats?'

'Only after prolonged torture. And Rosie too. Her survival is conditional on your submission. I didn't want to have to spell it out so starkly, but as you seem to be clinging to false hopes, it seems that I have no choice. So, let me be clear – if you refuse to submit, then Rosie Jackdaw will be tortured to death in front of you.'

Rosie's face paled.

'I've lived with threats all my life,' said Jade. 'Simon seems no different from my father; they are both violent bullies. If you let someone bully you once, then they'll keep doing it.'

Naxor smiled, but his eyes remained hostile. 'How brave, cousin. Noble, even. Though, perhaps also a little callous. Do you really not mind if Rosie is broken before your eyes? Will you shrug off her cries of agony, as her flesh is melted from her pretty little face?'

'I will curse Simon for doing it; and I will curse you for helping that beast.'

'But you can prevent it from happening, cousin! With a few words, and a gesture, Rosie will live. You can keep her by your side, if you desire. Simon will offer the same choice to the dragons – submit, or their children will suffer greatly; what do you think they will do? There is no shame in this. What mother wouldn't make a deal to save their children? Your cats are like your children, aren't they? And Rosie is a friend. You have it in your power to save them all.'

'Have you always been a bastard?' said Rosie.

Naxor regarded her. 'Yes. Sometimes, one must act in one's best interests. I knew immediately that Simon was too powerful for any of us to withstand, and I made my choice based upon reason. Dying for a noble cause has never been my ambition, and I will not apologise for that. If you want to live, Jackdaw, then perhaps you need to listen to this bastard's advice. Persuade my cousin to back down, and in a few days, you will be living in a palace. I will leave you now, to consider what I have said. Simon is anxious for an answer. I will tell him that you need a little more time to decide; but don't take too long.'

Naxor slipped away, passing between the Blade soldiers who were blocking the entrance to the cave.

'I think I've changed my mind,' said Rosie. 'Screw Naxor. Jade, don't submit because of me. I can die bravely. I'd rather die than live in Simon's new world.'

Jade glanced at her. 'Do you mean that?'

'I think so. Alright, I'm terrified. Not of dying, but of suffering first. But, I will try to be brave; I promise.'

'Do you think the dragons will submit?'

'I think that depends on Deathfang. If he's dead, then I guess that Dawnflame and Darksky might have to submit, to save their children. I don't know.'

'Would you blame them if they submitted?'

'No; how could I?'

'Then, I should do the same. You are the only mortal friend I've ever had, Rosie. You've changed the way I look at things. I don't want to lose you; you don't deserve to die. And, I couldn't bear the thought of him killing my cats; what kind of monster would do that? My beautiful little babies. It's the kind of thing my father or sister would threaten to do. Between them, they must have killed dozens of my cats over the centuries; sometimes as a punishment for something I did, sometimes just because they felt like it. They knew it was the best way to hurt me.'

A Blade officer appeared at the entrance. 'Lord Simon wants you both outside, now.'

More Blades squeezed into the cavern, and hauled Rosie and Jade to their feet.

'Take them out onto the grass,' said the officer.

'Traitor,' said Jade, glaring at him.

'That's funny, coming from you, ma'am,' said the officer; 'seeing as how you nearly destroyed the Blades while you were in charge of the Bulwark.'

The soldiers half-carried, half-shoved Rosie and Jade through the cave system, and out into the afternoon sunlight. Jade blinked, her eyes dazzled after the gloom of the cave. The two dragons were lying exactly where they had fallen, their eyes closed, while Flavus was conducting a training session of some kind, with twenty Blades sitting on the grass in front of him as he talked. Behind him, Jade noticed three soldiers were levelling their crossbows at his back, no doubt to encourage him.

Simon was rubbing his hands together as he watched the Blades pull Rosie and Jade toward him, while Naxor was lurking a few paces behind the Ascendant.

'Welcome back, Jade,' Simon cried. 'Naxor tells me that you are considering my terms. Well, what will it be? Shall I reward you for your loyalty, or will I start to destroy you and everything you hold dear?'

Jade glanced at the dragons. 'What about them?'

'I can deal with them first; is that what you want? I can see your thoughts. If the dragons submit, then you won't feel so bad doing it yourself; I see. Very well.'

He turned to the fallen dragons and raised a hand. Darksky awoke, her eyes blinking open. She raised her head, flames sparking round her jaws.

'Dragon,' said Simon; 'do not even think of fighting. Your three children are in my custody. If you attack, then I will tear them to pieces, slowly. Think, dragon. You can save your children's lives. I want nothing from you but a promise not to attack. You can live in your colony, in peace. Submit.'

Darksky's eyes fell upon Simon.

'There is no shame in being defeated by a more powerful enemy,' Simon went on. 'I am the father of all dragons; I created the magnificent bodies that house your spirits. You cannot resist me. Of all the Ascendants, it is I who best understands how dragons think. If you submit, then I will return two of your children to you this very day. If you refuse, then all three will die horrible deaths, and then you will also die, along with the rest of the colony. That is your choice.'

'You filthy insect,' said Darksky.

Simon laughed. 'Indeed.'

The dragon glanced at the still form of Dawnflame next to her.

'Dawnflame will have her son returned to her if she submits,' said Simon. 'I will only keep one of your infants in my custody if you both submit, as a little insurance policy.'

'Where are my children?'

'They're safe. For now.' He clicked his fingers, and Dawnflame's eyes also opened. She immediately rose up, her eyes darting around. She saw Simon, and opened her jaws to strike.

'No,' said Darksky. 'First listen. If we submit to this creature, then he will return Firestone to you.'

Dawnflame's eyes burned. 'He lies.'

'I am telling the truth, dragon,' said Simon. 'I have a Quadrant; I can return your son to the colony before nightfall. It would be wise of you to submit, and then I will allow you to fly back to your home, and I will bring your son, and two of Darksky's children, to you this evening.'

The two dragons looked at each other.

'That's right; take your time. You know that you are beaten; why not make the best of a bad situation?'

'My beloved mate Deathfang,' said Darksky; 'you wounded him deeply.'

'He tried to incinerate me. If he hadn't, he would still be alive.'

Darksky shuddered. 'Deathfang is dead? No.'

Simon nodded. 'Yes. The great grey lizard has breathed his last. He made a poor choice, and paid for it. Shall you do the same, or will you select a wiser course?'

Darksky's head lowered, as if she had been struck.

'Shall one dragon die this day,' said Simon, 'or all of you? That is your choice. Your children are crying for their mothers. Submit, and this nightmare shall be over.'

'You are loathsome,' said Dawnflame; 'my hatred of you will never cease.'

'I can live with that. Lower you heads and swear to me that you will be loyal servants, and then you can go.'

Jade stared at the two dragons. Darksky was distraught, her eyes wide, and she seemed smaller, as if her spirit had been broken. Dawnflame's expression was more defiant, but Jade could see the doubt and fear in her eyes. Nothing happened for a long moment, then both dragons lowered their heads towards Simon.

'You win, god,' said Dawnflame. 'We submit to you.'

'I need to hear Darksky say the same,' said Simon.

The dark blue dragon stared at Simon, pure hatred emanating from her eyes. 'I submit.'

'There, that wasn't so hard now, was it?' beamed Simon. 'Off you fly, then, and I will see you in the colony later this evening.'

The two dragons turned from Simon in disgust, then extended their wings and soared up into the sky.

Simon smiled, and turned back to Jade. 'And there you have it. Do you realise the extent of my powers now? For who else could have made two mighty dragons bow their heads and submit? I am the greatest, the wisest, the best. Now, if mere dragons can perceive the truth, how about you, young demigod? Has their example inspired you?'

Jade said nothing.

'Oh, I can see how much you hate me. That's not a good sign. If you are to serve me, then I need your heart to be with me.'

'My heart will never be with you.'

'Soldiers, prepare to torture the young Jackdaw girl. I warn you, Jade; this will get a little messy.'

Two Blades approached Rosie, and seized her by the arms.

'Last chance, Jade,' said Simon; 'or would you prefer to hear the screams of the only friend you have ever made? That's a little sad, isn't it? Nine centuries, and no friends. What a miserable life you have led. Soldiers, strip the mortal girl of her clothes; I want Jade to see the blood as it starts to flow.'

'Wait,' said Jade.

Simon smiled. 'Yes?'

Jade glanced at Rosie, who looked more frightened than she had ever seen her before. She noticed that Flavus had stopped talking; in fact, every eye in the valley was upon her, watching, and waiting.

Jade got down to her knees, and bowed her head.

'Sorry, Yendra,' she whispered. She glanced up, her face giving nothing away. 'I submit.'

CHAPTER 9

KEEPING SECRETS

Jezra, The Western Bank – 8ᵗʰ Mikalis 3423

'Please,' said Van; 'you don't understand. I just need one dose, so I can take the pain. My insides are burning up. One dose, that's all I'm asking for; please.'

Kelsey stood by the bed, her arms folded across her chest. 'Forget it; no chance.'

Van's eyes went to Emily, who was standing on the other side of the bed from Kelsey and Cardova.

'Your Majesty,' he said, his voice low and rasping; 'I'm begging you; show me some mercy. I'm in so much pain, and one dose of salve would help me sleep. I can't sleep like this; I haven't slept in days.'

Emily shook her head. 'No, Van. I'm sorry, but we are all agreed.'

'You bitch!' Van cried. He strained his hands, trying to free them from the restrainer straps that were keeping him to the bed, but he was too weak.

'Mind your language, sir,' said Cardova. 'Apologies for that, your Majesty.'

'It's quite all right, Captain,' said Emily. 'The major-general is not himself at the moment.'

'Just one damn dose!' Van yelled, struggling against the straps. 'I'm burning up,' he said, his anger turning to self pity. 'Please.' He started to weep, tears rolling down his ashen features. He had lost a lot of weight since his collapse, and he looked weaker than ever. 'Please.'

'Van,' said Kelsey; 'you've had no salve for eleven days. If we gave you some now, you'd be right back at the beginning. You're close...' She turned to Cardova. 'That's right, aye? Surely, he must be close to recovering?'

'Another couple of days,' said the captain, 'and the last of the salve will be out of his system. But as for recovery; that might take longer. It depends on his appetite; he needs to eat.'

'You try feeding him,' snapped Kelsey.

'I wasn't having a go at you. I know you've done your best, Kelsey.'

'It's been a fiasco,' she said. 'I can hardly get him to eat anything, and then he sicks up half of whatever he does manage to swallow.'

'His appetite should improve, as soon as his body is clear of the salve.'

Van glared at them. 'Stop talking about me as if I wasn't here. None of you understands how much pain I'm in; help me.'

'We are helping you,' said Kelsey; 'you just don't realise it yet.'

'You're cruel,' he said, his eyes burning with anger; 'you're letting me lie here in agony, when you know what would fix me. Please, just one dose.'

Kelsey sighed, then rubbed her eyes.

'Let's give the major-general a chance to rest,' said Emily.

'Rest?' he cried. 'How can I rest? Unfasten the straps; I'll behave. I swear it. I just need to get up for a minute.'

Emily glanced at Cardova and nodded towards the door.

'I'll stay with him,' said Kelsey, taking a seat by the bed.

'Don't leave!' yelled Van. 'Please; help me. I'm burning...'

Emily left the room with Cardova, and the captain closed it behind him, muffling the sound of Van's cries. They walked into the apartment's living room, where Vadhi was sitting with Silva and Lady Omertia, who was watching Maxwell play on the rug with a wooden greenhide toy.

Emily said nothing to them, and kept going, until she entered Van's office, which was empty. She waited for Cardova to follow her in, then shut the door.

'This can't go on,' she said.

Cardova nodded.

'We can't keep this a secret for much longer, Lucius,' she went on. 'The Combined Council is on the verge of breaking the door down. They know we're covering up something; half of them believe Van might be dead, and we're hiding his body in here.'

'Maybe we should let them see him, your Majesty.'

'In his condition? They'd remove him from office immediately.'

'We could give him something to make him sleep first. If we don't compromise soon, they might vote to terminate his position anyway. I would go down with him, of course; and then the Banner would elect a new commander.'

'But I am the damn Queen. What if I refuse to accept their decision?'

'The Banner are not your subjects, your Majesty; they are contracted employees. Unless their contracts specifically state otherwise, Banner rules override your orders. And before you ask, I've checked – their contracts have no such clause.'

'Then we need to hold out for as long as possible. But, we could try your suggestion. Perhaps we could invite a couple of council members, one from the Banner, the other from the Brigades, and they could see him for a minute while he sleeps. It might buy us a day or two.'

'Can I be blunt, your Majesty?'

'Please do.'

'What is best for Jezra? We've been lucky over the last few days, your Majesty. Simon could have captured Westrig by now, if he'd wanted to, and from there he could annihilate everyone who isn't within a hundred yards of Kelsey. We have to assume that his attention is elsewhere, and that he is planning on starving us out. Unfortunately, that won't take too long. The first harvest of summer is over a month and a half away, and our reserves will run out in ten days. My point is, perhaps we shouldn't be keeping Van's condition a secret from the Banner.'

'Tell me, Lucius, what would happen to you and Van if his addiction was discovered?'

'We would be removed from authority, and then arrested.'

'Followed by some sort of punishment, I assume?'

'Yes, your Majesty; for endangering the Banner. It's possible that we'd face execution; but you are the Queen – you have to do what's right for Jezra and its inhabitants.'

'I am, Captain. Despite Van's illness, he remains the best man for the job. Two more days, you said. That's how long it will take for the salve to leave Van's body. That's how long we have to continue with our deception. Then, we can let people see Van awake.'

'Very well, your Majesty.'

The door opened, and Silva glanced through. 'Apologies, your Majesty, but some Banner officers have arrived, along with a delegation of Blades sent by Simon.'

Emily's eyes widened. 'Simon has sent someone?'

'So it seems, your Majesty.'

Emily and Cardova left the office. Two lieutenants were waiting by the main doors of the apartment. They bowed to the Queen.

'Two Blade colonels have arrived by fishing vessel, your Majesty,' said one, 'and they were picked up in the harbour and brought here. They say that they have a message from Simon, for your ears.'

'Where are they?' said Emily.

'We've placed them into a secure room on this floor, your Majesty. Should we escort you there?'

'Yes. Captain Cardova and Lady Silva, please accompany me.'

One of the lieutenants glanced at the Queen. 'Should the major-general also attend, your Majesty?'

'The major-general remains too ill to move, unfortunately,' said Emily, thankful that no noise was coming from Van's room. 'Let's go.'

The two officers led them from the apartment, where a large squad of Banner soldiers was waiting to escort them the short distance to the room where the Blades were waiting. They went inside the small chamber. Two unarmed Blade officers were sitting at a table, surrounded by Banner soldiers.

'Everyone out, please,' said the Queen.

The Banner soldiers saluted, and filed from the room, leaving the Queen, Silva, Cardova and the two lieutenants alone with the Blades. Emily took a seat, her eyes on the faces of the Blades. They looked anxious, as if expecting to be arrested.

'We bear a message from Lord Simon,' said one.

'You should address the Queen of the City using her proper title,' said Cardova.

'We were instructed not to by Lord Simon,' said the Blade. 'Officially, we are not to view Emily Aurelian as royalty.'

Cardova frowned. 'This discussion is over.'

'Wait,' said Emily. 'If they have anything useful to say, I want to hear it. They can address you, Captain, if they do not feel comfortable talking directly to me.'

'Very well, your Majesty,' said Cardova. He narrowed his eyes at the two Blades as he towered over them. 'Address your comments to me from now on, if you are unable to show the proper respect towards your anointed monarch and sovereign. Your attitude, however, has been noted. Deliver your message.'

'Lord Simon wishes an end to the conflict,' said one of the colonels. 'He is prepared to offer the following pledges, if the leadership of Jezra is willing to surrender – firstly, the lives of the Brigade workers and all civilian Exiles will be guaranteed. They will be allowed to continue to live and work in Jezra unmolested, pending the appointment of a suitable governor. Secondly, the two dragons must leave Jezra, and return to their kin in the Eastern Mountains; Lord Simon pledges not to harm them. And, finally, Kelsey Holdfast and Emily Aurelian must be surrendered to Lord Simon, along with the entire Banner, to await judgement for their crimes against the City. You have until noon tomorrow to accept these terms.'

'We don't need to wait until then,' said Emily. 'Captain, inform the Blades that these terms are rejected.'

Cardova turned to the Blades. 'I assume that your ears are working? You heard the Queen. No deal.'

'But, Captain,' said one of the colonels, 'there are nearly twenty thousand Brigade workers and civilians living in Jezra. Will you sacrifice them, to protect two thousand Banner soldiers? This is the best deal you are going to get.'

'What does Simon intend to do with the two thousand Banner soldiers?' said Cardova. 'Every day, at dawn, ten of our comrades from the second regiment have been executed by the gates of Cuidrach Palace. Over a hundred prisoners from the Grey Isle have already died in this manner, and Simon expects us to put ourselves into his hands? And what will happen to the Queen? Without an absolute guarantee of her safety, these discussions are pointless.'

The Blade colonel smiled. 'I wonder if the Brigade workers and civilians will feel the same, when they learn of these terms. Aren't there several hundred young children now living here – the offspring of all those young Brigade workers? The surrender of your armed forces seems a small price to pay for their lives.'

'We will never surrender the Queen of the City to a usurper,' said Cardova. 'Simon does not belong here.'

'And you do?' said the colonel. 'Do I need to remind you, foreign Banner Captain, that you don't belong here either? The only people still loyal to Emily Aurelian are Exiles from Lostwell. Lord Simon may be an outsider, but he is clearly the most powerful god in the City. Opposing him is futile.'

Cardova turned to the Banner lieutenants. 'Did these delegates speak to anyone on their way here?'

One nodded. 'They shouted out some of the terms to the crowd by the harbour, sir; before we could stop them. The population will be aware of the gist of Simon's proposals.'

The Blade colonel smiled. 'I imagine there will be some strongly-worded debates taking place shortly among the common folk of Jezra.

How will the Brigades feel, to know that their leaders are abandoning them?'

'You are dismissed,' said Emily. 'Your attempts to divide us shall not succeed. Go back to your new master.'

The two Blades got to their feet. 'Noon tomorrow, Emily Aurelian. Send a boat to Ooste by then, if you see sense.'

The door was opened, and a squad of Banner soldiers escorted the Blades out.

'Treacherous bastards,' muttered Cardova, as the door was closed.

Emily bowed her head.

'The Banner will fight on, your Majesty,' he said. 'The daily executions outside Cuidrach Palace have assured that every soldier knows his fate if we surrender.'

'And the civilians? The Brigade workers?'

'Do you believe the promises made by Simon, your Majesty?'

'No.'

'Then the words of the Blades were meaningless. Think nothing more of them, your Majesty; they were merely trying to distract us.'

Raised voices sounded from outside the room, and Emily glanced at the door, her heart sinking.

The door opened.

'Your Majesty,' said a soldier; 'members of the Combined Council are here, demanding to speak to you at once. Should we let them in?'

Emily nodded. The door opened wider, and three officials from the Brigades walked into the room. They bowed low to the Queen, then Cardova gestured to the seats vacated by the Blades.

'Good afternoon,' said the Queen; 'how can we help you?'

'Is it true, your Majesty?' said one of the officials, a Shinstran by his accent. 'The town is rife with rumours.'

'Is what true?'

'The terms offered by Simon, your Majesty. Witnesses at the harbour claim to have heard that Simon has offered to spare the civilians and Brigades, if the Banner surrenders.'

'Simon's promises are worthless.'

'But he did offer that, your Majesty? This places us into a difficult position. I fear that the ordinary Brigade workers will demand that we at least open up more negotiations with Simon and the rest of the City. Food supplies are already being heavily rationed, and we are running out of basic items at an alarming rate. If we have been defeated militarily, then what else can we do but negotiate?'

'Simon will slaughter the Banner if we surrender,' said Emily. 'The same Banner that the Brigades have fought alongside for two years.'

'We don't know that for certain, your Majesty. Simon might show mercy.'

Emily shook her head.

'Might I ask, your Majesty,' said one of the other council members; 'what is the opinion of the Commander of the Banner? One would have thought that he ought to be involved in this discussion, even if he remains too ill to carry out all of his duties. Might we ask him in person?'

'Not today, I'm afraid,' said Emily. 'He is too ill.'

'Too ill, your Majesty? If that is so, then we should move to appoint a new commander. Jezra is facing the worst crisis of its short history; we need a commander who is capable of carrying out his duties.'

'I have every confidence that the major-general will recover soon.'

'In that case, you should have no problem in allowing us access to him, your Majesty, so that we might see his condition for ourselves.'

'Do you doubt the word of the Queen?' said Cardova.

'Not at all, Captain; however, her Majesty is not a doctor. We would be more than happy to assign some Brigade medical staff to provide a prognosis. A second opinion, as it were. We all want the major-general to recover, but if his illness is as severe as we suspect it is, then we need to get the process of appointing a new commander underway as soon as possible.'

'That will not be necessary,' said Emily.

'We think it is, your Majesty,' said the official. He took a breath. 'It pains me to say this, your Majesty, but unless we are granted full access to the major-general this very day, then unfortunately you leave us no choice but to seek his removal from office. The laws of Jezra, to which we are all subject, are clear on this. If the commander is incapacitated, then a replacement must be found.'

'Wait a few more days,' said Emily. 'I am sure that we shall see signs of improvement by then.'

'We shall discuss this with the rest of the council, your Majesty, but I fear that the situation demands that we take immediate action. We shall see ourselves out.'

The three Brigade officials got to their feet and trooped from the room.

Emily placed her head in her hands. 'It's over. I can't do this any more.'

Cardova gestured to the two lieutenants, who saluted and left the room.

'Don't despair, your Majesty,' he said.

'What else is there to do? The council will overthrow Van, and then they'll discover his addiction, and they'll realise that we've been covering it up. The people of Jezra will desert us when they find out. Simon's proposals will sound generous to their ears, and if even half of them are tempted to accept, then our rule here will collapse. I should have acted upon the warning signs from Van months ago, but I let it slide, because he was still able to carry out his duties. I have failed. Perhaps I should surrender, in person. Maybe Simon will spare the Banner soldiers if I hand myself in.'

'No, your Majesty,' said Cardova, his eyes widening. 'Simon will hang you in front of the entire City. I will not allow that to happen. And what about Kelsey? Will you hand her in too? Simon won't rest until she is also in his custody.'

Silva glanced up. 'There might be a way out of this, your Majesty.'

'Yes?' said Emily. 'Please tell me, Silva, for I cannot see it.'

'It is a risky course, your Majesty.'

'I would hardly assume it would be easy, Silva.'

'Your life might come into danger, your Majesty; but if it works, then we may be able to take Simon by surprise.'

'Please, Silva; stop prevaricating. I accept that I might be in danger; I am already in danger.'

The demigod leaned over, and lowered her voice. 'We should take Maxwell to Amalia.'

Cardova snorted.

'Hear me out, please,' said Silva. 'I still believe that Amalia is capable of doing the right thing, your Majesty. You have her child, and she has yours. She sent a messenger to Jezra, without Simon's knowledge or permission – this proves that she is willing to defy the Ascendant. If I am right about her, then she will be deeply unhappy about the current position in which she finds herself. She used to be the God-Queen, and now she has to bow before Simon. I believe that, if you went to Tara in person, and delivered Maxwell to her, then she would be open to an alliance. Keep Kelsey Holdfast here, in Jezra, so that Simon is unaware that you have left the town, then we can slip away by boat.'

'This is madness,' said Cardova. 'Amalia would hand the Queen over to Simon in a heartbeat.'

'I do not believe that,' said Silva. 'But, even if she did, would we be any worse off than if we rejected Simon's terms? If we do nothing, then Jezra's days are numbered, and the town will most likely fall into disorder, as soon as the Brigades rebel against the Banner soldiers. All we need are a few days; enough time to travel inconspicuously to Tara.'

'Say that you're right,' said Emily; 'what would Amalia demand as her part of the deal?'

'There is only one way to find out, your Majesty – to ask her in person, face to face. In my opinion, she would be content with little – an end to Simon, and a return to the way things used to be.'

'I will never bow before her as God-Queen.'

'And I fear that she will never bow to you as mortal Queen, your Majesty. Could you not find a way to co-exist? There must be a compromise available.'

'Alright; say we manage to sort out the details, face to face, as you say. What then? Simon would still be in Ooste.'

'We strike, your Majesty, quickly, and with every force at our disposal. Kelsey and the dragons from the air, the Banner from the sea, with Amalia advancing from Tara with the Roser militia at her back.'

'It's too risky,' said Cardova.

'Then please suggest an alternative, Captain,' said Silva. 'If you have a better plan, then don't hold your tongue.'

'Would you come with me, Silva?' said the Queen.

'Yes. I could alert you if Simon or any other god approaches, and I know Amalia, your Majesty. I can speak to her first, alone, and prepare her. She will, I believe, do anything to get her son back.'

Emily got to her feet.

'Your Majesty?' said Cardova.

'We need to bring Kelsey into this discussion. I want to see what she thinks, as she will be the one who has to stay here with Van, if we leave.'

'You can't seriously be considering this, your Majesty?'

'I am, Lucius, and you will be coming with us.'

Silva gave the captain a faint smile, then they left the room and walked back to the apartment. Emily glanced at Maxwell as they entered. The infant was trying to walk again, his hands clinging onto the edge of a chair as he swayed on his two feet.

Lady Omertia laughed. 'He's a determined little boy.'

Emily nodded, then went into Van's bedroom. She breathed a sigh of relief as she saw the major-general sleeping on the bed. Kelsey glanced up.

'Do you have a minute?' said Emily. 'Silva has a proposal you need to hear.'

'I look ridiculous, your Majesty,' said Cardova, gazing at his reflection in the tall mirror.

'You look like a civilian, Lucius,' said the Queen.

'Exactly, your Majesty. This is a bad idea.'

'You need to drop the "majesty" when you speak to me from now on.'

He turned to her. 'Please, your Majesty; I beg you to reconsider. I know what Kelsey said, but I doubt that she will be able to continue the deception for more than a day, and when the people of Jezra realise that you've gone, they'll think that you've deserted them. Van needs a few more days to flush the last of the salve out of his body; what will he say when he discovers this?'

'I don't know, Lucius. However, I believe that Simon will lose interest in Jezra when he discovers that I am no longer here. I also intend to be in Tara within a few days at the most. If we're quick, we can be in Maeladh Palace before the Combined Council has a chance to appoint a new commander. Kelsey will lock down the entire Command Post, allowing no one in or out of the building; that will give us the time we need.'

They went through to the living room of the apartment, where Silva was waiting, along with Lady Omertia and Maxwell.

Cardova frowned at the sight of Lady Omertia in her travelling clothes.

'I have decided to bring my mother along,' said Emily; 'we cannot leave her here alone; she would be at risk.'

Cardova said nothing, but his eyes were lit with anger.

'We will drop her off in Icehaven,' said the Queen. 'Lady Yvona will allow her to stay in Alkirk Palace, while we travel onwards to Tara. Has the boat been prepared?'

'Yes, your Majesty,' said Cardova. 'It is waiting for us by the pier at Westrig. The wagon to take us there is also ready.'

'Excellent, and remember to stop saying "your Majesty" all the time.'

Kelsey walked through from Van's bedroom. She glanced at Lucius and the Queen. 'You do look the part, I guess, though you should put your hood up, Queenie; your blonde hair is too recognisable.'

'I will when we leave, Kelsey.'

'Are you armed?'

Emily patted her side, where the Fated Blade was strapped.

'I have a sword too,' muttered Cardova; 'for all the good it will do us.'

'Cheer up, big guy,' said Kelsey.

'How are you so calm about this?' said Cardova. 'This plan is insane.'

'That's why it might work,' said Kelsey; 'it's the last thing that Simon would expect us to do. I also think that Silva has a point – there's a chance that Amalia wants nothing more than to get rid of Simon, as well as getting her son back. And, if we do nothing, then the end won't be far away. If it all goes to shit, then Frostback and Halfclaw will fly me and Van away.'

'How many "ifs" were in that statement, Kelsey?' said Cardova. 'I lost count.'

'Never mind him,' said Emily. 'Kelsey, are you clear on what you need to do?'

'Aye; I think so. As soon as you've left the building, I will seal up the doors to the Command Post and declare a state of emergency; martial law, with the Banner in control of the streets and a curfew for the civilians. I've already got Van to sign a few blank sheets of paper; I just need to fill in the details at the top of each page.'

'Have you informed the major-general of our plan?' said Emily.

'Aye. I thought it best. I'm not sure if he really understood everything I was saying, but I'll remind him when he wakes up.'

'The next few days are crucial,' said Cardova. 'You should see some improvement in the major-general's condition soon. If you can keep the Combined Council at bay until then, he should be able to do some light work.' The captain exhaled. 'This is a bad idea.'

'I know how you feel about this, Lucius,' said Emily, 'but I also need to know that I can depend on you. Will your doubts interfere with your duty?'

'Of course not, your Majesty. I will do my duty; I am under your command.'

'Thank you. Alright; I think we're ready. Mother, have Maxwell's things been packed?'

Lady Omertia gestured to a case on the floor. 'Everything is in here, dear.'

'Lucius, if you would, please?'

Cardova frowned, then picked up the case.

'You are making the correct decision, your Majesty,' said Silva, standing. 'I believe that this course of action is the best on offer.'

Cardova glared at the demigod.

'Have the stairs to the rear doors been cleared, Lucius? And don't say "your Majesty."'

'They have... ma'am.'

Emily turned to Kelsey. 'Thank you for agreeing to this. Your part will be essential to the success of our journey. Keep our secrets for as long as you can, and don't be afraid to flee if it comes to it. You will be needed, if we are to overcome Simon.'

Kelsey nodded. 'Good luck, Queenie. I'll await a message from you.'

Emily hesitated for a moment. Cardova looked deeply unhappy about their imminent departure, but Silva's optimism had given her some hope, and all she could do was cling onto it. She gazed at her travelling companions – a demigod, her mother, an infant and the Banner captain. Could they make a difference? What was the worst that could happen? Simon could catch them long before they reached Tara, or perhaps Amalia would instantly betray them rather than try to oppose the Ascendant. Then she thought about doing nothing. If they stayed in Jezra, then the town would fall, and there would be a bloodbath; the Banner would be slaughtered to the last man, and Emily would be strung up in public. She lowered her gaze; there was no alternative.

She tried to smile. 'Let's go.'

CHAPTER 10

TAKEN

Jezra, The Western Bank – 9th Mikalis 3423

'Tell me again,' said Van, his voice weak. 'The Queen has gone?'

Kelsey sighed in exasperation. 'I've already told you, several times. They left yesterday evening, as soon as it got dark. They took a fishing boat to Icehaven.'

'Are they in Icehaven?'

'I don't know! They got onto the boat; that's the last I heard.'

'Get Lucius; I need to talk to him about this.'

'Lucius has gone with them, Van; are you not listening to me?'

The major-general looked confused. Still, Kelsey thought, at least he wasn't pleading for salve.

'Sorry, Kelsey; my mind doesn't seem to be able to keep up with what you're telling me. What did the Combined Council have to say about this?'

'They don't know.'

'Didn't you say that martial law had been declared? Someone must have ordered that.'

'You did, Van. You signed the orders last night.'

'I did? I don't remember doing that. Whose idea was this... plan?'

'Silva's, I think. She believes that Amalia can be turned.'

Van tried to raise his hands, then remembered that they were strapped to the bed. 'Dear gods. And you just let them go?'

Kelsey eyed the straps, then leaned over and began to unbuckle them.

'Aye. It's a decent plan.'

'It relies upon Amalia deciding to help the Queen. It's not decent; it's ridiculous.'

Kelsey smothered a smile as she unfastened the last strap.

'Was Lucius happy with it?' Van said, rubbing his freed wrists. 'If he thought it was sensible, then perhaps I'm worrying about nothing.'

Kelsey leaned back in her chair. 'Lucius wasn't entirely enthusiastic, it must be said; but he went along with it.'

'Of course he did; he obeys orders.' He laid his head back on the pillow. 'I'm so tired.'

She stood. 'I'll let you get some sleep, and then I'll make you some lunch.'

He reached out and took Kelsey's hand. 'What you have done for me, Kelsey; I'm not sure if I'll ever be able to repay you. Even after I acted like a complete arsehole, you're still here, looking after me. I don't know what to say, except that I'm sorry for everything I've put you through.'

She shrugged. 'It was the salve.'

'It was, but it was my choices also. I was weak, and I succumbed to temptation. I don't deserve you, Kelsey.'

She leaned forward and kissed him on the forehead. 'I know.'

He closed his eyes, and she slipped out of the bedroom. The living room of the apartment was quiet, with just Vadhi there, sitting on a couch. Kelsey walked over and sat next to her, putting her feet up on the table.

'Peace and quiet, at last,' she said.

Vadhi said nothing.

'I might take a nap,' Kelsey went on; 'or maybe I should go up onto the roof and see if Frostback is around. Are you hungry?'

Vadhi glared at her.

Kelsey sighed. 'Aren't you speaking to me?'

'The Queen has run away, and you're just sitting there as if nothing has happened. She's betrayed us all; she expects us to stay here and fight for her, but she's too cowardly to hang around in person.'

'Pyre's arse, Vadhi, is that what you think? The Queen is putting herself at risk to try to save everyone. She could die for what she's doing.'

'And so will we. If she had surrendered, then at least the Brigades would be spared.'

'Don't you care about the Banner soldiers? Simon will kill them all if he gets his hands on them.'

'We don't know that. He might just put them in jail for a while.'

'Don't be an idiot, Vadhi. He slaughtered the entire Royal Guard when he took Pella, and he's killing ten Banner soldiers a day outside the ruins of Cuidrach Palace. It's nothing short of wishful thinking to imagine that he'll suddenly grow a conscience. What's more, I don't believe his promises. He'd say anything to divide us.'

'Aren't you angry? She's abandoned you too.'

'I'm angry at Simon, not Emily. He's the one that's put us into this position.' She glanced at the window clock. 'It's noon. The deadline for Simon's offer has passed.' She waited a moment. 'See? Nothing's happening. No fleet has appeared on the horizon. I'm going to make some lunch.'

She got to her feet and walked to the kitchen. The leadership had been receiving the same rations as everyone else in Jezra, but because the workers assumed that Van's apartment was still full, they had delivered enough for seven adults that morning. Kelsey looked through the meagre supplies, and prepared three plates with food. She made sure that Van's plate held the best of what was on offer; he needed the sustenance more than she or Vadhi did, then walked back into the living room, carrying a tray.

Simon smiled at her from the couch. 'Lunch? How thoughtful.'

Kelsey stared at the armoured god, her mouth dry. Vadhi was lying on the floor by his feet, her eyes closed.

'Your guard is sleeping,' said Simon. 'Where is the Queen? Why is she not in the Command Post?'

Kelsey decided to act as if everything was perfectly normal. She walked over to the table, laid the tray down, then sat opposite Simon. A long sword was resting across his knees, its blade glinting in the light.

'I do believe that I asked you a question,' he said. 'Where is the Queen?'

'She's gone. You've missed her.'

'I see. And where has she gone? Do I need to torture you, or perhaps your rather useless guard?'

'No. The Queen has fled. I don't know where she's gone, exactly. I'm supposed to cover it up; that's my job.'

Simon leaned forward, his eyes fixed on her. 'You're lying, aren't you? You fascinate me. You are the only mortal whose mind I have been unable to read, and it intrigues me that you are able to keep secrets from me. Anyway, that's enough chat for now.'

He withdrew the Quadrant, and glided his fingers across the copper-coloured surface. The air shimmered, and Kelsey found herself in the heat of a desert, with the sun glaring down at them. Simon was with her, while Vadhi's unconscious body was lying on the baking hot sand.

'We are still upon the world of the City,' Simon said, 'but I like the heat down here in the sunward desert. It crystallises my thoughts, somehow.'

'What do you want from me, Simon?' said Kelsey.

'Why are you not afraid of me?'

'I don't know. I've never been scared of idiot bullies who think they're wonderful. That's probably because my older brother was like that.'

'I have brought you here, Kelsey Holdfast, because I think we have more in common than you realise. Your world is at threat from Edmond, the Second Ascendant; you fought him on Lostwell. Your enemy is my enemy, Kelsey. We shouldn't be fighting each other; we should join forces. If I had you by my side, we would be able to destroy Edmond's grip on Implacatus; we would be unstoppable. You have my word that your home world will remain free; I'm not interested in destruction for the sake of it. No, what I want is simple – to remove Edmond from power. You want the same, yes?'

'If that's all you want, then why are you here?'

'I swore an oath to the ones who rescued me from Yocasta, a binding oath that I cannot break. I swore to return them to power, and I have done so. My next step is to oversee the removal of the salve from the Eastern Mountains. Once I have it in my possession, then I will make my move on Implacatus, using this world as a base from which to strike at Edmond. Emily and the Banner are in my way, and must be removed, before I will feel secure here. Do you see?'

'Aye. That makes sense, I guess.'

'Then, will you join me?'

'No. You're a murdering arsehole, and I don't make common cause with murdering arseholes.'

'But, Kelsey, surely you realise that I am your best chance to defeat Edmond? What would that mean to your family, friends and your fellow countrymen and women on your home world? They would be safe, for all time. They would never have to fear that Edmond would arrive, with his massed legions of Banners soldiers and greenhides, and his cohorts of death-powered Ancients and gods.' He stretched his arms out to either side, his skin glowing in the strong sunlight. 'When I sit upon the throne of Implacatus, I will give you full honours; you will have anything you desire – riches, palaces, slaves, or, if you prefer, a quiet life of peace and anonymity. Your skills are breathtaking, Kelsey; you might be the most powerful mortal who has ever lived.'

'My siblings might have something to say about that.'

Simon smiled. 'Perhaps we should recruit them too? The Holdfasts and I, together. I would give you worlds to rule. Do you have conditions? I am open to negotiation. Tell me what you want and, if I can grant it, I will.'

Kelsey said nothing.

'You do concede that I am your best chance of helping you get rid of Edmond?'

'You might be, but that doesn't mean anything. You're just as bad as Edmond, in your own way.'

Simon's eyes tightened. 'You have no idea what you're talking about.'

'Maybe not. I can only judge you both on what I've seen; and there doesn't seem to be much difference between you. Neither of you give a shit about mortals; you're only interested in power. Edmond has it, and you want it. If it was the other way around, I can imagine Edmond asking for my help to overthrow you.'

'I will not make this offer again, Holdfast. If you continue to spurn me, then I will have no choice as to what I do next.'

'Are you going to kill me?'

He shook his head. 'No. You're far too valuable to kill. I will put your skills to work, and you will end up helping my aims, even though you are unwilling.'

Kelsey frowned. 'You've lost me. If you're not going to kill me, then what are you going to do?'

He glanced down at the prostrate body of Vadhi on the sands. 'Do you wish to take this mortal girl with you?'

'Where?'

'Answer my question. Shall I leave her here to die in the desert, or do you want her to go with you?'

'I don't want her to die.'

'Then she goes with you. See? I am not a brute.'

'That's a matter of opinion.'

He looked her in the eyes. 'Join with me. If you say yes, then we will return to the City, to plan our takeover of Implacatus. Forget all the others; it is you I require. Join me.'

'No.'

'Why are you being so obstinate? I will destroy every soldier in the Banner, and I will catch Emily. Her reign is over, Kelsey; she lost. There is no need for you to continue being loyal to her.'

Kelsey turned away, and gazed out over the endless sands. She pictured herself by Simon's side as he rampaged through hordes of Edmond's minions, her powers blocking the gods from striking back. Simon was right; together, they would be unstoppable. She tried to imagine what her mother's response would be. What would Holder Fast do in the same situation? Never mind her mother; what would her sister do? Karalyn would destroy Simon in an instant, that's what she would do. Kelsey frowned. She wasn't her mother, or her sister; she had to come to a decision on her own.

'I will not work for you, Simon.'

'You fool,' he cried. 'You were on the cusp of greatness. Very well, Holdfast.' He took out the Quadrant. His fingers moved over the surface, and they appeared in a small room, with smooth, white walls, and a window that looked out over a thick bank of clouds.

'Do you know where we are?' he said.

She stepped round the body of Vadhi and walked to the window, but could see nothing but clouds, some of which were below them.

'No,' she said.

'We are on Implacatus, in a city by the name of Serene. Your new home.'

'What?'

He gave her a wry smile. 'This is where I leave you, Holdfast. The disruption you will cause here by your mere presence will be enough to send the gods who rule this place into paroxysms of frustration and anger. They will know something is wrong, but they will not be able to find you, or work out why their powers are intermittently failing. Lie low, that's my advice. If you do get caught, tell them that I am coming, and that my revenge will be overwhelming and complete. Preferably, however, don't get caught.'

He touched the Quadrant, and vanished.

Kelsey stared at the space he had just occupied, her mouth open. Despite his words, she had expected Simon to kill her for refusing to help him, but this? She had no money, no food, no possessions, and was stranded on the world of the Ascendants. She started to cry, then rubbed her face, pushing back the tears. She needed to stay angry; if she dissolved into self-pity, then she wouldn't last a day in Serene. From the floor, Vadhi let out a groan, and opened her eyes. She glanced around.

'Where are we?'

Kelsey stared at her.

'I don't recognise this room,' Vadhi went on, as she tried to get to her feet. 'The last thing I remember is you going off to make lunch. Did I fall asleep?'

Kelsey kept her eyes on Vadhi as she strode over to the window. The Exile's eyes widened at the view.

'Kelsey,' she said; 'are we still in the City?'

An hour passed before they dared to leave the room. Vadhi had wept for much of that time, unable to accept what had happened to her, while Kelsey had taken to pacing the floor, her mind overflowing with anxiety. Would she ever see Van again, or Frostback? What would they do when they learned that she had vanished without trace? Would they know that Simon had taken her, or would they think that she had run away? She knew there was no point in going over such thoughts, but she couldn't help it; whenever she tried to think of her own future, she fell into a near panic.

When Vadhi had stopped crying, she sat down on the floor, her knees up to her chin, swaying back and forward, her eyes wide.

'Get up,' said Kelsey. 'We can't stay in here forever.'

'We don't even know where "here" is,' Vadhi said.

'We're in a city. Van used to live here; so did Cardova, I think. If those two numpties can cope with Serene, then so can we. Are you hungry?'

'I can't think about food; not now. We've lost everything. There's no hope for us, is there? How are we supposed to get money to eat? Where are we going to sleep? I need the toilet.'

Kelsey reached down and helped Vadhi get to her feet. 'Just follow me,' she said. 'And try to look normal; you know, relaxed, as if you know where you are. We'll just go for a stroll, to get our bearings. Oh, and don't speak if you don't have to; I imagine that our accents will be out of place here.' Kelsey closed her eyes and took a breath. 'I am an aristocrat; I can handle this. I am a Holdfast; aye, a damned Holdfast. The poor bastards won't know what hit them.' She opened her eyes again. 'Alright; I'm ready.'

She walked to the door, then turned and glanced at Vadhi, who frowned and followed her. Kelsey eased the door open and peered out. The entrance led onto a long, perfectly straight corridor, also gleaming in white, with skylights directly above them. Down the left hand side of the corridor were dozens of identical doors, just like the one she had opened. The door in her hand had a number painted on it in black – 3471.

She stepped out into the corridor. No one was around, in either direction. She walked up to the next door along, and pressed her ear to it. The door fell open, and she toppled in, landing on the floor. Two men were in the room, sitting on low chairs eating a meal. They glanced up to stare at her.

'Whoops,' she said, getting up. 'Sorry, guys; wrong room.'

She noticed a pair of beds against the wall, then hurried out and closed the door. Vadhi was staring at her.

'I think these are tiny apartments,' Kelsey said, keeping her voice low. 'But there are no bathrooms or kitchens. Come on; let's get out of here before those guys get up to see who we are.'

They hurried down the corridor, then slowed when they came to an opening on their right. Through the entrance was a large canteen, with dozens of tables in neat rows along the floor, and a serving counter at the far end, where people were waiting in a queue. Kelsey glanced at a doorway inside the canteen, from which a woman was emerging, wiping her hands.

'Follow me,' Kelsey whispered to Vadhi, then she strode into the canteen, trying to pretend that she knew exactly what she was doing.

She reached the door and opened it, finding a bathroom inside. Vadhi joined her, and they locked the door.

'Go,' said Kelsey. 'I'll look away.'

She walked to a narrow window as Vadhi hurried to the toilet. The view was the same as it had been from the small room where they had arrived – nothing but clouds. She tried to remember everything that Van had told her about Serene. He had mentioned that it had been built high up on a mountain side, and that seemed to match what she was seeing. Behind her, she heard Vadhi get up and wash her hands.

'What now?' she said.

Kelsey shrugged. 'We need to steal some clothes. Everyone seems to be wearing the same drab outfits, and we stand out. If there's a communal canteen, then there will probably be a communal laundry service; we need to find it. From what I remember Van telling me, Serene is on many levels, all going down the side of a mountain. I suspect that we're in some kind of servants' district; maybe everyone on this level works for the gods, in which case, there are likely to be lots of immortals up here. We probably need to head downwards.'

She opened the door, and they hurried out, heading back into the long corridor. They kept walking, keeping a brisk pace, and passed countless doors on their left and right, all numbered. They heard voices coming from an arched opening on their right, and slowed. Beyond the opening was a vast room, where people were washing great heaps of uniforms. There were large tubs filled with steaming water, which workers were stirring with wooden paddles, while clothes were being rinsed in a succession of smaller tubs that stretched to the far end of the hall. On the right, the washed uniforms were being dried in the open air, next to carts filled with clean garments. The still-to-be-washed clothes were far closer than the laundered ones, and Kelsey and Vadhi slipped into the hall, hiding behind one of the heaps of dirty washing.

'Pick out something that doesn't stink,' whispered Kelsey, as she began rummaging through the pile.

'It all stinks.'

'Then hold your nose.'

They took their purloined clothes back to the room where they had arrived, and got changed, pulling on the slightly-stained grey uniforms while Vadhi pulled a face. They tied their hair back into pony-tails, as that seemed to be the style worn by most women they had seen, then stashed their own clothes in the corner of the room.

Kelsey opened the door and they stepped out. The long corridor was busier than before, with several small groups making their way in and out of the nearby canteen. Kelsey and Vadhi turned to the right, and walked away from the canteen and laundry. The gleaming white floor and ceiling made it difficult to see where the corridor ended, and Kelsey almost stumbled when they walked out into an enormous hall. It was roofed with a colossal glass dome, with windows running hundreds of feet down to the floor. They were on an upper level, and could look down at the dozen floors that lay below them. Each storey had a circular walkway that ringed the circumference of the dome, and there were plenty of staircases that seemed to almost float upon the air, connecting the various floors. A low hubbub of voices was echoing around the domed hall, from the dozens of people on the stairs.

Vadhi gasped. 'I've never seen so much glass in my life. Who could have built this?'

'The Ascendants, I guess,' said Kelsey; 'and never mind the glass; look at the statues.'

Rising up from the marble floor many feet below them were three human forms, each shining in polished gold. The figures were so gargantuan that their heads reached the upper level where Kelsey and Vadhi were standing. They walked to the rail by the walkway to get a better look. Two of the figures were women, and the other was a man.

'Who are they?' said Vadhi.

'That one's Belinda,' said Kelsey, pointing, 'and the guy is Edmond; although the statues make them look a lot older than they are now. I'm going to guess that the third figure is Theodora, because that would make the group represent the first three Ascendants.'

'Are they solid gold?'

'Who knows? Maybe they're just gold-plated; regardless, that's a shitload of gold. Belinda's sword alone could probably buy half the City. We need to get down those stairs, all the way to the bottom.'

'What about the soldiers?'

Kelsey squinted her eyes. 'What soldiers?'

'They're wearing a strange kind of armour. Look; there's two of them, on the level below us.'

Kelsey looked down. Two men were on the walkway a few yards to the left of them, on the level directly under where they were standing. Each was wearing a breastplate and armour of rippled pinks and reds.

'Pyre's arse,' muttered Kelsey. 'I see them now. That armour, it's not made of steel; in fact, it's not made of metal at all. It's stone.'

'Stone?'

'My mother once had an arm guard that a Rahain stone mage made for her. It was lost before my time, but she used to tell us about it. It was made of thin layers of compressed stone – light, but almost indestructible, and my mother said that you could see the colours of the polished stone. She said it was beautiful, but also extremely expensive.'

A woman in long robes approached the two soldiers as Kelsey and Vadhi were watching. Her expression was animated, and she was gesticulating wildly.

'Let's move,' said Kelsey, pulling Vadhi away from the railing. 'She's a god; I can sense her trying to use her vision powers.' She glanced around as they walked towards the nearest stairs going down. There were more men and women in similar robes, dotted around the hall, and positioned on many of the different walkways. Kelsey reached out, sensing for powers. 'Shit,' she muttered; 'there are gods everywhere, and I'm disrupting their powers.'

The sound of people running echoed through the hall as Kelsey and Vadhi descended the first set of stairs. More soldiers were visible, talking to the robe-wearing gods, who were staring around, wide-eyed.

'What is happening?' shrieked a god from the level below, his voice ringing across the hall. 'Are we under attack?'

'Keep walking,' whispered Kelsey, 'and keep your head down.'

Soldiers began appearing from doorways on every level, fanning out by the stairs. A god was trying to organise them, her face stricken with fear.

'No, I don't understand it,' shouted another god, as he strode up the same set of stairs that Kelsey and Vadhi were descending.

'Has everyone lost their powers?' said the robed goddess by his side.

'How should I know?' the man spat.

They passed Kelsey and Vadhi on the stairs without giving them a glance. The shouting increased, and many of the ordinary mortals were staring around at the panicking gods in the hall. Kelsey and Vadhi picked up their pace, hurrying down flight after flight of stairs. Gods were gathering, arguing among themselves; a few were weeping, while others were close to hysterics. Several soldiers looked unsure, as the gods around them grew more fearful.

Kelsey and Vadhi reached the bottom of the last flight of stairs, and walked past the giant feet of the three statues. A tall man in steel armour came striding out of an opening, dozens of soldiers at his back.

'Clear the hall of civilians!' he cried.

The soldiers spread out across the circular floor of the great hall. Two approached Kelsey and Vadhi, and gestured for them to leave by the closest exit. The two young women nodded, and ran for an archway. Beyond was another long, straight corridor, but it was far dingier than the one at the top of the hall, where they had arrived. A few families had emerged from their tiny apartments to see what was causing the noise, but soldiers were ordering them back inside. Kelsey and Vadhi pressed on, then stopped when they came to a huge plaza, with one side open to the elements. There were patches of grass, and a few trees, and they sat on a bench close to the edge of the mountain.

'We walked for more than a hundred yards,' said Kelsey, her voice low as she kept an eye out for more soldiers; 'their powers will have returned by now.'

'I don't get it,' said Vadhi. 'If you were causing that, then why didn't they stop us?'

'They had no idea it was us,' she said, 'and none of them would believe that a mere mortal could switch their powers off like that.' She rubbed her face. 'Simon was right; I'm going to cause chaos here. There must be hundreds, maybe thousands of gods and demigods in Serene; the city probably depends on them for everything; and wherever I go, there are going to be scenes like that.'

'Where are we going to go? I don't think we can go back to our room, not if we have to pass all of those gods and soldiers again.'

Kelsey nodded. 'I've been thinking about that. There's someone in Serene who might help us. It's a risk, but what else can we do?'

'Who?'

Kelsey exhaled. 'Van's father.'

CHAPTER 11

SURRENDER

Tara, Auldan, The City – 12th Mikalis 3423

'Thank you, Kagan,' said Amalia. 'I don't think I could bear to see the triumphant look on Simon's face.'

'It's fine,' said Kagan, standing by the carriage. 'It'll be good to get out of the palace for the day.'

'Better you than me.' She kissed him, then took a step back.

He smiled. 'Try not to kill the Aurelians while I'm away.'

'I'll try, but I'm not promising anything.'

Kagan turned, and climbed up into the carriage. A servant closed the door, and the four ponies got underway, the gravel crunching under the wheels of the carriage. Amalia gave a brief wave, then strode back into the palace, as the carriage rolled towards the iron gates by the edge of the courtyard. Kagan settled back into his seat. He was starting to regret offering to go to Pella in Amalia's stead, but he hadn't been lying about wanting to get out of the palace for a while.

The carriage slowed as it left the gates, and was joined by two wagons, both open-backed and filled with militia guards. The three vehicles set off down the steep road towards the streets of Tara, and Kagan tried to pay attention to what he was seeing. It was difficult, as his mind kept drifting back to dark thoughts about his future, and what might be happening to Maxwell. The answers might lie in Pella, he thought. Simon had summoned them; he had announced that the war was over and that all resistance from the rebels had ended. At first, Amalia and Kagan had been filled with hope by the message, thinking that it meant Maxwell's safe recovery, but they had been disabused of the notion by Felice, who had used her powers to tell them that their son had not been found.

The convoy reached the bottom of the cliffside, and they sped along the wide roads of the town, passing large whitewashed houses with red roofs on either side. Trees lined the route, and were in blossom, the light pink petals billowing in the warm breeze from the bay. They came to the main coastal road, where a group of Rosers stopped to stare at the carriage, then the convoy turned for Pella, heading into the rising sun. It would have been a lot quicker by boat, but the lack of available sea-worthy ships meant that almost everyone was travelling by the land route, and the road leading from Tara was busy with traffic. The waters of the bay were sparkling down to the left of the carriage, and Kagan glanced at the few vessels that were sailing that morning. Unlike the coastal waters off Alea Tanton, the bay was clear and he could see the bottom, where tiny silvery fish were swirling in little groups above the golden sand.

He had visited the Aurelians earlier that day, to tell them that the rebels had been defeated, but when Daniel had pressed him for details, he had been forced to admit that he had none – neither Simon nor Felice had deigned to tell them what exactly had happened, as if they delighted in keeping him and Amalia in the dark about what occurred in the rest of the City. Lady Aurelian had perceived his embarrassment, and had mocked him for it, but he was used to her pouncing on every opportunity to tell him that he was a fool.

The road began to turn left towards the east, following the shore as it curved in the direction of Pella. They passed the ancient walls of old Tara, and entered the Roser suburbs that continued without a gap. Row after row of neat houses rose up the gentle, terraced slopes of the Sunward Range to the right of the convoy, each with a little square garden at its front, covered in trimmed grass and perfectly arranged flowerbeds.

Kagan shook his head at the wealth on display. Even the poorer districts of Roser territory were richer than the richest mortal areas of Alea Tanton. The children he saw by the side of the road were healthy-looking and well-dressed; a world away from Kagan's own experience growing up in the Shinstran slums. After a mile or so, the convoy passed an unmanned checkpoint by the road, marking the boundary between Roser and Reaper territory. Kagan noticed the difference as soon as they crossed the frontier. The trees disappeared, and the streets were lined with red sandstone tenements, instead of detached villas. They passed a small market, filled with the last of the food that had been preserved over Freshmist. The first of many harvests would be coming soon, restocking the City's granaries with enough to tide them over to the following summer.

Reapers from the market were spilling onto the road, and the convoy slowed as it wound its way past them. Angry glances were directed towards the Roser flags flying from the carriage, and Kagan noticed the militia protecting the convoy grip their crossbows with a little more force. A few boos and jeers called out, then a section of the crowd began chanting 'Go home!' at his carriage. The convoy made its way through the crowd, and increased its speed, leaving the Reapers behind.

Kagan shook his head. They wanted him to go home? His home had been destroyed, along with the rest of Lostwell. The City didn't feel like his real home. Kagan felt his heart sink. He would do anything to return to the home that he and Sofia had made in Port Sanders.

They reached the walls of Pella, and entered the old town. The streets branching off to the right narrowed, but the coastal route was one of the main thoroughfares in Auldan, and remained wide, and busy. The large harbour began to spread out on their left, though there were far fewer boats than usual, and only the small fishing vessels were there in any numbers. The convoy slowed as they approached the ruins of Cuidrach Palace. Kagan stared out of the window at the sight of the blackened towers and collapsed roofs. It was the first time that he had seen the damage close up, though the smoke from the fires had been unmistakable from Tara while the inferno had raged. Amalia had told him that Cuidrach had been razed to the ground several times in its long history, and that it would soon be rebuilt, though Kagan wasn't sure what she had meant by "soon." A century was a short time to her.

A large crowd had gathered close to the front gates of the palace, and the convoy veered away to the right, entering a courtyard on the sunward side of Cuidrach. The damaged gates were well-protected by rows of armed militia. Beyond, stood a line of ten stakes that had been driven into the ground. Each stake was adorned with leather straps, and was heavily bloodstained. Kagan stared at the posts, his eyes wide. He had known that ten captured Banner soldiers were being executed each day at dawn, but he felt sickened at the sight. The wagons and carriage ground to a halt, and Kagan stepped down to the flagstones. Guards escorted him through the assembled crowd of militia, towards the enormous figure of Simon, standing head and shoulders above the others.

Kagan frowned at the armour the Ascendant was wearing. The shining steel had gone, replaced by a bright swirl of green and gold ripples. At first, Kagan assumed that it was enamel covering the metal plates, but as he walked closer to the Ascendant, he realised that the armour was made of a material he had never seen before.

'Greetings, favoured mortal,' said Simon.

Kagan bowed. 'Your Grace.'

'I see that you are admiring my new set of armour,' said the god. 'I will tell you my secret – I was on Implacatus. I had a few little jobs to do, and picked up one of my old sets of stone-crafted armour. If the false Queen is on the loose with that sword of hers, I thought it prudent to be better protected.'

'You were on Implacatus, your Grace?'

'Yes. It doesn't seem to have changed much since I was last there; Serene is perhaps bigger, though I didn't tarry too long. I want my return to be a surprise to Edmond.'

Felice approached from the right, accompanied by another woman in robes, whom Kagan didn't recognise.

'Ships have been sighted, your Grace,' said Felice.

Simon rubbed his hands together. 'Excellent. I think we are all here. Naxor is unavailable at the moment, while no one from Dalrig was able to attend; and it is a pity that Amalia has ignored my summons. Does she not care for my company, Kagan?'

Kagan's mouth went dry.

'Yes; perhaps it is best if you don't answer that question, mortal,' said Simon. 'Come; let us proceed to the other side of the palace. The ceremony is about to commence.'

Simon turned, and began striding away. Felice hurried to walk by his side, while Kagan fell in with the other woman in robes.

'Good morning, Kagan,' she said to him, as they walked.

'Sorry; do I know you, ma'am?'

'My name is Lady Lydia of Port Sanders. I'm not surprised that you don't recognise me, but I know much about you.'

Kagan nodded. 'Do you know why we're here, ma'am? Simon was a little vague on the details.'

'The Banner have surrendered, Kagan.'

'They have? Why now?'

'The Queen has vanished, for one thing; also, Kelsey Holdfast is no longer a problem. Without those two, the Banner have lost both their purpose and their protection.'

Kagan tried to digest the information. 'Is the Holdfast girl dead?'

'That, I don't know. As you said, Lord Simon wasn't clear regarding all of the details. No doubt, we shall discover her fate shortly.'

They walked around the perimeter of the ruined palace, along a path that led through a large, ornamental garden, with rose bushes coming into bloom. The gardens were full of militia guards, waiting in small groups on the grass in the sunshine. Each soldier jumped to attention and bowed low as Simon passed, and he rewarded them with smiles and nods. On the iceward side of the palace lay a vast courtyard, where a low wooden platform had been assembled. Upon it sat a large throne that had been removed from the interior of the palace, its sides charred black.

Simon ascended the platform, and sat upon the charred throne, while Felice, Lydia and Kagan took up their positions, standing to either side. In front of them was a great open space, the edges of which were ringed with militia. Over to their left, the harbour was visible, and Kagan noticed several tall masts approach over the fleet of fishing vessels.

'Here they come, your Grace,' said Felice.

'Indeed,' said Simon. 'Don't worry yourself, Felice; I keep my promises.'

'If he remains alive, your Grace.'

'He does. I could have easily killed him when I took Kelsey Holdfast, but I left him, for you.'

Felice bowed, a smile appearing on her lips.

'I must warn you, however,' Simon went on; 'his condition is rather fragile. If it's good sport you're after, you may need me or Lydia to heal him first.'

'I intend to torture him many times over, your Grace. It is his spirit I wish to break, rather than his body.'

Simon laughed. 'You rascal.'

'Felice,' said Kagan; 'thank you for letting us know that Maxwell wasn't found. It's bad news, but Amalia and I were grateful to know the truth.'

Felice shrugged.

'You sound a little ungrateful, mortal,' said Simon. 'Have I not fulfilled my pledges? Have I not returned the old regime to power? You are living in a palace, Kagan, amid servants and luxury.'

'I want my son back, your Grace.'

Simon's eyes tightened. 'The boy will be with the escaped false Queen. She will be caught; she has nowhere to hide. I, however, am a little busy at the moment, so perhaps you might consider looking for them yourself, or does the thought of work appal you?'

'No, your Grace, but...'

'Then it's settled. Find them by the end of the month, mortal. A lone woman and a child shouldn't be too difficult to locate. I have posted a large reward for anyone who reports seeing them, which should help.'

'Might I ask, my Grace,' said Lydia, 'what tasks are now occupying your time?'

'You can ask, Lydia; but that does not mean I am going to tell you.' He pointed in the direction of the harbour. 'Look; our guests are approaching.'

They turned to the large, open gates that connected the huge courtyard to the main road that ran by the harbour. The ships had docked, and streams of Banner soldiers were disembarking. The first batch of soldiers was entering the yard, led by a man using a walking stick.

'I see him,' whispered Felice.

'You were right about his health, your Grace,' said Lydia; 'I can sense his sickness from here.'

'Who are we talking about?' said Kagan.

'Major-General Van Logos,' said Lydia. 'The Commander of the Exiles.'

'Soon to be my personal slave,' said Felice.

They watched as the Banner soldiers made their way into the yard. They were dumping their weapons into an ever-growing pile by the gates, under the watchful eyes of the militia, while the leadership approached the platform. The man with the walking stick stood at the front, with officers on either flank.

'Good morning,' beamed Simon. 'What can I do for you, Major-General?'

Van kept his chin up. 'We are here to offer you our surrender, Ascendant.'

'About time,' said Simon. 'I would ask you for the location of the coward Queen, but I have already read your mind, and see that you don't know. She left by fishing boat from Westrig, did she? Kagan, mark that little fact. If she departed via the Cold Sea, that narrows down your options. So, Major-General, tell me; why should I accept your surrender? You are traitors to the City; perhaps I should execute you all, here and now.'

'The Banner do not fear death, Ascendant.'

'Is that supposed to impress me? How many soldiers are under your command?'

'I have brought every Banner soldier from Westrig and Jezra, Ascendant. They number over two thousand. You also have around six hundred still in custody that were captured upon the Grey Isle.'

'Yes. They have been providing entertainment each dawn to the inhabitants of Pella. Perhaps I should increase the daily execution count to fifty? That way, we'd work through the rest of the Banner in no time.'

'I request mercy for the soldiers, Ascendant,' said Van. 'We are prisoners of war, and the Banner charters clearly state that...'

'Enough. The Banner charters are not valid upon this world. You are rebels and traitors, and will be treated as such. You can talk all you like about contracts and obligations, but you are nothing more than a foreign army of mercenaries, hired by a usurping King and Queen.' He gazed out over the vast yard, where the last of the Banner soldiers were forming up into ranks. 'I shall place these rebels into the old barracks of the Royal Guard for now. It was built for five hundred, so it will be a squeeze. Then, I will decide what to do with them. I might execute them in batches, or perhaps all at once on an enormous pyre. Or maybe I will seal the doors and let them die of thirst. Two and a half thousand soldiers eat a lot of food, and I don't think they deserve any. What about you, Lydia; what do you think we should do with the Banner of the Lostwell Exiles?'

Lydia's face flushed. 'That is your decision, your Grace.'

'I know that, you fool. I asked for your opinion. Advise me.'

'Are they a danger to the City, your Grace?'

'Evidently so.'

'Then, I fear that you have no choice. If they are a threat, then they should be eradicated, your Grace.'

Simon laughed. 'Your thoughts are so transparent, Lydia; have none of you demigods learned how to shield your emotions? You are filled with revulsion at the thought of massacring these men, so why are you pandering to me? Is it out of fear?'

Lydia glanced down. 'Yes, your Grace.'

'Good. Better fear than disloyalty.' He turned back to Van. 'Do you see the quality of advisors I have to put up with? They tell me what they think I want to hear, while I can see their thoughts as clearly as I can see you hobbling in front of me, Major-General. Does the rest of the Banner know that salve addiction was the cause of your illness? It's rather pathetic, don't you think?'

Van's eyes tightened. 'Where is Kelsey Holdfast?'

Simon laughed. 'You love her? Oh, that's delightful. I didn't know that.'

'Does she live?'

'Probably.'

'Where is she?'

Simon leaned forward, as if about to impart a secret, a wide smirk on his lips. 'I whisked her off her feet. I thought she deserved a holiday. You are very familiar, I assume, with the city of Serene?'

Van's face paled.

'That's right,' said Simon. He laughed. 'I sent her to Implacatus. I thought it would be funny, and from the look on your face, I was correct in my assumption. How long do you think she will last? My own feeling is that she could hide successfully for quite some time, causing disruption and chaos wherever she goes. Can you imagine the vision gods, running around in panic, wondering where their powers have gone? Oh, I took her little friend along as well, so that she has some company; I'm not a brute.'

Van lowered his face, leaning on the stick. He looked broken.

'I have more good news for you,' said Simon. 'You can, no doubt, see the gorgeous young god standing to my right. I promised her that you would be hers, and I always keep my promises. You, Major-General, are now the property of Lady Felice. In order for my friend to enjoy this gift in the manner that she desires, I will have to heal you first.'

He raised a hand, and Van convulsed, dropping the walking stick and falling to his knees, as the other senior Banner officers stared.

'There you go,' said Simon. 'Felice, you may take him now.'

Felice gestured to a group of militia, who strode forwards and gripped Van by the shoulders. They hauled him to his feet and tied his hands behind his back.

'I need to request a small favour, Felice,' said Simon.

'Yes, your Grace?'

'Keep him alive until the end of the month; I want him to witness the execution of the Aurelians in Tara. I want him to see his false Queen die.' He glanced at Kagan. 'Of course, for that to happen, you need to do your job, and find her.'

'I'm not sure I understand, your Grace,' said Kagan.

'Come now, favoured mortal. Amalia has the entire Roser militia at her disposal, and she has a spy network in Medio. She must have, seeing how she managed to send someone to Jezra to talk to the false Queen.' He smiled. 'Did you really believe that I didn't know about that? If Amalia can use her wit to find Emily Aurelian once, then I'm sure she can do it again. I'll be keeping a very close eye on both of you, to see that you are not tempted to stray. Think of the capture of the Aurelian Queen as a little test, to prove your loyalty once and for all. Your reward will be my confidence in you, as well as the return of your son. When the Aurelians hang, the entire City will know the true extent of my power.'

'You would murder Elspeth, a child?' said Van.

'Silence, slave. You no longer have the right to address me. You are a walking piece of meat, nothing more, and your entire purpose is to satisfy Felice's sadistic urges. I'm sure you'll do a wonderful job.' He gestured to a group of militia. 'Lock the Banner away in the barracks of the sadly deceased Royal Guard. I'll decide what to do with them later.'

The militia bowed, then an officer blew on a whistle, and the Banner soldiers in the yard began to be herded away, flanked by cross-bow-wielding guards.

'I think our joyous ceremony is at a close,' said Simon. He stood, and raised his arms towards the crowds of Reaper civilians gathered by the gates. 'People of the City – the rebellion is over, and peace has returned to our land. However, we must always be on our guard, for traitors and saboteurs lurk among the dissatisfied and disgruntled. Every one of you must play your part in rooting them out from the shadows of the City. To this end, today I decree that each of the nine tribes must hand over ten enemies of the City every day, starting tomorrow, to be executed here, by the ruins of the false King and Queen's palace. I shall leave it up to each tribe to decide how these criminals are found; I care not for the details, but if any tribe does not deliver their daily batch of condemned men and women, then they will suffer. As for the Lostwell Exiles in Jezra, as they were part of an insidious rebellion, I cannot be so merciful. They will provide twenty criminals a day, without fail, until a hundred days pass. There are also great rewards on offer for any citizen who reports the location of either of the missing dragons, and, of course, for anyone who sees the false Queen. Stay alert, and loyal, and we shall all live together in harmony and tranquillity. Betray me, and you will bathe in the blood and tears of your loved ones. Worship me; love me; obey me.'

The crowd stared back at the Ascendant in silence, and Simon smiled, then stepped down from the platform. Kagan and the gods followed him, along with Van and the guards flanking him.

'That was pleasant,' said Simon, as they walked back into the ornamental gardens.

'Your Grace,' said Lydia, 'regarding this new decree; what if there are no traitors in Sander territory? How am I expected to find ten victims a day?'

'Use you imagination, Lydia,' said Simon. 'Fear will keep this City under control while I make my preparations for the next stages of my glorious plan.'

'But...'

'Be quiet, Lydia,' snapped Simon. 'Empty your jails; do whatever it takes. Round up beggars, for all I care. My plan will necessitate me leaving the City now and again, and I need to know that it hasn't fallen into anarchy in my absence.'

'Your Grace,' said Felice, 'am I responsible for fulfilling the quotas for the Scythes and Hammers as well as the Blades?'

'Yes.'

'I should inform you, your Grace,' she went on, 'that a mere two thousand Scythes exist. If the quotas run for a hundred days, then only half that number will survive.'

'Ah, so you can count, Felice. Well done.'

'No one will believe that half of the Scythes are traitors, your Grace.'

'I know. However, it will be your job to make it look convincing. Put on a few show trials; highlight any failure as an act of sabotage. Anyone who questions you is automatically put onto the list, for we cannot be wrong, and those who contradict us must necessarily be traitors by definition.'

Felice nodded. 'I will see it done, your Grace.'

'What about the Circuit?' said Lydia.

Simon came to a halt, and grabbed Lydia round the throat, lifting her off her feet.

'Haven't I warned you about forgetting my correct address?'

Lydia choked in his grasp, her face turning red as she struggled.

'You will call me "your Grace," at all times, without exception.'

He released Lydia, and the demigod fell to the gravel path, gasping, her hands on her throat.

'Now, the Circuit,' Simon said. 'For your impertinence, Lydia, I am assigning you to that lawless district. You will use Sander militia to snatch your ten Evaders each day, and deliver them to Pella.' He shook his head at her. 'Get up.'

Kagan extended his hand, but Lydia ignored him, and got to her feet unaided.

'That only leaves the Icewarders,' said Simon; 'a most disagreeable tribe, with a cowardly and ungrateful ruler. Yvona excels at one thing only – prevaricating. Not once has she left Icehaven to bow before me; apparently, I am to be satisfied with a mere letter. That will change today, for I intend to pay Icehaven a little visit, to ensure that they comply with my decrees.' He smiled. 'I also hear that they have a certain axe in their possession. That will go well with my new armour, I think.'

'Are you going to kill Lady Yvona, your Grace?' said Lydia.

Simon shrugged. 'Maybe. It depends how contrite she is, and if she begs for her life in front of me.'

They walked on, and came to the courtyard on the sunward side, where their carriages were waiting.

'Go back to your homes,' said Simon. 'And remember, tomorrow at dawn, I expect there to be ninety traitors standing here, awaiting their execution.'

Felice bowed, then led Van off to a carriage, accompanied by guards. Simon took out his Quadrant, and vanished, leaving Lydia and Kagan surrounded by dozens of militia soldiers.

She eyed him. 'I can only imagine the reaction in Tara to this latest decree. Good luck in finding a thousand Rosers to slaughter over the next hundred days.'

'It's insanity,' said Kagan.

'Don't say that; try not to even think it. This is Simon's City now, and we are all his slaves.' Lydia turned to go, then glanced over her shoulder. 'Oh, and the next time you find a stranded Ascendant on a desert world, my advice is to leave him there.'

Kagan said nothing as she got into her carriage. His thoughts turned to the new task he had been given – to find the Queen, and with her, his son. Despite the fear that had wormed its way into his guts, he clung on to the hope of seeing Maxwell again.

He tried not to think about Elspeth.

CHAPTER 12

FLAMES AT DAWN

The Eastern Mountains – 12th Mikalis 3423

Jade awoke to see Flavus scrape a stone against the wall of the small cavern, marking the ninth day since Simon had taken control of the valley. She sat up, pulling the thin blanket over her shoulders in the cool air of the mine.

'Good morning, ma'am,' he said.

'Why do you bother marking the wall like that?'

'It's all too easy to lose track of time, ma'am. How are you feeling?'

Jade felt for her powers, but nothing was there.

'I feel terrible,' she said.

'No sign of your powers yet?'

'No.'

'Simon told us that it takes several days for the anti-salve to wear off. When did you have your second dose?'

'Four days ago. I think Simon handed over the rest of the anti-salve to Naxor before he left, so I'm expecting that weasel to give me my next dose.'

'If we could somehow delay it, ma'am, then we might have a chance to escape. It will be too late when Simon returns.'

'It's already too late. I bowed before him. I am a traitor.'

'If Simon trusted you, ma'am, then you wouldn't be in this cell with Rosie and me. He knows that you submitted under duress; you only did it to save Rosie. When he returns to the valley, I expect he'll want a sign of your loyalty.'

'And I'll do it, if it stops Rosie from being hurt.' She stared at the floor of the dark cavern. 'I'm weak, Flavus. I always thought I'd be resolute, but all it took was him to threaten a mortal, and I crumbled. My father will be laughing at me.' She glanced at the sleeping form of Rosie lying on the ground next to her. 'If I was strong, I'd throttle her in her sleep, to show Simon that I don't care what he does, that he can't control me. That's what a ruthless god would do. But, I could never hurt her. What have I become?'

Flavus raised an eyebrow. 'A decent person, ma'am?'

Jade snorted. 'My newfound decency will get us all killed.'

'What does Simon want with so much salve, do you think?'

'I'm sure you can probably guess.'

'Alright. If I had to guess, ma'am, then he either means to destroy it all, to deny his enemies on Implacatus a chance to get their hands on it; or, he intends to use it to sow dissension among the gods, by controlling the supply of the substance that they covet above all others. With that kind of power, he might be able to prise away some of the Second Ascendant's support. He'll need more than salve, however, to overthrow the entire regime on Implacatus; he'll need an army too.'

'He's got the Blades now.'

'Then he'll need another Quadrant, so that he can open a portal between here and Implacatus, in order to move the Blades there. With only a single device, he'd have to ship a hundred at a time – a grossly inefficient way of doing things. With a portal, thousands could march through in a few minutes.' He lowered his voice. 'He also has access to an unlimited number of greenhides that he can control. He could flood the mountain cities of Implacatus with them, as a diversionary attack, while he moves the Blades to the palaces of the Ascendants. I fear that a frightful war is coming, a war that will result in the destruction of this world, and that of my home.'

'Unless we kill him first.'

Flavus nodded. 'Precisely, ma'am.'

Rosie shifted in her blanket, then opened her eyes.

'Good morning, Private,' said Flavus.

Rosie groaned. 'Your talking woke me up.' She glanced around. 'I prefer sleeping to being awake at the moment. Is there anything to drink?'

Jade passed her a waterskin.

'Thanks,' said Rosie, sitting up. She stretched her arms, then took a swig from the skin. 'They're going to kill us, aren't they? That's two days in a row that they haven't asked for our help or advice on refining salve. They don't need us any more.'

'They won't do anything until Simon returns,' said Flavus. 'They lack the authority.'

'Maybe,' said Rosie, 'but I don't trust Naxor. I wouldn't be surprised if he killed us, then told Simon we were trying to escape or something, and that he had no choice.'

'Simon can read Naxor's mind, Private.'

'Yeah, but Naxor's good at hiding stuff, sir. He managed to conceal the existence of this salve mine for quite a while before Simon sucked it out of his brain.' She glanced at Jade. 'Any powers yet?'

Jade shook her head.

'Damn it,' Rosie muttered. 'Bloody anti-salve. If only we could pour some of it down Simon's throat. Then we could feed him to a dragon. I hate him so much.'

Flavus tried to smile. 'I didn't think that you hated people, Private.'

'That was before he murdered Darvi and Inmara, sir. They were completely innocent, and that bastard killed them anyway.' She lowered her head. 'I hate him.'

They fell into silence as guards opened the rough wooden door that they were using to block the entrance to the cave. One by one, they were led outside, and given a couple of minutes under armed guard to relieve themselves, and to collect their rations. Once complete, they were herded back into the cave, where they sat with their meagre breakfasts on their laps.

Jade remained quiet as she ate. She had felt empty since being given anti-salve. With her first dose, she had thought that she was dying, and the sound of Naxor's laughter had echoed through her mind. With the second dose, at least she had known what to expect, but she felt stripped, and vulnerable. For her entire life, she had been able to count upon her self-healing powers; without them, it was as if she were mortal. It was humiliating. She was a mighty demigod, but, at that moment, a single crossbow bolt would probably be enough to bring her life to a painful end.

The door opened again, and Naxor strode into the cell.

'Greetings,' he said; 'it's a beautiful day outside – the summer sun is shining, and the birds are singing in the trees. Well, they would be if there were any trees left, but I'm afraid we've had to cut them all down. Sorry about that Jade; I know that you were very fond of them. The flowers have gone too, trampled by hundreds of boots...'

'Shut up,' muttered Jade.

Naxor laughed. 'I had no idea your company was so pleasant, cousin. All those centuries that I avoided you, thinking that you were nothing more than a weird, creepy child in an adult's body, and I could have been having fun. My, it's strange the effect that anti-salve has on different gods. Your father, Amalia and I all took to it quickly, using it to hide, whereas you and my brother Salvor seem positively upset by the experience. Your sister took her dose in her stride, but Amber was always the more level-headed of the two of you.'

'Do you want something?' said Flavus.

'Yes,' said Naxor; 'to be entertained. Frankly, this task is rather boring. All I do is supervise the dozens of Blades toiling in the mine, and make sure they don't make a mess of the refining process. Simon could have given this job to Amber, or Felice, but no – it fell upon my shoulders. It's got so tedious, that I have been amusing myself by listening in to your conversations. I liked your suggestions about Simon's plan. I mean, he hasn't told me anything about what he is intending to do with all that salve, and your ideas made some sense. Sending the Blades and greenhides to Implacatus? Seems reasonable. And another Quadrant? I'm not sure why I didn't think of that.'

'Because you're an idiot,' said Jade.

Naxor slapped her across the face, then smirked at the pain he had caused. Jade's hand went to her cheek, her temper rising.

'Do you feel that, cousin?' said Naxor. 'Mortal pain. That's what they feel when they get slapped. Strange, eh? Imagine living with the fear of pain and injury – it's amazing that any mortal can function. Amalia nearly had me killed when I was on anti-salve, and I can honestly say that I've never felt more alive.'

'It's a pity she didn't succeed,' said Rosie.

Naxor turned to her. 'Did I ever tell you how much I loathed your sister? Maddie is an utter imbecile. I had to pretend to like her, of course, as Blackrose was always close by. The number of times I had to bite my tongue, whenever she was prattling on in that moronic way she does. You are a lot like her, Rosie. She'll be dead by now, of course. She wouldn't last a month on Dragon Eyre. I hope that double-crossing bitch Sable is also dead. You don't know her, but let me just say that she is a prime example of why the Holdfasts should be exterminated.'

'Do you think you're hurting me with your bullshit?' said Rosie. 'Talk about prattling on.'

Naxor pulled out a knife. 'If I can't hurt you with words, I have other means.'

'You are a despicable fellow,' said Flavus. 'Like most bullies, I must assume that you are also a coward.'

'I heard what you said about me killing you all and telling Simon it was an accident, or that you were trying to escape. It's not a terrible idea. And you were right; I am good at burying things. It's easy; all I have to do is keep telling myself a lie over and over, and when Simon looks, that's what he sees. Corthie and Aila used to give me a telling off whenever I suggested torturing someone, but they aren't here now. I could do whatever I pleased to you; or, I could order the Blades to do it, while I watched.'

'Ignore him,' said Jade. 'All he wants is to see our reaction. Let's pretend he's not here.'

Rosie frowned. 'Pretend who's not here?'

'Exactly,' said Jade. 'So, Flavus, tell us more about where you grew up.'

'Certainly, ma'am,' he said. 'Serene is an enormous city, stretching for miles along the upper ridges of a great mountain, several miles above the sea. The gods do something to the air, I believe; otherwise it would be uninhabitable.'

'I know a secret about Serene,' said Naxor.

'When did you join the Banner, sir?' said Rosie.

'Oh, I had just turned fifteen,' said Flavus. 'That's the usual age for enrolment, although a few do enlist in their late teens or twenties. I did the same training as the others, but I was quickly advised to join the Banner's regiment of scouts, a specialist unit, as I seemed to have an aptitude for maps and remembering terrain. I'm terrible with faces, but I can always recall a landscape.'

'Someone you know,' said Naxor, 'is in Serene, right now.'

'I went on my first operation at eighteen,' Flavus went on, 'to a huge coalfield in the mountains of a world whose name I've never been able to pronounce. Local tribes were attacking the mines, and the Banner was employed to protect the miners, as well as to map the region.'

'Alright,' said Naxor, glaring at them; 'I get your point. Do you want to know who's in Serene or not?'

'It was a good life,' said Flavus. 'I heartily enjoyed my year there. The soldiers kept the troublesome tribes at bay, and I had peace to go out every day to chart the coalfields.'

Naxor stamped his foot on the ground, then turned to the guards by the door.

'Bind their hands and ankles and take them outside. Now.'

Blades barged into the cave, and shoved the three prisoners to the ground. Knees held them down as ropes were tied round each prisoner's wrists and ankles. Jade grunted in pain as her arms were twisted behind her back. Naxor had been right about mortals and the fear of pain. Jade was familiar with pain; the pain inflicted by her father had stamped itself on her mind for evermore, but it wasn't the same without self-healing. Jade had walked through the world with no thought for her personal safety, fearful only of other gods with death powers or, like Yendra, battle-vision. Yet mortals walked around knowing that each day could be their last; their lives could be blotted out by any number of random accidents. How did they cope?

The Blades carried the three prisoners from the cave, and they emerged into the blinding light of the sun. Jade blinked, dazzled, then felt herself be taken over to the banks of the pool, where a wooden structure housing the refining equipment had been built.

'Here will do,' said Naxor. 'Strap them to the side of the refinery. Don't be gentle.'

The three prisoners were hauled over to the wooden-framed structure, and strapped to it, each in an upright position.

Naxor smiled. 'Now, do I have your attention?'

'If you kill us in front of the Blades,' said Flavus, 'then you won't be able to hide what you've done from Simon.'

'You have a point,' said Naxor, 'though it is moot, as I do not intend to kill all of you. One will suffice. Right, where was I? Oh yes, crowing over our victory. Who is the only person capable of defeating Simon? Come on; don't dilly-dally. Name the person.'

Rosie frowned. 'Queen Emily?'

Naxor groaned. 'Are you as stupid as your sister? How could Emily defeat Simon?' He sighed. 'Take another guess.'

'The dragons?' said Flavus.

Naxor slapped his forehead. 'I am surrounded by idiots. You saw what the dragons were like in front of Simon. He had them eating out of the palm of his hand, and he still has one of Darksky's brats under lock and key. No, not the dragons. I'm going to have to tell you, aren't I? Very well – Kelsey Holdfast.'

'Of course,' said Flavus. 'She can block the Ascendant's powers.'

'At last. Yes. Well, Simon need fear no more, as Miss Holdfast is now in Serene. Ta-dah! Simon spirited her away by Quadrant to inflict chaos upon the inhabitants of Implacatus, and I can't work out if that means he's insane or a genius. Either way, I found it immensely funny. Anyway, with her out of the picture, the Banner have surrendered; in fact, they are surrendering to Simon right now, as I speak.'

'The Banner would never surrender,' said Flavus, 'not while the Queen is alive.'

'Emily ran off. She's not in Jezra.'

'What?' said Rosie. 'That can't be right.'

'Why, because it offends your sense of propriety, Miss Jackdaw the Younger? You may think it cowardly of her, and you'd probably be right, but the fact remains that she fled Jezra some nights ago. Is it any wonder that Van Logos had to surrender? Simon is gifting him to Felice, by the way, and she has all kinds of plans for him. Ironic, as Sable Holdfast was the real source of their quarrel. That bitch messed with Van's head, and he's going to pay the price.'

'You sound obsessed with this Holdfast woman,' said Jade.

'Yeah,' said Rosie. 'Did she reject you?'

'Don't be ridiculous. If you want to know the truth – she was in love with me, and I had to let her down rather firmly. She's never forgiven me for that. A spurned woman will always desire to claim her vengeance, and I was lucky to escape her clutches.' He frowned. 'You interrupted my crowing. I shall continue – the rebellion is over. Jezra has fallen, Kelsey is gone, the salve mine is Simon's, the Banner has surrendered. We can't stop winning.'

He grinned at them. 'My crowing is complete. You may cheer now. No? Alright then, we'll move straight on to the torture.' He pulled his knife out. 'One of you is going to feel this blade slide into your flesh. Who will it be? Choose carefully, and remember that Jade has taken anti-salve. If I were to cut off one of her ears, it would heal over in mortal fashion, and when her powers return, the scar tissue will have formed, and her self-healing won't be able to grow it back. In other words, if I maim her, she stays maimed. So, don't be picking little old Jade just because you think that she'll recover. She won't. Right; Flavus, you first. Who dies?'

'I'm not playing your silly games,' said the lieutenant.

'Alright, that's one vote for you,' said Naxor. 'Oh, and if the vote is a tie, everyone loses a finger, and then you vote again. And on and on, until you pick someone. Rosie?'

'I pick you, Naxor.'

Naxor raised an eyebrow. 'And that's one vote for Rosie. Jade? And remember, if you pick yourself, or give an answer as stupid as that of your companions, you all lose a finger, and we start all over again. I have plenty of time. None of these Blades will help you, or even care. They hate you, especially you, Jade. Any one of them would happily volunteer to slit your throat. So, my dear cousin, who do you choose?'

'Why are you doing this, Naxor?' said Jade. 'You're not trying to get information out of us, and Simon might be angry if you kill us. That leaves sadism. Are you a sadist, cousin? My father is; he gets pleasure from watching others suffer. Are you the same? I always knew that you were untrustworthy, but is this who you really are?'

Naxor stared at her. 'And that's one vote for Jade. We have a tie, and you know what happens if we have a tie.'

He brandished the knife and walked towards Flavus. 'You first, I think, Banner soldier.'

'Do your worst,' said Flavus; 'I am not afraid of cowards.'

Naxor lifted his arms, and took hold of the lieutenant's left hand. 'We'll start with the little fingers of each of you, and work up.'

'Stop,' cried Rosie. 'Please, Naxor; leave him alone.'

'That's better,' said Naxor. 'Beg. I like begging. Don't worry, Jackdaw; your finger will be next.'

He raised the knife, then stopped and frowned, as a shadow flitted between him and the low sun. Naxor turned his head to glance upwards, and a huge, scaled forelimb swooped down, and clutched him round the waist. The dragon soared back up into the sky, Naxor screaming and writhing in Dawnflame's grip. She rose up to a hundred feet, then hurled the body through the air. Naxor arced through the pink sky, his shriek of terror fading as he disappeared over the edge of the cliff.

All over the valley, Blades began to run for cover. A few reached for their crossbows, but Dawnflame hurtled back down, and opened her jaws. A great burst of fire exploded from her, the flames enveloping a large group of running Blades from behind, incinerating them. Dawnflame turned her head, hovering over the valley, the flames rising as she sent more flashes of fire at the fleeing Blades. The screams echoed off the cliffside as more soldiers went up in flames. Some tried to run as their hair and uniforms burned, while others were transformed into ash and smoke. A few jumped into the pool, and Dawnflame reached down, plucking them out one by one with her forelimbs, and ripping each body in two. A crossbow bolt struck her flank, and she turned back to the grass, and flooded the banks of the stream with more flames. The last of the Blades had run into the cave, so the dragon leaned down, her head by the entrance, and unleashed another torrent of fire, directly into the caverns. The flames rushed through the entrance, and smoke belched back out, thick and black.

Dawnflame paused. She turned her head, scanning the valley floor for movement. One Blade tried to get to his feet, and she went after him, her claws raking down his back and tearing him to shreds.

Jade, Rosie and Flavus stared at the carnage. Where a hundred Blades had been, only smoking and bloody human remains were left. Bodies were smouldering facedown by the stream, and guts were floating on the surface of the still pool, staining the clear water with blood. The dragon, satisfied that no Blades were living, lowered herself down to the valley floor, and turned to face Jade.

'I am here to save you, friend,' Dawnflame said. She raised a sharp claw, and sliced through the straps holding Jade to the side of the wooden frame. Jade fell to the ground, then pulled herself up.

'Thank you,' she said. 'Naxor?'

'I threw him into the pass the greenhides use to traverse the mountains,' said the dragon. 'He will not be troubling us again.'

Jade hurried to Rosie, and unbuckled her straps. She caught the young woman as she fell, then moved on to Flavus.

'That was perfect timing,' said Rosie.

'Yes,' said Flavus, as he was freed; 'most fortunate for us.'

'Fortune had nothing to do with it,' said the dragon. 'I have been watching, waiting for you to be brought outside. I didn't want to attack until I was sure of your location.'

'Are you here by yourself?' said Rosie.

'I am,' said the dragon.

'Does... does Darksky know you're here?'

'She does. She tried to prevent me from leaving the colony, but I prevailed.'

Jade helped Flavus down from the wooden frame, and the three humans turned to the dragon.

'Will you be in trouble with Darksky?' said Rosie. 'Simon still has one of her children.'

'I do not understand what you mean, little Jackdaw. Darksky was opposed to me intervening, but she does not own me.'

'But, what if Simon retaliates against the child he has in custody?'

'That is a risk, but my obligations were stronger.'

'Obligations?' said Rosie. 'What obligation did you have to save us?'

'My obligation is not to you, it is to Jade. She saved the life of my son, and I am in her debt. I would have been dishonoured to have allowed her to die. Darksky will rage, and she will hate me, but I had no choice but to act in the manner I did. Now, climb onto my back, all of you.'

The three prisoners glanced at each other, then began scrambling up the flank of the long, slender dragon, her lavender and blue scales shimmering in the sunlight. They clambered up onto her shoulders, then the dragon extended her wings and rose into the air. She hovered over the valley, then sent another great burst of flames downwards, smothering the refining equipment, and incinerating the stocks of refined salve that were ready to be transported back to the City. Flames and thick, black smoke rose into the sky, and Jade took a last look at the bodies scattered across the valley floor. Dawnflame turned, and soared away to sunward.

'Are we going to the colony?' said Flavus.

'You will see,' said the dragon.

They flew for half an hour, Dawnflame keeping low, her underside barely missing the tops of the tree cover. Behind them, the pillars of smoke began to fade into the distance, and it grew warmer. The dragon hugged the contours of the land, soaring along the bottom of valleys and keeping close to the ground. She followed a stream as it rushed down a ragged hillside, then descended next to a wide waterfall at the floor of a narrow ravine, her wings tucked in. She strode through the waterfall, soaking the three humans on her shoulders, and entered a high-roofed cave, where Bittersea and Firestone were waiting. The cave was dark, but light was shimmering through the curtain of falling water.

Dawnflame lowered her head to her mother and son. 'It is done. I have killed the soldiers and destroyed the mine workings.'

Bittersea held her gaze. 'And thereby earned the hatred of Darksky, daughter.'

'I had no choice mother; I am bound by ties to the demigod.'

'I know, daughter, but it is unfortunate all the same.'

'If Simon goes to the colony, Darksky can explain that we have left, and that she disapproved of my actions. The Ascendant will know she is telling the truth, and he will spare her child.'

'I hope you are right,' said Bittersea.

The elderly dragon glanced at the three humans sitting on her daughter's shoulders. 'You saved the Jackdaw girl too, I see. That, I understand, but why did you save the soldier? He has been to Dragon Eyre. Does he deserve to live?'

'Does anyone, mother? My mate Tarsnow deserved to live, and yet he is dead. The same with the mighty Deathfang. The brave die, while that coward Burntskull lives. I saved the soldier because he is an enemy of our enemies.'

'And I thank you for doing so, dragon,' said Flavus, bowing.

'Yes; thank you,' said Rosie. 'Naxor was going crazy.'

'Are you sure?' said Jade. 'Maybe he's always been like that.'

'Did you dispose of the demigod, daughter?' said Bittersea.

'I threw his body to the greenhides, mother.'

'Then, he might yet live?'

'He might. I hope he lives, mother. I hope he suffers. The greenhides will tear him to pieces.'

The three humans shuffled down onto the wet floor of the cave, the sound of the waterfall filling their ears.

'This is your new home, for now,' said Dawnflame. 'It's cramped, damp, and not very comfortable, but it is hidden from both Simon and Darksky. I have instructed Firestone not to hurt you, but he is young, and sometimes forgets what I tell him, so be on your guard.'

'What's next?' said Rosie. 'I mean, do we have a plan?'

'I have a plan,' said Dawnflame. 'Kill Simon.'

Rosie put her hands on her hips. 'That might be easier said than done.'

Dawnflame lowered her head until it was inches from Jade's face. 'What do you say, demigod?'

Jade looked into the dragon's eyes. 'I'm tired of being bullied. I want to fight back.'

'Yes,' said Dawnflame, her eyes flashing. 'Yes. Let's crush our enemies and burn their palaces. I will bring fire and you shall bring death. We will attack.'

'We might die,' said Rosie.

'We probably will, little Jackdaw,' said the dragon; 'but I would rather die with pride, than skulk in the shadows like a coward.'

'Before we rain fire down upon the City,' said Jade; 'I have one request to make.'

'Yes, friend?' said Dawnflame.

'Can we rescue my cats first?'

CHAPTER 13

DEEP IN THE SHADOWS

Icehaven, Medio, The City – 12th Mikalis 3423

'This is unacceptable,' said Cardova; 'we've been in Alkirk Palace for four days, and Lady Yvona is still too busy to see us?'

Major Hannia wrung her hands. 'It is unfortunate timing. Lady Yvona is dealing with one crisis after another.'

'Tell me, Major,' said Cardova, his back to the open window; 'are we guests here, or are we prisoners?'

'You are guests, of course.'

'Are we allowed to leave?'

'It is not safe for her Majesty to travel through the City at present, Captain,' said Hannia. 'For her own security, the Queen needs to remain here, under the protection of Lady Yvona.'

Cardova shook his head in exasperation.

Hannia attempted a weak smile. 'How are you finding the accommodation? It is the same suite that Corthie Holdfast stayed in when he lived here.'

'The rooms are fine,' said Emily. 'When do you think that Lady Yvona will be free to meet us?'

'I am unable to say, your Majesty.'

'Please let Lady Yvona know that we shall be leaving Alkirk first thing tomorrow, Major Hannia,' said the Queen. 'If she is unable to meet us in person, then we must be on our way. If anyone tries to prevent us from leaving, then I must warn you that we shall make an almighty scene. Captain Cardova is extremely proficient with both bow and sword.'

Major Hannia frowned. 'I hope that will not be necessary, your Majesty.'

'Then tell Yvona what I have said. I have already wasted more than enough time here. If Lady Yvona does not wish to help us, then she must let us go.'

The major bowed her head. 'I shall pass on your message, your Majesty.'

Emily watched as the major left the room, closing the door behind her.

Cardova sat down, then got up again and started to pace the floor. 'Will she betray us, do you think?'

'If Yvona was going to tell Simon about our presence here,' said Silva, 'she would have done so already, and the Ascendant would be here.'

'Simon thinks I'm in Jezra,' said Emily; 'and, as long as Kelsey and Van can keep it a secret, that will remain the case.'

'It feels safe enough here,' said Lady Omertia, holding Maxwell on her knee; 'and it's considerably more comfortable than the Command Post in Jezra.'

'It feels like a prison,' said Cardova. 'Were you serious about tomorrow morning, your Majesty?'

'Yes,' said Emily. 'Start working on ideas of how we can make our escape, ideally without killing anyone.'

'I already have a few schemes bubbling away at the back of my mind, your Majesty.' He paused and looked out of the window at the view over Icehaven harbour. 'Why won't she speak to us? I don't understand it.'

'She's terrified,' said Emily. 'Terrified of Simon, and terrified that he might discover that she is sheltering us here. I'm disappointed; I honestly believed that she possessed more courage.'

'She must have some courage, your Majesty,' said Silva. 'Didn't she help you overthrow Amalia a few years ago?'

'She did, but she had Corthie living here, as her personal champion. I think he imbued her with bravery. She has certainly not given me much support during my reign, with the exception of the Grey Isle, but she stood to gain a huge profit from that operation. Even then, it took Yendra and Kelsey to persuade her.'

'What a dismal-looking place,' said Cardova, his eyes on the view. 'Why would anyone choose to live in a town that doesn't get any sunlight?'

'It keeps outsiders from coming here,' said Lady Omertia; 'and the Icewarders like it that way. They have always been an odd tribe; never quite fitting in, as if they feel they are separate from the rest of the City. Between Yvona and her late mother, they have ruled Icehaven for almost one and a half thousand years, and Yvona has no intention of stepping down any time soon. Perhaps it was a mistake to come here; perhaps we placed too much faith in Yvona.'

There was a knock at the door, and it opened. Two servants entered, one pushing a trolley laden with plates, dishes and jugs.

The servants bowed. 'Breakfast is ready, your Majesty,' said one.

They wheeled the trolley over to a large table, and began to unload its contents.

'The fish was freshly caught this morning, your Majesty,' the servant went on; 'and the wine is a Sanders vintage, a delicate white from the slopes of the Sunward Range.'

They bowed again, then left the room, taking the empty trolley with them.

Emily got to her feet. 'At least we're being well fed.'

Cardova smiled as he walked to the table. 'Wine for breakfast? They're either decadent here, or they're trying to keep us mildly sedated.' He sat, and picked up the bottle.

Emily took a chair next to him, then they were joined by Silva and

Lady Omertia. Maxwell gazed at the food from Emily's mother's lap, and let out a gurgle.

'I'll cut up some tiny pieces of fish for you,' said Lady Omertia.

'Make sure there are no bones, mother,' said Emily.

Lady Omertia gave her daughter a look. 'I think I know what I'm doing, dear.'

'We should put some spare food aside during the next few meals,' said Cardova, 'so that we'll have a supply if we need to make a run for it.'

'Good idea,' said Emily. 'Silva, can you sense where Yvona is right now?'

'I could, your Majesty, but is it worth the risk? If Simon happens to be looking in this direction, then he would pick up traces of my powers, and he would know that I was here. I have been sparing with my powers since we departed Westrig, for that very reason.'

'Alright. A brief flash of powers tomorrow morning may be necessary, to make sure our way out of Icehaven is clear.'

'As you wish, your Majesty.'

Emily glanced around the table, watching the others eat. Despite everything, it felt good to be back in the City. She still had doubts about what she had done, and whether the course she had chosen was the wisest, but she was surrounded by the people she trusted the most. Captain Cardova still had misgivings, but his loyalty was beyond question, while her mother's support had never faltered. Silva too, had proved more loyal than most of the former Royal Family; only Jade, and poor Salvor had shown her the same level of support. She wondered if Salvor was dead. There had been no news of his condition for a long time, and she hoped he wasn't suffering terribly in prison.

'Aren't you going to eat something, dear?' said her mother.

Emily smiled, and picked up her fork.

The morning dragged by. There was little to do within the comfortable set of rooms they had been given. Lady Omertia occupied herself by playing with Maxwell, holding his hands as he attempted to walk across the floor; while Cardova sat by a window, staring at the view. When it was time for lunch, the doors opened, but instead of servants and more trolleys, Lady Yvona appeared in the doorway, wearing a long lemon-yellow dress that reached the ground.

Emily stood.

'Your Majesty,' said Yvona; 'may I come in?'

'Of course,' said Emily.

Cardova turned from the window and got to his feet as Yvona closed the door and walked into the room.

'Major Hannia tells me that you plan on leaving tomorrow,' Yvona said, 'against our advice, your Majesty.'

'Yes,' said Emily. 'We have been kept waiting for four days. Every time Major Hannia tells us that you are ready to see us, something else happens and the meeting is cancelled. I was starting to believe that we would never see you, Lady Yvona.'

'I will be blunt, your Majesty,' said Yvona; 'I wish you hadn't come here. You are putting me in a very awkward position; I have pledged my loyalty to Lord Simon.'

'You sent him a letter,' said Emily; 'you haven't bowed before him.'

'Does that make a difference, your Majesty? If he discovers that you are here, then Icehaven might be punished. My duty is to my people.'

'So is mine,' said Emily. 'The Icewarders cannot hide away and pretend that Simon is not here. At least, not while Jezra still stands against him.'

Yvona gave her a sad smile. 'Jezra has fallen, your Majesty. Lord Simon accepted the surrender of the Banner of the Lostwell Exiles this morning, in Pella. It's over.'

Cardova took a step forward, his eyes wide. 'The Banner surrendered, ma'am? Why?'

'Kelsey Holdfast was abducted by Lord Simon. Without her, the Banner could not defend Jezra. The Brigades and civilians remain on the Western Bank, but the soldiers and officers of the Banner are being held under guard in Pella, awaiting Lord Simon's decision on what is to be done with them.'

'And the major-general, ma'am?'

'Lord Simon handed the commander over to Lady Felice, whom, I believe, holds a personal grudge against him.'

Cardova collapsed into a chair, his head in his hands.

'Where is Kelsey Holdfast?' said Emily. 'Does Simon have her in custody?'

'I do not know where the Holdfast girl has been taken, your Majesty,' said Yvona. 'However, Lord Simon has issued a new decree, one that concerns me greatly. I am to deliver ten Icewarders to Pella by dawn tomorrow, where they are to be executed. Then ten the following day; and so on, for a total of one hundred days.' Her face fell. 'Lord Simon intends to kill a thousand Icewarders.'

Emily gasped. 'Why?'

'Every tribe has been given the same orders, your Majesty. There are to be ninety executions a day outside the gates of Cuidrach Palace, not counting the Exiles of Jezra, who are to provide twenty victims a day.'

'This is madness,' cried Emily. 'To what end?'

'To rid the City of troublemakers and anyone opposed to Lord Simon's rule, or so the words of the decree seem to state. This is a catastrophe. If I accede to Lord Simon's orders, the people of Icehaven will suffer, but if I refuse, then Lord Simon could easily make more severe demands.'

Lady Omertia clutched Maxwell to her chest. 'How are you going to find ten people a day for this bloodbath, my lady?'

'I'll start by sending the convicted murderers. The prison in Icehaven holds thirty-six men and women guilty of the crime of murder; but that will only take me up to day four. I am at a loss as to what to do after that.'

Emily sat. 'Every tribe?'

'Yes, your Majesty. Over ten thousand victims in all, if we include the Exiles. More, if Lord Simon also decides to have the Banner annihilated, as he did with the Royal Guard. The summer will be washed with blood.'

'Even the Scythes?'

'Even them, your Majesty. Lady Felice has been given the task of enforcing the decree among the tribes of the Bulwark.'

'We have to fight this; what else can we do?'

'We can submit to Lord Simon, and hope for better days to come,' said Yvona. 'If the choice is between losing a thousand Icewarders, and facing extinction, then there is no option but to comply. I'm sorry, your Majesty, but I cannot give you any assistance.'

'Then let us leave,' said Cardova. 'You don't want us here, ma'am; and with every passing second, I'd also rather be elsewhere. All we need is a covered wagon and a couple of ponies, and we could be gone in twenty minutes.'

Yvona glanced at the floor for a long moment. 'Very well,' she said in a low voice. 'I confess that I considered informing Lord Simon that you were here, in an attempt to buy his favour, and thereby better protect the people of Icehaven; but how can I place my trust in someone who acts as he does? I will not betray you, your Majesty; you are still the Queen in my eyes. Wait here.'

Yvona turned and strode from the room.

'Did you hear that?' said Cardova. 'She *almost* betrayed us. We need to get out of here as quickly as possible.'

'Agreed,' said Emily. 'Though, perhaps we shouldn't be too hard on Lady Yvona; she has a lot of responsibility to bear, and she came to the right decision in the end.'

Cardova got to his feet. 'Remain seated, ladies; I'll pack.'

Lady Omertia glanced at Emily. 'I assume this means we shall not be asking Lady Yvona if I can stay here, while you walk off into danger?'

'I don't think we can risk it, mother. I wouldn't like to leave you here on your own; Yvona might decide to sacrifice you to save Icehaven.'

'I concur. What do you make of Simon's decision to take ten people from each tribe? The man's mad.'

'He's making a mistake. The people of the City will see him for who he really is.'

'Is that a bad thing, your Majesty?' said Silva. 'I mean, of course, from Simon's point of view. He's probably right, in a way – there most likely does exist a certain segment of the mortal population opposed to his rule. If he can eliminate hundreds of his most ardent enemies from the City, then he won't care about the thousands of innocents who will also perish. This decree will keep the mortal masses too frightened to resist. Anyone who speaks out against it will be liable to find themselves marked down for execution, so the natural response will be to stay silent. As a tool of control, this decree will be quite effective.'

'It will certainly empty the City's prisons,' said Lady Omertia.

'It's disgusting,' said Emily. 'I can already imagine Lydia, Amber, and others, using it to get rid of anyone they don't like; anyone who has ever spoken to them with disrespect. It surprises me that he has included the Blades in this scheme. One might have thought that he'd protect them.'

'Felice will use the decree to eliminate every officer who remains loyal to you, your Majesty,' said Silva.

Emily bowed her head. 'How can we fight this? Especially with Kelsey captured. She was our only real hope of success.'

'Kelsey had her uses, your Majesty,' said Silva, 'but she suffers from the same weakness as Simon.'

'What weakness?'

Silva smiled. 'They can only be in one place at a time, your Majesty. To defeat Simon, we must avoid confronting him at all costs. We strike wherever he is absent, and eliminate his allies. Furthermore, if we can separate him from his Quadrant, then our chances increase tenfold.' She leaned forward. 'The Quadrant is the key, your Majesty.'

Cardova hauled their trunk over towards the table. 'We're all packed up and ready to go.'

Emily eyed the door. 'Hopefully, Yvona is arranging our transport.'

An hour passed, but Lady Yvona had not returned to the rooms where Emily and the others were waiting. Maxwell had been unsettled, and was whining and fidgeting on Lady Omertia's knees, which wasn't helping anyone's mood.

Emily got to her feet. 'I'm going to see what's happening.'

'Are you sure, your Majesty?' said Silva. 'A Queen should not be wandering about on her own.'

'I think we can abandon decorum for ten minutes,' said Emily. 'We need to find out what's causing the delay. I know Yvona said that she wouldn't betray us, but I'm starting to get nervous. Lucius, stay here, but be ready to move. If we have to, we'll head directly down the stairs and take a wagon from the courtyard, by force if necessary.'

Cardova nodded. 'Understood, ma'am.'

Emily walked over to the door. She listened for a moment, but heard nothing, so she eased it open and peered out into an empty corridor. The silence seemed unusual, and Emily's heart began to race. She closed the door, then stole along the passageway. She reached a landing, where stairs went down to the next level, but, again, it was deserted. She carried on, entering the part of the palace where Yvona had her quarters. She went into a small anteroom, then froze as she heard voices coming from Yvona's private study.

'I know you're keeping something buried inside that tiny mind of yours,' came a voice.

Emily shrunk back against the wall. It was Simon, his tone unmistakeable.

'I can either inflict more pain on you than you can endure, or I will rip it out of your head, Yvona,' he said.

Emily crept forward, fear hammering at her insides. The door to the study was slightly ajar, and she squinted through the gap. Lying on the floor in front of her was the body of Major Hannia, her head missing. Blood and fragments of tissue and bone spread out from her shoulders, forming a circle on the carpet. Two yards from the body, Simon was standing, wearing strange armour of green and gold. On her knees in front of the Ascendant was Yvona, her face tinged with grey. Her hands were at her throat, and foam was emerging from her lips. Emily stared in horror. She wanted to help the demigod, but her feet refused to move.

'You displease me, Yvona,' Simon said. 'First, you refuse to attend my court, in order to pay me the respect you owe, and now I find that you're keeping secrets. One might conclude that you are not as loyal as your pathetic letter claimed.'

He lowered a hand, and Yvona collapsed to the floor, gasping for breath. Simon stepped over her, and walked towards a large tapestry on the wall. Next to it, the Axe of Rand was hanging. Simon reached up and grabbed hold of the axe with both hands, then brought the dark blade close to his face to examine it.

'A fine weapon,' he said. 'I'll take it.' He glanced down at Yvona, 'Now, are you going to tell me what you are hiding from me, or do I need to scrub your mind for it?'

Yvona struggled up to her knees, a hand on the surface of the desk. 'I have nothing to say to you, Lord Simon,' she gasped. 'Nothing at all.'

Simon swung the axe down, cleaving through Yvona's forearm, and slicing her hand off. Yvona screamed, her yellow dress spattered with blood as she clutched the raw wound at the end of her limb.

'That should soften your resistance somewhat,' said Simon. He gripped Yvona's chin and stared into her eyes.

Simon's face darkened. 'The false Queen is here? In the palace?' He bared his teeth. 'You make me sick, demigod. You are the worst sort of traitor, one who lies and pretends to be loyal.' He raised the axe above his head. 'There is but one appropriate punishment.'

Emily stared through the slender gap in the doorframe, her heart pounding. Simon gripped the handle of the axe in both hands. Yvona glanced up, her eyes red. She opened her mouth to speak, and Simon brought the axe down. Emily looked away, unable to bear the sight. She closed her eyes for a moment, hearing Simon's breath as he swung the axe down again, and again. Emily opened her eyes. Simon was standing over the bloody remains of Lady Yvona, his arms covered in blood. He withdrew the Quadrant from behind his armour, and vanished.

Emily remained where she was, her feet frozen to the floor. Then, without making a conscious decision, she ran. She sprinted down the deserted corridors, and burst through the door of their rooms.

'Simon's here!' she cried. 'Run!'

Cardova jumped to his feet. He picked up the huge trunk with both hands.

'Forget the trunk,' shouted Emily. 'Run.'

Silva frowned. 'Where is Lady Yvona, your Majesty?'

'She's dead,' said Emily, pulling her mother up from the chair. She shoved her towards the door.

'Let's move,' said Cardova. 'Stay together; straight down the stairs. Your Majesty; you lead. I'll cover the rear.'

Emily drew her Fated Blade, the dark metal glistening in the same way that the Axe of Rand had done, then ran back to the door. Behind her, Cardova was shepherding the other two women. Lady Omertia had Maxwell clutched to her shoulder, while Silva seemed unconcerned, her expression neutral.

Emily glanced back out into the corridor. It was still deserted, so she ran out, heading towards a set of narrow stairs that connected every floor of the palace. They reached the stairwell, and hurried down, descending several flights in a few minutes. Two members of the Icewarder militia were guarding the bottom of the stairs on the ground level, and they stared up with open mouths as they saw the small group running down towards them.

'Evacuate the palace,' cried the Queen. 'Simon is here; get everyone out.'

The two guards moved to block them.

'We have had no orders from Lady Yvona, ma'am,' said one; 'you will have to remain here while we make some checks.'

Cardova leaped down the last few stairs, his sword drawn. He bundled one of the crossbow-wielding guards to the ground, then plunged his sword into the guts of the other guard, shoving him to the side as he fell. Lady Omertia gasped in horror, and Emily pushed her forwards, keeping her moving.

They ran on, and reached an open archway that led out onto a courtyard. Several wagons and carriages were lined up, and Emily paused by the shadows near the opening.

'A carriage would be too obvious, ma'am,' said Cardova, 'and too easy to stop at a road block. We'll need to split up and go on foot.'

Emily frowned. 'Split up?'

'Yes, ma'am. If Simon knows we're here... I'm assuming he knows we're here?'

'He does.'

'Then he'll be looking for a group our size. I should go with you, and Maxwell, while Silva and your mother go by a different route.'

'It's pointless,' said Silva; 'he'll find us. As soon as he realises that we've fled, he will use his powers to search everywhere close by. We won't get far.'

'I'm not giving up,' said Emily. 'Yvona died trying to save us. Then Simon vanished.'

Cardova narrowed his eyes. 'How do you know this, ma'am?'

'I'll tell you later, when there's time; we need to go.'

'Why would he vanish?' said Lady Omertia.

'To collect reinforcements, presumably,' said Cardova. 'He'll be back in a few minutes with a hundred Blades, or greenhides.'

'I shall remain here, your Majesty,' said Silva. 'I will hide in the palace somewhere, then use my powers. They will light up like a beacon for Simon, and he will come to me. The distraction might give you enough time to make it out of Icehaven.'

'No, Silva,' said Emily. 'He will kill you too.'

'Not if I surrender to him.'

'In which case,' said Cardova, 'he will discover the purpose of our mission. He'll know we're going to Amalia.'

'That can't be helped,' said Silva. 'It's either that, or he catches us all.' She smiled at Emily. 'Your Majesty, it has been a pleasure to serve you. Hold true to our objectives – Amalia will help you, I truly believe it. Farewell.'

The demigod turned, and hurried back along the corridor and up the stairs.

Cardova sheathed his sword, and glanced at Emily. 'It's now or never, ma'am.'

'What should we do, Captain?' said Lady Omertia.

'We walk out of here, in a straight line, and head for the gates. As soon as we're out of the palace grounds, we run.'

Emily nodded, and pulled her hood up to cover her hair.

They stepped out into the afternoon shadows. A group of Icewarders was working close to a few wagons, loading crates and carrying out repairs. A few glanced in the direction of Emily and the others, but their civilian clothing seemed to fool them, and they went back to their work. Emily frowned, then realised that Lady Yvona had kept their presence a secret from her own people as well as Simon. The Icewarders had no idea who they were.

Cardova kept their pace steady, and they walked across the cobbles, leaving the palace grounds by a small gate. The guards on duty were there to prevent anyone getting in, and no one tried to stop them as they strode out onto the street. They carried on, reaching a corner where rows of grey housing blocks stood, then Cardova picked his pace up, and they raced down the road. He turned left, then right, weaving through the houses, then skidded to a halt as they approached an open-topped wagon. A few barrels of heating oil were stacked up on the rear of the wagon under a large sheet of tarpaulin, and ponies were hitched to the front, but there was no sign of the wagon's owners.

Cardova scanned the street, then pulled up the tarpaulin.

'Get in,' he said. 'Hide. I'll drive.'

Emily pulled herself up onto the back of the wagon, and slipped under the wide tarpaulin. Lady Omertia handed her Maxwell, then Cardova helped her climb up to join her daughter. Emily was plunged into darkness as Cardova secured the sheet, then she felt the wagon start to move. She closed her eyes, anxiety and fear coursing through her. Since Yvona's murder, she had been too busy to take in what had happened, but now that she was huddling in the darkness, it all came back to her, and she relived the savage death of the demigod over and over as the wagon pulled through the streets.

Yvona had not betrayed them. She had tried to hide their presence from Simon, and he had cut her down for it. Tears spilled from Emily's eyes, and she felt her mother's arm go over her shoulder. Maxwell was wriggling in her mother's grasp, but the sounds he was making were drowned out by the rumble of the wheels on the cobbled streets. Emily lost herself for a while. She burrowed into her mother's arms, sobbing for Yvona and Silva, her mind replaying the moment Simon had swung the axe.

The wagon stopped. Emily blinked, unsure how long she, her mother and Maxwell had been hiding. The tarpaulin sheet was lifted.

'We're walking from here,' said Cardova. 'Someone will report the missing wagon, and Simon will find it.'

He helped them down to the ground, and Emily glanced around. They were still in Icehaven. Cardova had parked the wagon next to a large junction, close to the town walls.

'We'll have to spend tonight out in the open,' said Cardova, as they began to walk towards a set of gates in the walls. 'Hopefully, Simon won't know which direction we've taken.'

'Which direction are we taking, Captain?' said Lady Omertia. 'Maxwell will need to be fed soon.'

'He might have to do without for a while,' said Cardova. 'We have three options – turn west, and go via the coastal route to Fishcross; go east, and enter the Bulwark through the Middle Walls; or carry on ahead, and climb the Iceward Range.'

Emily tried to think. They needed to get to Tara, but Simon would know that Maeladh Palace was their ultimate destination, and any direct route would quickly be searched.

'The Bulwark,' she said. 'We'll go to Tara the long way round.'

They fell into silence as they approached the town walls. Icewarder guards stood around on duty, but their attention seemed focussed solely on the wagons and carriages entering and leaving the town, and those on foot were ignored as they passed through. Beyond the walls was a wide road that followed the line of walls. They turned left onto it and started to walk east, the dark slopes of the Iceward Range stretching off to their right.

'It's five miles to the Middle Walls,' said Cardova, as they walked. He glanced at Emily. 'Tell me, ma'am; how did you know what happened between Simon and Yvona?'

Emily lowered her gaze. 'I watched it.'

'How?'

'Through a crack in a doorway. Simon was questioning Yvona, trying to make her tell him that we were here, and...'

'Wait a minute,' he said, his eyes tightening. 'You saw Simon, and stood around to watch?' He halted on the street and turned to her. 'Are you insane?' he cried. 'How am I supposed to protect you if you put yourself at risk like that? What if Simon had seen you?'

'He didn't.'

'Dear gods.'

Emily watched him. His eyes were tight, and his fists clenched. He put a hand to his face and took a breath.

'Is everything alright, Captain?' said Lady Omertia. 'Shouldn't we be pressing on?'

Cardova said nothing. He stared at Emily, then turned to look at Lady Omertia and the child in her arms.

'Lucius,' said Emily; 'don't give up on us.'

He blinked. 'Never, ma'am. Only, if you see Simon again, then, I beg you, run. If he catches you and Maxwell, then all hope is truly lost. As it is, we're hanging on by the narrowest thread.'

'Let Silva's sacrifice mean something,' said Emily. 'And Yvona's.'

Cardova nodded, then took another long breath. He turned, and they started walking again, the thick, dark shadows of the Iceward Range smothering them.

CHAPTER 14

THE DARKER CORNERS

Serene, Implacatus – 13th Dunninch 5255

Kelsey crouched in the dank, squalid alleyway, keeping an eye on the street ahead, as Vadhi rummaged in the row of large bins behind her. For four days, they had survived by eating garbage, and hiding out in the darker corners of Serene, which were plentiful on the lower levels of the city.

Vadhi clambered down from the bin, and joined Kelsey, a stained canvas bag in her hands. She passed Kelsey a chunk of stale bread.

'You might be an aristocrat,' the young Exile said, 'but I know how to find food in a slum. Your privileged upbringing probably didn't teach you that.'

Kelsey shrugged. 'You're right. If we wanted food, we'd ring a bell and servants would bring it. What do you want me to do – apologise?'

'No,' said Vadhi; 'just acknowledge that, without me, you'd be starving, or captured.' She gestured at their surroundings. 'I'm from Alea Tanton – I know how to survive in a place like this. I was lost on the upper levels of the city, but down here feels almost like home.'

Kelsey tore off some bread and chewed it. 'Fine,' she said. 'I acknowledge it.'

Vadhi smiled. 'Thank you. Now, I have some doubts about your plan.'

'We have no choice. Van's father is the only person in this city who might be willing to help us.'

'He could be dead.'

'Van told me that he was still alive. Sure, he might have died in the last couple of years, but the odds are with us. I'm more worried that he'll hand us over to the authorities, but I think it's worth the risk. If we are ever to get back to the City, you know, the City of Pella, then we'll need a Quadrant. Van's father could give us the information we need to get one.'

'The Quadrants will be in the hands of the gods,' said Vadhi. 'Even if he knows where they are, they'll be too well protected to steal.'

'We have to try. I don't accept that we're stuck here forever; I refuse to accept it.'

They finished eating, and Kelsey stood, leaning against the side of the crumbling building to her right. On the upper levels of the city, everything seemed clean and symmetrical, but the lower levels were decayed and filthy. Along to the left, a large sheet of thick glass was letting in the last of the day's light. Once the sun had set, the streets would exist in a state of semi-darkness, with only a few lamps to provide a dim illumination. Their first night in Serene had been terrifying. Groups of young men had harassed them, and they had been followed several times. Since then, one of them would always stay awake while the other slept, and part of the reason for Kelsey's desire to find Van's father was the prospect of a decent night's rest.

They went out onto the busy street, Vadhi with her bag slung over her shoulder. They passed hot food stalls, and grimy-looking bars and taverns. Beggars sat by most corners. Some of them displayed signs, informing the public that they were maimed former Banner soldiers, and several had the dilated pupils of salve addicts. Kelsey could smell dreamweed in the air, and many of the slum dwellers were also smoking tobacco, but after two years without, she felt no desire to start again.

A huge set of wide stairs came into view, leading up to a higher level. A couple of gods were there, along with a detachment of soldiers, preventing anyone without authorisation from ascending. Kelsey and Vadhi hung back, watching from the shadows of a narrow back street.

'Any moment,' said Kelsey, her eyes on the gods.

A small group of workers began to climb the steps, and one of the gods stepped out in front of them, ready to read their minds. He glanced into the eyes of the group, then his face fell. He turned to his colleague, and they spoke together. The soldiers gathered round, as the two gods became flustered. Over four days, Kelsey had disrupted the powers of the gods throughout the city, and they all knew something was wrong. The two gods started to argue, then one stormed away, with tears rolling down his face. The other chased after him, leaving the soldiers alone on the stairs.

'Now,' said Kelsey.

She and Vadhi slipped back out into the crowds of people on the street, and they hurried towards the stairs. With no gods present, the soldiers were allowing anyone to climb the steps, and Kelsey and Vadhi joined the rear of the small group. They passed the soldiers, who were frowning but did nothing to stop them. Kelsey kept her head down, and they made it to the next level. They turned left, entering the Banner district. It was their first time in that part of the city, though they had scouted out its approaches the day before. The streets were clean again, and much wider than the slum level they had just left behind. Recruitment offices clustered along one side of the road, each displaying garish standards and flags denoting the different Banners. She saw one that had a large black crown on a white background, and they slowed.

'That was Lucius's old Banner,' said Kelsey. 'Let's start here.'

They walked through a doorway and entered the office. Behind a desk, a man in uniform glanced up at them.

'Good afternoon, ladies,' he said. 'How can I help you? If you are thinking of enlisting, then you should try next door at the Banner of the Coiled Serpent; the Black Crown only accepts male recruits.'

'I'm trying to find someone,' said Kelsey, 'but I can't see the office for the Banner of the Golden Fist.'

'The Golden Fist?' said the man. 'That Banner was disbanded a couple of years ago.'

'Disbanded?'

'That's right; after the fiasco in Lostwell. Is it an active soldier you're after? If so, they will have been transferred to another Banner, but there are still several thousand missing from the Lostwell operations.'

'What about records of past soldiers? Are they kept somewhere?'

'You could try the Banner Registry Office; they keep records of most service personnel. They handle payments to widows and so on.'

'That sounds perfect,' she said. 'Where is it?'

'If you're planning on going today, then you'd better hurry, as they close soon. Head up the main street, then take a right at the junction. The Registry Office is a tall building on the left, next to the headquarters of the Banner of the Ironheads.'

Kelsey glanced at the man's uniform. 'Thank you very much, Lieutenant.'

He smiled. 'You're welcome. If you have any younger brothers or cousins who want to enlist, make sure you send them my way.'

'Will do.'

The two women left the shop, and hurried along the wide road.

'We can't smell that bad,' said Vadhi. 'That man didn't seem to notice.'

'Banner officers are always polite,' said Kelsey, 'unless they're trying to kill you.'

They turned right at a crossroads, avoiding a few carriages as they trundled past. On their left was a large complex of buildings, enclosed by a high wall. Halfway along was a huge sign above an arched entrance, naming the place as belonging to the Ironheads. The next building along was set back a little from the road, and was so tall it almost brushed the smooth ceiling of the cavern.

'This is it,' said Kelsey, as she gazed at the building. Its unadorned sides were blank, with no windows anywhere. They walked up the front steps and entered through the doorway.

'Hello,' said Kelsey, as she approached a long reception desk, where several clerks in uniform sat. On either side of the hall were several doors, all marked *Private*.

A young man glanced up and smiled. 'Yes?'

'I'm looking for someone that used to serve in the Banner of the Golden Fist,' said Kelsey, 'but I don't know where they live.'

The man nodded. 'Are you a close relation of this person?'

'Eh, no.'

'Sorry, ma'am; our policy is not to divulge personal details regarding members of the Banners. Some occasionally get death threats, and we wouldn't want to lead an assassin to their front door now, would we?'

'Perhaps you could pass on a message? It's very important that I see him.'

The man took a pencil and a piece of paper out of a drawer.

'Name?' he said.

'Logos.'

'Banner?'

'The Golden Fist; I think.'

The man raised an eyebrow. 'Rank?'

'Eh, unsure.'

'I see. Age?'

'No idea. I'm going to guess fifty.'

The man put down the pencil. 'I think I know who you mean, even though the details you have provided are a little scant. Do you know his first name?'

Kelsey cringed on the inside. 'No.'

'Have you ever met him?'

'Never.' She sighed. If they knew who Van's father was, then they would probably know about Van as well. She considered leaving the office, but that would also look suspicious. 'Listen,' she said; 'it's his son that I know. Van and I were going to get married before he disappeared.'

'He did more than disappear, ma'am. Van Logos was officially expelled from the Banners for cowardice and disobeying orders. It is on record that he assaulted members of three different Banners on Lostwell before its destruction. If he were alive, there would a warrant out for his arrest.'

By then, every clerk at the long reception desk was paying attention to the conversation. Kelsey became self-conscious of the state she and Vadhi were in. Neither had washed properly in days, and their drab uniforms were stained, and their hair bedraggled.

'I know all that,' said Kelsey. 'That's why I have to see his father. Van left me with nothing.' She started to cry, surprising herself that she was able to weep upon command. 'Please show me some pity; I didn't know that Van was going to turn out the way he did. He promised me the world, and now I'm practically destitute. If only I could speak to his father, even for a few moments, to tell him how much I loved his son. It might give him some comfort.'

The man sighed. 'Name?'

'I already told you that.'

'No, miss; your name.'

'Uh, Clementine Garo.'

'Right you are, ma'am; I'll see that a message is passed on to Sergeant Logos this evening.'

'*Sergeant* Logos?'

'That's right, ma'am. If he wishes to respond, he will leave a message for you here. Come back the same time tomorrow, but don't get your hopes up. Sergeant Logos likes to keep himself to himself.'

'Thank you,' said Kelsey.

The man glanced back down at his work, so Kelsey and Vadhi trailed back out of the office and onto the road.

'I saw you crying in there,' said Vadhi; 'nicely done.'

'I didn't know I could do it; I'm quite impressed with myself.'

'What now? Should we go back down a level and find somewhere to rest for the night?'

'No. Didn't you hear? They're going to send him a message tonight.

That means, well, hopefully it means that we can follow the guy I spoke to when he comes out.'

Streetlamps were being lit as the glow from the deep skylights faded. Kelsey and Vadhi snuck in between the Registry Office and the walls of the Banner of the Ironheads, keeping to the shadows.

'The guy you spoke to might not be the one who delivers the message,' said Vadhi.

'I know, but it's worth a try. Frankly, I'd do almost anything to avoid another night in a cold alleyway that reeks of piss.'

They waited for half an hour in the darkness, then the doors of the Registry Office opened, and a handful of uniformed men and women emerged into the street. They chatted for a few minutes, then dispersed, heading away in different directions. Kelsey kept a close eye on the young man that she had been speaking to, and watched him walk past the narrow lane where they were hiding. They waited a few seconds, then crept out. They watched him turn right at the crossroads, then they hurried to the junction, peering round the corner.

They were so used to skulking about Serene, that they managed to follow the man along several streets without being noticed. They passed more huge complexes surrounded by walls, and then came to an area with rows of high housing blocks, cut into the side of the vast cavern. The man disappeared through one of the entrances, and Kelsey ran to the door. Her finger went down the list of names on a card affixed to the wall.

'Got him,' she said. 'Logos – apartment 3b.'

She rushed back to Vadhi, and they waited in the shadows of the next door's entrance. After a few minutes, the man emerged, a deep frown on his face. He took a breath, then walked back the way he had come.

'We're good at this,' said Vadhi; 'we could be spies.'

Kelsey gave her a look, then they walked up to the entrance. The hall inside was badly-lit, and held a smell similar to many of the alley-ways in the slums below. They crept up to the second floor, and Vadhi spotted a faded nameplate on one of the apartment doors.

'This is the one,' she said.

Kelsey joined her by the door. She knocked, and the door eased open a foot.

'Hello?' she said. 'Sergeant Logos? Anyone home?'

There was no response, so she pushed the door open another foot, then froze. In the dark entrance hall, a man was sitting behind a loaded ballista, the yard-long bolt aimed at the doorway.

'Don't move,' said the man, his face in shadows. 'If one of these bolts hits your head, it will take it clean off. Put your hands in the air where I can see them.'

Kelsey and Vadhi glanced at each other, then raised their arms.

'Now,' said the man, 'walk into the hallway, and close the door behind you.'

'Please don't kill us,' said Vadhi.

'I will if you don't do as I say. Walk into the hall, and close the door.'

The two women entered the apartment, and Kelsey shut the door behind them.

'Good,' said the man. 'There is now a small chance of you surviving. The next thing you have to do is tell me who sent you here.'

'No one,' said Kelsey.

The man laughed. 'Right. Which one of you claims to be Clementine?'

'That'll be me,' said Kelsey.

'My boy was never going to marry a Clementine. Your intelligence is faulty. Anyone who knew Van would know that he had no time or inclination for that kind of commitment. Prostitutes, yes; he was in and out of the Banner brothels, but a fiancé? No.'

'I lied to the man in the Registry Office. I'm not called Clementine, and I wasn't engaged to Van.'

'I've already guessed all that, little lady. Who sent you, and why?'

'I knew your son on Lostwell,' said Kelsey, 'and... after Lostwell.'

'There is no after Lostwell. My son was killed along with the others when the Ascendants obliterated that world.'

'Some of us escaped. Listen to my voice – do I sound like I come from Implacatus? Van is alive.'

The man said nothing, his expression unreadable in the shadows.

'And, I do actually love him, and he loves me; well, I think he still does. We've been on and off, you know? He's quite hard to get along with at times, and I'm... I'm not exactly easy to be with either. The truth is that we've probably argued more times than we've got on. I slapped him once, and he didn't speak to me for months. Mind you, he didn't deserve it, not that time. I could have slapped him for a hundred other things.'

'What's your real name, girl?'

'I'm not sure I should say. There are gods in this city that would like to find me.'

'And you're telling me this? Which gods?'

'Oh... Edmond, for one.'

The man coughed and spluttered for a moment. 'You're wanted by the Second Ascendant? Get out, now! You can't be here – the Ascendants see everything; they probably already know that you're here, in my apartment. Dear gods; you stupid girl. You'll bring them down upon my head as well as your own.'

'They don't know I'm here.'

'You fool; of course they do.'

'Alright; I have an idea. We wait. If you're right, then Banner forces, of which there are plenty nearby, will soon come bursting through your door, along with several gods. If they do so, then you will be aiming a ballista at us, holding us so that we couldn't escape. You'll be a hero. Edmond has tried to catch me before, and failed. How does that sound?'

'It sounds ridiculous.'

'Maybe so. However, if no one comes here tonight, then you can be certain that I'm right, because they'll not want me to slip through their fingers again.'

The man said nothing for a while. Eventually he grunted.

'Have a seat,' he said.

'Where?' said Vadhi.

'On the damn floor, girl!'

The women crouched down and sat on the bare floorboards.

Kelsey smirked. 'This is still better than an alleyway.'

Two uncomfortable hours passed. The man said nothing the entire time, his eyes never leaving Kelsey and Vadhi, and his hand close to the trigger mechanism of his ballista. After a while, he shifted in his chair.

'I need to relieve myself,' he said.

'Fine,' said Kelsey. 'We'll stay right here.'

'No; you'll run for it.'

'We won't; I want to speak to you about Van; that's why I'm here. By the way, what kind of person has a ballista in their hallway?'

'The kind of person who has spent their entire life annoying the wrong people.'

'Van's a major-general now,' she said. 'That came out wrong. I wasn't comparing him to you. There's nothing wrong with being a sergeant. I know plenty of sergeants who...'

'Shut up, girl,' said the man. He emitted a low laugh. 'A major-general, eh? Not that it means anything. No Banner would have him, not after Lostwell, which means that he's the major-general of some two-bit operation.'

'He formed a new Banner, from the survivors of Lostwell.'

'No? He did, did he?' He sighed. 'What am I saying? I'm starting to believe your bullshit. Right, tell me something about my son that only his father would know.'

'What? How am I supposed to answer that? He hardly told me anything about his childhood, except that his mother died in an operation a few years ago. He's told me all about his four trips to Dragon Eyre; does that count? He also told me about the prostitutes, and the narcotics, and the booze, and, I guess, the salve. I couldn't stand him when I first met him; he was so arrogant. I still can't stand him at times.

After Lostwell, he knew he couldn't return to Implacatus; he knew that he would be arrested if he set foot in Serene; so he followed me to this other place, because...' She puffed out her cheeks; 'because, he said he loved me. I wasn't ready then. Oh wait; he had a silver cigarette case, that you gave him on his eighteenth birthday. He lost it. He loaned it to a friend of mine who went to Dragon Eyre, of all places. He was quite upset about that.'

'I'll admit that much of what you've said rings true. But, I have to know – why is the Second Ascendant looking for you? What have you done?'

'He wants me for the same reason that he can't find me; if that makes sense. I have a unique ability; alright, not quite unique, as my big sister can also kind of do it, but anyway; I block the powers of the gods. Any god within a hundred yards of my location can't use their powers. That's why no one has burst through the door. They can't sense me.'

'Are you claiming to be a god?'

'Nope. I'm a plain old mortal; except, with powers.'

He got up and strode away, leaving the two women alone in the hallway.

'Should we get out of here?' said Vadhi. 'I don't think he likes us.'

'We're staying,' said Kelsey. 'I've already told him too much; we have to win his trust.'

'How?'

'I'm making this up as I go along, Vadhi; I don't know.'

'You don't know what?' said the man.

Kelsey looked up. The man was standing, leaning against the far wall of the hall. His face was visible for the first time, and Kelsey could see a resemblance to Van in his features.

'I don't know what in Pyre's name I'm doing,' she said. 'I want to trust you, but I'm worried that you'll hand us over to the gods. I came to you because I've been abandoned here, in Implacatus, and I want to get back to Van, and my dragon, and my friends. You are the only person I've heard of that lives here, and I'm asking you for help.'

'There are always rumours in Serene,' the man said; 'but I have a good memory for them. I recall my son's involvement in Lostwell under Renko; I kept an eye on any news coming in, as a father does. When it all went bad, a rumour ran around, a strange tale of a family of mortals with powers. That, at any rate, was the excuse that Renko gave the Ascendants to explain his failure. News dried up after that. I suspect that the Ascendants didn't want the citizens of Serene to hear about their failures on Lostwell. Then, over the last few days, more strange rumours have been circulating. Gods, suddenly losing their powers; panicking, weeping like children. Banner soldiers not knowing which way to turn. Then, it passes, and their powers come back. The authorities are taking it seriously. Some think it's a disease; others that a hostile power from another world is trying to attack. I have yet to hear anyone suggest that a mere mortal has been causing this chaos, but memories are short. There was a name attached to those earlier rumours, and I remember it.'

'You do?' said Kelsey.

'Yes. Holdfast. Are you one of them? Are you a Holdfast, girl?'

'Pyre's arsehole,' said Kelsey. 'If you can deduce this, then, no offence, but so will others.' She rubbed her forehead. 'Have you got a drink? If you're going to hand me over to Edmond, then I'm going to need a drink first.'

The man snorted. He walked along the hall, then reached down, took Kelsey's hand, and hauled her to her feet. He did the same to Vadhi, then turned and strode back down the hallway. The two women followed him, and entered a small living area, with a few chairs, and a shuttered window. The man sat down, and reached for an earthenware jug. He found a few mugs, and poured out three measures.

He handed the drinks to Kelsey and Vadhi.

'Sit down,' he said. 'Drink.'

Kelsey and Vadhi took the offered mugs, and sat on the only other chairs in the room.

'I gave the Banner of the Golden Fist twenty years of my life,' the man said, 'and look at my luxurious surroundings. A tiny, rat-infested apartment, and a pittance for a pension. My knees gave out first, then my back, and then my wife died. Did Van tell you how she died?'

'No,' said Kelsey, clutching the mug in her hands.

'It was a month before Van's fourth posting to Dragon Eyre, and that's where my wife happened to be. My boy didn't want to return to that place, but, with his mother already there, we thought that the fourth time would be better than the first three. Have you heard of an organisation called Unk Tannic?'

'No.'

'They're dragon-worshippers. Fanatics. On Dragon Eyre, they had infiltrated the civilian support network for the Banners, and began a wave of terror and killings. They massacred thirty-two people by burning down a tavern. They sealed the doors and threw incendiary devices through the windows. My wife, Van's mother, was one of those inside. She was having a meal and a drink with her friends from the regiment. The Banner returned her remains to me in a small box. Van wanted to walk away, but I, his father, told him that he would not dishonour the Golden Fist in such a manner; that he would go and do his duty.' He shook his head. 'And so, Van went, and spent the next nine months on that cursed world. He was never the same after that. He'd done things, in a rage born of grief; terrible things. I lost them both. When Van departed for his fifth operation upon Dragon Eyre, a year later, I believed that he would never return. I hardly saw him again, when he did get back. Alcohol, salve, dullweed... the brothels. It ripped my heart out to see how low he had fallen.' He stared at Kelsey. 'And you say that he is in love with you? If you're lying to me, I won't hand you over to the Ascendants, girl; I'll kill you myself.'

Kelsey sipped the raw spirits from the mug.

'How did you meet?'

'The first time?' she said. 'My brother, Corthie Holdfast, was killing a bunch of Banner soldiers, who had broken into a castle. He wouldn't stop, not even after the soldiers had laid down their weapons, so I, stupidly, ran out, my arms waving like an idiot. Van was one of the three soldiers who survived.'

'You admit that you are a Holdfast?'

'My name is Kelsey, and aye; I'm a Holdfast. The rumours were true – my family has powers. So do plenty of folk on my home world, but my family's powers are special. My brother killed hundreds of Banner soldiers on Lostwell, and a few gods as well. After Van had spent fifty days in captivity, my brother hired him to protect me. I think he hated me at first, but I guess I must have worn him down, without meaning to, and by the time Lostwell was destroyed... I want to get back to him. He's ill.'

'Ill?'

'Salve.'

The man nodded.

'He was just coming off it when I was snatched and brought here.'

'Do you love him?'

'This is the first time that I've admitted it, even to myself; but aye, I do. We've been through so much together. He drives me crazy, but I don't want to live without him. I broke it off when I learned that he was addicted to salve, but I couldn't stop myself from going back. I can't promise that our future will be filled with joy and happiness, but aye; I love him.'

The man took a drink, his eyes lowered. 'You have eased my pain.'

Kelsey and Vadhi shared a glance.

'You have done the worst thing imaginable,' he went on; 'you have given me hope.' He began to cry, silent tears wetting his cheeks. 'My boy; my stupid, beloved boy.'

Kelsey said nothing, watching as the powerfully-built man sobbed in front of her.

'The Ascendants,' he said, a slow rage building in his eyes; 'what is your opinion of them?'

'They want to destroy my home world, and the world where I now live with Van,' she said. 'I hate them.'

He stared at her. 'Everyone hates them, girl. Two of them were killed on Lostwell, an unspeakable, and unbelievable event.'

'I was on the back of a dragon when one of them died. Leksandr, his name was.'

'You helped kill one of them?'

'Aye.'

'Leksandr invented the greenhides.'

'I know.'

'And you killed him?'

'Aye; well, the dragons delivered the flames. I blocked his powers, and the dragons turned him into dust.'

'I am looking at an Ascendant-killer? No wonder Edmond is after you. If I were to hand you over to the Ancients, I imagine that my reward would be generous. A better apartment, a rise in my allowance; perhaps even a measure of the respect I deserve – all would be mine.'

'I guess so.'

'You're a lucky girl; very lucky indeed.'

Kelsey frowned. 'Why?'

'Because you'll struggle to find anyone in Serene who hates the Ascendants more than I do.' He reached out a hand, and placed it firmly onto Kelsey's shoulder. 'My name is Caelius, and I will help you.'

'You could be putting yourself at risk.'

He emitted a grim laugh. 'Do you think I care about that? I have waited my whole life for a chance to fight back against those bastards; a life filled with fear; a life spent knowing that the gods control everything we say and do; and in you walk – a woman, against whom the terrible powers of the Ascendants are useless; and a woman who loves my son.'

He shook his head. 'Kelsey Holdfast, a day may arrive when I curse the moment you walked into my apartment; but until that day comes I will hide you, I will feed you, and by all the gods, I will protect you – for my son, and for the redemption of my own, dark soul.'

CHAPTER 15

THE DINNER

Tara, Auldan, The City – 17th Mikalis 3423

'Two quick taps, today, sir; followed by three slow,' said the guard by the doorway.

'Thank you,' said Kagan. 'Summon a few more guards; we'll be escorting the captives upstairs.'

'Yes, sir.'

The guard unlocked the door, and Kagan entered the small apartment. The air held a stale odour of nappies and unwashed flesh, and he crinkled his nose.

'Good evening,' he said to the Aurelians. 'I have something different for you today.'

The family glanced up at him, their eyes weary.

'Don't you want to know what it is?' he said.

Lady Aurelian gave him a look of contempt. 'Are we being executed?'

'No. Just dinner.'

She raised an eyebrow. 'Amalia has invited us to dinner?'

'Not quite,' he said. 'Simon has. He'll be arriving in Maeladh soon, and he wants you upstairs.'

Lady Aurelian glanced away. 'No, thank you.'

'At the very least, you'll get some fresh air,' said Kagan. 'And some sunlight.'

'What if we refuse to attend?' said Lord Aurelian. 'Tempting as it sounds, of course.'

'Then, Simon will come down here and drag you up by the hair.' Kagan shrugged. 'That's what he said. He said other things too, about making your teeth fall out and so on. The usual threats.'

Lord Aurelian shook his head. 'Why you remain loyal to that beast is beyond my comprehension. Are you sure that it isn't a trick? He doesn't want us upstairs purely to have us killed?'

'He says that you won't be executed until Emily Aurelian has been caught. He wants me to find her. I have until the end of the month.'

'And, if you fail?' said Lady Aurelian.

Kagan shrugged again. 'Are you coming?'

She glanced down at her unkempt clothes. 'In this? Are we allowed to wash and dress first?'

'No.'

'I see. The purpose of this dinner is to humiliate us. Very well.' She glanced at Daniel, who was holding onto Elspeth. 'Son, shall we humour the beast?'

'I don't see that we have a choice, mother.'

'We shall go,' said Lady Aurelian, 'though I can't promise to be polite.'

Kagan nodded, then returned to the door and gave the correct sequence of knocks. The door opened, and Kagan saw half a dozen guards standing outside. A few moments later, the Aurelians got to their feet, Daniel keeping a firm hold of Elspeth, and they all began walking along the basement corridors. They climbed two sets of stairs, then paused by an open window. Kagan watched as the Aurelians gazed out at the view, a fresh breeze blowing through their untidy hair. The guards went to move them on, but Kagan raised a hand.

'Let them enjoy the air for a minute,' he said.

'Yes, sir.'

Elspeth laughed in Daniel's arms as the sunlight touched her pale skin, and Daniel gave her a look filled with love. Kagan felt his emotions tear inside him, and he glanced away, blinking.

'I say,' said Lord Aurelian, pointing in the direction of Pella; 'what's causing that smoke, old chap?'

Kagan turned, and saw the thin pillar of grey smoke rising from across the bay.

'It's the pyre by Cuidrach Palace,' he said.

'Pyre?'

'Yes, to burn the bodies of those executed each morning. There are a hundred and ten victims every dawn; five hundred and fifty in total so far.'

Daniel choked back a sob, his hands trembling with rage.

'Simon is a monster,' said Lady Aurelian. 'You, Kagan, are no better than he, for you know the crimes he is committing, and yet you do nothing.'

Kagan had no answer to that, so remained quiet.

'How are the Roser victims being selected?' said Lord Aurelian.

'I don't know.'

'You don't know? Aren't you and Amalia responsible for choosing them?'

'Amalia asked the Roser leadership to decide. She told them to clear the prisons first, but after that they'll have to work it out on their own.'

Lady Aurelian lowered her gaze. 'Lord Chamberlain will pick his personal enemies. He won't waste an opportunity such as this. I've seen enough; can we please move on?'

Kagan nodded to the guards, and they resumed walking. They came to a huge dining hall, large enough to seat a hundred people. At the far end of the hall, a single, long table had been set for dinner. Amalia was already there, sitting two chairs along from Lady Lydia, who was wearing an expression of extreme distaste.

Amalia stood. 'There you are. Praise the gods; I thought Simon was going to pull your teeth out.'

'Pretending you care again?' said Lady Aurelian. 'How thoughtful.'

'I was more concerned about the mess it would make of the carpets, my dear Lady Aurelian.'

'Shame is harder to remove than blood.'

'Then it is fortunate that I feel no shame.'

The two women glared at each other for a moment, then Amalia smiled. 'Please, be seated.'

The Aurelians sat opposite Lady Lydia, who ignored them, while Kagan went round the table and took a chair next to Amalia.

'Simon should be here soon, I imagine,' said Amalia; 'and then we can get this dinner over with.' She sniffed. 'What is making that awful smell?'

'We are,' said Daniel. 'It's what happens if you don't allow us to wash or change our clothes. What did you expect?'

'It's lucky that I don't have an appetite,' said Amalia, 'for I doubt I could face eating with that odour present.'

Lydia sighed. 'Let them wash, for pity's sake, grandmother. At least allow them to bathe the child.'

'Simon wants them in this condition,' said Amalia; 'he wants them looking wretched for their execution.'

'Then, defy him.'

'Really, Lydia? Defy Simon? Tell me; how exactly have you been defying him? Have you written him a stiff letter of complaint? Yvona sent him a letter, and look what happened to her.'

Daniel frowned. 'What did happen to her?'

'Simon hacked her to pieces with the Axe of Rand.'

The Aurelians gasped, and Daniel looked sick.

'Mortals are running Icehaven now,' Amalia went on, 'and they've been dutifully dispatching their ten victims every dawn to Pella, along with everyone else.' She glanced at Lydia. 'Apart from you. Of course, that has more to do with incompetence than defiance.'

'The Evaders have been resisting the decree with great violence,' said Lydia. 'They have attacked and killed many of the Sander militia I've sent into the Circuit to collect the daily quotas; it's impossible.'

'I hope Simon agrees with you. Have you thought up some suitable excuses? A grovelling apology is probably in order as well. I imagine we'll be seeing you on your knees at some point over dinner.'

'Do be quiet, grandmother. You don't scare me any more; you're not the God-Queen. In Simon's city, you are just another slave.'

Lady Aurelian laughed. 'This might be more entertaining than I had heretofore assumed.'

'Be careful,' said Amalia; 'I wouldn't want you choking to death on your food.'

'Oh, please. Threats? We've been locked in the basement of the palace since winter – do you think your threats have any effect? Lady Lydia has helped me see your position more clearly. You're terrified, aren't you? Terrified of Simon. That nugget of information has lightened my mood. Is there any wine?'

Kagan reached across the table for a bottle, and pulled out the cork. He filled a few glasses, and passed one to Amalia, who was drumming her fingers on the tabletop. Lord and Lady Aurelian each took a sip, but Daniel refused. Elspeth started to cry, and the hall fell into an uncomfortable silence, as Daniel rocked her on his knee.

Lydia shifted in her chair. 'Is anyone coming from Dalrig?'

Amalia shook her head.

'How do they get away with it?' Lydia said. 'Simon told me he would increase the Sanders' daily total to twenty if I refused to come.'

'Well, he hates Montieth,' said Amalia.

'Who doesn't?' said Lady Aurelian.

'He's my son,' said Amalia; 'I have an obligation to like him. As for Amber, I have no idea why she doesn't have to attend. I have heard nothing from her in a while.'

The air at the other end of the hall crackled, and four figures appeared. Behind them, another, far larger presence materialised at the same time, and Daniel rose from his seat in horror, an arm out to protect Elspeth.

'Greetings,' beamed Simon. 'I do hope you are all hungry. I am. Oh, and pay no attention to the young greenhide queen that I have brought along. I bagged her over on the Western Bank this morning, but she'll behave herself.'

He strode forwards, leading the other three humans, while the huge greenhide queen stood sentinel by the entrance to the hall. Kagan shifted his eyes from the monstrous beast to the others that Simon had brought. He recognised Naxor, but the other two faces were unfamiliar. Both had been severely beaten, and were keeping their heads down.

Amalia narrowed her eyes. 'Silva?'

'Indeed,' said Simon, standing by the head of the table. 'Naxor, sit to my left. Silva, Salvor, sit anywhere you like.'

Silva sat down between Amalia and Lydia, while Salvor shuffled to the other end of the table, his legs in obvious pain.

Simon grinned at everyone, then took his seat. 'I am smiling,' he said, 'but do not be fooled. Inside, my heart is bursting with rage. Naxor, tell them why I am angry.'

The demigod looked up. He wasn't injured like Silva and Salvor were, but he had a sheepish expression on his face.

'A dragon destroyed the salve mine and freed Jade.'

'That's right,' said Simon. 'A dragon. No sooner had I left the valley in the Eastern Mountains, than a damned dragon appeared – a dragon who had earlier submitted to me. Now, Jade is on the loose. She also bowed before me.' He shook his head. 'You just can't trust anyone any more. Worse, they destroyed over forty tons of refined salve; the entire stock that had been excavated from the mine thus far. I've had to transport a further two hundred Blades to the mountains, along with ballistae, and nets that can be launched by catapult, so that mining can recommence. What a waste. I will kill Jade and the dragon, naturally, with great suffering. However, that is merely the first of my disappointments. Silva, why don't you explain how you tricked me?'

The demigod glanced up, her face covered in bruises.

'Come on, Silva; don't be shy, or I'll give you more anti-salve and cut your fingers off.'

'I allowed myself to be captured,' she said, her voice low, 'so that Emily Aurelian and Maxwell could escape Icehaven.'

Daniel's eyes widened. 'Emily was in Icehaven?'

'Your slut of a wife is sleeping with a Banner officer,' said Simon; 'a certain Captain Cardova. Do you know him, false King?'

'I don't believe you,' said Daniel.

Simon laughed.

'It's not true,' said Silva. 'Captain Cardova is an honourable man, and your wife would never betray you, your Majesty.'

Simon slammed his fist down onto the table, then pointed at Silva, who screamed in agony and fell off the chair.

'That's what you get for ruining my joke,' Simon said, glancing at the writhing body of Silva on the floor. He gestured towards Salvor. 'You should be more like him. Salvor gives me nothing. Of course, that might be down to the fact that I melted half his brain. He may never speak again, isn't that right, Salvor?'

The demigod said nothing, keeping his eyes on the table.

Simon turned to Amalia. 'I have a question, young goddess – take a guess. What do you think the false Queen is trying to do?'

Amalia shook her head. 'I don't know, your Grace.'

'That's why I asked you to guess.'

'Perhaps she is hiding, your Grace? Maybe she wants to rally support for her cause?'

Simon eyed her closely. 'You can do better than that, goddess. I can see you pondering the correct answer in your mind.'

Amalia frowned. 'She's coming here? For Elspeth?'

'You're close. She wishes to exchange Elspeth for Maxwell, and hopefully forge an alliance with you. What do you say to that?'

'I don't know what to say, your Grace.'

'I thoroughly scoured through Silva's mind. The false Queen believes that you might be willing to help her. Now, wherever would she get an idea like that? She loathed you just a short time ago; she took your throne! And then, behind my back, you sent a messenger to Jezra to fill little Emily's head full of hope. If she makes it to Tara, I trust you know what to do with her?'

'Lock her up with the rest of her family, your Grace?'

'Precisely. If you don't, then you will take her place on the gallows in Prince's Square; do you understand?'

'Yes, your Grace.'

Lady Aurelian sighed.

Simon turned to her. 'What's the matter? I thought you would enjoy seeing the former God-Queen bow to my wishes. She is your enemy, is she not?'

'Oh, I find it most amusing. Amalia is a vile creature, nourished by the blood and pain of her many victims. She ruled the City as a tyrant, without any heed for the laws; she appointed her imbecilic children and grandchildren into positions of power; and, finally, her greatest crime of all – she allowed the greenhides to breach the walls of the City, causing the slaughter of over a hundred thousand of its citizens.'

Simon nodded. 'Then, why did you sigh, Aurelian?'

'Because I came to the awful realisation that, even with her many faults, she was a better ruler than you will ever be.'

Simon raised his hand, his eyes flashing with rage. Lady Aurelian sipped from her wine glass, unperturbed.

He lowered his hand, and let out a low laugh. 'No. That's what you want. You want to die here, to spare yourself the agony and humiliation of being tortured and executed in front of the people of Tara. For that, I will ensure that you live long enough to see Elspeth take her last breath, before I crush her tiny skull between my hands.'

Lady Aurelian smiled.

Silva struggled back into her seat. Blood was streaming from her nose, and she held a napkin up to her face.

'Glad to see you joining us again, Silva,' said Simon. 'I thought you were taking a nap down there.' He grinned. 'Do you want to know what Silva really thinks of Emily? She's using her. Silva doesn't really care about the Aurelians, or the City, or anything else for that matter. She has one objective in mind – to find the Third Ascendant. Unlike most of the Exiles from Lostwell, Silva has never given up hope of one day leaving this world, and she would do just about anything to get back to Belinda. It's ironic, in a way, because if she had come over to my side in the beginning, then I would have helped her accomplish that. Once I am in control of Implacatus, I would have found the world of the Hold-fasts, and reunited Silva with Belinda. But now?' He stared at Silva. 'Look at me, and listen carefully. Silva, you will never see Belinda again. You will never leave this world. I will chain you to a mountainside and leave you there, forever.' He glanced at Amalia. 'Where's dinner? I'm starving.'

Amalia reached behind her, and pulled a cord. Moments later, the doors of the hall opened, and a line of servants began to enter, wheeling laden trolleys. They halted, the lead servants backing away in terror from the monstrous greenhide queen standing by the entrance.

'Don't mind her,' said Simon. 'Get over here with the food.'

The servants eyed each other, and pressed on, diverting around the bulk of the greenhide queen, and trying to keep as far away from the long claws as possible. They reached the table, and began to unload the trolleys. Simon rubbed his hands together.

'Let me tell you about my plans for Matilda,' said Simon. 'That's the greenhide's name. I decided to name her, as she will be the founder of the first greenhide nest within the walls of the City. Those quarries in the Iceward Range where the dragons used to live – they'll be perfect for a greenhide nest. That way, whenever I have to leave the City, I can be sure that order is being maintained in my absence. A fine idea, don't you agree?'

No one spoke.

'Naxor?' said Simon. 'Flatter me.'

'Yes, your Grace,' the demigod said. 'It is a wise proposal. However, it seems to depend on your control over them. Might I ask; how will you maintain that control if you are away from the City?'

Simon rolled his eyes. 'I think you need to take some lessons in flattery; that was pathetic. However, in answer to your question, I can imprint a set of commands into their minds, that will last for a while in my absence. If there is a nest involved, then the queen is the key, as she can control her own young. I've already been working on Matilda. Watch.'

He glanced at the greenhide queen, and she began to move. With disturbing speed, she raced towards the table, then came to a halt next to the trembling servants.

'Lydia,' said Simon, 'pick out one of the servants.'

'I'm sorry, your Grace?' she said.

'I know you're sorry, Lydia; that can't be helped. Pick out one of the servants, or they all die.'

Lydia pointed at an older man, and within seconds the greenhide queen had snatched him in her long forelimbs. She raced back to the entrance of the hall, ripped the man to pieces amid the terrified screams of the other servants, and began to feast on his remains.

Kagan glanced away. He was shaking, with both fear and anger; his thoughts turning to how he could escape this nightmare. He was a coward, but they all were. Even Lady Aurelian looked shocked and upset, her steely smile disintegrating at the sound of the greenhide's jaws devouring the servant. Across the table from her, Amalia said nothing.

'The rest of you servants,' said Simon, 'leave. Run, before I change my mind.'

The servants abandoned the trolleys and sprinted for the door, as Simon laughed.

Silva glared at Lydia. 'You shouldn't have picked someone.'

'I had to,' cried Lydia.

'She's right,' said Simon. 'If Lydia had refused, it would be her that the greenhide queen was eating right now. Talking about eating; tuck in. I had the meat especially brought over by boat from Ooste this afternoon for us to enjoy. Everyone; eat; and yes, that's an order.'

Slowly, everyone began to pick up their cutlery and start on dinner. Kagan glanced at the food on his plate. A huge slab of meat was sitting next to a few vegetables. The steak had been lightly cooked, and blood was pooling under it.

'Come on; eat,' said Simon. He pushed a chunk of meat into his mouth and chewed. 'Oh yes. Very nice; very tender.' He glanced around. 'That's right. Good. Now, let me tell you a little story while we feast. I had to return to the Eastern Mountains, as you know, to retrieve the unfortunate Naxor from the bottom of the ravine where the dragon had thrown him.' He laughed. 'Picture that for a moment – Naxor flying through the air. Anyway, once I had finished at the mine, I paid the dragon colony a little visit as, naturally, I wished to question them about the attack on the valley. The dragon who had carried out the attack wasn't there. She has fled, along with her mother and her young son. Only two adult dragons remain at the colony, both of whom swore to me that they had tried to stop the other dragon from attacking the mine. I read their minds. They were telling the truth. All the same, I felt that a punishment of some sort was in order.' He paused. 'Are you all enjoying the food? Good. Where was I? Oh yes; now, what appropriate punishment could I deliver? One answer was obvious. I was holding one of the dragon's young infant children in a dungeon under the Royal Palace in Ooste.' He picked a bit of meat from his teeth. 'My, young dragon flesh does taste gorgeous, doesn't it? Meat from the older ones tends to be a bit tough and stringy.'

Daniel retched, while Lydia and several others threw down their cutlery in disgust. Kagan backed away, his guts churning, as the sound of Simon's laughter echoed round the hall.

'You utter beast!' cried Lady Aurelian.

Simon slapped his thigh, shaking with laughter.

'He's lying,' said Silva. 'I have eaten dragon flesh, and this is not it.'

Simon leapt up from the table, his eyes blazing, and strode round to where Silva was sitting. He pulled her from her chair and punched her in the face, then threw her to the ground. He began kicking her, and stamped on her arm.

'What did I tell you?' he screamed at her, as his boot landed on her side. 'Don't spoil my jokes.'

He picked her up by the throat, and dropped her into her chair, where she slumped, blood covering her face. She cradled her wounded arm to her chest, softly weeping.

Simon went back to his chair and sat, his face like thunder.

Naxor coughed. 'What are we eating, your Grace?'

'Veal,' the Ascendant muttered. 'I spared the dragon child. I told Darksky, the mother, that she must hunt down and kill Dawnflame, or I will rip all of her children to pieces. She swore she would do it, and dragons always keep their word.' He frowned. 'That's what surprised me about the attack on the mine – I have never known a dragon to forsake an oath. Humans, both mortal and immortal, on the other hand, break their word so often that I expect it.' He turned to Lydia. 'You, for example, young demigod – why have the daily quotas of Evaders been late to arrive in Pella? Didn't you promise that they would be delivered on time, before dawn, for the public to witness the executions?'

Lydia swallowed. 'Ten Evaders have been sent every day, your Grace.'

'I know that!' he cried. 'I asked you why they were late. What's the point of having a mass execution each dawn, if the Evaders aren't getting there until later? Two days ago, they arrived well past noon. Why?'

'The Circuit, your Grace, has not been cooperating. I have already lost eight members of the Sander militia – killed by Evaders resisting the collection of the quota...'

'Are your soldiers idiots? Are they incompetent?'

'No, your Grace.'

'I see. So, are they deliberately holding back? Are there saboteurs among your militia? If incompetence doesn't explain your failure, Lydia, then the only other option is disloyalty. Perhaps I should introduce a new quota, targeted at the traitors in the Sander militia.'

'But, your Grace; the Circuit is a special case. It is utterly lawless. The mortal monarchy did nothing to impose discipline or the rule of law into the territory of the Evaders. They are governed by anarchy.'

Simon turned to Daniel, who was clinging tightly onto Elspeth. 'Is this true, false King?'

Daniel glanced up. 'I have nothing to say to you.'

'You don't need to speak,' said Simon; 'I can see your thoughts. You feel guilty that you allowed the Circuit to slip out of your grasp during your so-called rule.' He nodded. 'Very well. If the Circuit is indeed as anarchic as your thoughts suggest, then I think I might pay the Evaders a visit in person.'

'It is good for a noble ruler to see all of their realm,' said Naxor. 'Might I ask what the purpose of your visit would be?'

Simon gave Naxor a withering look. 'You are a vile little snake, aren't you, Naxor? I can see the calculations going on in your mind, as you try to devise a way of increasing your power and influence.'

'Your Grace,' said Naxor, 'I am merely running through every contingency. My wish is to secure your rule over the City; my own interests are secondary to yours.'

'Yes? Then, young Naxor, please tell us all why you decided to hide the existence of the salve mine from me.'

Naxor glanced away. 'I... uh, yes, well, I didn't... you see, your Grace...'

Simon shook his head. 'I think you shall accompany me to the Circuit, Naxor. Lydia – you shall come too. We will travel there via Yocasta.'

Lydia's eyes widened. 'Yocasta, your Grace?'

'That's what I said. The greenhides there have already been trained, and are obedient. Bringing them here would save me the effort of having to train the wild greenhides that roam the lands beyond the City walls. Let's see the difference a hundred of them make to the security of the Circuit. Once we have installed them inside the territory of the Evaders, then you, Naxor, shall take over as governor of the Circuit, and you will be responsible for the new quota of twenty victims a day. With greenhides at your back, you should have fewer difficulties than Lydia experienced.' He turned to her. 'As for you, I am stripping you of your responsibility to collect the quota from the Evaders. However, failure must be punished. I want a hundred officers from the Sander militia, delivered to Pella for dawn tomorrow, where they will join the executions.'

Lydia gasped. 'A hundred, your Grace? That would encompass the entire officer class; the Sander militia is one of the smallest in the City and…'

'Shut up, Lydia; I have grown tired of your excuses. You will obey me without question. Do you understand?'

Lydia bowed her head. 'Yes, your Grace.'

Simon stood. 'My appetite has gone. Amalia, your hospitality has been delightful. Aurelians, I look forward to the great day when the citizens of the City will be able to witness your bloody executions. I have thought up a dozen unusual and agonising torments for you to suffer; each of you will beg for death before the end. Kagan; my, you have been quiet today, but I can sense your fear. Remember, you have until the end of the month to find the missing false Queen, and your son. Failure will be punished. Goodbye.'

He took out the Quadrant, and vanished, along with Naxor, Lydia, Salvor and Silva. Over by the entrance to the hall, the monstrous greenhide queen also disappeared, leaving the remains of the servant scattered in bloody pieces across the floor.

Kagan glanced round the table. Only he, Amalia and the Aurelians remained. For a moment, no one spoke, then Amalia stood, and strode from the hall without a word.

Daniel and his parents stared at Kagan, their eyes boring into him.

'I can also sense your fear, Kagan,' said Lady Aurelian. 'I don't need to be a god to see how terrified you are of Simon. Amalia too, and Lydia. Together, you have delivered the City into the hands of a monster. I hope you are proud.'

'We delivered nothing,' he said. 'Simon took the power for himself, and there was nothing we could do to stop him.'

'Does that mean you have to help him? For that is what you are doing. History will judge you harshly, Kagan; very harshly indeed, if, in fact, the City has a future where histories are still written.'

A servant was lurking by the main doors, keeping away from the blood and gore left behind by the greenhide queen.

Kagan signalled to him. 'Bring a squad of guards – the Aurelians are being returned to their rooms.'

The servant bowed, then hurried away.

'Set us free, Kagan,' said Daniel. 'Simon will be busy for hours. You could say that we over-powered you.'

Kagan snorted. 'Simon would read the truth from my head in an instant.'

Daniel smiled. 'You're considering it though, aren't you? You still know the difference between right and wrong. Kagan, you are not yet lost, not entirely.'

'Don't patronise me. In a few months, you will all be dead, and Simon? Simon could be gone. He wants to conquer Implacatus. Win or lose, he can't be here and there at the same time.'

'You coward,' spat Lady Aurelian. 'You hope to survive this by being an obedient slave? Would you not prefer to die with honour than live with such shame?'

The guards entered the hall, and approached the long table.

'I'd rather live.' He signalled to the guards. 'Escort the Aurelians back to their rooms.'

The guards waited until the Aurelians were standing, then shepherded them from the hall. Kagan sat alone, the words of Daniel and Lady Aurelian ringing in his mind. The King had been right – he wanted to help the Aurelians. But, if the price of that was death, then he wasn't willing to pay it. Could he live with the shame of serving Simon? He poured himself a full measure of wine, downed it in one, then refilled his glass.

He recalled what Simon had read from Silva's mind. If the information was correct, then Emily would be coming to Tara, bringing Maxwell with her. If she was stupid enough to hand herself over to Amalia, then she deserved what she got. They would take Maxwell, and Emily would be sent to the gallows along with the rest of her family.

And then? Perhaps then, Simon would let them live in peace.

He gulped down the wine. It was a fool's hope, and he knew it.

Simon would never allow them to live in peace, but what could Kagan do? He was a mere mortal; tiny and insignificant next to the immense power of the Ascendant. Any act of resistance would be crushed, and he would lose Amalia and Maxwell forever.

Lady Aurelian was right – he had no desire to die as a hero in a pointless cause. He would rather live as a coward. He broke down as the realisation struck him, and wept in the empty, bloodstained hall.

CHAPTER 16

BY ACCIDENT

The Sunward Desert – 17th Mikalis 3423

The dragon soared over the desert, the sun hanging just over the horizon. Jade clung onto Dawnflame's shoulders, her eyes on the endless sand below them. The dragon had not spoken to her since they had departed the cavern behind the waterfall that afternoon, her attention focussed on flying. Jade didn't mind; she preferred the quiet – it gave her time to think about what she needed to do.

Without warning, the dragon began to arc to the right, heading iceward.

'Are we close to the City?' she said.

'I am aiming to cross the walls over the Sunward Range, and the hills lie directly ahead of us.'

'How do you know that?'

'I am a dragon, demigod; I know how to navigate.'

The ground beneath them changed, with shrubs and patches of greenery sprouting among the sands, then the marshlands began. Flocks of birds lifted up into the sky at the dragon's approach, filling the air. Dawnflame increased her altitude, soaring over the startled birds.

'You don't talk much,' said Jade.

'I am concentrating on flying.'

'Good. I thought that you were still unhappy about helping me today.'

'I am not unhappy. I merely believe your plan to be foolish. However, if you truly value your tiny, furry animals, then I am obliged to assist you in the task of rescuing them. You say they are like your children. That seems ludicrous to my mind, but you saved my son. I will return the favour.'

'Once we get my cats back to our hiding place, then we can start attacking the City. I need to know my babies are safe first.'

'Little Jackdaw also thought the idea was foolish. Do you never take the advice of your friends, demigod?'

'Rosie's wrong about this. She's just worried that we'll get ourselves killed.'

The dragon paused for a moment. 'There is one other aspect of your plan that is flawed, demigod. If we are successful today, then four small mammals will be sharing our living space. To Firestone, they will be indistinguishable from food. He may eat them. I will tell him not to, but he is a child, and children do not always obey their parents. The temptation may be too strong for him to resist.'

Jade frowned. Two days previously, Firestone had been caught trying to eat Flavus's leg while the lieutenant had been sleeping. Dawnflame had severely reprimanded the young dragon and, fortunately, Flavus's injury had been easy for Jade to heal. How was she going to protect her cats from the young, red dragon?

'We'll work something out,' she said.

'I admire your optimism, demigod.'

The marshy ground raced beneath them, Dawnflame's speed impressing Jade.

'You're faster than Halfclaw.'

'Of course I am. Halfclaw is still growing. In time, he may become quicker than me, but I outmatch him for now.'

'Where is he, do you think? And Frostback too?'

'I do not have an answer for you. I have seen no trace of either of them since Jezra fell to Simon's forces. I suspect that they have fled to a remote region, perhaps among the icy wastes beyond the Cold Sea; somewhere out of sight of the Ascendant. If Frostback is aware that Kelsey Holdfast has left this world, she will not be searching for her here.'

'Have they abandoned us?'

'Frostback is tied only to the Holdfast witch, and Halfclaw is tied to his betrothed. They have no obligation to defend the City from an Ascendant.'

'Then, why are you doing it?'

'I am driven by hatred, demigod; that, and my duty to you as the one who saved my son. Those are reasons enough for me to act.'

The dragon fell into silence again as she sped over the marshlands. Compared to the vast expanse of swamps, the Warm Sea was small. The sun was setting behind them as they rushed over the water, the high ridges of the Sunward Range ahead of them. Dawnflame kept low. A few fishing vessels were out on the sea, but Jade knew that she and Dawnflame would have gone by the time the boats could return to the City to report what they had seen. The cliffs of the Sunward Range grew nearer, and Dawnflame reared up, hugging the side of the steep rocks. At the top of the ridge was a high wall, but it was never guarded, and Dawnflame landed on the hillside on the other side of it. Jade clambered down to the grass, and the dragon placed a wooden box onto the ground next to her that she had been carrying.

'You have three hours, demigod. Return here with your animals, and we shall go back to the mountains.'

The dragon took off without another word, and flew off to sunward, her sleek form racing back over the waters of the Warm Sea. Jade turned. The hills of the Sunward Range were laid out in front of her. Three hours would be tight to walk all the way to Pella and back. She wondered where Simon was, then pushed the thought from her mind, picked up the box, and began walking.

Two hours had passed before Jade finally trudged past the walls of Old Pella. The hike through the Sunward Range had taken her a lot longer than she had imagined. It might only have been a few miles as a dragon flies, but on foot she had faced valleys and high ridges, along with plenty of Roser estates full of workers out labouring in the last of the day's light. Darkness had descended long before she had reached the main road, but at least no one had recognised her.

She spotted the ruins of Cuidrach Palace ahead of her as she walked along the narrow streets of the ancient town. She had a hood up to cover her hair, and had swapped her dark green dress for the more nondescript clothing that Rosie had been wearing. Jade hated it. She felt like a peasant, rather than a mighty demigod, but no one on the streets of Pella paid her any attention, which was what she had wanted. Still, the fact that she had been forced to adopt a disguise rankled with her. The stupid mortals brushing past her on the cobbles had no idea who she was, and that offended her dwindling sense of immortal entitlement.

Her nose caught a terrible odour coming from the front of the palace. She squinted in the dim lamplight, and caught sight of a huge, smouldering bonfire, being tended by a group of Reaper militia. The awful smell grew worse, then she noticed that the bonfire was made up of dozens of bodies. Guards were pouring oil onto the corpses, encouraging them to burn, and a pillar of thick, black smoke was rising into the night air. In front of the bonfire was a long row of large stakes that had been driven into the ground, stretching across the entire front of the ruined palace. Bloodstained leather straps were hanging from the wooden posts, and the ground at the base of each was spattered with blood and gore.

Jade frowned. It was obvious that the stakes were being used for mass, public executions, but she had no idea who the victims were, or what they had done.

She took a right, heading away from the harbour front, and walked along the sunward edge of the palace. She passed a heavily-guarded gate, and kept walking. She turned left again, at the far end of the palace grounds, then dived into the shadows. The wall ringing the grounds was low and crumbling in places, and she scanned the area for people. Seeing no one, she threw the wooden box over the wall, then she pulled herself up onto the low barrier and slipped into the palace grounds, keeping to the thick bushes that lined the wall. The gardens seemed deserted, though many of the flowerbeds had been trampled, and the grass was a muddy mess. Jade crept along by the wall, keeping low, the box clutched in her arms, until she spotted the little cottage where she had stayed after resigning from the Bulwark. No lights were on within the cottage, despite the fact that a couple of the windows were lying open.

Jade ran across the last stretch, breaking from cover to sprint over the gravel path. She reached the back door of the cottage, and pushed it open. She listened. Nothing. She stole through the back room of the small building. The place had been gutted, with everything of value stripped. Even the wooden doorframes had gone, presumably to feed the bonfire. Jade glanced around, her spirits falling. There was no sign of the woman who had been looking after her cats, and she wished she had learned her name.

She heard a noise and jumped. She looked down, and saw Tab-Tab amble across the dirt floor. Jade burst into tears, and fell to her knees, dropping the box.

'My precious baby,' she said, picking her up and holding her to her chest. 'You're so skinny; what have you been eating?' She reached into a pocket and produced a handful of dried meat, which she placed on the floor. She released Tab-Tab from her grip and the cat began to eat, purring loudly. The smell of the food and the sound of Jade's voice soon attracted Fluffy and Ginger too, and Jade gave them each some of the meat. She waited until they were all eating, then quietly opened the box. Then, in a flurry of movement, she grabbed each cat, and shoved it into the box. She pushed Ginger in, while he protested loudly, and shut the box.

'Sorry, babies; I'm sorry. You won't be in the box for long. Mummy needs to take you far from here. Now, I just need to find Poppy, and then we can go.'

The cats meowed inside the box, and Jade could hear their claws scratch at the wood. Jade felt terrible for them, but she had no choice. She turned.

'Poppy! Poppy! Mummy's here.'

She saw a glint of cat's eyes shining in the hallway.

'There you are; come over here, Poppy, there's a good girl.'

Poppy stepped forward, saw the box, then turned and raced away.

Jade sighed. 'Damn it. Poppy, you naughty cat. Come back here.'

She got up, and walked into the hallway. Poppy darted by her feet, heading into Jade's old bedroom. Jade went in, and closed the door, her eyes searching the shadows. Poppy was in the corner of the bare room. Jade approached, and the cat hissed.

'How dare you?' said Jade. 'I'm trying to rescue you, ungrateful baby.'

She dived into the corner of the room, her arms sweeping Poppy up. The cat struggled, her claws out, and scratched Jade down her arms and hands. Jade grunted, then ran back to the rear room. She opened the box with one hand, pushed Tab-Tab back in, then shoved Poppy inside. She closed and latched the box, then sat down, watching as the scratches on her arms healed.

'Right,' she said. 'Now, all I have to do is carry you lot all the way back to the Sunward Range in the next half hour.' She glanced at the box. 'We're not going to make it, are we? The box was heavy enough without you four in it. Sorry, that sounded like I was calling you fat.' She stood, and picked up the box. It was hard to balance, as the four cats inside were moving around, and she struggled with the weight. Rosie had tried to explain some of the practical difficulties with Jade's plan, but the demigod had ignored her. Unfortunately, it seemed that the mortal girl had been right.

Jade carried the box to the back door of the cottage and peered outside. The gardens were still deserted, but the cats were yowling from inside the box, and were sure to attract attention at some point over the five miles back to the ridges of the Sunward Range. She strode outside, trying to keep the box level, then staggered along the path, her boots crunching on the gravel. She heard a strange whooshing noise, and her heart pounded, then a giant, scaled forelimb gripped her round the waist and her feet left the ground. She shrieked in fright, her voice echoing across the palace grounds.

'Be quiet,' said Dawnflame, plucking the loaded box from Jade's arms with her free forelimb.

Jade looked up. 'What are you doing in Pella? Simon might see you.'

'Simon is in the Circuit,' the dragon said, as she ascended into the night sky. 'I saw him while I was circling the City. Don't worry, I was too high for human eyes to see, and the Ascendant was too busy to notice me. He has brought greenhides with him, and they are slaughtering the Evaders.'

'Why?'

'Do you expect me to understand the mind of an insane Ascendant, demigod? I have no knowledge of his motivations, but, while he is distracted in the Circuit, I suggest that we go onto the attack.'

'But, we have the cats.'

'Yes, we do. However, that fact does not prevent me from unleashing an inferno upon our enemies.'

'I suppose that's true.'

'And you can use your death powers,' said the dragon. 'I will keep a safe grip on the box containing your animals. They might enjoy watching the flames.'

'I doubt that.'

The dragon soared over the Union Walls, keeping sunward of the Circuit. Jade turned to look, and saw a few fires in the central region, close to the Great Racecourse.

'Did you say he brought greenhides?'

'I did. I counted around a hundred of the beasts. Simon is controlling their movements. When I was circling, I saw him order them into Redmarket Palace. Then I noticed how late it was, and waited for you to leave the cottage. Simon will learn that we were in the City, but not until long after we have left.'

They crossed the Middle Walls, and started to pass Hammer territory. Dawnflame carried on, and Jade realised what their destination was.

'We're going to the Fortress of the Lifegiver?'

'Yes,' said the dragon. 'The Lostwell goddess lives there now. She shall be our first target.'

'Felice?'

'Yes. Do you object?'

'No. Not one bit.'

They reached the dark and silent fields of the Scythes, and the giant fortress loomed ahead, shrouded in the shadows of night. Dawnflame plunged downwards, until she was skimming the hedges and trees that bordered the fields.

'I will deliver flame,' said the dragon. 'Your role is to pick off any who try to loose ballista bolts at us.'

'Alright.'

Jade flexed her fingers, feeling for her powers. She glanced at the box, held in the grasp of the dragon's left forelimb.

'Don't watch, babies. You don't want to see mummy kill people, do you? You might get frightened.'

'Demigod,' said the dragon; 'do your animals understand your words?'

'Eh, no.'

'Then why speak to them?'

'They recognise my voice, and my tone. I'm trying to comfort them; they must be scared. They've never flown before.'

The dragon laughed.

They reached the Scythe Wall, and Dawnflame surged upwards, then opened her jaws. An enormous blast of fire erupted from the dragon, enveloping the gatehouse of the fortress. Blades on the perimeter wall screamed in panic, but a few ran to the ballista stations on the battlements, and started to turn the machines towards the dragon. Jade raised her right hand, and sent her death powers towards them, clearing the top of the wall. The Blades fell down, into the rising flames.

Dawnflame soared up, passing the burning gatehouse, and sent another long blast of fire down into the fortress's large courtyard, incinerating everything that moved.

'Look out,' cried Jade. 'The ballista platform, next to the Duke's Tower.'

Dawnflame aimed her stream of fire upwards, and the top of the platform erupted in flames. The catapults and ballistae were consumed in the inferno, along with the dozen Blades operating the machines.

'Can you deal with Felice on your own, demigod?' said the dragon.

'Yes.'

'Then I shall set you down. Be quick about it, and I will destroy the rest of the fortress.'

The dragon landed in the middle of the burning courtyard, and released Jade from her grip. The demigod sprinted for the tower, dodging the smoking bodies littering the ground, as the dragon ascended back into the air. The two guards by the entrance to the Duke's Tower were already dead, their bodies smouldering and charred as they lay by the front door. Jade entered the tower, and saw the damage that had been caused by Frostback's attack a few months before. Much of the stonework was blackened with soot, and a stale odour of smoke lingered in the air. She heard raised voices, and looked up. Blades were on the stairs, their eyes wide with panic, while orders were being yelled from the floor above.

Jade swept her hand from left to right, and the soldiers fell, toppling down the steps into a heap at the bottom, their eyes lifeless. Jade climbed over the bodies, and crept up the stairs. A Blade officer was standing on the landing above, his arms outstretched as a soldier strapped his armour on. They turned, and saw Jade.

'Hey; you,' yelled the officer. 'What are you doing here?'

Jade raised a finger, and the officer's head half-melted. His hair slid off his scalp, and his eyes fell out as his skin dissolved. The soldier next to him screamed, and Jade ended his life, causing his heart to stop. Jade looked at her hands for a moment. It had been a long while since she had used her powers to kill, and it felt different than before. She wondered if the men had families. Rosie's brother was a Blade. She blinked. Why was she feeling that way? It was almost as if she regretted killing them.

A noise from above distracted her, and she gazed up to see Felice. The god was on the next floor up. Their eyes met for a moment, then the god vanished, running into a room and closing the door. Jade raced up the steps, and barged through the entrance. A crossbow bolt slammed into her waist, sending her flying backwards. She hit the floor. Another bolt whistled past, inches from her face.

'Damn it,' muttered Felice, as she tried to reload.

Jade pulled the bolt from her waist and charged at Felice. The god's hands fumbled on the crossbow, and Jade bowled her over. They fell into the room, their limbs tangled together. Jade closed her eyes, knowing that Felice had the power to send her to sleep. The god writhed beneath her, then Jade felt a punch land on her face. Fighting the pain, Jade placed a hand onto Felice's cheek, and began to draw the god's life force out of her.

Felice screamed. She kicked and punched, but Jade kept her hand steady. She felt her own strength grow inside her as she took from the god. The wound in her waist healed, and she felt no pain from the punches that struck her. Felice began to weaken; her struggling grew less, and she gasped in agony, too feeble to use her powers to self-heal.

Jade withdrew her hand, and stood over the god.

'Do you know what this is called, Felice?' said Jade. 'Revenge. You brought Simon to the City, and now you'll pay for it.'

'No,' gasped Felice, her strength diminished. 'Please, Jade. Simon is insane. Even you bowed before him.'

'I did,' said Jade, 'and I'm ashamed of it. He would have killed my friend if I hadn't.'

Felice turned her head to glance out of the window. Flames were rising all over the fortress, and the sound of Blades dying echoed through the air.

'Simon will kill you for this,' Felice gasped. 'Save me, and I will help you.'

Jade shook her head. She walked over to a wall, where two crossed swords, the symbol of the Blades, were hanging. She took one down, feeling the weight of the weapon in her hand.

'You don't need to do this, Jade,' Felice said, her eyes on the sword. 'I am already too weak to resist.'

'I know, but if I leave you here, you'll recover. And then you'll go right back to helping Simon. This is the only way, Felice. Any last words?'

'Simon will kill you.'

'You already said that. Seems a waste of your last words, don't you think?'

She raised the sword in both hands over Felice, then glanced down at the god's neck. She knew what she had to do, but she had never killed a mortal with a weapon before, let alone a god. It felt wrong, and horrible; somehow more horrible than killing by death powers.

'Please,' said Felice, as tears came from her eyes. 'Please, Jade...'

Jade closed her eyes, and brought the sword down, almost flinching as she did so. She felt the blade strike something, and Felice's voice cut off in a last, gargled gasp.

She opened her eyes. Felice's head was half-severed, and blood was dribbling from her lips. Jade wanted to throw up at the sight. Was it enough? Did her head need to be completely cleaved from her body for her to be truly dead? Jade didn't know. She dropped the sword, and it fell to the floor. Jade staggered away from the body, then collapsed to her knees and vomited over the rug. Her hands started to shake, and her forehead was clammy. A scratching noise disturbed her, and she jumped in fright, thinking that Felice had healed herself already.

She turned, and saw the body on the floor, lying motionless. The scratching noise came again, and Jade scanned the room. Maybe Felice had a cat. She saw a long, coffin-shaped wooden box lying against the wall, and listened. The scratching was coming from inside. Jade hauled herself to her feet, and stumbled over to the box. It had a latch on the lid.

'Who's making that noise?' she said. 'Cats?'

'Help me,' came a muffled voice from inside the box.

Jade released the catch, and removed the lid. Inside the box was a man. She blinked in surprise. The man was covered in blood and open sores, and his ragged clothes were stinking.

Jade grimaced and pulled away. 'Who are you?'

'Van,' the man whispered, his face a broken mess.

'Major-General Van Logos?'

'Yes. Jade, kill me or heal me, but don't leave me like this.'

'What did you do to be put in a box? Did Felice do this to you?'

'Yes.'

Jade felt her stomach turn. The man looked like one of her father's experiments. She raised her hand, and felt the huge reserves of power that she had pulled from Felice. She shot out a sustained burst of healing, and the man convulsed, his entire body shaking violently. Jade backed away, watching.

The man sat up. His face was still covered in blood, but Jade recognised him at last. He looked at his hands, then at the rest of his body. He rubbed his face.

'Thank you,' he said.

'You're welcome.'

'What's happening?'

'Dawnflame and I are destroying the Fortress of the Lifegiver. I killed Felice, though I don't think I'll ever hold a sword again. It was horrible.'

Van stared at her, then he noticed the body lying on the floor. He clambered out of the coffin, and stared down at Felice. He leaned over and picked up the sword that Jade had dropped.

He glanced at Jade. 'You mean you almost killed Felice.'

'Will she recover from that? I wasn't sure.'

'Neither am I,' he said; 'but let's make certain.'

He brought the sword down with a powerful lunge, severing the god's head from her body. He then picked the head up, and threw it out of the nearest window.

Jade frowned, feeling sick again.

'Now, we're certain,' said Van. 'What's the plan?'

'We fly back to the Eastern Mountains.'

'Where's Simon?'

'In the Circuit.'

'He'll be here soon.'

'Yes. We should leave.'

He looked her in the eye. 'Jade, thank you.'

'Stop talking, and let's go.'

She left the room, and glanced down the stairs of the tower. She had killed an enemy and rescued an ally, but she felt wretched, the image of Felice's half-severed neck stamped onto her mind. Her guts churned as they hurried down the steps to the ground floor. Outside was a scene of devastation. The tall barrack blocks were afire, smoke and flames tumbling upwards from every window, while bodies lay all over the courtyard. The dragon soared down, and landed amid the carnage.

'Felice is dead,' said Jade.

'Good. Now, quickly, Jade,' said Dawnflame. 'Simon will be coming for us.' The dragon glanced at Van. 'Why have you brought this man?' she said. 'He commanded the Banner the day Tarsnow was killed.'

Van bowed before her. 'Dawnflame, I am willing to answer for my mistakes. Tarsnow was a noble and magnificent dragon, and his loss was a bitter blow. The ones who killed him suffered for it.'

'Can we discuss this later?' said Jade. 'Van knows lots about military tactics, and stuff like that. He could help us plan our next attack.'

'Do you mean to attack again?' said Van.

'We do,' said the dragon. 'However, Jade is in charge of the humans; will you obey her orders? I will not suffer a Banner soldier as leader.'

'I'm happy to serve Jade, if we're taking the fight to Simon.'

The dragon's eyes burned. 'This sits ill with me, but we must leave. Climb up.'

'Me too?' said Van.

'Yes, Banner insect,' said Dawnflame. 'You too.'

Van smiled. 'Thank you.'

'Don't thank me yet, insect. I will decide what to do with you when we return to the mountains.'

Van's eyes went to the wooden box grasped in the dragon's claws.

'What's in there? Supplies?'

'No,' said Jade; 'my cats. I came to the City to rescue them. I only saved you by accident.'

Van raised an eyebrow, but said nothing.

They clambered up onto the dragon's shoulders, and Dawnflame ascended into the air, the fires raging through the fortress surrounding them. Dawnflame soared through the thick banks of smoke, and crossed the Great Walls, the conflagration lighting up the night sky as they raced towards the east.

CHAPTER 17

METALLURGY

S ector Seven, The Bulwark, The City – 18th Mikalis 3423

Emily felt a hand gently shake her shoulder, and her eyes opened. Cardova was crouching over her in the dark room, a finger on his lips. He glanced upwards, then headed towards the stairs. Emily yawned, then stretched her arms. It was a warm, humid night, and she had been dreaming about her time in the Rats.

Cardova stopped at the stairs, turned, then gestured for her to follow him.

Emily pulled the thin blanket from her, and crept across the small room, careful not to wake either her mother or Maxwell. She went up the stairs after Cardova, and they came out on to the flat roof of the squat building. All around them were the derelict Blade houses of Sector Seven, abandoned since the greenhide incursion three years previously. Cardova pointed at the horizon, halfway between sunward and the east. Emily squinted. The sky in that direction was glowing red, despite the fact that dawn was still a few hours away.

'The Fortress of the Lifegiver is burning,' said the captain.

Emily frowned.

'Now,' said Cardova, 'what could cause an inferno like that?'

'Do you think Frostback and Halfclaw have returned?'

Cardova shook his head. 'I doubt that they will return, ma'am. Their only connection to us is Kelsey Holdfast, and if she isn't here, then they won't get involved. But, if it's not them, then who?'

'Perhaps Deathfang has rallied the other dragons?'

'Perhaps. Whatever the reason, it's a blow against Simon. However, Van might be inside that fortress, if Felice took him back there. Or maybe not; I don't know. It might make a difference to the numbers of Blade soldiers guarding the gates on the Hammer Wall, though. I think we need to be ready. If there's a chance of getting through those gates today, we have to take it.'

'Agreed, Lucius. We can't stay here any longer; we're running out of food, and the Blade patrols will find us eventually. Alright; we'll try today. We need to get down to the gates before they're opened at dawn.' She paused. 'Try not to think about Van – he could be anywhere.'

Cardova nodded, his eyes troubled. They crept back downstairs, and changed their clothes in the darkness, pulling on the spare Blade uniforms that they had found in an abandoned house a couple of days previously. They packed their civilian clothes into a bag, then Emily woke her mother, and, together, they shared the last of their food as the light towards sunward started to grow.

When they were ready to leave, Cardova slung the bag over his shoulder, and Lady Omertia picked up the sleeping form of Maxwell, wrapped in a blanket. They emerged from the derelict house, and walked through the overgrown and deserted streets of Sector Seven. The Blades had abandoned several of their old housing sectors following the greenhide incursion, clustering the survivors, and withdrawing from entire areas. Many of the houses had been stripped of their roofs, and every wooden item had been taken, from floorboards to window frames. A few stray cats prowled the neighbourhood, their eyes glinting in the predawn light.

They left the streets behind, and crossed the large training grounds that lay between Sector Seven and the long wall that sealed off Scythe and Hammer territory. The path was filled with knee-high weeds, until they reached the main road that led from Arrowhead Fort to the Middle

Walls. A few wagons were passing, and Emily and the others waited for the way to be clear before rushing across. They picked up their pace for the last mile, hurrying along the road that ran directly to the main gates in the Hammer Wall.

A large group of Blades were stationed by the gates, and Cardova slowed as they approached.

'I hope your Blade accent is convincing,' he whispered.

'It'll be more convincing than yours, Lucius,' Emily said, 'so stay quiet.'

A few Blades glanced in their direction as they neared the gates. Emily noticed that there were fewer Blades than normal, and they seemed subdued, even angry.

Emily strode forwards, leaving Cardova with her mother and Maxwell.

She saluted the officer on duty.

'Morning, sir,' she said. 'We have a woman and child to return to Hammer territory; they were found wandering through the Iceward Range.'

The officer frowned at her. 'Wait your turn, Private,' he said. 'We'll get the daily convoy out first, and then you can escort them in.'

'Yes, sir.'

The officer's eyes narrowed a little, and seemed to bore into her.

'Sir?' said another Blade. 'The convoy's on its way.'

The officer gestured to the others. 'Open the gates!'

Emily slipped back to where Cardova was standing, and they moved aside as the Blades removed the long crossbeam from the front of the double gates. They hauled the huge gates open, revealing a cobbled street, lined with brick buildings. A large crowd of Hammers had gathered, and began moving forwards, surging towards the opening.

'Get back!' screamed the officer. 'Sergeant, loose over their heads.'

A squad of Blades aimed their crossbows, and loosed over the crowd. The Hammers cried out, and many fled, while others threw stones at the Blades. Down the street, a long convoy of wagons was slowly making its way to the gates, flanked by heavily-armoured Blades.

Stones were battering off their shields, while Hammers were hurling roof slates at them from the tops of the brick houses.

A few Blades came over to where Emily and the others were standing, watching the Hammers as the convoy approached.

'Did you hear about the Fortress of the Lifegiver?' said one of the Blades.

Emily nodded.

'Bastard dragons. They killed hundreds; whole battalions wiped out. My cousin was garrisoned there.'

'What happened to Felice?' she said.

'Who knows? The fires are still raging and no one can get close to the Duke's Tower. They'll have to reshuffle entire battalions, otherwise that whole stretch of the Great Walls will be undefended. Just when we thought things were settling down again, and this happens. Why can't the dragons leave us alone?'

Emily said nothing. They quietened to watch as the convoy reached the opening in the walls. Wagons filled with the produce of the Hammers rolled out of the gates – leather, crossbows, ceramics, uniforms, cement and dozens of other items, all stacked up in crates, or heaped in sacks. The Blades formed a thick, armoured line to prevent any of the Hammers from leaving the territory, and the last of the wagons pulled out in a hail of stones.

'Let's go,' said Emily.

'Be careful in there,' said the Blade standing next to her. 'The Hammers will eat you alive.'

The officer glanced over, and gestured to Emily. She saluted, then pushed her mother forward. Maxwell had awoken from the noise, and was crying and struggling in Lady Omertia's grip.

'Report to the forward station when you've dropped the woman off,' the officer said to Emily. 'Then get out with the next convoy – we need every Blade out here and on duty, in case the dragon comes back. Understood?'

'Yes, sir.'

The officer frowned at her again, then signalled for them to go.

Emily and Cardova flanked Lady Omertia, and eased through the line of soldiers. The gates were pushed shut, leaving them on the other side, along with two dozen of the heavily-armoured Blades. Stones were still bouncing off the cobbles, but most of the Hammers had retreated with the departure of the convoy.

A sergeant eyed Emily. 'Wait a minute before you go in any deeper. The Hammers like to give us a little show each morning, but they always disperse afterwards. Where are you going?'

'Tanner's district,' said Emily. 'Returning this escaped Hammer to her home.'

The sergeant raised an eyebrow. 'Just drop her off here and make her walk back on her own.'

Emily shrugged. 'Orders, Sergeant. We were told to take her home.'

'By whom, Private?'

'By the commander of the Second Gate on the Middle Walls, Sergeant.'

The sergeant shook his head. 'Idiot. Is he trying to get you killed? Do you want an escort as far as the Candlemaker's district?'

'No thanks. All that armour will just attract attention. We'll be quick.'

'Do you know the forward station?'

She shook her head.

'It's an enormous concrete fort two hundred yards east of here. Make your way there once you've dropped the woman off. Good luck.'

Emily nodded, then she set off, Cardova and Lady Omertia by her side. As soon as they left the protective line of armoured Blades, they started to receive looks of hatred and contempt from the remaining Hammers on the street.

An old woman spat at them. 'You don't belong here, Blades.'

'The dragon will get you next,' laughed a child, who was sitting by the side of the road. 'The dragon will roast all the Blades.'

Emily kept walking, her head down, the helmet uncomfortable. Cardova kept his eyes on the Hammers, his hand close to the hilt of his sword. They reached a junction and followed a narrow street flanked with brick houses, their fronts blacked by the soot spilling from dozens of chimneys. A large group of young Hammers stepped out onto the road in front of them, blocking their way.

Emily glanced over her shoulder. Another group had emerged from the narrow, shadow-filled alleyways that ran between the rows of houses behind them.

A man stepped forward from the crowd, wielding a large iron-worker's hammer.

'You shouldn't have come here, Blades,' he said. 'Let the woman and child go, then drop your weapons.'

'We are not Blades,' said Emily.

The man snorted. 'Right.'

'Listen to my voice,' said Emily, dropping her attempt at a Blade accent. 'Do I sound like a Blade to you? Cardova – speak to them.'

'She speaks the truth, Hammers,' said Lucius. 'I am a Banner officer. We are not Blades.'

'And, I'm not a Hammer,' said Lady Omertia, her aristocratic Roser accent piercing the air.

Voices began to murmur among the assembled Hammers.

'We entered Hammer territory illegally,' said Emily. 'I'm looking for an old friend. We are on the same side.'

The man walked up to them, the hammer leaning on his shoulder. 'Two Rosers, an Exile, and a baby?' He squinted at Emily's face. 'Do I know you?'

Emily lowered her voice. 'We need to get off the streets.'

'Take your helmet off.'

Emily shook her head. 'No. Hammers don't tend to have blonde hair, and I'll attract too much attention.'

The man frowned, then his eyes widened. 'Your Majesty?' he whispered.

'Keep it quiet,' said Emily. 'Please.'

The man said nothing, his face revealing a wealth of emotions, and for a moment Emily thought he was about to start weeping.

'You saved my family at the Eighth Gate, your Majesty,' the man said, his voice cracking. 'You saved all of us... You... I...' A tear rolled down his cheek, as the other Hammers stood around in silence.

'Who are they?' shouted one.

The man glanced up. 'Friends. They're friends. Clear the road.' He turned back to Emily. 'What do you need?'

'I'm looking for a man named Achan. He works at the Metallurgical Institute.'

'Achan? I know who he is, your Majesty. He was a friend of Corthie Holdfast, and he's well known among the Hammers. We'll take you to him.'

He gestured to a few of his comrades, and they came forward.

'We're escorting them to the Metallurgical Institute.'

'Why?' said one. 'Who are they?'

'Never mind that for now. Let's go.'

They set off down the street, a dozen armed Hammers flanking them. People watched from their windows or front doors as they passed. To them, Emily realised, it would look as though two Blades had been captured and were being led away to their doom, but no one tried to intervene.

'Things are as bad now as they ever were, your Majesty,' the chief Hammer whispered to her as they walked. 'The Blades have sealed up Hammer territory again, and they cut our rations if we fall behind our production schedules. They're bleeding us dry. The gods have won, haven't they? After all the blood that was spilled, and all the pain and loss, the gods have returned. Was it all in vain? Under your rule, we had a glimpse of freedom, and now it's worse than ever.'

'We will beat them,' Emily said.

'How, your Majesty? Simon is more powerful than any of the gods that used to rule us. There are rumours that even the former God-Queen is nothing but a slave next to him. And with Yendra dead...'

'I know it looks bleak, but we can't give up. Look at me. I've been driven from Pella, and then from Jezra, but I refuse to surrender. I will never surrender to Simon. You must have heard what happened to the

Fortress of the Lifegiver last night – the fight back against Simon has begun.'

They reached a large, concrete and brick structure next to a main road. To sunward, the light had increased, and dawn had come. Emily took a long breath of the smoky air, her memories stirred.

'Guard the entrance,' the chief Hammer said to his comrades. 'I'll take our guests inside.'

Emily noticed several of the Hammers whispering among themselves, and guessed that a rumour of her being in Hammer territory would soon spread, even to the ears of Simon. Along with the Reapers, the Hammers had always been the most loyal to the Aurelian Crown, and she knew that they would try to shield her from Simon's wrath if he came for her.

'I'm putting you all at risk,' she said, as they entered the building. 'If Simon discovers that I am here, he will come for me.'

'We'll try to keep you presence here quiet, your Majesty,' said the Hammer. 'You did well in keeping the helmet on. You have to remember that almost every Hammer here owes their life to you, and they all saw you at the Eighth Gate that day.'

The rundown old building was quiet, and they ascended two flights of stairs, and then the chief knocked on a door. To Emily's surprise, a green-skinned Fordian opened the door.

'We're looking for Achan,' said the Hammer.

The Fordian man eyed Emily and Cardova, then noticed the child in Lady Omertia's arms. He frowned.

'Who is it?' said a man's voice, then Achan appeared at the door, wearing a set of Hammer overalls.

Emily grinned. 'Hello.'

Achan squinted at her. 'Hello. Who...?' He paused, his face flushing. 'What? No.'

'Yes,' said Emily.

Achan stared, his mouth open.

'Do you know these people, Achan?' said the Fordian.

'Know them?' he said. 'I... it's the damn Queen. It's the Queen!'

'Keep your voice down,' said Cardova. 'Let's not announce it to the entire City.'

'Of course; sorry. Yes,' said Achan. He moved to the side. 'Come in; please. Are you hungry?'

They entered a large laboratory, filled with machinery and work-benches. A small group of men and women in overalls were sitting, and Achan's face flushed with excitement as he closed the door.

He fell to his knees. 'Your Majesty.'

The others in the room glanced at each other, then stared at Emily as she took her helmet off. Four others dropped to their knees immediately, while the others looked confused.

'It's the Queen,' said Achan, to those still sitting; 'the saviour of the Hammers.' He smiled at Emily. 'They're Exiles, your Majesty; they don't know you like we do.'

'Stand, please,' said Emily. 'There's no need to kneel.'

'You mentioned food?' said Lady Omertia. 'The child is hungry.'

'Yes, my lady,' said Achan, springing up. 'Yordi, fetch some breakfast for our guests. Your Majesty, please sit. That Blade uniform looks strange on you.'

'I used to be a Blade, for a short while,' said Emily, taking a seat.

The others in the room crowded round. Two of them were Fordians, and she recognised other Lostwell accents among some of the rest.

'Are there many Exiles working here?' she said.

'Oh yes, your Majesty,' said Achan. 'Princess Yendra sent us thousands of skilled workers from Lostwell when they first arrived. The Exiles might be discriminated against by the other tribes, but the Hammers have always welcomed them. They've brought us so many new ideas, from metal-working to ceramic production, and ballista design; their range of skills is adding to our knowledge daily. We're already producing a new type of iron plough for the Scythes; it's twice as efficient as the traditional designs we've used for centuries. It's been like having your eyes opened. Why have we never done this before? Sorry, your Majesty; that was a rhetorical question; I'm just a little over-excited by your sudden appearance here.' He glanced away, and wiped his eyes. 'It's good to see you, your Majesty. You don't know how much this means...'

He started to cry. Cardova put an arm on his shoulder.

'Who are you?' said Achan.

'My name is Lucius.'

One of the Fordians scowled. 'Banner?'

Cardova nodded. 'Yes.'

'Were you in Yoneath, Banner soldier?'

'I was.'

The Fordians tensed.

'Those days are long gone,' said Emily. 'In Jezra, the Fordians, Torduans and Shinstrans had made their peace with the Banner. We're all on the same side now. We have to put the past behind us, if we are to beat Simon.'

One of the Fordians turned to her. 'The Banner slaughtered thousands of my people in Yoneath – women, children, old folk. The streets ran with blood. They desecrated our holiest shrine, and left it in ruins.'

'Lostwell has gone,' said Cardova, 'along with Fordamere and everything else. And now Simon has the Banner jailed in Pella. I can live with your hate, but can we work together?'

'I went to Jezra,' said someone with a Torduan accent, 'before Simon took it. The Banner had changed. They were protecting the Exiles, not persecuting them.'

The Fordians looked unconvinced.

'Captain Cardova's loyalty is beyond question,' said Emily. 'Without him, I would be in the hands of Simon.'

'They have your family, your Majesty,' said Achan. 'Simon announced that they are going to be executed in Tara, as soon as you are caught. If that happens, the Hammers will rise up, and burn half the City down. Many are already hoarding weapons, ready to fight.'

Emily nodded. 'Can you help me get to Tara, Achan?'

The man blinked. 'What? You want to go to Tara, your Majesty? No. You can't. Stay here, in Hammer territory, where the people love you.'

'Achan, if Simon finds out where I am, then you are all in danger. He would kill every Hammer to get to me, and I already feel terrible about involving you in my secrets.'

The door opened, and Yordi hurried in, carrying a tray.

'Leave the food here,' said Achan; 'then everyone please leave. I would like to speak to the Queen alone for a moment.'

Yordi put the tray down onto a workbench, then accompanied the other workers out of the room. Achan walked over to the tray.

'There is food here for you all, including the child.' He glanced at Emily. 'Amalia's child, your Majesty?'

'How did you know that?'

'I have more jobs here in Hammer territory than merely working in the institute, your Majesty. I'm a member of the ruling council, and have access to a lot of intelligence that most people are unaware of. We have contacts in the Circuit, and in Pella. I knew that Amalia's son was in Jezra, and there was no mention of him when the town surrendered. You were lucky the Blades didn't stop you at the gates.'

'I think the fires at the Fortress of the Lifegiver distracted them,' she said, sitting by the workbench.

Her mother joined her, and started to cut up vegetables for the child.

'Can we trust the others to keep her Majesty's presence here quiet?' said Cardova.

'Everyone in this institute works for me,' said Achan. 'I will make sure none of them breathe a word of it. The Exiles here hate Simon; they think the world is going to end, just like Lostwell did. And the Hammers would never betray the Queen.'

Cardova nodded. 'I estimate that we have a day before Simon finds out.'

'Can you help us get to Tara?' said Emily.

'I could, your Majesty,' said Achan, sitting, 'but I would hate myself for it. You'd be delivering yourself into the hands of our enemies. Can I ask why you wish to go there?'

'I need to speak to Amalia.'

Achan stared at her. 'The God-Queen? The one who tried to

slaughter every inhabitant of Medio? She closed the Union Walls to the Hammers and Evaders; don't you remember, your Majesty? If she had prevailed, there would only be four tribes left in the City.'

'I know, Achan, but I have intelligence that she hates Simon as much as we do.'

'I'm sure she does, your Majesty. And? Are you hoping to strike a deal with her? She is nothing but pure evil; what kind of deal would she be satisfied with? She will want the City back; that will be her price for helping to overthrow Simon. You cannot trust her.'

Cardova looked like he wanted to say something, then he turned away.

'The captain agrees with you, Achan,' said Emily. 'So does my mother.'

Lady Omertia glanced at her. 'I have never voiced my opinion on the subject, dear.'

'Yes; I know, mother. That's what you do when you don't agree with me. Look; if I had other options available, I would snatch at them. Without Kelsey Holdfast, no mortals can stand up to Simon; if he came here, to Hammer territory, it would be a slaughter. Amalia might be our only chance.'

Achan shook his head. 'No, your Majesty. That sounds like a counsel of despair. There is a rumour that Simon doesn't really want to be here – he wants to leave and rejoin the other gods. If that's true, then perhaps we should lie low and wait. We can re-emerge from the shadows as soon as he has gone.'

'That could be a hundred years from now, Achan.'

Cardova turned back to face them. 'Have there been any large orders for weapons placed recently?'

Achan nodded. 'Yes. Armour, crossbows, ballistae, swords, packs, boots – you name it, the Blades have ordered it. The Hammer armament factories are working at full speed; we've had to drop several civilian projects to accommodate their demands.'

'Simon is building an army,' said Cardova. 'If I'm right, then he's planning to take the Blades with him when he leaves.'

'Good,' said Achan; 'let him have them. The Blades have been rotten since Marcus ruled them; even Yendra was unable to really change them – she didn't have enough time to finish the job before Montieth murdered her.'

'The Blades are not rotten; they are a tribe of the City,' said Emily, 'and I will not allow Simon to lead them to their destruction on another world. More importantly, if Simon travels to Implacatus, then the gods will discover where we have been hiding, and they will come here. Simon's departure will not be the end of them. The only safe course is to kill him before he can leave.'

Achan frowned. 'If Corthie were here...'

'Corthie isn't here,' said Emily, her temper fraying. 'We'll have to do this on our own. Therefore, no matter how distasteful it is, for me and for you, I have to try to come to an arrangement with Amalia.'

Achan said nothing.

Emily sighed. 'You think I've lost my mind.'

'No, your Majesty,' the Hammer said, 'but perhaps the strain and tension is taking its toll. When I was in Icehaven with Corthie, I knew that my family was trapped in Hammer territory, and I would have done anything to save them from the greenhides; anything. Your family are captive, your Majesty. Is your desire to be reunited with them overriding your wisdom?'

Emily glanced down. 'Tell me about the ships that leave Salt Quay each day.'

Achan stared at her, then sighed. 'Only one boat leaves Salt Quay each day for Auldan, your Majesty – the predawn vessel that takes the thirty victims to Pella to be executed – ten Hammers, ten Scythes and ten Blades. I could get you onto that boat, as Hammer guards, then you could get off at Tara on the way back.'

'That sounds perfect, Achan.'

'No, your Majesty; it's far from perfect. You would be walking into a nest of vipers. You may be right that Amalia hates Simon; if so, then she probably fears him too. She will deliver you up to him, as a sign of her loyalty, or to deflect accusations of disloyalty. She will not help you.'

'Then I will die,' said Emily. 'But at least I will have tried; at least I will have done everything within my power to save the City from Simon, just as I did everything I could to save the City from Amalia.'

'Are you ordering me to assist you, your Majesty?'

'Yes, Achan; if that helps.'

'It's what I'll tell the rest of the Hammers when they find out. I doubt it will save me. If your plan fails, they will hang me too; either that, or my name will be added to the list of daily victims. I will go down in infamy, as the man who sent Queen Emily Aurelian to her death.'

'I need you to look after my mother once we've gone,' said Emily. 'I am trusting you with her.'

Lady Omertia glanced up. 'Am I not coming to Tara, dear?'

'No, mother. Just me, Lucius and Maxwell.'

Her mother nodded. 'So be it. I hope you know what you're doing, dear.'

Emily sighed. 'So do I, mother; so do I.'

CHAPTER 18

COFFEE AND A CAKE

Serene, Implacatus – 18th Dunninch 5255

The smell of coffee filled Kelsey's nostrils as she dressed for the day. Her hair was still wet from the shower, and she was dripping water onto the threadbare rugs of the apartment. Barefoot, she walked into the tiny kitchen, where Vadhi was standing by the stove, watching the coffee pot.

'You were singing in the shower again,' said Vadhi.

'I know,' said Kelsey. 'I felt like it.'

Vadhi frowned.

'What's the matter?' said Kelsey. 'Is my singing that bad?'

'Well, forget the fact that the walls of this apartment are so thin that the neighbours are probably wondering why there's a woman living here; what is there to sing about? This apartment has one window, and it overlooks the inside of a cavern – we haven't seen the sky in days.'

'Aye,' said Kelsey, 'but there's warm water and coffee; a considerable step up from sleeping among the rats of the alleys.'

Vadhi picked up the pot from the stove and filled two mugs. 'And where's the old guy? Five nights we've slept here, and every morning when we get up, he's not here. Don't you think that's a bit strange? Where does he go?'

Kelsey shrugged, and gripped the handle of the steaming mug of coffee. She sipped the scalding liquid, and sighed.

She gazed at the mug, then gave it a kiss. 'I missed you. If only there was milk and sugar too, then you would be perfect. And maybe a shot of whisky.'

'Did you get drunk with him again last night?'

'We shared a bottle of wine, Vadhi; we were hardly shrieking through the streets in our underwear. Old Caelius can talk, all right. I've learned more about Van's past in a few days than I ever learned from him. Did you know that the Banners have a system of boarding schools for children to go to when both of their parents are away on operations? Van spent several years in one, because his mother and father were always getting sent to one place or another.'

'They would leave him here, on his own?'

'They could hardly take him with them. And, he wasn't on his own – there were hundreds of other children at his school who were in the same position. Cardova used to say that the Banners were like an extended family.'

A key rattled in the lock of the front door, and they turned, hearing Caelius enter the apartment. He strode into the kitchen, a large linen bag over his shoulder.

'Good morning, ladies,' he said. 'Sleep well?'

'Aye,' said Kelsey.

He smiled. 'It brightens my day to see two such beautiful young women in my home.'

'We're not ornaments,' said Kelsey.

'No, but you are very beautiful. Van is a lucky man.'

He walked to the kitchen table and dropped the bag onto it. He began to unpack the contents, laying out fresh bread and other food.

'I went to the market this morning,' he said; 'and got us all something nice for dinner. I'll cook. It makes a change to be preparing meals for more than one person after so long.' He glanced at Vadhi. 'Is there any of that coffee left?'

Vadhi nodded, and filled another mug.

'Thank you.' He took the mug, and sat next to the unpacked array of food on the table. He took a sip, and raised an eyebrow. 'Very strong, young lady.'

Vadhi shrugged. 'Sorry. It was the way we made it on Lostwell. Do you want me to put on a fresh pot?'

'No, no; it's fine,' he said; 'I needed something to wake me up.'

Kelsey eyed him. 'You're in a good mood today.'

'I am,' he said. 'Dredging up the past with you has been both painful and joyful.' He sipped his coffee again. 'Would you like to leave the apartment today?'

'What do you mean?' said Vadhi. 'Are you throwing us out?'

Caelius laughed. 'Of course not; wherever did you get that notion? I meant come out with me for a walk?'

'Is it safe?' said Kelsey.

'I think so. No gods ever come round these streets, so for five days there have been no mysterious cases of them losing their powers. I was watching a couple of them this morning; they were acting as if nothing's happened; as if it was all a bad dream.'

'That'll change if we go back outside.'

'Yes,' he said.

'I get it,' said Kelsey; 'it's a test. You want to see if I was telling the truth about my ability to block powers. That's alright; if you weren't suspicious then there would be something wrong with you.'

'I'm not suspicious,' he said; 'I believe you. Having said that, I would very much like to see it happen. I have my own reasons. One of them is purely selfish – I want to be able to walk through the city knowing that no damn god can read my mind. I want my thoughts to be free for once. That's what I was thinking about when I came in; that's what was making me smile.'

'Can we go somewhere to see the sunlight?' said Vadhi.

'Certainly.'

'Is there any sunlight on this level?'

'There's sunlight on every level of the city, Vadhi. Serene is built on a series of long terraces. It's true that much of the city is dug deep into the side of the mountain, but every level has access to the open air, even the slums.'

'And the gods live at the top?'

'Not quite. The gods live on a neighbouring peak, called Cumulus. No mortals are allowed there, unless expressly invited, and there's no way to get there without powers. The gods build little bridges from stone to connect Cumulus to Serene, then destroy them when they've finished with whatever business they had with us.' He laughed. 'Imagine Kelsey standing there, at the place where the bridges connect to Serene. The gods would fall a thousand feet down the mountainside. I'd pay good money to see that.'

Vadhi's eyes widened. 'Is that where we're going?'

'No,' he said; 'not today, at any rate. Let's just go for a simple stroll, and get a bit of fresh air. Sound good, girls?'

Kelsey hesitated. She had successfully skulked around the city for days, but that had been just her and Vadhi. If Caelius was fairly well-known in the Banner district, then people might begin to wonder who she was.

'I think it sounds great,' said Vadhi. 'Are there shops?'

Caelius smiled at her. 'Thinking of buying something?'

Vadhi's face flushed. 'Just a hairbrush and some make up. I hate looking at myself in your bathroom mirror; I'm a mess.'

'You are not,' he said. 'But, if you insist, then we can visit a shop or two; I'll buy whatever you need.'

'Thanks.'

'What about you, Kelsey?' he said.

'I think we should be very careful,' she said. 'We don't want to attract too much attention.'

'I know a few ways in and out of the Banner district that are quiet and out-of-the-way.'

'What about your neighbours?'

'I haven't spoken to any of them in years.' His eyes narrowed. 'Everyone in this block is ex-Banner of the Soaring Eagle; I got put here after the Golden Fist was disbanded.' He glanced away, and Kelsey could sense his anger return.

'When shall we go?' she said.

'How about now?' he said, a smile coming back to his lips.

———

Caelius Logos led them out of the Banner district by a narrow set of stairs that descended from the rear of a fortified complex close to where he lived. Unlike the main stairs, there were no gods present, and only a handful of Banner soldiers were on duty. They nodded to Caelius, and let him pass. They glanced at Kelsey and Vadhi, but made no comment.

Caelius took them to a street lined with market stalls, and bought a few things for Vadhi, spoiling her as if she were his daughter, while Kelsey remained quiet, her anxiety growing deeper the longer they were outside. There were no gods nearby that she could sense, but Caelius seemed to know a lot of people, and chatted to a few.

'I thought you didn't mingle with people,' Kelsey muttered, as they walked along the street, Caelius carrying the linen bag over his shoulder.

'I talk to ex-Golden Fist veterans,' he said. 'This is where a lot of the Banner soldiers do their shopping. Now, if I recall correctly, Vadhi was asking to see the sunlight.'

'It is close?' said the Torduan.

'Just a couple of minutes away.'

They turned left at a crossroads, and walked between high housing blocks, cut into the sides of the cavern. Ahead of them, Kelsey could see a patch of light, and the air quality improved. At the end of the street, the ground opened up into a long, wide terrace, open to the sky. A few little cafés were dotted about amid the grass and trees, and Vadhi grinned.

'Can we stop for a coffee?' she said. 'And, maybe a cake? Look at the cakes that café has; can we go there?'

'Perhaps not that café,' said Caelius. 'Follow me; I know a good place.'

They strode out onto the grass, and Kelsey felt the sun on her skin. She gazed out at the view. Clouds were hugging the side of the mountain below them, but the sky above was clear and blue. Caelius led them to the right for a few minutes, passing little orchards and gardens, until they reached a café next to a large archway, where a few stone buildings sat. Caelius took a seat facing the archway, and gestured to Vadhi and Kelsey to join him.

'This is great,' said Vadhi. 'It's so good to be outside again; and it's nice to see a blue sky, instead of a red one.'

Caelius raised an eyebrow, but said nothing.

A waiter approached, and passed them some printed menus.

'Cakes and coffee, please,' said Caelius. 'No, I'll have a tea; that coffee this morning is still making my head buzz.'

The waiter bowed his head, and walked into the café. Kelsey kept an eye on Caelius. He kept glancing over at the archway, as if expecting to see something.

'What's in those buildings?' she said.

He shrugged. 'Administrative goings-on,' he said. 'Offices and clerks and suchlike.' He gave her a funny look. 'Your range is a hundred yards, yes? Is that the total diameter, or the radius?'

'The radius,' she said. 'I cover a hundred yards in every direction around me.'

He nodded.

'Any particular reason for that question?'

'Over thirty thousand square yards, eh?'

'I haven't done the calculation.'

'It's a simple one – three and a bit times ten thousand.'

'I know how to work it out.'

Vadhi gave her a look.

Kelsey ignored her. 'Caelius, are we at this particular café for a reason?'

'Yes. I like it.'

'Is that the only reason?'

He laughed. 'You're very suspicious this morning. You are also correct; I'm waiting for someone.'

Kelsey glared at him. 'Who?'

The waiter returned at that moment, and placed a pot of coffee, a pot of tea, and a plate of cakes onto the table.

'I'll pay now,' said Caelius, reaching into a pocket.

'Certainly, sir,' said the waiter. 'That will be eleven silver pennies.'

Caelius counted out the small coins, and dropped them into the waiter's hand, along with a generous tip.

The waiter bowed. 'Many thanks, sir.'

'I thought you had very little money,' said Kelsey, once the waiter had gone. 'How are you affording to treat us like this? Eleven silver pennies would have bought Vadhi and me food for three days in the slums.'

'Shut up,' said Vadhi. 'Why are you trying to ruin our day out? Caelius is being nothing but kind to us.'

Kelsey looked away, feeling shame bite her. 'Sorry.'

'It's alright,' said Caelius. He glanced back at the archway, and his eyes tightened. 'Kelsey, come with me, please. Vadhi, stay here and keep our table. Kelsey and I won't be long.'

'Why?' said Kelsey.

'I'll explain later,' said Caelius, standing. 'Now, please, Miss Holdfast.'

Kelsey sighed and got to her feet. Caelius began to stride away towards the archway, and Kelsey hurried to keep up.

'Where are we going?' she said.

Caelius nodded ahead of them. 'We're following that man; the one I was waiting for.'

Kelsey peered ahead. A man was walking down the street, wearing long, flowing robes.

'He's a god,' she whispered; 'I can sense him.'

'He's not just a god, Kelsey; he's an Ancient. Do you know what that means?'

'Aye. Why are we following him?'

'How are you in stressful situations? Can you remain calm?'

'It depends.'

'You've been in battles, though?'

'From the back of a dragon.'

'That should suffice. Stay close, and whatever you do, don't panic.'

They followed the man for a hundred yards, their pace slowly catching him up. When they were right behind him, his head turned, and he glared at Caelius.

'You?' he said. 'I'd hoped I'd seen the last of you a long time ago, Logos.'

Caelius bowed his head. 'Great Ancient; what a coincidence, seeing you here.'

The Ancient glanced around, but the street was deserted. He smiled. 'I could kill you, Logos, with a snap of my fingers, and no one would know.'

'Try it.'

'Don't tempt me.'

Caelius pulled a knife from the inside of his coat. 'Does this tempt you?'

The Ancient's face twisted with fury. 'Are you threatening me, you pathetic mortal? Have you lost your mind?'

Caelius sprang at the god, his speed startling Kelsey. The mortal man bundled the Ancient into the shadows of an alleyway, his knife clenched in his right fist.

He glanced over his shoulder at Kelsey. 'Stay there, and keep a watch on the road. This won't take long.'

Kelsey stared. The Ancient was struggling in Caelius's grip, his eyes wide with terror and panic. Caelius raised the knife, and Kelsey looked away. She heard the sound of the blade striking home; once, twice, then she put her hands to her ears, her eyes scanning the street for signs of anyone approaching; her hands shaking.

She felt a tap of her shoulder and jumped.

Caelius nodded to her. 'All done; let's get out of here.'

They hurried back down the road, Caelius with a hand on Kelsey's lower back to steer her.

'What... Who...?' she muttered. 'Caelius, you have blood on your face.'

He halted, and removed a handkerchief from a pocket. He handed it to her.

'Could you?'

Kelsey wiped the blood from the man's cheek, her fingers trembling.

'You kept calm,' he said. 'Good girl.'

'You bastard,' she said. 'You dragged us out here purely so you could use me to kill that god, didn't you?'

'Yes.'

She glared at him. 'Did you make sure? Did you finish the job?'

'Do you think I'm an amateur, Kelsey? I removed his head and cut out his heart. He won't be coming back.'

'You've killed gods before?'

'No. That was my first.' He smiled. 'It felt... wonderful. The moment when he realised his powers weren't working will live with me forever. The look on his face... was perfect.'

They resumed their pace, and emerged through the archway into the sunlight. Caelius smiled at Vadhi as they sat back down at the table.

'Where did you go?' said the Torduan. 'I didn't like being left alone.'

'Sorry about that,' said Caelius; 'but it's done now.' He sipped his tea. 'Lovely.'

Kelsey slumped in her chair, her eyes on the clouds drifting by, and her anger growing.

———

They walked back to Caelius's tenement block after finishing their drinks. Caelius chatted the entire way, regaling Vadhi with stories of the Banners, while Kelsey trudged along in silence. For every step she took, she half-expected soldiers to come rushing towards them, but she heard no sounds of alarm. Once back in the Banner district, Caelius handed over a single copper coin for a printed news sheet, folded it, and placed it inside the linen bag.

They reached the tenement and ascended the stairs to his apartment, and Kelsey almost broke down as soon as the door was closed behind them.

'You'd better explain yourself!' she shouted at Caelius, as he locked the door.

'Explain what?' said Vadhi.

Caelius glanced at the Torduan. 'Go into the bedroom for a moment. I need to speak to Kelsey about something personal to do with Van.' He handed her the linen bag. 'You can try on some of your new clothes; I bet you look stunning in them.'

Vadhi glanced from Kelsey to Caelius, then walked away.

'Let's go to the kitchen,' said Caelius.

Kelsey nodded, and followed him into the tiny room. Caelius sat, and stretched his arms.

'A great day,' he said, 'and you made it possible, Kelsey.'

Kelsey remained standing. 'I don't like what you did.'

'I thought you hated the gods as much as me.'

'I do. That's not what I meant. Why did you trick me into it? It's the lies I don't like.'

'I wasn't sure if you'd panic. Would you have been able to walk calmly through the market, looking at clothes, if you'd known what I was going to do?'

'It was just so... cold-blooded. You know what? You remind me of my mother, and not in a good way.'

'She sounds like the kind of person I'd like to meet.'

'She has battle-vision; she'd kick your arse. Oh, and there's one detail you should know about how my powers work, before you try anything like that again. If that Ancient had touched your skin with his fingers, he would have killed you. My ability only blocks powers that go through the air.'

Caelius's face paled. 'I see. I didn't know that.'

'Well, if we'd talked about it first, I would have told you. Gloves, next time; aye? Now, who in Pyre's name was he?'

Caelius let out a long breath. 'Hold on, I need a drink.' He lifted a bottle of wine from the table and opened it, his hands shaking.

'You were lucky,' she said.

'I now realise that,' he said, pouring himself a drink.

'I'm not a girl,' said Kelsey; 'I've been fighting the gods since I was a teenager; for ten years. I've been involved in wars and sieges, and I'm a damn dragon-rider for Pyre's sake. Don't treat me like a child.'

Caelius downed his wine. 'I'm sorry, Kelsey. I should have told you. You seem so young and innocent to me that I thought... never mind; I was wrong. Now, that man I killed; that Ancient – his name was Sabat, and I've longed to make him suffer for years.'

'Why?'

'It was his orders that disbanded the Banner of the Golden Fist.'

Kelsey frowned. 'You killed him for that?'

He refilled his glass. 'Yes. He deserved to die. The Golden Fist was my family, especially after my wife died. It was all I had left, and he took it away. I can see from your expression that you don't understand. The Golden Fist was in existence for over seven hundred years, and they closed it down because of one mistake. The failure of that operation was Renko's fault, not the Banner's. I lost my home, most of my pension and benefits, and, worst of all, I was no longer around my old comrades. They helped me get through my wife's death, and then Van's disgrace; and now they've been scattered to a hundred different Banners, all because the gods were embarrassed, and they had to blame someone. I tried to speak to Sabat about it many times, but he laughed in my face, and called my son a traitor.' He glanced at Kelsey. 'If that's not enough for you, then there are plenty of other cruel and callous things he did. I could sit here all day and recite them to you, but one example should suffice. You're aware of the on-going war on Dragon Eyre? It was Sabat who sanctioned the first massacres of the indigenous population, in order to make way for new settlers from Implacatus. Half a million were killed in six months – on his orders.'

'Alright, I get it; he was a bad sort. Fair enough; I'm not going to judge you for killing Sabat.'

'I did it, though, didn't I? I wasn't dreaming – I killed an Ancient?'

'You did. I bet you wish you could tell all of your old Banner comrades, but you're going to have to resist the temptation.'

'I know. Ha! I really killed him.' He refilled his glass. 'It doesn't bring the Banner back, but I know that all the Golden Fist veterans will hear of his death.'

'So will Edmond.'

'They'll suspect another god; for who else could kill an Ancient?'

'I don't know; Edmond's not stupid, and he knows who I am, and what I can do. Which is, you know, why he's after me. He might put two and two together.'

'No doubt. Let's hope his wedding preparations keep him occupied for a while.'

'He's getting married, is he?'

'Yes. To another Ascendant. She was on Lostwell; you might have heard of her – Belinda.'

Kelsey blinked. Her mouth opened, but no words came out.

'I see that you've heard of the Third Ascendant. She used to be a rebel, many years ago. Edmond brought her back here before he destroyed Lostwell, and they've announced that they are going to get married later this year. They're in love, apparently, although I doubt that Ascendants can really feel love.' He sipped his wine. 'Did you fight against her on Lostwell?'

'Wait. Belinda is on Implacatus?'

Caelius laughed. 'That's what I said.'

'Have you seen her?'

'Of course not. Sergeants don't get invited to Cumulus. In my entire life, I have never once caught a glimpse of an Ascendant in the flesh. Ancients, yes, but never an Ascendant. Obviously, I'm aware that two of the bastards were sent to Lostwell, but that was a tremendous breach of tradition, and to imagine that both of them lost their lives there is almost beyond my comprehension. Are you hoping to get invited to the wedding?'

Kelsey stared at him. 'This can't be true. Could Edmond be making it all up?'

'I haven't heard any rumours that contradict her being in Cumulus. I know a few senior officers who have been there, and they seemed to believe that she was there; they said that many gods were talking about her return to Implacatus.'

'This is hard to accept. I was with Belinda on Lostwell. We didn't always get on, but she was a good friend of my little brother. More importantly, she was on our side, or at least I think she was. And now she's marrying Edmond? That doesn't make sense.'

'I'll tell you what doesn't make sense, Kelsey – the way you're talking about her. Belinda is the Third Ascendant – she's your enemy. All of the Ascendants are your enemy; there are no "good" ones among them.'

'No. She's not like the others. Wait; let me explain. My sister utterly wiped her mind, and she had to learn everything again, from the beginning; how to speak, everything. She has no memories of the previous thirty millennia; my sister destroyed it all. Then she helped us in the fight against the gods who had come with her from Lostwell, and she fought again for us on Lostwell.'

'What can I say? All I know is what I read in the news sheet. The Second Ascendant brought the Third home, to Cumulus, where she's been living ever since. And then, a few months ago, they announced that they were engaged to be married. There's going to be an enormous party; even the mortals in Serene are getting the day off. Maybe her memories have come back.'

'Karalyn told me that was impossible.'

'A few days ago, I thought mortals having powers was impossible. I'm sorry that this news seems to have upset you. To me, Belinda is just another Ascendant. Did you perhaps place too much faith in her?'

Vadhi came striding into the kitchen before Kelsey could respond.

'That's a very smart outfit, young lady,' said Caelius, smiling. 'You were right; your hair does look better brushed.'

'Never mind my hair,' said Vadhi, her eyes wide. She held out the news sheet in front of them. 'Look; they know we're here.'

Kelsey grabbed the news sheet. It was folded open on page two, where a small article sat beneath a drawing of a woman's face.

'Shit,' she groaned. 'I think that's meant to be me.' Her eyes scanned the text. The article was assuring the public of Serene that the cause of the strange disturbances in the gods' powers had been discovered. The Blessed and Sacred Second Ascendant, Lord Edmond, had announced that an aberrant mortal, a sub-human created by Nathaniel, the disgraced Fourth Ascendant, was roaming the streets of Serene. The abomination had the power to hinder the powers of the gods, but was of no threat to mortals. If seen, she was to be apprehended and handed over to the Banners.

She glanced at the last line – an enormous reward was being offered for her capture, and the picture of the "abomination" was given a name – Kelsey Holdfast.

'How could they have discovered we were here?' said Vadhi, her face pale.

'I don't know,' said Kelsey.

Caelius frowned. 'If Belinda knew you well, could she have sensed you?'

'No. It'll be down to all those times I've blocked their powers. Edmond recognises the pattern, even though he can't see me, and now he's plastered my face all over the news sheet.'

'But,' said Vadhi, 'does this mean we have to stay indoors again? It's not my picture in the news sheet. No one will recognise me if I go out.'

'No,' said Caelius, 'but any god could read your mind once you'd gone a hundred yards from Kelsey. I think it's best if we all stay in for a while. It's lucky I bought so much food this morning.'

Vadhi sat, and put her head in her hands. 'Will they find us?'

'Only if they do a house-to-house search,' said Caelius, 'which is exceedingly unlikely.'

'Or,' said Kelsey, 'if someone you spoke to today saw me there with you, and then reads the news sheet.'

Caelius squinted at the drawing of Kelsey, then shook his head.

'We'll be fine,' he said. 'They got your nose all wrong.'

CHAPTER 19

SURVIVAL INSTINCT

T ara, Auldan, The City – 19th Mikalis 3423

'Here you are,' said Kagan. 'I've been looking for you for half an hour.'

Amalia glanced up at him from an armchair. 'It's a large palace.'

'What are you doing in here?' he said, glancing into the chamber.

'Thinking.'

'Lord Chamberlain was waiting for you, along with a few others from the Roser council.'

'Did I miss them? What a shame.'

'They wanted you to approve a list of names for execution. They have identified a hundred people to cover the next ten days. I was no good to them; I didn't recognise any of the names.'

'I don't care who is on the list. They want my approval so that they can blame me for the deaths.'

'That's what I thought too. Lady Lydia delivered her hundred Sander officers to Pella yesterday; the entire leadership of her militia. Apparently, she begged for mercy in front of Simon, but he killed them anyway.'

'Of course he did. I assume Lydia went crawling back to Port Sanders?'

'Yes. Lord Chamberlain said she was weeping.'

Amalia said nothing, so Kagan walked in and sat down on a chair next to her.

'Do you know the significance of this room, Kagan?'

He glanced around at the dust-sheets covering the furniture. 'No.'

'This is where Aila killed Marcus. It was their honeymoon suite. She murdered him after the wedding, as soon as they were alone. It was the moment my world fell apart. Prior to that, I was triumphant over my enemies, and my plans were coming close to fruition.' She shook her head. 'I didn't think the little bitch was capable of overcoming Marcus. She melted half of his face off with salve, and then beheaded him. I underestimated her. What a mistake. That wasn't my worst, however. Elevating Marcus in the first place was a bigger mistake, though I'd never admit that to any of my grandchildren. He was an oaf, blinded by desire for his cousin, and I made him Prince of Tara.'

Kagan sat in silence, his eyes on her.

'Going back further,' she went on, 'I was also mistaken to trust my husband. I believed Malik when he told me that he had executed Yendra for slaying Michael. Why didn't I insist on proof? I wanted to believe him, that's why; just as I wanted to believe that Marcus was capable of ruling the City. So stupid of me.'

'Is it wise to sit in the darkness, dwelling on your old mistakes?' said Kagan.

'Probably not, but what else is there to do? When you have a memory as long as mine, you have more room for mistakes. The errors of a god can ripple outwards for centuries, and we are living through the consequences of mine. It's my fault that Simon is in control of the City. If I had acted differently when I had the power to do so, none of this would have happened.'

'True, but at the same time, Maxwell wouldn't have been born.'

'Perhaps that would have been better.'

'Don't say that.'

'Why not? For all the joy Maxwell has brought me, I now live in fear – fear of what might happen to him.'

'I don't think Emily will hurt him.'

She glanced up. 'It is not Emily I'm scared of. If we get Maxwell back, then he will fall under Simon's control. The Ascendant will use him to force us to do his bidding. It sounds terrible, but I trust Emily with his safety more than I do Simon. Emily wants Elspeth back; that's her motivation for keeping Maxwell from harm. What will stop Simon from hurting him?'

'Dear gods; you're right. I've been so focussed on getting him back, that I hadn't thought about what comes afterwards.'

'This leaves me with a dilemma.'

'You mean, if Simon was right, and Emily is making her way here?'

'Yes.'

'Should we...?'

'Don't say it, Kagan. It's bad enough that you're thinking it.'

'You're thinking it too.'

'No, I'm not. I was wrong; there's no dilemma. If Emily is foolish enough to come here, then she will die with the rest of her family in Prince's Square. That's the thought you need to keep in your mind, Kagan; that, and nothing else. Do not give Simon any excuse to kill you.'

'There's still hope,' he said. 'There's Jade, and the dragon.'

Amalia glared at him. 'Jade is making it worse, not better. Simon wants salve and Blades, and she has attacked them both. We want Simon to leave the City as soon as possible, and all she has achieved is to delay his plans.'

'She's showing more courage than anyone else.'

'Jade isn't courageous – she's a fool. It's not entirely her fault; nine centuries in Greylin Palace would turn anyone into a fool. She doesn't understand the consequences of her actions. If she did, she wouldn't leave her mountain hideout. Instead, she kills Felice and burns the Fortress of the Lifegiver to the ground. Nearly a thousand Blades were incinerated, to add to the three thousand killed in the failed first attack on Jezra. How does that help the City?'

Kagan eyed her. 'You sound like you care about the mortals.'

Amalia snorted. 'Do I? Oh dear. I suppose I do care about them, in a political sense. Without Blades, there would be no one to guard the Great Walls from the Eternal Enemy.'

'But you opened the walls to the greenhides.'

'I know, but I evacuated the Blades from Medio first. I'd rather a hundred thousand Evaders perish than ten thousand Blades.'

'Sometimes, I think that you're developing a conscience, and then you say something like that.'

'Sorry to disappoint you.'

'Are you?'

'No. I am what I am, Kagan. I am the ruthless, mass-murdering God-Queen, and I am also the mother of Maxwell, who wants to live in peace. I am both of those things. On Lostwell, I was different. There, I was on the run, and no one cared that I used to be the Queen and ruler of this City, but here? Here, I am forever trapped by my past. That's what Naxor and the others don't understand – they only see one side of me, the side I revealed to them, and they ignore or forget the hundreds of years when I never left my palaces. I created this City; I built the Union Walls, the Middle Walls, and the Great Walls. I made it possible. I slaughtered the greenhides and killed their queens; me. What is my reward? Everyone loathes me. You are the only person I trust, Kagan. You know me, and yet you haven't walked out.'

Kagan said nothing, thinking of the times he had been close to running.

A sound of crashing and raised voices echoed through the corridors outside the chamber.

Amalia lowered her face. 'Simon. What does he want now?'

They stood. Kagan took her hand, and they kissed.

'Whatever it is,' Kagan said; 'we'll face him together.'

'Clear your thoughts; empty your mind, then think of something positive. The angrier he is, the less likely he'll be focussed enough to delve too deeply into your head.'

Kagan nodded, and they left the room. They followed the source of the shouting, and Simon's voice rang through to Kagan's ears. The Ascendant was in a rage, that seemed clear. They reached the throne room with the long, curving window. Naxor was sitting on the floor by the wall, his eyes wide as Simon was unleashing his fury on the furniture. He was wielding the Axe of Rand, and using it to destroy the pair of thrones that sat on a raised platform. The dark blade was slicing through the gilded wood, and fragments were flying all over the room.

Simon turned, and paused, the axe mid-swing.

Amalia bowed. 'Greetings, your Grace.'

'Shut your stupid mouth,' Simon snarled. 'I should have sent you to the Bulwark, and kept Felice here. The swine cut her head off! Felice was the only trustworthy and competent servant I had in this filthy City; her death has left me with nothing but the dregs. The losers. The worthless.'

'Her death was a blow, your Grace.'

'You disgust me. You didn't even like Felice. You were always jealous that I chose her to share my bed, rather than you. You desire me, don't you?'

'No, your Grace.'

'Don't lie to me. You are attracted to power, and I am the most powerful being you have ever known. I hold the lives of every mortal and god within the palm of my hand, and the thought of being with me makes you giddy. Admit it.'

'There is nothing to admit, your Grace.'

'Liar. Whore.'

'Don't call her that,' said Kagan.

Simon turned to him, and raised a finger. Kagan fell to his knees, choking. His fingers clutched at his throat, but no air was reaching his lungs. Simon took a few steps towards him, smiling.

'I will call her whatever I please, mortal,' he said. 'Now, why haven't you fulfilled the one task I set you? Where is the false Queen? The days of Mikalis are passing, and yet I see no sign that you are any closer to capturing her. Do you know what happens if you fail to apprehend her before the end of the month? You will be gutted on the gallows of Prince's Square in her place, that's what, after I've forced you to kill Elspeth with your own hands.'

Kagan's sight started to fade, and he felt himself weakening. He swayed.

Simon snarled out a laugh, and released him. Kagan toppled to the floor, gasping for air, as Amalia crouched by him.

'Look at the two of you,' Simon said; 'crawling on the ground like insects.'

Amalia glanced up at him. 'Did you come here for a particular reason, your Grace?'

'This is my City – I go where I please. But, as you asked, I came here to present you with Naxor. I can't abide him for a moment longer, and if he stays with me, then I will kill him.' He turned to the demigod sitting by the wall. 'I have almost killed him several times. If I didn't have such a need for servants, his brains would be all over the Royal Palace.'

'I thought you had assigned him to the Circuit, your Grace.'

'That didn't even last a day. No sooner had I left him in charge, than I had to return to rescue him from hordes of Evaders who were storming Redmarket Palace. I would have let them have their way with him, but I learned of Felice's death. This is your last chance, Naxor. When I return here, you will prove your loyalty to me, or you will die.'

Naxor spluttered. 'But, your Grace...'

'Silence.'

'Where are you going, your Grace?' said Amalia.

'Yocasta, first,' he said, 'to collect more greenhides for the Circuit. It's time that the Evaders learned to fear me. Then, I shall once more travel to the Eastern Mountains, to hunt for Jade and the renegade dragon, and to transport a batch of refined salve back to the City for safekeeping. I also need to check on Matilda, to ensure that she has settled into her new home in the Iceward Range.' He sighed. 'I weary of this City. I might destroy it when I leave.' He smiled. 'Did I say that out loud? Whoops.'

He brandished the Quadrant and vanished.

Kagan felt a burst of healing power from Amalia's touch, and the pain disappeared from his throat.

'Did you hear that?' cried Naxor. 'Did you hear what he said?'

'Shut up, Naxor,' said Amalia, as she and Kagan stood. 'If you think I am remotely interested in anything you have to say, then you are gravely mistaken.' She glanced at the destruction of the two thrones. 'They were over a thousand years old. Now, they're firewood.'

Naxor leapt to his feet. 'I don't think you're taking this seriously. Simon is insane. He's going to kill us all.'

Amalia shrugged. 'Hopefully, he'll start with you.'

'We have to do something, grandmother.'

'Is this a joke, Naxor? You were the one who gave Simon the salve in the first place. Come on, Kagan; the voice of my grandson is starting to irritate me.'

She and Kagan walked from the room, and Naxor rushed after them.

'I have to remain in Maeladh Palace,' the demigod said. 'You heard what Simon said – I have to be here when he returns.'

'So?' said Amalia.

'Well, that could be days from now. Where will I sleep?'

'I don't care, Naxor. There are dozens of empty rooms in the palace. Find one, and crawl into it.'

'Slow down, grandmother,' he said, as he hurried after them; 'we need to talk.'

'No, we don't.'

'Are we going to sit back and allow Simon to destroy the City?'

'You don't care about the City.'

'Alright, but I care about my own life.'

'Simon will read these thoughts from your head when he gets back.'

'He's going to kill me anyway. He hasn't trusted me since I withheld the knowledge of the salve mine from him. I thought he was going to kill me that day, but he gave me another chance. I'm all out of chances, grandmother.'

'Do you expect me to feel sorry for you?'

'No, but I do expect you to act in your own interests. Why do you think I kept the salve mine a secret? Because I was thinking ahead, to a time when Simon is no longer here, but with every day that passes, that future looks less likely. He's never going to leave us in peace. Even if he goes to Implacatus to fight the other Ascendants, then he will keep returning here, for salve, soldiers, weapons, and greenhides. We'll never be free of him. Grandmother. We made a terrible mistake!'

Amalia came to a halt in the corridor, turned, and slapped Naxor across the face.

'Your rash words will get us all killed,' she said. 'Is that what you want? You think Simon is going to kill you, so you wish for me and Kagan to die by your side?'

Naxor held his cheek. 'No, grandmother. I don't want to die.'

'I don't think Simon cares what you want. You can stay inside the walls of the palace, but I don't want to see you. And stay away from the Aurelians.'

She strode away. Kagan glanced at Naxor.

'Speak to her, Kagan,' said the demigod. 'She listens to you.'

'And tell her what? That, despite your record of treachery, we should now trust you? Do you think we're stupid?'

'No. Cowards, maybe, but not stupid.'

'You hypocrite,' said Kagan. 'I didn't see you object when Simon was torturing Silva, or when the greenhide queen ate the old servant. You are the biggest coward of them all.'

'I am; I admit it freely. I am also terrified. I thought, we all thought, that Simon could not possibly be any worse than the Aurelians. And, even if he was, then he would be leaving soon, so it wouldn't matter. All we had to do was hang on long enough for him to go, and then we would be free again. We were wrong, Kagan. I know it was me who gave him the salve, but you would have done the same; we are all responsible for bringing the Ascendant to the City. I think that means we also have a responsibility to rid the City of him.'

Kagan laughed. 'You almost had me for a moment there; right up until you mentioned feeling responsible for the City.'

'You don't know me, Kagan. You think you do, but you don't.'

Kagan watched as Naxor stormed off down the corridor, heading in the opposite direction from Amalia, the heels of his boots clacking off the marble floor.

Amalia raised an eyebrow as she sipped from her glass. 'Please don't tell me that you've fallen for his lies.'

'No,' said Kagan; 'but I do believe that he's scared. He isn't making that up.'

'Of course he's scared. Who isn't?'

'The question is, can we use his fear?'

'To do what?'

Kagan sat back on the long couch. 'I don't know. Could we arrange a situation where Naxor might do something rash? If he could distract Simon, even for a few moments, then we might be able to act.'

'I don't think you quite understand how this works. Simon will read this plan from your mind the moment he looks at you. It is impossible to take him by surprise, unless your name ends in Holdfast.'

'Is that it? We've given up?'

'No. We can hardly give up something we haven't started. Resisting Simon is futile; we knew that the moment we released him from Yocasta. My sole aim is to get Maxwell back, and then try to survive.'

'Even if he wipes out the City?'

'I don't have the answers, Kagan.'

'I have answers,' said Naxor, from the doorway.

Amalia glared at him. 'I thought I told you that I didn't want to see you?'

'I know,' said Naxor, coming into the room, 'but how can I stay away when I have a million thoughts running wild through my head?' He produced a vial from a pocket. 'My last concentrated salve. Simon doesn't know I have it. If we threw it into his face, then he would be blinded for a few minutes. It's how Aila got Marcus.'

'I am perfectly aware of that,' said Amalia.

'We'll need a distraction for it to work,' Naxor went on, approaching the couch and sitting. 'Something that will draw his attention, to give me time to throw the salve at him. We'll also need to do it somewhere with access to weapons, or something sharp enough to cut his head off. Three jobs, and there's three of us – one to distract, one to throw, and the other to chop.'

Amalia started to laugh. 'You're mad.'

'Kagan's a strong lad,' said Naxor; 'he can wield the sword, or whatever we use. That leaves you, grandmother. Think of something that will distract Simon. I know, tell him that you do actually desire him. He loves to hear things like that. When he turns to you, I'll act next, and then Kagan will have a few moments to finish him off.'

'Let's play along,' said Amalia; 'let's pretend that I am intrigued by your plan. It's a terrible plan, but let us imagine that it isn't. Even if I wanted Simon dead, then what makes you think I would trust you to play your part, Naxor? Do you remember the salve mine behind the Royal Palace? Or, the cavern in Fordamere? They are but two examples of when you have betrayed my trust. There comes a time in every liar's life when no one believes them any more, and I passed that stage with you a long time ago.'

Naxor nodded. 'Do you have any brandy?'

Amalia narrowed her eyes. 'Weren't you listening to me?'

'All I heard was that you're considering my plan.' He stood, and walked to a row of cupboards, which he began opening. 'Now, where are you hiding the brandy?'

'What happened in Fordamere?' said Kagan.

'Naxor tried to steal my Quadrant.'

The demigod looked up from the cupboards. 'You were about to flee. I was trying to stop you.'

'What nonsense! I was actually trying to help Corthie, Blackrose and the others, for once. Van and Silva had persuaded me to help rescue Kelsey Holdfast, and we did, from right under the noses of the Ascendants. For one tiny moment, I was on the same side as my former enemies.' She shook her head. 'And then Naxor ruined it all. I panicked, and fled. If he hadn't interfered, then things might have turned out very differently, for all of us.'

'Wait,' said Kagan; 'you were helping the Holdfasts?'

'It sounds crazy now, but yes. The Ascendants had taken Kelsey, and I returned her to her brother. Naturally, few believed my motives were honest, but we were facing a common enemy.'

'What would have happened if Naxor hadn't tried to steal the Quadrant?'

'We would have tried to rescue Belinda next, or we would have escaped, together. I admit that my motives were partly selfish; I wanted Belinda back.'

'That doesn't sound selfish.'

'I had a plan at the time to bring Belinda here, to the City. I was going to need her to retake power.'

Naxor laughed. 'See? You wanted to bring an Ascendant back to the City. You succeeded; well done!'

'Shut up.'

'Tell him what you did next. No hypotheticals this time; tell Kagan what you actually did.'

'I panicked, as I said. I fled, and took Kelsey Holdfast with me, along with Aila, though that was an accident; she was clinging onto me at the time. Kelsey was insurance, to make sure the Ascendants couldn't find me. It worked well, until they escaped.'

Naxor opened another cupboard door. 'Ah, here we are. At last.'

He walked back to the couch with a bottle and some glasses clutched in his hands. He sat, opened the bottle, and poured.

Kagan eyed him. 'Why did you try to steal the Quadrant?'

'To stop my grandmother escaping.'

'Stop it. Can you not tell the truth, for once in your life? What would you have done if you had managed to get the Quadrant in Fordamere?'

Naxor sipped from his glass. 'Splendid.'

'Answer me, Naxor.'

'Fine. I would have transported us out of that hideous cavern immediately. Belinda didn't want to be saved; she had gone over to the Ascendants. Leksandr, Arete and thousands of Banner soldiers were attacking. We needed to leave. Once I had taken everyone to a safe location, then I would have disappeared. I had plans to develop the salve mine in the Eastern Mountains, and then I could have started up a very lucrative trade with Implacatus. You can make a lot of money with a Quadrant.'

'I don't believe you,' said Amalia. 'You would have disappeared, on your own, and left us there to die.'

Naxor shrugged. 'I might have done; who knows? So what? It's in the past, along with your myriad crimes, grandmother. Shall we talk about some of the things you've done, like marrying off two of your grandchildren to each other? Or, how about the time you had my mother murdered?'

'I have apologised to you for that.'

'And that makes everything fine? Look, we could sit here all day, trading insults and reciting each other's despicable acts; or, we can plot Simon's death. I know which I'd rather discuss.'

'You are a weasel.'

'So you've decided to continue with the insults? Sad. How about you turn your mind to what we should do once we've killed Simon? There are a few loose ends that we'll need to deal with quickly. There's the Quadrant, obviously.'

'My Quadrant.'

'Quite, grandmother. Then... there are the Aurelians.'

Amalia smiled. 'Do go on. I'd love to hear your plans for them.'

'Simple. We dispose of the adults, and go back to the old scheme of putting Elspeth and Maxwell back together. Agreed?'

'No,' said Kagan.

Naxor smirked. 'I don't recall asking for your opinion.'

'I don't care. If this happens, then you're not executing the Aurelians.'

'Ha! You said "if" it happens. That sounds like Kagan agrees with my plan to kill Simon, doesn't it, grandmother?'

She shrugged. 'A slip of the tongue.'

'Look; I get it. You can't openly say it, and you don't even want to openly think it. We are all terrified of Simon, so terrified that we monitor our own thoughts all the time. I can't live like this.' He stared at Amalia. 'I can see what you're thinking. You are worried about Maxwell; you are scared that Simon will hurt him. You're right to be afraid of that. Simon will hurt him. Why? Because he knows that you would crawl over broken glass to protect your boy. He will own you if Maxwell is returned. Can you live like that?'

Amalia said nothing.

'If we do nothing,' Naxor went on, 'then Simon's power will only grow and grow. He will probably take Maxwell into custody, to ensure your good behaviour; and he will kill me sooner or later. The Aurelians will die; the dragons will die; the Banner will die. He will remove half of the Bulwark to Implacatus, where most of them will die. The wars of the gods will spread here, as the Ascendants counter-attack. This is the future you face, grandmother.' He paused. 'Or, we kill him.'

'We are sitting in the room he usually appears in,' said Kagan. 'I could hide a sword under one of the couches.'

Amalia turned to him. 'Be quiet. Don't say it. Simon might be listening to us, right now. For all we know, this whole thing is a trap.'

'I know you will never trust me,' said Naxor. 'That's fine; I wouldn't trust me either. But, this is not about trust; it's about survival. Our survival, and Maxwell's survival. That, I assume, does interest you?'

Amalia put her head in her hands.

'I don't need to hear your agreement, grandmother. Your silence will do. When Simon returns, we do not hesitate. We make sure we meet him here, in this room. You will confess your lustful feelings towards him, then I will blind him, and Kagan will cut off his head. If we fail, we will be dead in seconds, but if we succeed? If we succeed, we will be heroes.'

'I hate you,' whispered Amalia.

'I know. Is that it? Is that all you have to say?'

Amalia remained silent.

Naxor nodded to Kagan. 'Simon could return at any time. Fetch a sword.'

CHAPTER 20

OPPORTUNE

The Eastern Mountains – 19th Mikalis 3423

Jade sat on the grassy bank of the rushing stream, surrounded by wild flowers in bloom. The air was still, and the cloudless sky was almost blue, with tendrils of peach and pink. Ginger was lying in a patch of sunlight, sprawled out on the grass, his eyes on a butterfly flitting by the tall flowers, while Poppy was sitting on a rock by the edge of the stream, cleaning her paws. Of Tab-Tab and Fluffy, there was no sign, but Jade wasn't worried; she knew they would be close by. The four cats had lasted only a few seconds inside the hidden cavern after Jade had released them from the confines of the box. They had taken one look at the dragons and bolted, going faster than Jade had ever seen them move before. She had rushed out after them, and it had taken a while before they had emerged from their various hiding places in the valley, attracted by her voice, and the food she had brought for them.

'They seem to like it here.'

Jade turned, and saw Rosie standing next to her.

'It's beautiful,' she said, 'but I'm concerned about Sweetmist. Where will they go when the rains come?'

Rosie made a face. 'Do you really think we'll still be here over Sweetmist? It's three months away.'

'Where else will we be? I love it here; why would I move back to the City?'

'Well, I kind of miss my brother and my friends. I thought we would be back before last Freshmist, and here we are, more than halfway through Mikalis already. Oh, I almost forgot – Dawnflame wants to speak to you. She got back ten minutes ago.'

'I saw her shadow overhead as she arrived.'

'She sent me to get you.'

'What for?'

Rosie shrugged. 'Something dangerous, probably.'

Jade nodded.

'Is it worth it?' said Rosie. 'Is it worth risking your lives to attack Simon?'

'That's a strange question. What would make it worth it? If we kill him?'

'He's too powerful, Jade. We could, you know, just hide here.'

'Until when? Do you think someone else will kill him for us?'

'No, I don't.'

'Then, someone has to try.'

'But why you?'

'Why not me? Simon is worse than my father, but I'm not scared of him.' She got to her feet. 'He's just a bully.'

They followed the stream up the gentle slope, high cliffs on either side. The grass was abundant and bees were mingling with the butterflies. The ravine wasn't as neat and ordered as the salve valley had been, but to Jade it seemed perfect. The sound of the waterfall drowned out any further conversation, and they ducked through, entering the large cavern. The air was cool inside, and the cave smelled of dragon. Dawnflame was holding court in the centre, while Bittersea was watching Firestone over by the far corner. Flavus and Van were speaking to Dawnflame, but they turned as Jade and Rosie approached.

'We should leave at once, demigod,' said Dawnflame.

Jade raised an eyebrow. 'Why?'

'I have been out, monitoring the valleys and mountains. Simon is at the salve mine; I saw him with my own eyes. An opportunity to attack the City has arisen; an opportunity we should not waste.'

Van rubbed his chin. 'It takes four hours to fly to the City, yes?'

'Yes,' said Dawnflame. 'Simon could be at the mine for days.'

'Not if we attack the City,' said Van. 'I imagine that he will use his powers to check Auldan every few hours.'

'True. That still gives us time.'

Rosie frowned. 'What's the point?'

'Private Jackdaw,' said Flavus; 'please remember who you are addressing. Major-General Van Logos is the Commander of the Banner of the Lostwell Exiles.'

'Sorry. What's the point, sir?'

'The point of attacking the City?' said Van.

'Yes, sir.'

'We are harassing the enemy, Private; trying to frustrate and hinder his work here. Ideally, we push him into making a mistake, but we also want to show him that he hasn't yet beaten all of us. There is also Queen Emily Aurelian to consider. She is on the run, somewhere in the City. Our attacks can serve to distract Simon, to buy her some precious time so that she can remain uncaptured. Lastly, it is to prove to the ordinary citizens of the City that the fight goes on. Do those answers satisfy you, Private?'

'Yes. Actually, they do, sir.'

Van smiled. 'Flavus and Rosie will remain here, and I will accompany Lady Jade on today's operation.' He glanced at the dragon. 'With your kind permission, of course.'

'You can come along,' said Dawnflame; 'it makes no difference to me. Climb up; let us go.'

'Good luck, sir,' said Flavus.

'Stay hidden within the cavern while we're gone,' said Van. 'If Simon is at the mine, he will probably also take some time to search the mountains for us.'

Flavus saluted. 'Yes, sir.'

Jade and Van clambered up onto the dragon's shoulders, then Dawnflame strode through the waterfall, soaking them. Jade shook her head, her long hair sending more water over Van. As soon as the dragon was outside, she extended her wings in the narrow ravine and soared into the air. She kept low, and flew sunward over the mountains, keeping to the valleys.

'What should we attack?' said Jade.

'How about Simon's own home?' said Van. 'The Royal Palace in Ooste. Let's hit him where it hurts.'

'A fine idea, soldier,' said Dawnflame. 'I have always wanted to burn a palace.'

'An attack there should minimise civilian losses,' said Van. 'Militia soldiers can be targeted, but we should spare the civilians, if possible.'

'And if Simon turns up, we leave?' said Jade.

'That would seem to be the most sensible course of action,' said Van, 'but we should keep an open mind, and take any opportunity that presents itself.'

Jade nodded. Despite Dawnflame's earlier insistence that the demigod was in charge of the humans hiding in the cavern, Jade had been happy to let Van think up their strategy. After all, she had already achieved her goal - the rescue of her cats, whereas Van seemed as keen as Dawnflame to inflict more damage on Simon's rule. She closed her eyes as the warm breeze swept through her drying hair, and settled down to enjoy the journey.

Dawnflame took them via the sunward deserts, where the temperature soared, then they turned towards iceward, and crossed the miles of marshlands. They emerged over the Warm Sea, then cut across the spur of the Western Bank, keeping well clear of Jezra to the east. At the coastline, Dawnflame dived low, skimming the surface of the Cold Sea, the fog and winds of the Clashing Seas just to their right. They crossed the

Straits in a few minutes, then climbed the steep cliffs of the Shield Hills. The fog enveloped them as the dragon surged sunward along the line of hills, then they broke through. The town of Ooste lay below them, spreading out in the early afternoon sunshine. Dawnflame made straight for the harbour. Positioned on the roofs of several tall buildings by the quayside were several ballista batteries, all pointing towards the bay.

'We've caught them off-guard,' cried Van. 'Burn them now, before they can turn those machines.'

'I know what I'm doing, soldier,' said the dragon.

Dawnflame soared over the houses of Ooste. Screams drifted up to them from the inhabitants, and civilians were running through the streets in panic at the sight of Dawnflame overhead. The militia by the ballistae were frantically trying to re-position their machines, but Dawnflame was too fast for them. She reared up, opened her jaws, and sprayed a wide burst of fire over the roofs of the harbour buildings. Bodies toppled to the ground, wrapped in flames, some splashing into the waters of the bay, others landing on some of the small fishing vessels berthed by the piers.

Dawnflame turned her head, her eyes scanning for more targets. The town was in chaos. A bell was ringing somewhere, its peals competing with the screams of terror. The dragon rose up into the air, then soared towards the Royal Palace, its white façade gleaming in the sunshine.

'The palace, I assume?'

'Yes,' said Jade. 'The home of the God-King and God-Queen for centuries.'

'Keep a lookout for more ballistae, humans, while I see how well the home of the gods burns.'

The dragon hovered close to the palace entrance. The militia on duty were trying to seal the heavy doors at the front, their crossbows useless against Dawnflame. The dragon watched them for a moment, as sparks shot across her glistening teeth, then the flames began. The dragon aimed for the doors, and they disappeared in the inferno, incinerated along with the militia. Windows shattered, and smoke belched out from the upper floors as the flames continued. The front of the palace blackened as Dawnflame aimed a little higher, then the high roof of the building caught fire, sending thick, dark smoke up into the cloudless sky.

'Keep going,' said Jade. 'The palace stretches back into the cliffside, and goes underground as well. At least, I think it does – I've never been inside the Royal Palace in my life.'

The dragon didn't respond, but she increased the flow of fire. Parts of the palace façade cracked, and tumbled to the ground, the fiery pieces exploding on the flagstones of the courtyard before the main entrance. A tower collapsed, sending thousands of bricks spilling down into the open roof in a crash of noise.

Dawnflame closed her jaws, and admired her handiwork. The entire building was wreathed in flames and smoke.

'I would be lying if I said I didn't enjoy that,' said the dragon. 'To me, it feels like revenge for Lostwell, as well as an assault on Simon. I missed the fight upon Old Alea, but now I, Dawnflame, also have a palace to my name.'

'Simon will return as soon as he sees the damage,' said Van. 'We should leave.'

'Perhaps not,' said the dragon.

Van blinked. 'What do you mean?'

'You said to keep an open mind. I have a better idea.'

She soared upwards, circled the town in full view of the citizens, then soared off over the Shield Hills. As soon as she was out of sight of the town, she reversed course, hugging the tops of the ridges, then slipped back into the town via the cliffs, dropping behind the palace, close to the edge of the Royal Academy. She tucked her wings in, her back to the cliffside. Ahead of them, there was a narrow gap, through which the courtyard in front of the palace could be seen.

'We shall await him here, I think,' said the dragon.

'Is this wise?' said Van.

'It's an opportunity,' said the dragon.

Van glanced at Jade, a concerned look on his face.

'It's up to her,' said the demigod.

'But, he's an Ascendant.'

'So?' said Jade. 'I'm not scared. Are you?'

'Frankly, yes. Didn't we talk about this yesterday? I thought we agreed that our best tactic was to avoid Simon – to attack locations when he's not there?'

'I listened to all of that,' said the dragon, 'but I didn't necessarily agree.'

'I don't mind waiting for Simon,' said Jade, 'especially if we have a chance to surprise him.'

Van said nothing, his eyes wide.

Jade smiled. 'I used to fancy you. Do you remember?'

'Eh, what? Yes, I guess so. You used to proposition me when I first arrived in the City.'

Her smile faded. 'You rejected me.'

'I was in love with Kelsey Holdfast.'

'Was? Does that mean you aren't any more?'

His face fell. 'I'm still in love with her, but she's not here, is she? I mean, she's on bloody Implacatus, thanks to Simon.'

'The Ascendant stole your mate?' said Dawnflame. 'Surely that is reason enough to want to attack him?'

'Oh, I want to attack him; don't doubt that for a second, but he could knock us out of the sky from a hundred yards away. Or, he could use the fires in the palace to send flames up at us.'

'He might.'

'If he sees us, close your eyes.'

'I shall, soldier. He has tricked me once, by sending me to sleep; he will not do so again.'

'Damn dragons,' muttered Van. 'This is the same stubborn streak that has seen so many of your kin killed on Dragon Eyre.'

Dawnflame slowly turned her head round to face him. 'Do you think it wise to mention this to me? My mate died at the hands of insects; do you think I have forgotten?'

'No. I'm sorry.'

'At the moment, our enemies happen to coincide, soldier; but do not think that I like you. I wouldn't want you to get the wrong impression. Jade and the little Jackdaw are the only humans I have met that I have any respect for – you are just another Banner insect.'

'A handsome Banner insect,' said Jade.

Dawnflame eyed her, then turned back to face the gap leading to the courtyard. To their right, the smoke was continuing to belch upwards, filling the sky.

Two hours passed. The grounds by the Royal Academy remained deserted, and no one from the citizenry approached the inferno engulfing the palace. A few militia soldiers came into the courtyard by the front entrance, but the heat was too fierce for them to get any closer. Dawnflame kept her eyes on the narrow gap, waiting, as Jade and Van sat upon her shoulders. Van stayed quiet, and Jade wondered if he was day-dreaming about Kelsey. She couldn't understand what he saw in her. The mortal girl was rude, ungrateful, and seemed to delight in being contrary and obstinate. No wonder she didn't seem to have any friends. How could Van be so besotted with her? It made no sense.

Just as Jade was considering sliding down to the ground to stretch her legs, Dawnflame tensed.

'There,' whispered Van, his eyes narrow.

Jade peered through the gap, and saw Simon. The Ascendant was standing in the middle of the courtyard, staring at the flames. He was dressed in full armour, but it was strangely-coloured, with green and gold lines and swirls; and he had a large axe over his shoulder. Even from that distance, it was clear from his features that he was enraged, and the nearest militia soldiers were cowering in fear behind him.

'Hold on tight,' said Dawnflame, then she sprang into the air, opening her jaws at the same time. The moment she was clear of the buildings, the dragon unleashed the greatest torrent of fire Jade had yet seen. It hit Simon like a tidal wave, bowling him over and covering him in flames. Around him, the militia were incinerated within seconds, but Simon was writhing and struggling, trying to get back to his feet as the flames roiled over him.

Jade reached out with her hand, and blasted her death powers at the figure in the flames. Simon screamed, then collapsed to the ground, motionless.

Dawnflame closed her jaws, and the flames died down, leaving Simon's body charred and smoking on the ground.

'Take me closer,' said Van. 'Quickly; he'll recover in a moment.'

'Are you going to take his head, soldier?'

'If I can,' said Van, as the dragon lowered to the flagstones of the courtyard.

Jade watched as Van clambered down. He unsheathed the sword he had taken from the Duke's Tower, and ran towards Simon. The smouldering body of the Ascendant began to move as Van reached it. The soldier raised his sword above his head, then hesitated. Instead of swinging the blade, he fell to his knees, and began rummaging around the Ascendant's body.

'What is the fool doing?' cried Dawnflame. 'If he doesn't kill the god, I will have to burn them both.'

'Give him a moment,' said Jade.

Van shoved something into his clothes, then got back to his feet. It was too late. Simon raised his head, then lifted a hand. Jade blasted more death powers at the Ascendant, distracting him for a second, then Dawnflame swooped. She soared low over the courtyard, a forelimb outstretched, and plucked Van from the ground. She ascended, just as Simon was getting to his feet. Dawnflame turned, to unleash more flames, but the Ascendant raised his hand. Jade did so at the same time, and their death powers collided. Jade cried out in pain.

'Go!' yelled Van from the dragon's forelimb. 'Now!'

Dawnflame gave a burst of speed, soaring off in the direction of the Union Walls. A wave of death powers struck her from behind, and she began to plunge downwards. Jade placed her hand onto the dragon's scales, feeding her with healing powers, and Dawnflame struggled onwards. They sped over Auldan, then the dragon turned for iceward. She tried to scale the slopes of the Iceward Range, her flanks crashing into the tops of the trees, as Jade continued to send healing into her body. Beyond the heights of the hills, the death powers from Simon ceased. Dawnflame hurtled down, heading straight for Icehaven, but managed to pull up at the last second. They cleared the town, and then there was nothing below them but the waters of the Cold Sea.

Dawnflame stabilised, and Jade removed her hands. She flew on, the temperature dropping with every minute, until they reached an enormous iceberg drifting through the sea. The dragon hovered above it, then released Van from her grasp. He landed heavily onto the ice, then Dawnflame set down next to him.

'You imbecile!' the dragon shouted at him. 'You almost killed us all! Give me one reason why I shouldn't end your life now.'

Van groaned.

Jade slid down to the ice, and crouched by Van.

'Why didn't you kill Simon?' she said.

Van struggled up into a sitting position. 'The sword wouldn't have got through his armour; the blade would have broken on his neck collar.'

'Didn't you know that before you jumped down?' said the dragon.

'I miscalculated,' he said.

The dragon's eyes burned with fury. 'You miscalculated?'

'Yes. I made a mistake. He's in full armour, and it's made from a material stronger than anything my sword could have got through. I could have stabbed him in the face, but that wouldn't have killed him. His armour is practically indestructible.'

'He'll be looking for us now,' said Jade. 'He could be here any second.'

Van smiled. 'No, I don't think so.'

'Why not?'

Van slipped his hand into his clothes and withdrew a metal device, its surface the colour of polished copper. 'Because I snatched this from him.'

Jade laughed. 'You got his Quadrant?'

'I did, as soon as I realised that I wouldn't be able to kill him. The Eastern Mountains will be safe; he has no way to get there any more. Or, anywhere else, for that matter.'

'Can you take us right back to the cavern now?' said Jade.

Van's grin faded. 'Eh, no.'

'You don't know how to use it, do you?'

'No. Do you?'

Jade shook her head.

'So,' said the dragon; 'you stole something that you don't know how to use? This day has been a disaster.'

'Not so, dragon. We've hurt Simon more than you know. This Quadrant was essential to him; it was the only way he could travel to ten places in one day. Without it, he'll be stuck in the City. Believe me, he'll be angrier than ever.'

'We could destroy the salve mine again,' said Jade, 'and there would be nothing he could do to stop us.'

'Exactly. We should be celebrating.'

'My body is still aching from the Ascendant's powers,' said Dawn-flame; 'I do not feel like celebrating.' She turned to Jade. 'Once again, demigod, I have you to thank. At least one of you has some sense. I am tempted to leave the Banner soldier here, lest he lead us into another catastrophe.'

'He did the best he could,' said Jade. 'Simon will miss the Quadrant. He's probably weeping and wailing about it right now.'

'Well, that pleases me a little,' said the dragon. 'Still, I had hoped for a better outcome. Did you hear him scream when your death powers hit him? That was my favourite moment.' She glanced back towards Van. 'Very well, Banner soldier; I will not leave you here. Climb back up, both of you, and I will take us home.'

The journey back to the Eastern Mountains was far colder than the outward leg had been, and Jade was shivering by the time they reached the foothills, her energy almost spent. Dawnflame soared sunward, flitting over the snow-covered peaks until the temperature began to rise again. Van had spent the hours examining the Quadrant, though Jade noticed that he was careful not to brush his fingers across the surface. Jade had caught only a few glimpses of a Quadrant in the past, and she had been unaware of their existence until she had fled Greylin Palace. It seemed too small to be so powerful; just a scrap of metal, though the studded jewels and strange engravings intrigued her.

They got soaked again as they went through the waterfall. Bittersea was close to the entrance, standing guard, while Firestone was curled up sleeping in the corner of the cavern. Flavus and Rosie jumped to their feet at the approach of Dawnflame, the Blade girl with a huge grin on her face.

'You were away for so long that I was worried,' she said, as Jade and Van climbed down to the floor of the cavern.

'We attacked Simon,' said Jade.

Rosie's mouth fell open.

'And you survived, ma'am?' said Flavus. 'Well done. Not many who face an Ascendant live to tell the tale.'

'Dawnflame burned him to a crisp,' said Jade.

'Is he... is he dead?' said Rosie.

Jade shook her head. 'No. But we burned the Royal Palace to the ground, and gave him a good scare.'

'We did more than that,' said Van, brandishing the Quadrant.

Flavus's face split into a wide grin. 'You stole that from him, sir? Congratulations; that is fantastic news.'

'Is it?' said Dawnflame. 'I would have preferred to have brought Simon's head back for Firestone to play with.'

'But Madam Dawnflame,' said the lieutenant; 'his power is greatly diminished without his Quadrant. His plans are in ruins.'

'But, he is still here. I want to see his corpse, not a silly piece of metal.'

'Don't underestimate this achievement, daughter,' said Bittersea. 'This cavern is now safe from Simon. Even an Ascendant cannot walk through two hundred miles of greenhides to get here.'

'I don't desire safety, mother; I crave revenge.'

'And you burnt his palace. There is no harm in drawing out your revenge. You would be dissatisfied if it was over too soon.'

'I doubt that, mother.'

'What is more,' said Flavus, 'we can now use the Quadrant to attack him.'

'Can we, sir?' said Rosie. 'That will save all the hours of flying back and forth.'

'Unfortunately not,' said Van. 'No one here knows how to use it. I was always kept away from Quadrants, even as a captain in the Banner of the Golden Fist. They were for gods only, not for mortals.'

'Should we destroy it?' said Jade. 'If it's no good to us, then we should put it out of use forever, so that Simon can't steal it back.'

'Might I intervene, sir?' said Flavus. 'I know a little about how to operate a Quadrant.'

Van blinked. 'You do, Lieutenant? How?'

'Well, sir, as a scout, I was often sent out as part of an advance group of Banner specialists, to reconnoitre the area before the main body of soldiers appeared. On one operation, I was stranded on a remote island on Dragon Eyre, with only a god for company, while we waited for reinforcements to arrive. We had been ordered to stay, and, quite frankly, we thought we were going to die on that island. Rebels and dragons had surrounded our position, and so the god showed me how to perform two actions upon the Quadrant, in case he was killed.'

Van stared at Flavus. 'What did he show you?'

'The two simplest actions, sir, or so he said. The first returns you to the location where the Quadrant was last activated. If Simon travelled from the salve mine to Ooste, then this action would take us back to the salve mine, if you follow me, sir.'

'And the second action?'

'The second action, sir, returns you to the location where the Quadrant was first activated.'

'First activated?' said Jade. 'Where would that take us?'

Flavus glanced at her. 'To the same location where every Quadrant was created, ma'am.'

'Alright; where's that?'

Van's eyes tightened. 'Implacatus.'

CHAPTER 21
PAYING THE PRICE

S alt Quay, The Bulwark, The City – 20th Mikalis 3423
Emily stood on the dark quayside, watching from the shadows
of the high harbour buildings as the condemned prisoners were herded
onto a long, slender galley. A crude leather helmet was covering her
hair, and she was handling her militia crossbow with care. There was
no sign of the sun, and the air had a slight chill to it, which would be
dispelled as soon as the summer's day began. Over to her left, beyond
the thick ranks of militia, a small line of passengers was also waiting to
board the ship; among them, Lucius Cardova was standing, his big
arms enveloping Maxwell. Emily glanced in their direction, then looked
away, conscious that she wasn't supposed to know either of them. She
took a breath, trying to calm her nerves.

Achan had stayed away, having given her a tearful farewell a few
hours previously. He had begged her not to go through with her plan,
but her mind was made up, and, despite his misgivings, he had
provided her with all the assistance she had required. In a breast
pocket of her militia uniform was a pass, stamped and signed by the
Hammer council, allowing her to enter Auldan, and Lucius had a
similar one, along with a small purse of gold. Maxwell was dressed in
the drab grey common to the Hammers, and had a fake tribal tattoo on

his upper left arm. Emily smiled as she imagined Amalia's reaction to seeing it.

She felt a presence by her side and turned to see her mother, her features shrouded in a long hooded cloak.

'I wanted to see you off, dear,' she whispered.

Emily said nothing.

'Your grandmother would be very proud of you.'

'What about you, mother?' Emily said, her voice low.

Lady Omertia's eyes glanced away.

'You think I'm making a mistake, don't you?'

'It's not my place to say, dear.'

'Of course it's your place; you're my mother. If I can't rely on you to tell me the truth, then who can I rely on?'

'Very well. I agree with Achan's opinion. You are needlessly putting yourself in grave danger. You-know-who hasn't changed, and I think you're being a little naïve to suppose that she will entertain any serious thoughts of allying herself to your cause. She will betray you as soon as she has Maxwell in her clutches.'

'Maybe, but I have to try.'

'You're wrong, dear; you don't have to do this. You could remain hidden in the Hammer lands, and wait for the right moment.'

'That moment will never come,' said Emily.

'Patience was never your strong point, daughter.' Lady Omertia tried to smile. 'Good luck.'

A low whistle sounded, and the militia began to follow the prisoners up the gangway onto the vessel. Emily glanced at her mother for a final time, then got into line. She and the other soldiers tramped up the wooden plank and stepped down onto the deck of the galley. The prisoners had been taken below, and the militia made room on the deck for the small number of passengers. Lucius was easy to spot, his height marking him out among the others, and Emily watched from the corner of her eye as he sat down by the deck railings, Maxwell in his arms. Blade sailors unfurled the main sail and threw off the ropes connecting them to the quayside, and the ship began to edge away from the harbour. Emily turned back, her eyes scanning the crowd on the docks, but her mother had gone.

A militia sergeant noticed Emily.

'You,' he called; 'guard the aft hatch. If any of the prisoners escape, you'll be taking their place on the scaffold.'

Emily nodded, gripped her crossbow, and made her way to the rear of the vessel, passing the crew, guards and passengers filling the open deck. The aft hatch sat in front of the small quarterdeck, and two other Hammer guards were already there, crouching by the metal bars. Emily glanced down into the dark hold, and saw over a dozen faces staring back up at her. The ten Hammer prisoners represented the last batch of hardened criminals to be taken from the territory's jails; for the following day's quota, thieves rather than murderers would be sent to Pella.

'Mercy,' cried up a Scythe victim from the hold, her eyes red. 'I've done nothing wrong.'

A Hammer guard next to Emily narrowed his eyes. 'You must have done something.'

'Our prison was emptied after three days,' said the Scythe woman. 'I was selected because I complained about the executions. I'm being killed because I spoke out.'

'You should have kept your mouth shut,' said the Hammer guard.

'I can't believe I'm hearing this from a Hammer,' said the woman; 'shame on you. Shame on this City, and on every coward that dwell within its walls.'

'Shut up,' said a Blade prisoner from the darkness of the hold. 'Your prattling is doing us no good. Do you think you're the only one down here who is being executed for their opinions? I supported Yendra, and then Jade, for all the good it did me. Where are the Aurelians now, eh? One's a prisoner, and the other one ran away. The gods were never going to allow us to rule ourselves; it was a dream, and the dream is over.'

Emily pulled her gaze away from the hold, her heart filling with bitterness. The galley was pulling out of Salt Quay's small harbour, and the wind picked up in the rougher waters of the Warm Sea. Running along the sides of the vessel were banks of oars, but they wouldn't be needed for the outward voyage; the strong breeze from sunward would guide them to Pella unaided.

They passed the lights of Port Sanders to their right, then the land rose into the heights of the Sunward Range. In the distance ahead of them was another vessel, presumably carrying that day's allotment of Sander and Evader victims, and the larger Bulwark ship began to close on it as they rounded the corner of the hills and turned for iceward. Their speed picked up as the sails were fully opened, and they passed the Sander vessel before they turned again to enter the huge bay. To their right, the sky was brightening, and Emily could see the towns of Tara, Ooste and Pella spreading out in a continuous line of houses, harbours and streets. The ship tacked to iceward, then slowed as it neared the harbour of Pella.

Emily almost sobbed at the sight of Cuidrach Palace. Its roofs had gone, and the remaining walls were blackened and ruined. Her home had become the City's execution site, the place where Simon's daily victims were slaughtered. A long row of large posts lined the waterfront between the ruins of the palace and the harbour, and crowds of Reaper militia were on hand, ready to greet that morning's arrivals. Cries rose up from the hold as the vessel bumped against the quay, then the sergeant strode forwards, his hand grasping a great set of iron keys. Emily stood back as the hatch was opened. Reaper militia boarded the vessel, and began pulling the prisoners out onto the deck. Some were struggling, while others seemed resigned to their fate.

The Scythe woman was one of those refusing to resist. She kept her head high as the Reapers led her and the others across the deck and up onto the stone quay, her eyes brimming with contempt at the acquiescence of the soldiers in Simon's insane orders. Emily, too, was taken aback. A few short months before, the Hammer and Reaper militia had been loyal to her, and she would never have believed that they would passively go along with the daily ritual of executions. They were still good people, she told herself; they were the same kind, generous folk she had known for years, and yet fear had turned them into Simon's willing accomplices.

The vessel cast off the moment the last of the thirty prisoners had disembarked, as if the Blade captain wished to be gone from the grisly sight of the executions posts as soon as possible. The ship turned in the harbour, then set off towards Tara. Not one of the sailors or guards glanced back at Pella, and Emily turned her back on the ruins of the palace, not wanting to stand out. She felt guilt and shame course through her. She was the Queen, and she had stood by as innocent citizens of the City were being led off to die. Did that make her as much of an accomplice as the others? She had a good reason to remain quiet, she told herself, but then she imagined that every one of the guards and sailors had also rationalised their choices.

The spirits of the crew rose as they left Pella harbour and crossed the bay, as if a shadow had departed, and the sun rose above the horizon, splitting the sky in pinks and reds.

Emily walked up to the Hammer sergeant, and showed him her pass. He took it from her hand and squinted at it.

'You're getting off at Tara?' he said.

Emily nodded.

'And how are you getting back to the Bulwark?'

'Tomorrow's boat.'

He frowned at her accent, then handed her the pass back. 'Alright. Behave yourself, Private. The Rosers aren't too keen on outsiders; stay out of trouble.'

'Yes, Sergeant.'

He strode away, leaving Emily standing alone by the railings of the galley. He had picked up on the way she had spoken, and she wondered what he was thinking. In the old days, he would have asked, but under Simon's rule, everyone had learned that it was better to keep your mouth closed. Emily turned towards Tara, watching as the sunlight spread across the town and the cliffs where Princeps Row and Maeladh Palace stood. Her husband and daughter were up there, and her heart began to pound.

The galley drew into the harbour of Tara, and docked at a long pier. The small group of passengers all showed their passes to the Roser guards on duty by the gangway, and Emily followed them down onto the pier, keeping her head low. The Rosers examined her pass, then waved her through. She kept her distance from Lucius as they walked towards the town, then followed him as he turned for the iceward tip of the promontory. The day was warming up, and the houses of Tara were gleaming in the light. Lucius turned right before reaching Prince's Square, and Emily frowned as she noticed a large wooden platform that had been constructed in the centre of the large plaza. A line of gallows stood at the rear of the platform, and Roser soldiers were clustered in groups, keeping the civilians away.

Emily shuddered, then picked up her pace. She made her way to a small park, enclosed by buildings on every side, where Lucius was waiting for her. High trees and thick bushes were shielding them from the windows of the buildings, and Lucius handed her the bag he had been carrying. She took it without a word, then quickly changed out of her Hammer uniform, dressing as a Roser housemaid under the shelter of the branches of a beech tree, while Lucius kept an eye on the park entrance. She handed her crossbow to him, and he gave her the sheathed Fated Blade.

'Thank you, Lucius.'

The officer gazed down at her. 'It's not too late to change your mind, your Majesty.'

Emily removed her leather helmet and replaced it with a shawl to cover her hair.

'Do you remember the address of the hostelry?' she said.

'Yes, your Majesty.'

'Good. You will wait for me there. If all goes well, I will send a message; and, if I don't return by the time of tomorrow's boat, you will know that I have failed. Make your way back to Hammer territory and look after my mother.'

Cardova crouched on the grass in the shade of the tree and set Maxwell upon his feet. The child cried, and reached for him.

'I know you think I'm making an error, Lucius,' said Emily.

'I am under your orders, your Majesty. If you insist on doing this, then I ask permission to come with you into the palace. If things get violent, I should be there to protect you.'

'If things get violent, Lucius, then I've already lost. I see no point in you being captured or killed.'

He glanced up at her, a hand round Maxwell's shoulder. 'This is the hardest order I've had to follow, your Majesty. If they kill you, I will never forgive myself, no matter how long I live. You have a kind and generous heart, and I know how much you want to believe that Amalia can be reasoned with, but she has led you into a trap. Part of me wants to throw you over my shoulder and make a run for it. We could leave Maxwell in Tara and send a message to the palace, telling them where he is. To go in person, on your own, is madness.'

'Did you see the execution posts in Pella?'

'Yes.'

'That is the future of the City if I do nothing. Every day, Simon's grip tightens a little more. Without Kelsey, the only hope we have lies with the native gods of the City. If the price for ridding us of Simon is my life, then I'm prepared to accept that. I am the Queen, and it is my duty to put my people first.'

Lucius tore his glance from her, and stared at the ground. Emily crouched down next to him, and gathered Maxwell in her arms.

'Lucius,' she said, 'you have been faithful and true, and I'm grateful I got to know you. I'm proud of you, proud that you are my best officer, and proud that you are my friend.'

She stood, Maxwell clinging to her chest. 'Don't worry, little Max; you'll be seeing your mother and father soon.'

Lucius put a hand to his eyes, as if unable to look at her.

Emily placed a hand on his shoulder. 'Go to the hostelry, and wait.'

The big soldier nodded.

Emily turned, and walked from the small park before she could start to cry. She didn't look back, and kept her eyes down, as befitted a servant of her position. The streets were a little busier than before, with early morning deliveries of food and drink arriving at the fronts of the elegant townhouses. A flower-seller was setting up her stall in a small square, and the woman smiled at Emily as she passed. A well-dressed couple strode along the street towards her, and Emily moved off the pavement, keeping her head bowed until they passed. They hadn't glanced in her direction; most Rosers treating servants as if they were invisible.

Emily continued on her way, heading towards the colossal statue of Prince Michael on the headland, a place she had visited countless times as a child, when she had read every book that existed about the former ruling god of the City. She reached the enormous pedestal that supported the statue, and took a moment to gaze out over the bay towards Ooste. The waters were sparkling in the dawn light, and the only thing ruining the view were the thin pillars of smoke rising from the vicinity of Pella. Another day, another hundred corpses, burning in the summer sunshine.

She edged around the rocks to the far side of the pedestal, then clambered along the side of the cliff, her left arm keeping a tight grip on Maxwell. Within moments, she was out of sight of anyone close to the statue, making her way across the rough landscape, as the waves surged against the shore a few yards to her right. It took her longer to find the hidden quay than she had expected, but, after a twenty minute search, she came across the narrow gully where Montieth had carried her and Daniel away after he had killed Yendra. She followed the path to the sheer cliffs, and climbed the rough steps. The doorway had been blocked up with fresh beams of wood, and she crouched by it. She pulled at the beams, but they had been nailed to the doorframe.

'Try not to wriggle, little Max,' she said, as she drew the Fated Blade. The dark metal glistened in the light as she raised it above her head. She brought it down, hacking through the wood, which parted beneath the strokes of the sharp blade. She sheathed the sword and pulled the broken fragments away, then kicked the door open. She peered into the darkness beyond, then crawled through the gap, entering the mines that ran under the cliffs. Maxwell let out a whimper.

'Don't be scared,' said Emily; 'this is the way to your mother. Think how happy you'll be to see her. She's missed you, you know, and she'll probably spoil you. I would, because you're such a brave boy. Now, let's be brave for a little longer, yes?'

The light from the open door cast illumination down the tunnel, and Emily crept along, her left arm round the child as her right hand felt for the tunnel side. It levelled off and grew wider, and she kept going, using touch to feel her way through the darkness. It grew cold, and fear rippled through her as she concentrated on moving one leg in front of the other. The wall on her right hand side came to an end, and her fingers felt nothing. She slipped, and fell to the rough ground. She clenched her teeth shut to avoid crying out, then got back to her feet and stumbled onwards. Her hand found another wall, then she worked her way along it, until she reached a door. She pushed and pulled it, but it was locked, so she took out the sword, and rammed it into the slim gap by the handle. The lock gave way, and she eased the door open, her eyes blinking from the dim lamplight. She crossed over into the basement of the palace, and closed the door behind her.

She took a moment to gather her wits, putting the darkness out of her mind. She listened, but could hear nothing, so she carried on, creeping along the passageways of the basement cellars until she reached a set of stairs. They creaked under her boots as she ascended two flights, then she smiled as she saw daylight coming through a set of shutters. She was in the palace. Of all of the palaces of the City, Maeladh was one that she knew well, but it was so large that there remained many areas that were unfamiliar to her. She hid her sword beneath her servant's cloak, and walked on, keeping her eyes and ears open. She turned a corner, and a man saw her. He was dressed as a servant, and was equipped with all kinds of gardening tools.

He frowned at her. 'Are you new, girl?'

She nodded.

'You can't be bringing your children into the palace,' he went on. 'If her ladyship finds out, you'll be sent home.'

'He's ill,' she said, trying to soften her aristocratic accent. 'I want to speak to Lord Kagan or Lady Amalia about him.'

'That is a bad idea,' said the gardener.

'Where are they?'

'You're a fool,' he said. He shrugged. 'But, if you want to lose your job, you'll find them in the oval living room, where they always sit for breakfast.' He pointed. 'That way.'

'Thanks,' she said, then walked past him. He shook his head, then carried on, in the opposite direction.

'Don't expect any sympathy from them,' he called after her.

Emily kept her pace steady, following the corridor as it ran along the sunward flank of the palace. She reached a large hallway, and saw a servant wheeling a trolley out of a room with double doors. Emily walked on, trying to show confidence, and was almost at the doors when the servant raised an arm to block her way.

'Who are you?' he said 'You can't go in there.'

'Is Lady Amalia in there?'

'She is, and you are not allowed in. Who hired you? I wasn't told that we had any new servants. Where is your permission slip?'

Emily drew her sword, and the man's eyes widened.

'Get out of my way,' she said.

The servant shrieked. 'Alarm!' he cried. 'Intruder!'

Another man burst through the door. His eyes went from the servant, to the sword in Emily's hands, and then he saw the child. His mouth opened.

'This woman is an intruder, my lord,' the servant shouted.

Emily ripped the shawl from her head. 'I am not an intruder.' She turned to the other man. 'Are you Kagan?'

'I am,' he said, raising his hands. 'Put the sword down. Amalia! Get out here.'

The doors swung open, and Emily froze. The woman standing in front of her looked younger than she had imagined, and her eyes opened wide at the sight of Emily with Maxwell.

Amalia turned to the servant. 'You are dismissed. Say nothing to anyone. Go.'

The servant gulped, then hurried away, abandoning the trolley in his haste.

Amalia turned to Emily, then gestured to the double doors. Emily, the sword still gripped in her right hand, walked into a large room, with a long, curving window overlooking Tara and the bay. Behind her, she heard Amalia and Kagan also enter the room, and then the doors were closed.

'She came,' said Kagan, his voice almost a whisper.

'She did,' said Amalia.

Emily turned in the middle of the room. 'Where are Elspeth and Daniel?'

'Safe,' said Amalia. 'For now.'

'They're in an apartment in the basement,' said Kagan. 'Please, don't hurt Maxwell; put the sword down.'

'She's not going to hurt Maxwell, Kagan,' said Amalia. 'She wants her daughter.'

'I do,' said Emily. She sheathed her sword. 'I am not one for making deals where children are concerned.' She held out Maxwell. 'Take him; here is your son. He belongs with you.'

Amalia raised an eyebrow. 'No tricks? You don't want to bargain first?'

'No. Take him.'

Amalia stretched out her arms, and took the child. She pressed him against her, her eyes welling, as Kagan put his arms round them both, his joy mixed with his own tears. Emily watched them for a moment, then walked to the window, leaving them alone.

It was done.

She gazed down at the town of Tara – her home for so many years. She picked out the street where she had been raised, then her eyes went to the gallows in Prince's Square. Behind her, she could hear the sound of sobs and tears as Amalia and Kagan were reunited with their son, and it made her heart ache.

A hand touched her elbow.

'Thank you,' said Kagan.

Emily glanced at him. 'It was the right thing to do.'

'The right thing? Are you mad? You can't stay here; if Simon comes back, he will kill you; he is...'

'Quiet, Kagan, please,' said Amalia. She was smiling, but her eyes were troubled as she embraced her child.

'I want to talk,' said Emily; 'Queen to Queen.'

'Neither of us are queens any more, Emily Aurelian,' said Amalia. 'This is Simon's City.'

'Then we should take it back from him.'

'We?' said Amalia. 'There is no "we." Don't get me wrong; I am grateful that you have returned our son to us, but you shouldn't have come here. Simon has Silva – he knows that you were planning to travel to Maeladh, and his orders to us were quite clear on the subject.'

'I imagine they were,' said Emily. 'The question remains – are you going to follow those orders, or is there a better path to take? Are we slaves in this City? Together, we could wrest control from the Ascendant. Tell me what you want.'

Amalia laughed. 'What I want? Oh dear. I doubt that you'll be happy to hear it, but if you insist. Please, Emily, take a seat. Kagan, get our guest a glass of water.'

The former God-Queen sat, keeping Maxwell close to her. She gazed into his face, her eyes welling again.

'You're so big,' she said; 'I missed you, my beautiful boy.'

'He can walk,' said Emily.

'Can he? Sit, Emily.'

Emily glanced around the room, and sat on a couch across from Amalia and Maxwell. Kagan returned from a table, with a glass of water for her.

'Thank you,' she said.

'You are now my prisoner,' said Amalia. 'You will join the rest of your family in the basement, where you will be able to spend a few days with them, before Simon has you all executed. That, I'm afraid, is that.'

'Wait a minute,' said Kagan; 'should we not think this through?'

'What is there to think about?' said Amalia. 'Naxor is in the palace, so he probably already knows what has occurred. If we do anything other than follow Simon's orders, then we will be on the gallows with the Aurelians.'

Kagan's face fell. 'But, she risked her life to come here.'

'Exactly,' said Amalia. 'She knew what she was doing.' She glanced back at Emily. 'Did you happen to get a good look at Ooste on your way here?'

Emily shook her head.

'The Royal Palace is a smouldering pile of ashes, courtesy of Jade and a disgruntled dragon. Simon is in a frightful temper, and we are expecting him to arrive here later today. He is moving into Maeladh. You certainly picked an auspicious day to make your appearance here.'

'Jade and a dragon attacked the Royal Palace? As well as the Fortress of the Lifegiver?'

'Indeed. You should have remained hidden, Emily.'

Kagan's features cracked. 'We should tell her about the plan.'

Amalia glared at him.

'What plan?' said Emily.

'Nothing,' said Amalia. 'There is no plan.'

The double doors opened, and Naxor rushed into the room.

'Malik's ass,' he cried, staring at Emily. 'What do we do?'

'We obey Simon's orders, of course,' said Amalia. 'Summon the guards.'

Naxor turned to Kagan, and they shared a glance. 'But...'

'But, nothing, Naxor,' said Amalia. 'Summon the guards.'

Emily watched as Naxor's feet remained frozen to the floor, his hands twitching.

'Dear gods,' sighed Amalia. 'Do I have to do everything myself?'

Naxor's eyes glazed over for a second, then he collapsed onto a chair. 'It's done.'

Emily glanced at Amalia. 'I thought better of you.'

'I know you did,' she said. 'Sorry to disappoint.'

Half a dozen militia burst through the doors, their crossbows pointed at Emily.

'Take her to her family,' said Amalia; 'oh, and remove her sword first.'

Emily stood, and unstrapped the Fated Blade from her belt, then laid it down onto the couch. The militia surrounded her, and escorted her from the room. Naxor and Amalia were looking in the other direction, but Kagan stared at her as she was led away, his face stricken with doubt and fear.

The militia took her down some stairs, and back into the basement of the palace. They came to a door at the end of a long corridor, where more guards were on hand to unlock it. The door swung open, and Emily was pushed through. She came into a small room that stank of nappies and unwashed clothes.

'Emily?' said Daniel, getting to his feet.

Emily ran to Elspeth, then knelt and picked her up, hugging her as her tears fell. Around her, Lord and Lady Aurelian stood, and Daniel crouched next to her, his arms round her. Emily closed her eyes, her tears mingling into the hair of her daughter.

She had made many mistakes over the course of her life, mistakes she wished she could undo. She had been rash when she should have been cautious, and had learned many bitter lessons along the way. Despite that, feeling her child in her arms, she knew that whatever she had done that day, it wasn't a mistake.

She kissed Elspeth, and surrendered to her tears.

CHAPTER 22

EXTRACTION

Serene, Implacatus – 20th Dunninch 5255

Caelius winked at Vadhi, blew on his hands, then rolled the dice. He laughed, as the young Torduan groaned.

'Just what I needed,' said the veteran Banner sergeant; 'and the game is mine. That makes it six games to none, I believe?'

Vadhi turned to Kelsey. 'He's cheating.'

Kelsey sipped her coffee. 'I don't see how.'

'But, if this game is just luck, then how could he win six in a row?'

'I played this game for twenty years in the Banner mess halls,' said Caelius; 'it's not mere luck; there's skill involved too. Shall we reset the board?'

Vadhi folded her arms across her chest. 'No. Kelsey can play you. I don't play cheats.'

'Those are strong words, young lady,' he said, as he tipped the game pieces into a velvet bag. 'I never cheat. I might bluff a little, but the Banner would have barred me from the mess if I'd cheated. Just be thankful we're not playing for money.'

Vadhi sighed. 'Fine. One more game. Anything to relieve the tedium of being stuck in this tiny apartment. Can I open a bottle of wine?'

Caelius raised an eyebrow. 'Dawn was only a couple of hours ago, and you want to start drinking? We should hold off until lunchtime.'

'Aye,' said Kelsey, 'because that worked out so well yesterday. Vadhi could barely walk by sunset.'

Vadhi frowned. 'You weren't much better; you got all teary about your dragon.'

'So? I miss her. At least I didn't throw up all over the bathroom.'

Caelius shook his head as he placed the pieces back onto the gaming board. 'And I thought that being trapped in here with two beautiful young women would be an enjoyable experience. You certainly bicker a lot. It's clear that neither of you have had to spend much time in enforced isolation. One time, when I was on a barren rock of a world, we had to stay in a damp, rotten barracks for six months while the storms raged outside. We had to entertain ourselves, or go mad.'

'I have plenty experience of that,' said Kelsey, 'which is probably why I have a low tolerance of it now. I was chained up for months, with only an annoying Rakanese guy for company.'

'You've told that story before,' said Vadhi. 'Could we not go for a little walk?'

'Aye,' said Kelsey. 'I want to go to Cumulus, to see if the rumours about Belinda are true. Maybe Edmond is making it all up.'

'Impossible,' said Caelius.

'Which bit?'

'All of it, young lady. You would never get into Cumulus. You would need a god to build a bridge, and how could they do that with you around? Their powers wouldn't work. And, no matter how hard it is for you to believe it, you're going to have to accept that Belinda is marrying the Second Ascendant. It's best that you forget all about her; she might have once seemed like a friend, but it was an illusion. Ascendants aren't the same as us, none of the gods are. They don't make friends with mortals, just as we don't make friends with mice.'

'Get us some books, then,' said Kelsey. 'I'd happily read all day.'

'I will, as soon as it's safe to go back outside. Why don't you tell us more about your dragon? I have some questions about a few of the things you said yesterday.'

'Like what?'

'You said that you were a dragon rider.'

'Aye?'

He gave her a look that reminded her of a parent admonishing a child for lying. 'You bonded with a dragon, did you?'

'Aye, I did.'

'On Dragon Eyre...'

Kelsey sighed. 'Here we go again.'

'On Dragon Eyre,' Caelius repeated, 'riders spend at least a decade being groomed by their chosen dragon. They go through a whole series of convoluted rituals, progressing in stages. Then, the selected rider has to wait until the previous rider retires or dies. It's a lifelong commitment.'

'So? The dragons on Lostwell didn't have any of those weird traditions. They were wild. That doesn't make my bond to Frostback worth any less.'

'Hmm.'

'What's that supposed to mean?'

'A dragon rider,' he said; 'a *true* dragon rider, is not allowed to have any other relationships. That includes lovers, boyfriends, whatever. They are permitted to have but one passion – their dragon. They can't afford to split their loyalties, and dragons can get extremely jealous. Yet, you claim to love my son. Let me ask you a question, young Kelsey – if you had to choose between Van and this Frostback, whom would you pick?'

'And why would I have to choose?'

'What a strange question. Let me put it into simple terms – if your dragon wants to go north, and Van wants to go south, who would you follow? A slighter cruder question – where do you spend your nights? Dragons expect their riders to share their lairs, to keep them clean, as well as to provide company. Is my son to return home to an empty bed every evening?'

Kelsey cringed. 'I don't know.'

'Perhaps you should think about it. I once knew a few riders. They would have rather died than be separated from their dragons, and their dragons would destroy anything in their paths to get their riders back. It was a known weak spot, that we used to target. Capture a dragon's rider, and that dragon would become unstable, and their sense of honour would lead them into making all kinds of foolish mistakes.'

'Shut up and play the damn game,' said Kelsey.

There was a loud rap on the front door of the apartment, and Caelius got to his feet.

'Think about my words,' he said, as he walked towards the hallway.

Kelsey scowled at his back as he left the room.

Vadhi narrowed her eyes. 'Who would you choose?'

'Not you as well, Vadhi,' said Kelsey. 'Both – that's who I choose. I want both.'

'But, what if...'

Kelsey raised a hand. 'Quiet; I'm listening.'

They fell into silence, and Kelsey strained her ears to hear what was going on in the hallway. Caelius was talking with someone in a low voice; a man by the sound of it. Their words were too quiet to make out, and she felt her anxiety return. Caelius seldom received visitors, excepting the occasional delivery of supplies.

They waited, and then heard the front door close. Caelius walked back into the sitting room, with a bag, which he placed onto the table.

'This should last us a few days,' he said, opening the bag. 'Bread, wine, cheese...'

'What were you talking about?' said Kelsey. 'Who was it?'

'An old friend from the Golden Fist.'

Kelsey frowned. There was something in Caelius's eyes that signalled alarm, despite the calm tone in his voice.

'And?' she said.

Caelius sat. 'Nothing; just rumours.'

'What rumours?'

'Gossip. It appears that my old friend somehow knew that I was harbouring at least one person in this apartment and, if he knows, then, well, I guess that most of my old Banner know.'

'Of course they know,' said Kelsey. 'This is exactly what I said would happen. Dozens of folk saw me and Vadhi out shopping with you a couple of days ago, and the walls in this apartment block are paper-thin. We're in danger here, aren't we? We should move.'

Caelius rubbed his chin. 'Where? This is still the safest place for us. No gods will be able to use their powers with you here, and my ballista will keep anyone from getting inside.'

'But there's nowhere to run. If the Banners come round, we'll be trapped.'

'Then we'll make a last stand worthy of a mess hall song.'

Kelsey stared at him.

He opened a bottle of wine. 'Perhaps we should start early today.'

'Are you out of your mind?' said Kelsey. 'You want to be drunk when they turn up?'

'No one is going to turn up, young lady.'

Another knock came from the front door, and Caelius blinked.

'Are you expecting anyone else?' said Vadhi.

Caelius shook his head.

'Shit,' muttered Kelsey.

'Remain calm,' said Caelius, standing. He picked up a loaded crossbow from by his chair. 'Get under the table, and stay there. We'll not go down without a fight.'

Kelsey and Vadhi got to their feet, then crouched under the table. Caelius checked the crossbow, took a breath, then walked out into the hallway. Vadhi began to tremble under the table.

'Yes?' came Caelius's voice from the hall. 'Who is it?'

A muffled voice replied, and Kelsey heard the front door open.

'Enter, and close the door behind you,' said Caelius.

The door clicked shut.

'You haven't changed,' said Caelius. 'Who's the girl?'

'What?' said a voice. 'I turn up here after all this time, and that's what you ask me?'

Kelsey's heart soared. It was Van. She grinned at Vadhi.

Caelius sighed. 'Welcome home, son. Who's the girl?'

'Her name is Jade, and she's a friend,' said Van. 'Jade, tell my father that we're only friends.'

'What?' said the demigod's voice.

'Tell my father that we're not romantically involved.'

'Oh. No, we're not. Are we friends? I didn't know that. I did try to seduce Van when I first met him, but he's in love with someone else.'

'You're in love with someone else, son?' said Caelius. 'Who?'

'Can we come into the apartment, father?'

'You are in the apartment, son.'

'Yes, we're standing in a hallway in front of a loaded ballista. I have some questions about that, but they can wait.'

'Tell me who you're in love with, and then we can all have a drink together.'

'Dear gods!' cried Van. 'Fine. Her name is Kelsey Holdfast, and we're looking for her.'

'Stop there, son. Follow me.'

Kelsey wriggled out from under the table as the door to the sitting room opened. Caelius walked in, followed by Van and Jade. Van's eyes scanned the room, then he halted as he saw Kelsey, his mouth opening. Kelsey's face split into a wide smile and she ran to him across the sitting room floor. He opened his arms and gathered her up, pulling her close to his chest.

'You're alive,' he said; 'you're here.'

'Shut up and kiss me.'

His lips found hers and she closed her eyes as they kissed, her heart bursting with relief and joy. She felt his arms round her waist and back; they were strong again, and he seemed back to his old self.

'Please stop,' said Jade.

Caelius laughed, and slapped his son across the back. 'Well done, my boy.'

Kelsey and Van parted, their eyes still locked together.

Van smiled down at her. 'You're so beautiful. I never want to let you go.'

Kelsey flushed. 'How did you get to Implacatus?'

'We stole Simon's Quadrant,' Van said. 'How did you get here? I mean, how did you find my father?'

'It wasn't that difficult,' she said.

'We should return to the waterfall cavern,' said Jade. 'I think we were followed here.'

'What?' said Caelius. 'No. You can't leave just yet; I haven't seen my boy in years. I thought you were dead, Van, until Kelsey told me that you still lived. Sit down; have a drink before you go.'

Van seemed oblivious to everyone else, his eyes never leaving Kelsey's face.

'Please,' said Caelius.

'Alright, father,' said Van, 'but we'll need to be quick. Jade's right. I think that someone might have recognised me as we entered the Banner district. We appeared on one of the upper levels of the city, and we had a long walk to get here.' He noticed Vadhi. 'Hello.'

'Hello, sir,' she said. 'What's going on in the City?'

Van said nothing as they sat, his arm remaining round Kelsey's waist. Caelius picked up the open bottle of wine and looked around for glasses.

'We're wasting time,' said Jade. 'We've already spent too long on Implacatus.'

'We won't be long,' said Caelius. 'So, son, how have you been getting on?'

Van glanced around at the shabby apartment. 'They put you in here?'

'Yes. After the Golden Fist was disbanded. They cut my pension too. They decided I was the father of a traitor.'

Van gave his father a wry smile. 'Sorry about that.'

'You were never the kind of boy who gave much thought to the consequences of his actions. Still, let's not dwell on that. I killed Sabat.'

'You did what? You killed an Ancient?'

Caelius nodded. 'He deserved it.'

'Tell him the whole story,' said Kelsey.

'I cut his head off and ripped out his immortal heart.'

'That's not what I meant,' said Kelsey. 'Tell him how you tricked me.'

'Alright. I may have taken advantage of Kelsey's blocking powers to get close to him. For which, I have apologised, several times over. Still, it was worth it to kill a god. If I had my way, I'd kill every last one of them.'

Jade glared at him. 'You would, would you? Nasty old man.'

'Jade is a demigod, father,' said Van; 'as well as a friend.'

'You keep saying that we're friends,' said Jade. 'When did this happen? Why did no one tell me?'

Caelius eyed her. 'A demigod, eh? Why didn't you know that Kelsey was in the apartment?'

'Because I wasn't trying to use my powers.'

'What powers?'

'Death, old man, so don't push me.'

'I think we're safe enough, what with young Miss Holdfast here.'

Jade reached forward, and grabbed Caelius's hand. 'She can't stop my powers going through touch. Now, say sorry.'

The colour drained from Caelius's face.

'Leave him be,' said Kelsey. 'We owe him, despite what he did to trick me.'

Jade glanced at her. 'I will, as soon as he apologises.'

'I... I'm sorry,' said Caelius.

Jade released her grip with a smile. 'There. That wasn't so difficult. Oh, your heartbeat is irregular, old man, and you have an ulcer forming in your stomach. Well, you did. I healed them both for you, and I also fixed your knees. Now, what do you say?'

'Thank you,' said Caelius, rubbing his hand, his eyes wide.

'That's right.' She turned to Van. 'Let's go. I've had enough of this old bastard.'

'He's my father, Jade.'

'So? My father is a monster.'

'But, I haven't finished,' said Caelius. 'My son goes on an operation and doesn't return, and you expect me to catch up with him in five minutes?'

'It would take too long to explain everything about the world where we're now living,' said Van.

'Oh, I know all about the City,' said Caelius; 'Kelsey and Vadhi have told me. I want to know about your old Golden Fist colleagues. How's Sohul? He was always your best friend among the officers.'

Van glanced down. 'Sohul died on Lostwell. He drowned, on the morning of the last day.'

'I'll have to tell his mother. What a shame. How about...'

'There's no one from the Golden Fist, father. My new Banner consists of Black Crown and Undying Flame soldiers, mostly. The Golden Fist were pulled out after Renko's failure. Did you hear about all that?'

'Yes.'

'Belinda's here,' said Kelsey.

Van's eyes widened. 'How?'

Kelsey shrugged. 'She's getting married to Edmond, apparently.'

'No. Really? I would have thought that unlikely.'

'Why, son?' said Caelius. 'She's an Ascendant. She's back in Cumulus, living a life of splendour and luxury, while the rest of us scrabble about in the dirt. So, are you going to marry Kelsey?'

Van's face flushed.

'She has a tongue on her that could wither an Ancient,' Caelius went on, 'but I think she'd make a good wife. Your mother would have liked her. She certainly beats any of your previous girlfriends.'

Jade stood. 'Come on. Get the Quadrant ready. This mortal nonsense is making my head feel funny.'

Van nodded. 'Perhaps we should go.'

'I thought you didn't know how to use a Quadrant,' said Kelsey.

'Flavus showed me a couple of things.'

'Who?'

'Lieutenant Flavus, a scout. Never mind, you'll be meeting him and the others soon.'

'Frostback?'

Van shook his head. 'She disappeared after Simon snatched you. We haven't seen her or Halfclaw since then.'

Kelsey's face fell. 'What? She ran away?'

'You're the only reason she stayed as long as she did,' Van said. 'She doesn't care about the rest of us. Who knows – she might come back if she discovers you have returned.'

'I've been riding on Dawnflame,' said Jade.

'No way,' said Kelsey. 'That sounds like horse shit. You're claiming to be Dawnflame's rider?'

'I didn't say that. The dragon and I have come to an agreement, based on a mutual desire for revenge. We've burned the Fortress of the Lifegiver, the salve mine, and the Royal Palace, so far. I killed Felice. While the rest of the City has been cowering in terror, Dawnflame and I have been leading the resistance.'

'You? And Dawnflame? Pyre's sweaty crotch, Jade, I would have thought...'

Jade leaned over and stared at Kelsey. 'You thought what?'

'Nothing.'

'Say it, Holdfast. You thought what? That I would be a coward? That I would serve Simon? I've always known that you hated me, but you don't know me. Everyone was weeping and wailing when they heard that you'd been taken, but I didn't. We had no need of you, or your strange powers; Dawnflame and I have been managing fine without you.'

Kelsey narrowed her eyes. 'Then why did you come here to rescue me?'

'Van asked,' she said. 'He wanted someone with real powers to protect him in Serene. He said please. He was very polite. Unlike you.'

Kelsey stared at the demigod. 'What about Deathfang?'

'Deathfang's dead,' said Jade. 'Simon killed him.'

'Frostback's father is dead? No wonder she ran away.'

Jade turned to Van, her eyes tight. 'The Quadrant. Now.'

Van pulled the metal device from his clothes. Caelius squinted at it.

'I'm sorry, father,' Van said, 'but we should leave. We're placing you in danger.'

Caelius snorted.

'Did you hear something?' said Vadhi.

Caelius got to his feet, and walked over to the narrow window.

'It appears that the tenement building is surrounded,' he said. 'Lord Bastion is outside.'

'Shit,' cried Van, jumping to his feet. He joined his father at the window. 'Looks like an entire regiment is breaking down the doors.'

'I'll man the ballista,' said Caelius. 'That should give you time to get out of here.'

'And then what?' said Van. 'They'll kill you.'

Caelius faced his son. 'It'll be worth it to know that you all got away.'

Shouts rang out from the stairwell of the building, along with the thump of boots.

Kelsey grabbed the crossbow. 'Van; now, before they burst through the front door.'

Van stared at his father, who narrowed his eyes.

'I don't like that look on your face, son,' he said. 'Whatever you're planning, stop it at once.'

There was a crash from the hallway as the door was kicked down. Van glided his thumb over the Quadrant, and the air shimmered. Kelsey slipped on the wet ground as the view around her was plunged into darkness. She panicked for a second, then saw that they were in a large cavern, a low glow coming from a tall waterfall on one side. Van helped her to her feet.

'What did I just say?' cried Caelius, waving his arms.

'I couldn't leave you there, father,' said Van. 'Bastion would have tortured you.'

'I'm a grown man; I can make up my own mind.'

Jade rolled her eyes. 'You should have left him.'

'Where are we?' said Vadhi.

Kelsey glanced at the small group that had gathered in front of them. There were three dragons – Dawnflame, Bittersea and Firestone, along with two humans. She recognised Maddie's sister from the roof of Cuidrach Palace, but the man was a stranger.

'We're in our waterfall cavern,' said Jade. 'This is Rosie, Flavus and the dragons. Everyone, this is Kelsey, Van's grumpy old father, and a mortal girl that no one has bothered to introduce me to.'

'Her name is Vadhi,' said Kelsey. 'She's an Exile from Lostwell.'

Flavus bowed his head. 'I am delighted to see you all back safe and sound. I trust the Quadrant performed as desired, sir?'

Van nodded. 'It worked just as you said.'

'You were away for hours,' said Rosie; 'we thought you were dead.'

'We had to trek for miles in Serene,' said Jade.

Bittersea stretched out her neck and sniffed Kelsey. 'You are back, Holdfast.'

'Hi, dragons,' said Kelsey. 'I heard about Deathfang. What about Darksky and Burntskull?'

'They have been swayed by Simon,' said Dawnflame. 'Darksky is now my sworn enemy.'

'The Ascendant is holding one of Darksky's children as a hostage,' said Van; 'it's not her fault.'

'She is a coward,' said Dawnflame. 'Her sense of honour buckled and broke. If she were a true friend, she would sacrifice one of her children to keep her obligations.'

Caelius chuckled. 'That's the dragons I remember.'

'Silence, worm,' said Dawnflame. 'Van, is this being of value to you?'

'He's my father, Dawnflame.'

'I know; I heard Jade's words. Answer my question before I kill him and give his flesh to my son to devour.'

Van nodded. 'Yes, he is of great value to me.'

'What talents does he possess? Can he help us?'

'I am an old soldier,' said Caelius, puffing out his chest, 'and I have faced your kind many times. I do not fear you.'

'He killed a god,' said Kelsey.

Dawnflame closed her jaws. 'Did he? That is a useful skill to have. I shall allow him to live.'

Kelsey felt Van's hand on her arm. He nodded towards the waterfall, and they walked away from the others. They passed to the left of the main flow of water, and emerged into the red sunlight. Kelsey squinted until her eyes adjusted, then looked around at the verdant valley.

'This is where we've been hiding,' said Van. 'We're to the west of the salve mine and the old dragon colony, but with the Quadrant in our possession, we should be safe from Simon.'

She glanced at him as he took her hand. 'How are you feeling? About the salve, I mean. You seem better.'

'I am better. I owe you, Kelsey, for looking after me. I was an idiot; I thought I could control it, but I was wrong. Are we... are we alright?'

'Aye.'

He smiled, and they kissed again.

'Why aren't you in Jezra?' she said.

'Jezra fell after you were taken. With the Queen gone, there was nothing we could do but surrender. Kelsey, I thought I'd lost you forever. How did you survive on Implacatus? I mean, before you found my father?'

'We rummaged through the garbage for food, and caused a lot of annoyance to the gods. Simon was right about that; that's why he sent me there. If Caelius hadn't killed that Ancient, then I reckon we could have stayed hidden for ages. Your father just couldn't help himself.'

'Did he treat you alright?'

'Aye, once he believed my story. You don't seem very happy to see him.'

'My father and I have had our problems; mostly since my mother died. I said some cruel things, and he acted like an idiot. All the same, there was no way I was going to leave him to die. Bastion would have... well, let's not think about that. Are you sure about Belinda?'

'No, but Caelius is.'

'The Belinda I knew in Shawe Myre would never have agreed to marry Edmond.'

'I know. Still, I guess people change. She was always an Ascendant at heart. Wait. If you surrendered to Simon, then how did you get here?'

'Jade rescued me from the Fortress of the Lifegiver.'

Kelsey frowned.

'Don't be like that. Jade's unorthodox, but I think her heart is in the right place.'

'She has a heart? Are you sure it's not just because she fancies you?'

'Those days are long gone. She cares more about her cats than any of us.' He pointed. 'Look; there's one of them.'

Kelsey noticed a large ginger tomcat sprawled out on a rock in the sunshine.

'She brought her cats here?'

'She rescued them before she came for me.'

'That doesn't surprise me.'

'At the same time, she and Dawnflame have all but wrecked Simon's plans. They burnt the stocks of salve taken from the mine, and now we have his Quadrant.'

'And the Queen?'

Van shrugged. 'No idea. Cardova is with her, though, so she should be safe, as long as she keeps her head down. It's up to us to topple Simon. You, me, Jade, and Dawnflame.'

'Can we use the Quadrant to get back to the City?'

'No. I only know how to go to Implacatus and back; that's all Flavus was taught.'

'Silva knows how to use a Quadrant; where is she?'

'With the Queen? I'm not sure.'

Bittersea's head plunged through the waterfall, and Van and Kelsey were soaked by the spray.

'Holdfast,' said the dragon, staring at her.

'Aye?'

'Do you wish to see Frostback again?'

'Of course. Do you know where she is?'

'I do.'

'You do?' said Van. 'Why didn't you tell us this?'

'What business is it of yours, soldier?' said the old dragon. 'Frost-back is in mourning for her father, and has isolated herself with her mate. The Holdfast girl is the only human I would reveal the truth to – she is Frostback's rider; she deserves to know.' The dragon pulled herself through the waterfall, watching as the ginger tomcat bolted into the undergrowth. She turned back to look at Kelsey. 'I shall fly to her location, and inform her of your return, Holdfast. She will come, if she wishes. Or not.'

'Thank you, Bittersea,' said Kelsey. 'Tell her I love her; tell her I've missed her.'

'I shall.'

Bittersea extended her wings, and ascended into the red sky, then soared away to the west.

Kelsey grinned. 'With Frostback and Halfclaw added to our little band, we might have a chance.'

They walked back into the cavern, hand in hand.

Dawnflame stared at them. 'We should plan our next attack.'

'I'm ready to leave now,' said Jade.

'Let's wait for Bittersea to return,' said Dawnflame.

'Why?' said the demigod.

'That is not your concern, demigod.'

Jade glared at her, then looked at Kelsey, who shrugged.

'Something's going on,' said the demigod. 'I don't like secrets being kept from me.'

'Secrets?' said Caelius. 'What secrets?'

'Let's all eat first,' said Rosie. 'A bit of food will make us all happier.'

'Don't let Caelius cook,' said Kelsey. 'No offence.'

The old soldier frowned.

'I can cook,' said Rosie. 'Everyone, sit down. Well, not the dragons, obviously, they can remain crouching. Does everyone like goat?'

Caelius groaned. 'A damp cave, hostile dragons, no beds or chairs, and only goat to eat? If you'd told me your plan, son, I could have grabbed all of our provisions first, but no; you knew better, didn't you?' He shook his head. 'When will you learn to think things through?'

Van brandished the Quadrant. 'I could always send you back to Lord Bastion's warm embrace?'

'Don't fight,' said Rosie. 'We're all friends.'

'No, we're not,' said Jade. 'Would people please stop saying that? Rosie, you are my friend. Flavus... you're alright, I guess, though I wouldn't stretch it to "friend". I don't even like the rest of you. Van is useful, I suppose, but Caelius and Kelsey are mean and rude.' She frowned at Vadhi. 'And I don't know anything about you. Probably for the best.'

'That's why I have a grudging admiration for you, demigod,' said Dawnflame. 'You care not for niceties. Those of us gathered here may not be friends, but we are bound together, by one thing – revenge. We will burn the City and its gods, and we shall not cease until Simon's smouldering and beheaded corpse is lying before me. On this, can we all agree?'

'Fine by me,' said Jade.

'Alright,' said Kelsey. 'Let's have some of that goat, and then we can wreak some bloody revenge.'

Rosie's glance fell. 'Revenge is an unhealthy motivation. I'll fight, but to save the people I love, and to protect my home; not for hate. If we let hate rule us, then we will never win.'

Van nodded. 'That's good enough for me. Flavus?'

The lieutenant bowed his head. 'I am ready to receive your orders, sir.'

'Thank you. Vadhi?'

The Torduan woman looked up from where she was sitting on a dry patch of rocky ground. 'What?'

'Are you with us?'

Vadhi sighed. 'Yes, sir.'

'Are you not going to ask me, son?' said Caelius.

'What – ask you if you're prepared to fight against the gods? It's what you've wanted to do all your life, father.'

'Ask me anyway.'

Van rubbed his face. 'Fine. Father, will you help us fight the Tenth Ascendant?'

Caelius grinned. 'Count me in.'

CHAPTER 23

TORMENTED

T ara, Auldan, The City – 20th Mikalis 3423

Kagan stared at Emily as she was led out of the room by the Roser guards, his hands shaking with frustration and anger. He turned to Amalia and Naxor as soon as the door was closed.

'What are we doing?' he cried. 'What about our plan? Are we handing Emily over to Simon? We can't; she risked everything to bring Maxwell back to us. We can't betray her.'

'Sit down, Kagan,' said Amalia. 'Don't get flustered.'

'I'll admit to being a little confused myself,' said Naxor, pouring himself a large brandy.

'Is that supposed to surprise me?' said Amalia.

Naxor picked up the Fated Blade in one hand as he sipped his drink. 'This is a far better sword than the one Kagan procured for our plan. It should slice right through Simon's armour.'

'I don't understand,' said Kagan. 'Are we going through with the plan or not?'

'Please don't shout in front of Maxwell,' said Amalia. 'We don't want to frighten him. He must be scared, getting passed around and taken on strange journeys.' She held the child up and kissed him. 'Everything's going to be fine now; you'll see.'

'Is it?' said Kagan, sitting down next to her, his eyes on Maxwell. 'What about what Naxor said – that Simon would use Maxwell against us?'

'That is why we're going to kill him, Kagan.'

'So, we are going through with the plan?'

'Of course,' said Amalia. 'Emily Aurelian is a different matter altogether. If we succeed against Simon, then we can decide what to do with that troublesome family. However, it made no sense whatsoever to let her go. Simon would know, and he would punish us. She'll be fine in the basement for a while.'

Kagan shook his head.

'Have some brandy,' said Naxor. 'That'll cheer you up.'

Kagan glared at the demigod, who smirked back at him.

'The timing will be delicate,' said Amalia. 'If we assume that Simon will use the Quadrant to appear here, in this room, then we need to stay ready and prepared. Grandson, hide that sword, if you would. Thank you. Do you have the salve with you?'

Naxor pushed the Fated Blade under the couch, then patted a pocket.

'Excellent.'

'And are you ready, grandmother?' he said.

'Ready for what?'

'Ready to declare your passion for Simon? That's your role, remember? You're going to have to make it convincing; otherwise he'll know it's a trick.'

'I'm sure I'll manage.'

Naxor turned to Kagan. 'Don't get too jealous. Actually, no; get jealous – that would be more realistic. Now, it might be the case that Simon has already seen Emily arrive; if so, then we'll have to think on our feet. Afterwards, we should kill the Aurelians. We could blame it on Simon.'

'I disagree,' said Kagan.

'I thought you might,' said Naxor. 'Still, there isn't room in this City for two Queens; am I right?'

'You are,' said Amalia.

'Thought so. So, either you will have to bow to her, or she will have to bow to you. As neither seems particularly likely, then getting rid of them discreetly would appear to be our best option. We could reduce their bodies to dust, so there's no evidence.'

'At times, grandson,' said Amalia, 'I think you are as twisted as Simon.'

Naxor smiled. 'But not as twisted as, say, someone who opened the gates in the Middle Walls to the greenhides?'

'One tiny mistake, and you cast it up at every opportunity?'

'I'm not sure the good people of Medio would think it amounted to a tiny mistake, grandmother. Let's face it; your heart is as sour and dark as any Ascendant's. I'm talking about murdering one family. I have a long way to go before I can compete with you.'

'Maxwell doesn't want to hear these things about his mother,' she said, standing. 'I'm going to give him a bath, and get him out of these horrid clothes. At least he looks well fed.'

A servant opened the door. 'My lady,' he gasped.

Amalia frowned. 'What's wrong? If you are here to tell me that the Aurelians have escaped, then I advise that you start running.'

'No, my lady,' said the servant, his hands trembling. 'Lord Simon has arrived.'

Kagan jumped to his feet. 'Where?'

'He has come by carriage from Ooste, my lord. Along with... along with about a hundred greenhides, including the enormous creature that he brought to dinner. They're at the front gates of the palace.'

'He arrived by carriage?' said Amalia. 'Why?'

'I don't know, my lady. I ran here to tell you as soon as I saw them approach.'

Amalia, Kagan and Naxor glanced at each other. Kagan strode to the window, and gazed out. Simon was marching up a gravel path towards one of the side entrances to the palace, while a mass of greenhides was accompanying him. Towering over them was the young greenhide queen. Kagan felt his heart lurch, and he thought he was going to vomit.

'Thank you,' said Amalia to the servant. 'That will be all.'

The servant turned, and ran from the room.

'Stay calm,' said Amalia. 'This changes nothing.'

The three of them waited in silence. Voices boomed through the doorway, then the sound of boots rapping off the marble floors. The doors swung open, and Simon entered, wearing an expression of rage.

'Your Grace,' said Amalia, bowing her head. 'What a pleasure it is to see you here.'

'I live here now,' said Simon. 'Maeladh is mine, after those bastards razed the Royal Palace to the ground. I have brought Matilda along, in case any dragons come for me here. I have ordered my greenhides to surround the palace, and have removed every ballista and catapult from Ooste and Pella – they will be placed onto the roofs of Maeladh.'

'Of course, your Grace,' said Amalia. 'Will you be requiring Roser militia to assist with this?'

Simon stared at her. 'They're my militia, and I have already passed on my orders. I've also brought Doria, Silva and Salvor; they will need somewhere to stay here instead. That idiot son of yours...' His eyes flitted to Maxwell, and he frowned. 'I meant Montieth,' he said after a moment. 'Montieth is here. He followed me from Ooste.' He pointed at Maxwell. 'Explain.'

'Certainly, your Grace. Emily Aurelian arrived here this morning, just as you predicted. She is being held with the other Aurelians in the basement.'

Simon collapsed into a seat. 'That's the first piece of good news I've had in a while. I shall take the entire sunward wing of the palace – have your things moved out by sunset.'

'Yes, your Grace. Apart from Salvor, Doria and Silva, did you bring much luggage?'

'No. It's all burnt.'

'Then, your Grace, might I ask why you took a carriage?'

'They stole my Quadrant.'

Naxor gasped. 'What? Apologies, your Grace; I was just startled by the news. Jade has the Quadrant?'

Simon turned his head to stare at the demigod. 'She does. I sense disappointment in you. That's good; I had imagined that you might be gloating.'

'What happened, your Grace?' said Amalia.

'The renegade dragon ambushed me, and while I was recovering from the inferno, someone took the Quadrant. Then they flew away. I am going to impale Jade upon a stake; I imagine it will take several days for a demigod to die from that. The dragon I will chain and muzzle, and then I shall dangle her in front of the greenhides.'

'What if they remain in the Eastern Mountains, your Grace?' said Naxor.

'They won't. They have a taste for fire and death now; they will be back. And when they return, I will be ready. I do not believe that Jade knows how to use the Quadrant; it is nothing but a useless scrap of metal to her. My biggest fear is that she destroys it. If she does, then I will be stranded here for all eternity.' He shrugged. 'I lasted millennia on Yocasta – a desert wasteland. The City is a great improvement on that, at least.'

Montieth walked into the room, his eyes tight. He noticed Amalia. 'Mother.'

She nodded to him. 'Welcome back to Maeladh, son.'

'He's not staying long,' said Simon. He turned to him. 'Well? What do you want? You followed me all the way here, so I presume you want something.'

'Yes, your Grace,' said Montieth, striding forwards. 'I want you to fulfil your promises.'

'What promises, you ignorant wretch?'

'You promised me, your Grace, that you would provide me with a steady supply of salve from the mine in the mountains, and yet I have sat patiently in Dalrig all these months, waiting in vain for the salve to appear. Where is it?'

Simon leapt to his feet with a roar. He gripped Montieth round the throat with his left hand, and began punching the god in the face, over and over. Montieth tried to struggle and scream, then he hung limp, his face a bloody pulp, as the Ascendant's fist pounded him. Simon tossed him to the corner of the room, where he hit the wall and slid to the floor. Simon barked out a laugh, then sat back down again.

'Yet another of my rescuers betrays me,' he said. 'First, Naxor hid the existence of the salve mine from me, and now Montieth makes demands.' He glanced at Amalia, then Kagan. 'With the loss of Felice, only you two remain loyal to me. A bitter queen and a pathetic mortal.'

'I am loyal, your Grace,' said Naxor.

'Are you?' Simon said. 'Then why don't I trust you?'

'You can trust me, your Grace; I swear it.'

'We shall see about that.'

Montieth groaned from the corner of the room and pulled himself to his feet. His face had healed, but was caked in dried blood.

'Get on your knees,' said Simon.

Montieth glared at the Ascendant, but obeyed. He slipped back down to his knees, and bowed his head.

'Now,' said Simon; 'let's try that again, shall we? What do you want?'

'Most glorious and beloved Lord Simon, mighty ruler of the City, foremost in wisdom and mercy, hear my plea.'

Simon pulled a face. 'Don't overdo it.'

'Apologies, your Grace. I humbly beg that you spare some salve for me; just a little, please.'

'That's better. Salve, you say? I am a generous ruler, and would be delighted to give you some; however, the renegade dragon has destroyed the stocks at the mine, and I currently find myself with no means to travel back there. I daresay that one could walk there in a few years, once the local greenhides have died out, but until then you must help me regain the Quadrant.'

Montieth blinked. 'There is no salve, your Grace?'

'Is that all you heard?' Simon sighed. 'Naxor, give Montieth the vial of concentrated salve that you have hidden in your pocket. Oh, and pass me the Fated Blade from under the couch at the same time – we wouldn't want it falling into the wrong hands now, would we?'

Naxor froze.

Amalia turned to him. 'You rat!'

'I had no choice, grandmother,' Naxor cried; 'he knew everything; there was nothing I could do.'

'You liar,' said Simon, laughing. He turned to Amalia. 'The truth is that I asked him to test your loyalty, Amalia; a test which you have spectacularly failed. Let me see if I get this right – Naxor was going to throw the salve into my face, and then poor little mortal Kagan was going to chop my head off?' He laughed again, louder. 'And your role in this sordid conspiracy, my beautiful queen?' He stood, and walked slowly towards Amalia. 'You were going to attempt to fool me into thinking that you were passionately in love with me. Are you going to deny it?'

Amalia said nothing, her eyes shining with terror as Simon approached. He leaned forward, and she clutched tightly onto Maxwell.

'Give me the child,' he said.

'No, please. Your Grace, please don't hurt him.'

'Me, hurt a child?' he said. 'The very idea.'

He plucked Maxwell from her arms, then slapped her across the face as she tried to resist. He held up Maxwell and gazed at him.

'So fragile,' he said. 'Kagan, take your son.'

Simon handed the infant to Kagan, who wrapped his arms round him and backed away.

'Now, Amalia,' said the Ascendant; 'where were we? Stand up.'

Amalia got to her feet.

'Naxor, Montieth; take her arms. Ensure she doesn't struggle.'

'No,' cried Kagan. 'Leave her alone.'

'Be quiet, mortal,' said Simon, as Naxor and Montieth took hold of Amalia's arms. 'As of this moment, I have decided to let you live – I need someone to look after little Maxwell for me, and who better than his father?' He pointed in Kagan's face. 'But, if you cross me again, I will crush your son's skull in front of you.'

'Say nothing, Kagan,' cried Amalia, as Simon turned back to face her.

'That's right,' said the Ascendant; 'listen to Amalia, Kagan.' He reached over to the couch and picked up the Fated Blade. 'Now, young goddess, the time for your plotting and conspiring is over. In a few days, your body will be swinging from the gallows, along with those of the Aurelians, while your son and mortal lover watch. You will hear the crowds cheer as I torture you. "Down with the God-Queen!" they will chant. "Death to the tyrant." I will gut you in front of them, but we have plenty of time before then, so let's give you a little foretaste.'

He gripped the hilt of the Fated Blade, and slowly pushed it into Amalia's stomach, twisting the sword as he stared into her face. Blood came from her mouth, and she choked and gasped, her eyes burning with her agony. He pushed the blade in further, smiling, then pulled it out, and a spray of her blood spattered the front of his stone armour. Amalia's head lolled, then she began to heal. Simon reached into a pocket and withdrew a vial. He flicked the lid off with a thumb, then waited for a moment, watching as the wound in Amalia's waist began to close.

'Not too soon; not too late,' he said. 'Now, I think.'

He held the vial out and forced Amalia's chin upwards. A few drops of the thick, red liquid fell onto her tongue, and she cried out.

'Release her,' said Simon.

Naxor and Montieth let go of her arms and she collapsed to the floor, her hands reaching for her bloody stomach as she sobbed and gasped in pain.

'What have you done to her?' cried Kagan.

Simon pointed the Fated Blade at Maxwell's throat. 'Did you forget something, mortal?'

Kagan froze, his eyes on the sharp blade brushing against his son's neck. 'Your Grace.'

'That's better,' he said, pulling the sword away. 'I gave her some anti-salve, to stop her healing too much, and, of course, to rob her of her powers.' He placed a boot on her stomach, and pressed down a little, causing her to scream out in pain. 'Ah yes. It seems to have worked.' He leaned over her. 'Such is your treachery rewarded, young goddess. How different things could have been, if only you had remained loyal.'

Montieth knelt by Amalia. 'Fascinating,' he said. 'I have never had the opportunity to experiment with anti-salve on a god as powerful as you, mother.'

Something in Kagan snapped. He clenched his right fist and punched Montieth in the face, cracking the god's nose open. Before anyone else could react, he did the same to Naxor, sending the demigod sprawling to the floor.

Simon chuckled. 'Quite right, Kagan. Both of them deserved a good thumping. And how embarrassing for you two; felled by a mere mortal with a baby in his arms.'

Montieth jumped to his feet and raised his hand.

Simon shook his finger at him. 'Don't even think about it, you pathetic wretch. Take Naxor's concentrated salve, and be on your way back to Dalrig.'

'But, he struck me, your Grace.'

'Yes; it was most amusing. You have ten seconds to leave this room, or I will kill you.'

Montieth held his hand out to Naxor, who passed him a vial of silvery liquid, then the god ran from the room.

Simon eyed Naxor. 'Are you thinking of retaliating against Kagan, too?'

'No, your Grace. I deserved it, just as you said.'

'There's a good boy. Now, carry your grandmother to her cell in the dungeons. I will post a few greenhides down there, to make sure no one thinks about trying to help her escape.'

'Yes, your Grace.'

Simon turned to Kagan. 'And you, my lad, I think you'd better go and find yourself some new quarters. As I said, I am taking the entire sunward flank of the palace as my own. Oh, and don't try to get out the building, as I have ordered the greenhides to kill anyone on sight who tries to leave without my express permission.'

Kagan hung his head. Naxor picked up Amalia in his arms, and she cried out in torment, then Kagan followed them out of the room. As soon as they were out of sight of Simon, Kagan turned to the demigod.

'You treacherous bastard, Naxor. I will kill you for what you did today; understand? I will rip your head off.'

'I had no choice, Kagan.'

Kagan gripped Amalia's hand, and crouched by her face. 'I love you, and I will come for you, somehow.'

'No, Kagan,' she gasped. 'Save yourself, and save Maxwell.'

'He's watching us,' said Naxor. 'Just thought you should know.'

Kagan stood, holding onto Maxwell with both arms. The infant started to cry, and Kagan rocked him, as Naxor disappeared down the corridor, Amalia in his arms.

'My lord,' said the servant, her eyes lowered; 'your new quarters have been cleaned, and are ready for you to move into. We have placed the cot by the end of your bed, and set out some food and milk for the child.'

'Thank you,' said Kagan.

The servant bowed. 'Please let us know if you require anything else.'

She strode away, leading another two servants with her. Kagan turned, his arms sore from holding onto Maxwell for so long. He entered his new rooms, and glanced around. His living room had a window, and he walked up to it. The view was to iceward, and he could see the upper half of the massive statue of Prince Michael, and to the left, the grand houses of Princeps Row. He placed Maxwell down onto the rug, and sat, his mind filled with nothing but the image of Simon driving the dark sword into Amalia's waist. He had let her down. He had stood there, like a fool, and had done nothing as the woman he loved was tortured by the god. Punching Montieth and Naxor had been vaguely satisfying, but it was the Ascendant he hated above all else.

He had done nothing, but it had been for a reason. He glanced at

Maxwell, as the infant boy crawled along the rug. Simon would have killed his son if he had resisted, but something didn't make sense. Simon must have known that Kagan had played a full part in the conspiracy, so why had the Ascendant allowed him to live? Why wasn't Kagan in the dungeons along with Amalia? It was probably another trick, or a game.

He put his head in his hands. If only Jade hadn't stolen Simon's Quadrant. The stupid demigod might have doomed the City to Simon's rule for millennia by her actions; what had she been thinking? Compared to her, Kagan had nothing but sympathy and respect for Emily. There was a true Queen, a woman prepared to sacrifice everything to do what was right. And now she was in the dungeons along with Amalia, while Kagan, a coward, was free to roam the palace. He hated himself for a moment, then shook the idea from his mind. He had to be strong, for Maxwell. Perhaps the dragon would come to Tara, with Jade on her shoulders, and Kagan would be able to escape in the confusion, with Maxwell clutched in his arms and Amalia by his side. Even better, maybe he would have a chance to free Emily too, along with the rest of the Aurelians.

It was hopeless. Simon would see; Simon would know, and he would strike them down as easily as swatting a fly.

'Good afternoon,' said a voice. 'May I come in?'

He glanced up, and saw a woman standing by the door. He squinted, recognising her from the dinner with Simon.

'Silva?' he said.

'Yes, Kagan.'

'Come in; take a seat.'

The woman limped over to a couch, and he noticed the bruises on her face.

She sat down, and sighed. 'Thank you.'

'Are you in pain?'

'Just a little. It's nothing. How is Maxwell?'

Kagan looked down at the child. 'Fine, I think. I hope he doesn't remember anything he saw today.'

The infant gazed up at Silva, and smiled. She smiled back, and extended a hand. The child grasped it, and pulled himself up to his feet, beaming from ear to ear.

'Good boy,' said Silva. 'I have to admit; I missed you.'

'You know my son?' said Kagan.

'I was in Jezra with Queen Emily, and Pella before that. The Queen's mother was chiefly responsible for little Maxwell's welfare, but I was around.'

'You were with him for five months,' said Kagan, watching as his son took a step.

'Yes. You should know that the Queen commanded that he be treated as if he were her own child. He wanted for nothing, except his parents, naturally. The Queen did her best.'

'I know she did.'

'Did you care for Elspeth in the same manner?'

'No. Simon had the Aurelians for the first two months, then he brought them here. We put them into an apartment, rather than the dungeons, but it's not a great place to live. I've checked on them most days, for all the good it's done. Can I ask – why are you not in the dungeons? I thought you were Simon's prisoner.'

'I am, but so are you, it seems. I've been dosed with anti-salve, and my leg was badly hurt, so I won't be running anywhere. Simon told me I could walk the halls of the palace. He also informed me that I would be torn to pieces by greenhides if I stepped outside.'

'At the dinner,' Kagan said, 'Simon told us that you didn't care about the Aurelians, or anything but getting back to... sorry, I can't remember the name.'

'I think you're referring to Queen Belinda, the Third Ascendant. Part of what he said was true, I suppose, as I long to see my Queen, but he was lying about the rest, just as he lied about us eating dragon flesh, or when he told the King that Queen Emily was sleeping with a soldier. It's Simon's way, to spread lies about us, to keep us divided.'

'He could be listening to us now.'

'He's read the contents of my soul, and seen everything I have ever done, said or thought. My words to you would not surprise him.'

'Why hasn't he killed us?'

'I'm not sure. I think he needs people around him to bully, people who will fawn over him, and praise his name. People like Naxor.'

Kagan scowled. 'That filthy bastard.'

Silva shrugged. 'He is what he is. I knew he was rotten from the start, and when he betrayed Queen Belinda, I vowed never to trust him again. But forget about him for a moment. I have a question for you. When we arrived, it was by carriage. Did Simon tell you why?'

'Jade stole his Quadrant.'

Silva's face lit up. 'Yes!' She beamed at Maxwell. 'What a clever girl Jade is, little Max.'

'What are you talking about?' said Kagan, his eyes narrowing. 'This is a disaster. Without a Quadrant, Simon could be here for thousands of years.'

'No, Kagan,' she said. 'Lady Jade is turning the tide. Three times she and the dragon have struck, and each time has hurt Simon more. He will have to travel by carriage and boat, and the Eastern Mountains are now completely out of his reach.' She raised her eyes to the heavens. 'Let it be here that Jade strikes next.'

A floorboard creaked by the doorway, and Kagan and Silva turned. A young woman was standing there, a terrified and haunted look on her face.

'This is Lady Doria,' said Silva to Kagan.

'Another demigod?'

'Yes. However, Lady Doria possesses no powers beyond self-healing, and, correct me if I'm wrong, but until today, she hadn't left the Royal Palace in Ooste for a thousand years.'

'That's not true,' said Doria, her voice almost a whisper. 'I was at the coronation of the Aurelians in Pella a few years ago, and I'm only eight hundred years old.'

'My apologies,' said Silva.

'Can we help you?' said Kagan.

'I heard voices... I... Can I come in?'

'Alright,' said Kagan. He frowned. 'This seems a little strange. Why are you all coming here?'

'Safety in numbers,' said Doria, as she sat on a couch. She stared at Maxwell on the rug. 'I don't want to be alone, not when Simon is prowling the sunward wing. He released me from his harem when we arrived, and told me to pick some rooms for myself. So, I came here to the iceward wing, to be as far away from him as possible. He makes my skin crawl.'

'You poor girl,' said Silva.

'I'm not a girl.'

'Of course not. Did you pick some rooms?'

'Not yet.'

'And Salvor; have you seen him?'

Doria shook her head.

Silva pursed her lips, then turned to Kagan. 'This may seem like a dreadful inconvenience, and if it is, then please tell me, but perhaps we should all stay in these quarters? Doria and I could help look after little Max, and we could keep each other company.'

'I don't know,' said Doria.

'We could share a room,' said Silva, 'and Kagan and little Max can have the other. Listen to me, both of you – Simon wants to keep us divided, and he wants us to be terrified. Each of us has been tormented by him in our own way...'

'No,' said Kagan. 'You have both had a far harder time than I.'

'Is that so? Were you not forced to watch, with your son in your arms, as the woman you love was tortured? That wasn't nothing, Kagan, and there is no profit in trying to rank our miseries. Look to your strength instead, the strength to be found in simple friendship. Together, we are stronger than we are apart.'

'You don't understand. I'm partly responsible for Simon being here. I was there, on Yocasta, when we revived him.'

'It doesn't matter any more. The future is all that should occupy our thoughts.'

Kagan cast his eyes downwards. 'Alright. I'd be happy if you both stayed. If you want to.'

'I do,' said Silva. 'Doria?'

The demigod said nothing for a moment, then nodded.

'That's settled, then,' said Silva.

'What about Amalia, and the Aurelians?' said Kagan. 'Simon's going to execute them. How do we stop him?'

'You cannot plan ahead when there's an Ascendant around,' said Silva.

'So, what do we do?'

'We wait.'

'For what?'

Silva smiled. 'An opportunity.'

CHAPTER 24

GETTING PERSONAL

The Eastern Mountains – 21st Mikalis 3423

Jade stood in the shade of the cliffs, her eyes on the young, silver dragon. Kelsey was also outside, crouching by Frostback on the grassy banks of the stream that rushed down the valley. The Holdfast witch had been crying, and Jade presumed the tears were of joy at seeing her dragon again.

'They look so happy together,' said Rosie.

Jade turned, and saw the young Jackdaw woman next to her.

'Don't you think?' said Rosie.

Jade shrugged. 'I don't see why it was a secret. Bittersea could have told us that she was going to fetch the two young dragons from wherever they've been hiding. We've wasted a whole day waiting for them.'

'Yes, but now we have three dragons who can attack Simon; is that not better?'

'Dawnflame's been enough so far. We didn't need Kelsey, or any other dragons, to burn the Royal Palace. And, Dawnflame's bigger than either Frostback or Halfclaw, and faster; and more powerful.'

'You sound like you want to defeat Simon on your own.'

'I do. I've been fighting, while everyone else has been hiding, and I don't want to share the credit. Now, if we beat Simon, then everyone will think it was because of Kelsey and her tiny, silver dragon.'

'Frostback isn't tiny; she's enormous.'

'She's tiny compared to Dawnflame.'

'Are you jealous?'

'Yes. I'm supposed to be the leader of this expedition, and the others are trying to take over. It's not fair. Worse, Frostback has scared my cats away; who knows when they'll come back?'

Rosie raised an eyebrow. 'Come on, Jade; don't be like that. Your cats will be fine. They'll return as soon as Frostback enters the cavern. You're still the leader, but Caelius and Van seem to know a lot about tactics and stuff; there's no harm in taking their advice.'

Kelsey's laughter echoed up through the ravine, and Jade's frown deepened.

'Flavus is alright,' she said; 'but now there are three know-it-all Banner soldiers, as well as that idiot Kelsey.'

'She's not an idiot.'

'She's mean.'

'You can be mean too, sometimes. Not to me, but to the others.'

'Why are you defending her?'

'We're on the same side, Jade. We're all trying to fight Simon's rule. We all want things to go back to the way they were before he arrived.'

Jade glared at her. 'I don't. Do you think I enjoyed my old life in the City? I was ridiculed, shunned, and treated like a child. I do *not* want to go back to that.'

Dawnflame pushed her head out through the waterfall. She glanced around, and saw Jade and Rosie.

'I deem that Frostback and the Holdfast girl have had ample time to get re-acquainted,' the dragon said. 'We should be planning the next attack.'

'I agree,' said Jade.

'Good.' The dragon turned towards the ravine. 'Frostback; it is time. Join us in the cavern.'

The silver dragon glanced up. 'We will be there in a moment.'

Dawnflame tilted her head, then disappeared back through the waterfall. Jade turned, and strode along the ravine, Rosie by her side. They passed through the driest gap in the waterfall marking the entrance to the cavern, and walked into the dimly-lit interior. Over to their left, Caelius, Flavus and Van were poring over maps of the City, each of which had been drawn up by the Banner scout, while Vadhi was sitting by herself, keeping her distance from the cluster of dragons by the right hand wall. With the addition of two extra dragons, there was very little space left in the cavern, and Halfclaw was squeezed in next to Bittersea and Firestone, who was playing with the carcass of a goat.

Behind Jade, Frostback and Kelsey also entered the cavern, and everyone got settled, as Dawnflame lifted her head.

'Comrades,' she said. 'The day is wearing on, and we have yet to plan our next attack.' She glanced at Jade. 'Demigod, which target would you prefer?'

Jade walked into the centre of the cavern, feeling the eyes of the humans and dragons on her.

'I propose that we strike at Dalrig,' she said; 'against my father and sister.'

'That seems reasonable enough,' said Dawnflame.

Kelsey raised her hand. 'Wait a moment,' she said. 'Can I speak?'

Dawnflame paused for a moment, then angled her head slightly.

'Thank you,' said Kelsey, stepping forward. 'Back in winter, Frostback and I tried to attack Greylin Palace, just after Simon had arrived in the City. It was hopeless. Dalrig is ringed with ballista batteries. We tried from above, and then from the harbour, but we couldn't even get close to Greylin. Instead of Dalrig, why don't we go straight for Tara? That's probably where Simon is lurking, but if he's not there, we can still hit Amalia where it hurts.'

'I agree,' said Frostback. 'Tara is the obvious choice.'

'I also agree,' said Van.

Jade simmered with growing anger. 'No. We should attack Dalrig.'

'May I ask why, ma'am?' said Van. 'Are you sure it's not personal?'

'Our tactics were working fine before you lot joined us,' she said.

'We've been wearing Simon down, hitting his allies, the salve mine, the fortresses on the Great Wall. My father and sister are among the only allies Simon has left. If we can eliminate them, he will be weakened, and almost alone.'

'Weren't you listening to me?' said Kelsey. 'Dalrig is too heavily defended.'

'Maybe for your little silver dragon,' said Jade. 'Dawnflame's already taken on Simon; she'll have no problem getting to Greylin.'

Frostback reared her head, sparks flashing across her jaws. 'I did not come here to be insulted.'

'No?' said Jade. 'Why did you come here? Don't pretend that you care about the City – you ran away, when we stayed here to fight. If Kelsey wasn't here, you and Halfclaw would still be hiding.'

'How dare you?' roared Frostback. 'Simon killed my father, the mightiest dragon on this world; whereas you wish to kill your own father. Have you no shame?'

Jade narrowed her eyes. 'No. My father is not redeemable. The only shame I feel is that I am his daughter. You may have failed to breach the defences of Dalrig, little dragon, but my death powers will destroy any soldier who remains by their ballista. We will do what you could not.'

Frostback's eyes burned red.

'Enough,' said Dawnflame. 'Jade is correct, and that is the end of the matter.'

Frostback turned to her. 'You are siding with this wretched demigod?'

'I am,' said Dawnflame. 'She has the necessary spirit to win this fight; do you?'

'I fought for two years in Jezra,' said Frostback; 'are you questioning my courage?'

'Any dragon can fight greenhides, Frostback,' said Dawnflame. 'I have yet to see you take on an opponent of any worth.'

The two dragons faced each other, and the cavern stilled.

'Please,' cried Rosie; 'don't fight! There has to be an answer that we can all agree to.'

'I have a suggestion,' said Caelius, striding forwards. He walked right up to the narrow gap between Frostback and Dawnflame, and folded his arms across his wide chest.

'You?' said Dawnflame. 'Such arrogance! You have been on this world for one day, Banner insect.'

'And what do you think I've been doing in that time, dragon?' he said. 'Lieutenant Flavus has a fine collection of maps, and I have been involved in over twenty operations throughout my career, on a dozen different worlds.' He glanced around the cavern. 'You folk, you've been on this world too long to see what's obvious. You imagine the City to be enormous, because it is all you know. A mere four miles separates Dalrig from Tara, as the dragon flies. Four miles! I could walk the distance in an hour. I have a solution that should satisfy everyone. We leave under cover of darkness, a few hours before dawn tomorrow, and strike Dalrig at sunrise, just as Lady Jade suggests. Then, once the objectives have been fulfilled, we turn immediately for Tara, as Miss Holdfast suggests, and strike there too. In other words, we hit both on the same day. We could end the war tomorrow.'

'You are forgetting one thing, soldier,' said Bittersea. 'If anything goes wrong, then the dragons who go would be too exhausted to return to the Eastern Mountains.'

Caelius smiled. 'I've thought of that, madam dragon. If a retreat is required, then the strike force concentrates, and retires across the Straits to Jezra. From what I've been told, the populace there is entirely from Lostwell, and they used to be your friends. It is the ideal location to fall back to, if necessary.'

'For the sake of compromise,' said Van, 'I can accept that.'

Caelius beamed. 'Thank you, son.' He gazed up at the dragons.

'This plan still ignores the defences at Dalrig,' said Kelsey. 'For all Jade's boasting, the fact remains that the town has dozens of ballistae.'

'That's where Jade and Dawnflame come in,' said Caelius. 'They fly ahead of the formation, out of range of your blocking abilities, and Lady Jade uses her death powers to clear the way. Then, and only then, do the other two dragons – Frostback and Halfclaw, approach, so that

Kelsey's abilities can negate those of Montieth and Amber. There are risks, of course, but no operation is risk-free.' He glanced around at the others. 'My plan utilises our strengths – we have Lady Jade, and we have Miss Holdfast. Deployed appropriately, they could be an extremely effective combination.'

Jade and Kelsey glared at each other.

'I acquiesce,' said Frostback, breaking the uncomfortable silence. 'It is a good plan, Van-father.'

'Thank you,' said Caelius. 'Lieutenant Flavus should take much of the credit; I didn't come up with it on my own. We should pool our skills, and put our pride to one side, for the greater cause.'

Rosie nudged Jade with her elbow.

Jade sighed. 'Very well. If Dawnflame agrees, then I suppose I do too.'

Dawnflame raised her head. 'Can we be certain of a welcome in Jezra?'

'I'm not sure,' said Van. 'I can't imagine that the Exiles have any love for Simon, but they might be too scared to help us.'

'They'll help us, sir,' said Vadhi. 'If I was still in Jezra, along with the rest of the Brigades, I'd be watching the skies for dragons every day, praying that they would appear. The Exiles love Frostback and Halfclaw.'

'Even after they fled?' said Dawnflame.

'You shame me,' said Frostback, lowering her head. 'When my rider was taken, something inside my heart died, and I acted irrationally. And then, when I learned what had happened to my father, I turned my back on the City in disgust. Halfclaw is not to blame; I persuaded him to come with me.'

'I was worried about you,' said Halfclaw; 'I couldn't have left you alone.'

'Thank you, my beloved,' she said. She turned to Kelsey. 'Now that you have returned, my spirit has been renewed. I cannot explain it.'

'I can,' said Caelius. 'Maybe I was wrong, Kelsey, when I questioned your bond with Frostback, for she acted just as other dragons have done in the past when they have lost their riders. Frostback, if, for instance, Kelsey had been held prisoner within the City, would you have fled?'

'No. I would have died trying to rescue her. But... when I was told that she had been taken to another world, I felt nothing but endless despair.'

Caelius nodded. 'You are bonded. Kelsey, please accept my apologies for my earlier words to you; they were spoken in ignorance.'

'It's fine, Caelius,' said Kelsey.

'I shall not pretend to understand this,' said Dawnflame. 'To my mind, this bond is unhealthy, for it seems to lead to a crippling dependence upon each other, and a dragon should never have to depend upon an insect.' She paused. 'A human. All the same, I would grieve if Jade were killed.'

'You would?' said Jade, narrowing her eyes.

'Yes. I admit that you are becoming dear to me. In you, I see my own fears and desires reflecting back at me.'

Jade stared at the dragon, afraid to speak in case she started to cry. She ran from the cavern, ducking through the waterfall, then slumped to the grass. She wiped her eyes. What was happening to her? The others must think that she was stupid, and she had probably offended Dawnflame. Did the dragon mean what she had said? Dragons weren't supposed to be able to lie, but she found it hard to believe that Dawnflame felt anything towards her.

The dragon pushed her head through the waterfall. 'Did I speak ill?'

Jade shook her head.

'Then, I think I understand. You do not feel the same as I do, demigod. That is fine. I shall bear my hurt deep within, so that it does not interfere with our plans.'

'That's not it,' said Jade. 'Don't say that.'

'Then, what is the problem?'

'I don't make friends,' said Jade; 'no one likes me, except for Rosie, and she's different from the others – more forgiving. I don't deserve her. I am a bad person, don't you understand?'

'Jade,' said the dragon, 'do you think anyone likes me? Even

Bittersea, my own mother, thinks that I'm too headstrong and rash. My former best friend, Darksky, is hunting these mountains to find and kill me, and none of the humans think fondly of me. I am an outcast, just as you are.'

'I like you.'

'I believe you; why do you not believe me?'

'You helped me, because I saved Firestone.'

'That is true, but we have moved beyond that. You and I fought alone, against everything Simon could wield against us, and we have survived. Your powers, and my fire. Accept the truth, Jade.'

Jade started to cry, and the dragon moved her face against her, nuzzling the weeping demigod.

'Is everything alright?' said Rosie, appearing through the gap by the waterfall.

'Yes,' said Dawnflame. 'All is well.'

'Good. I'm glad you're not fighting. Listen, Caelius wants you back inside, Dawnflame. He wants you to be involved in the planning for tomorrow. He said that a dragon's perspective is essential.'

'He is correct,' said the dragon. 'I will see you soon, Jade.'

Dawnflame pulled her head back through the waterfall, and Rosie sat down next to Jade. She put her arm round the demigod's shoulders, saying nothing, for which Jade was grateful.

That night, four hours before dawn, three dragons emerged into the moonlight of the ravine. Atop Dawnflame's shoulders sat Jade and Rosie; Kelsey and Van were buckled into the harness on Frostback, and Flavus, Caelius and Vadhi were strapped onto Halfclaw's harness. Bittersea and Firestone, who were remaining behind, watched from the waterfall, as the three dragons extended their wings and lifted into the cool, dark sky.

The Banner officers had spent the entire afternoon and evening with Dawnflame, planning every stage of the operation, while Jade and

Kelsey had avoided each other, which had been tricky within the tight confines of the cavern.

The dragons turned for iceward, and sped off, soaring over the mountain range. The temperature steadily fell, and the snow on the tips of the mountains shone in the light of the two moons. Jade wrapped her blanket round her, feeling the chill wind bite.

'What a beautiful night,' said Rosie.

'I'm not sure that you should have come along,' said Jade. 'You would have been safer in the cavern with Bittersea.'

'It's not fair that you've had to do all the fighting. I want to take part; I want to help. And help more than just cleaning and cooking dinner, not that I begrudge doing all that.'

'But you're not a warrior.'

'I'm a Blade. Fighting to protect the City was drummed into me from my youth; it's part of who I am. Alright, I might not be as professional as the Banner guys, but I've killed greenhides. I'm not scared.'

Jade glanced at her. 'Don't die.'

Rosie laughed. 'I'll try not to.'

They kept a tight formation as they soared over the snow and icefields at the iceward end of the mountains, then they turned for the west, crossing over the ragged coastline until they were above the Cold Sea. Winds whipped across their flanks, and slivers of frost formed on the dragons' wings. They passed gigantic icebergs, where seals were clustering under the purple skies, then the dragons banked as one, and headed sunward, towards the City.

'We shall begin our descent,' said Dawnflame. 'We shall fly low for this last stage of the journey.'

Ahead of them, the sky was turning pink, and Jade saw the coastline slowly emerge from the predawn haze. They passed the town of Fishcross to their left, a cluster of golden lights sprinkled along the shore, then they saw Dalrig approach. Dawnflame increased her speed, leaving Frostback and Halfclaw trailing behind, her belly just yards above the swelling waves below them.

'Ready your powers, demigod,' said the dragon. 'We will strike directly through the harbour.'

Jade flexed her right hand.

'How do you know where the ballistae are?' said Rosie. 'I can't see any.'

'The Holdfast girl told us that they were positioned onto the sterns of the larger ships,' said Dawnflame; 'but take no chances, Jade. Kill them all.'

Rosie frowned, but looked away, saying nothing. Jade glanced at her, then hardened her heart. It would be Gloamer militia, and Gloamer sailors and harbour workers that she would be killing – her own people. They had never liked her, but did that mean they deserved to die? Probably not, she reasoned, but that wasn't going to stop her from doing what needed to be done. The bay that led to Dalrig narrowed, and she saw the masts of the ships lined up in the harbour. There was no noise or alarm coming from the docks, and she smiled as she realised that they had surprise on their side.

'Fire will alert them,' Dawnflame said, 'so I will refrain. Jade, this task is yours.'

Jade raised her hand, feeling for the lives of those on the decks of the ships. Dawnflame flashed across the entrance to the harbour, and Jade unleashed her powers, sweeping her hand from left to right in a wide arc, sending a burst of silent death upon the Dalrigian fleet. There were a few splashes, as bodies toppled into the waters of the harbour basin. Rosie pointed up at the roofs of the tall buildings flanking the quayside, and Jade saw the massed ballistae positioned there. She raised her hand again, directing her powers onto the harbour front, and more bodies fell, hurtling down from the rooftops. At the same time, the sun split the horizon, bathing the town in pink light, and the first screams began.

Dawnflame wheeled round, coming close to the side of Greylin Palace, and Jade sent her powers down onto the roof, slaughtering the soldiers by the six ballistae that were occupying the space where her garden had once been. A bell began to peal, then another, as the town awoke to the attack. Two ballista bolts whistled by Dawnflame's left wing, and she turned her head, her jaws opening. Fire poured from the dragon's mouth, and a large merchant ship exploded in flames, its deck and masts engulfed, and the ballista station was incinerated. More flames rose up along the iceward edge of the harbour, as Frostback and Halfclaw sped through the gap that Jade had created. A few bolts were being loosed, but most splashed down harmlessly into the cold waters of the basin. Frostback and Halfclaw veered apart, each taking a different flank of the harbour, and within a minute, every ship was ablaze. Dawnflame swept over the roof of Greylin, burning the ballistae, then she retreated, banking round in a wide arc to come in behind Frostback. The three dragons clustered together again, and approached the palace. Frostback alighted first, dropping off Van and Kelsey, then Dawnflame lowered herself to the burning roof.

'Do what you have to do, Jade,' the dragon said. 'We dragons will remain above, and keep the militia from getting too close.'

Jade slid down to the roof, and Rosie followed a moment later, a crossbow gripped in her hands. Halfclaw descended next, and Vadhi jumped down, along with Flavus and Caelius, who looked as though he was having the time of his life.

'Kelsey and Jade to the centre,' the old sergeant called out; 'crossbows on the flanks. Lady Jade, lead the way.'

Jade stared at the stairwell turret in the corner of the roof, then started to run. Caelius was on her right, his crossbow ready, while she could hear Kelsey and Van a few paces behind her. They reached the stairs and ran down them. Three militia soldiers were at the bottom of the steps, about to ascend, and they gazed up in alarm. Caelius dropped to a knee and loosed a bolt into the throat of the first, then Rosie and Van also loosed, striking the second soldier. Van reloaded, loosed again, and the third fell.

'This time,' said Kelsey, 'can we please burn this place to the ground? I'm so sick of coming here.'

'It will burn,' said Jade. 'I want to see it burn, but we must find my father and sister first.'

'And then what? We kill them both?'

Jade felt everyone look at her. 'Yes.'

'That's cold,' said Kelsey. 'Are you sure? Montieth might deserve it, but what about Amber?'

'Her too,' said Jade.

'Are you sure this isn't personal?'

'We have little time,' said Caelius; 'we should be pressing on.'

Jade nodded. 'Follow me.'

She headed along a corridor, then led them down the service stairs, towards the basement. She tried to ignore the familiar sights and smells, but Kelsey's words echoed round her mind. Was it personal, or was she doing the best thing, strategically? Her hatred of her father and sister had spanned centuries, and she had nursed her grievances against them for as long as she could remember. Between them, they had made her life a misery, and had left her almost incapable of forming normal relationships with other people; and she had grown more in the previous three years than she had in her first nine centuries.

They reached the bottom of the stairs, and she forced such thoughts from her mind. She raised her hand, then remembered that her powers were useless, thanks to Kelsey Holdfast. Despite that, she led from the front, the others following her as she crept down the dark passageways under Greylin Palace.

'You stupid girl, Amber!' cried her father's voice from a side room. 'I told you to divide the concentrated salve into four containers, not three, and look; you've spilled some. Do you realise that I had to degrade myself in front of Simon to receive this? It was humiliating.'

Jade slowed in the passageway. Light was coming out from the open doorway ahead of her. She recalled the chamber that lay beyond – one of her father's laboratories. She glanced at Van, and he nodded, then signalled towards those armed with crossbows. Only she and Kelsey had no weapon, and they stayed at the rear as the others moved forward into position.

'I should punish you, idiot child!' shrieked Montieth. 'Do it again, only this time, do it right – do you understand me?'

Van raised a finger, and the group rushed off, covering the last few yards to the open doorway. Jade watched as they sprinted to the opening. Van, Caelius and Rosie loosed their bows into the room, then hurried inside, and Jade ran to follow them. She barged past Flavus into the laboratory, and saw Caelius loose another bolt, directly into Montieth's face. The god staggered backwards, hitting a table loaded with equipment, and sending the glass vials and tubes crashing to the floor.

'Nobody go near him,' Van cried, his crossbow aimed at the prostrate body of Montieth on the floor. 'He can still use his powers through touch.'

Kelsey let out a cry, and she grabbed Jade's arm. The demigod moved to brush her off, then she saw where Kelsey was staring. To the left of another table, stood Amber. Jade's eyes widened. Her sister's skin was a greyish-green colour, and her eyes were empty. She stood motionless, vacantly staring at the ground in front of her.

'Pyre's arse,' muttered Kelsey. 'She's… Is she…?'

Van kicked Montieth. 'What did you do to Amber, you bastard?'

Montieth ripped the bolt from his face, and crawled away, shrieking. He reached the corner of the room, then turned to see four crossbows pointing at him. He raised his hand, but nothing happened, then he noticed Kelsey.

'You!' he cried. 'Filthy witch!'

Jade pulled her gaze from her sister. She stepped forward, pushing Kelsey to the side.

'Father,' she said.

'Who are you speaking to?' Montieth called out. 'I am not your father.' He spat at her. 'You are dead to me.'

'What about Amber?' said Van.

'She's gone,' said Jade.

Montieth laughed. 'She thought she was better than me; she bowed to Simon, and he rewarded her by placing her in charge of Dalrig. I couldn't let such an insult stand. I taught Amber the truth, that I rule Dalrig; me, and no one else, for all eternity. Now, get out of my palace!'

'You killed your own daughter?' said Rosie, her face pale. 'And then you... brought her back?'

'It was the only way to guarantee her everlasting obedience,' said Montieth. 'She was always a stubborn girl.'

'I've heard enough from this piece of shit,' said Caelius, his crossbow at his shoulder, aimed into Montieth's face. 'Let's end it.'

'How?' said Van. 'We have no anti-salve, and we can't risk touching him.'

Jade walked over to the table where the vials of concentrated salve sat. She picked up the one with the most in it, then returned to the others.

'You see this, father?' she said. 'You have lived for salve; it has been your one obsession. My earliest memory is of you forcing some down my throat, while Amber held me down. Do you remember?'

Montieth shrugged. 'No.'

She tipped the vial over, and the salve flowed out, dropping onto Montieth's face. He raised his hands to protect himself, and the salve burned through the skin of his fingers in seconds. A large drop hit his chin, and he screamed in agony. He tried to wipe it away, but his fingers were already withered and burning. He roared, and writhed on the floor, lashing out with his arms and legs, as smoke rose from the bare skin of his face and hands.

'You always thought I was weak, father,' Jade said, as she crouched down by him. She reached out, and rammed her index finger directly into his right eye, driving it deep into the socket. 'Tell me; am I weak, father? Tell me.' She started to rip his weakened life force out of his body, and he flailed in agony as she kept her finger steady. 'Am I weak, you bastard?' she cried, feeling the body of her father start to fail. He gasped and groaned, foam appearing around his bloody lips and chin, while she felt her own power build and grow.

Her father gasped a final time, then lay still, his body withered and dried up, like a husk. Jade pulled her finger from his eye socket, and wiped it onto her leg. She stood, noticing for the first time that everyone in the room was staring at her in silence.

She glanced at Caelius. 'Take his head, just in case.'

The old veteran gulped. 'Yes, ma'am.'

She looked at the others, as Caelius drew a sword from his belt. Rosie was weeping, while Kelsey was gazing at her with an expression of terror mixed with grudging respect. She heard the swing of the sword behind her, but didn't turn to look.

'It's done, ma'am,' said Caelius. 'He isn't coming back from that.'

Jade turned to face Amber, who had remained motionless the entire time.

'Sister,' she said. 'I know you can't hear me, but father is dead. We're free, Amber; we're free.' She started to cry. Kelsey put a hand on her shoulder. 'Get off me!' she cried. 'Don't touch me. I know what I have to do. Please leave me alone to do it.'

'Everybody out,' said Van.

'I'll be waiting for you in the hall, Jade,' said Rosie through her tears.

Jade waited until the others had left, then she walked the few paces to her sister. She took her hand.

'I'm sorry,' she said, sobbing. 'You should have been a better sister, but I should have been better too. We let each other down.' She lifted her free hand, and moved a strand of lank hair from Amber's face. 'You didn't deserve this, but it'll be over soon; I promise. I wish we had more happy memories, but all I remember is the pain, and the loneliness. Why couldn't you have been there for me? All the same, sister, I loved you. Goodbye, Amber.'

She sent her powers through her hand into her sister's body, and Amber toppled to the floor, her unnatural life ended. Jade's vision went blurry from the tears, and she sank to her knees, weeping over her sister's body.

CHAPTER 25

SLEEPLESS

Tara, Auldan, The City – 22nd Mikalis 3423

The floorboards creaked next to the couch where Emily and Daniel were lying, and she opened her eyes.

'Sorry, Emily,' whispered Lord Aurelian; 'it's just me, popping to the bathroom.'

Emily nodded, then he crept by the cot where Elspeth was sleeping. Emily checked that the child hadn't awoken, then lay on her back with her eyes open.

A few moments later, Lord Aurelian re-appeared, and Emily watched him enter the kitchen. She pulled back the blanket and snuck off the couch. She padded over to the kitchen, and saw Daniel's father lighting a candle.

'I didn't mean to wake you,' he said, keeping his voice down.

'I was already awake,' she said, closing the door. 'It's too hot and stuffy down here to sleep.'

Lord Aurelian smiled. 'You get used to it. You should have taken the bedroom; it can't be right that the King and Queen have to sleep on a couch.'

'No. I wouldn't dream of throwing you and Lady Aurelian out of your room. The couch is fine.'

'Apart from me waking you up to visit the lavatory, I suppose.'

Emily sat on a kitchen chair, and wiped the sweat from her fore-head. After two days and two nights being locked in the basement apartment, she longed to feel a fresh breeze against her face. She sniffed her clothes. She could do with a bath as well. Still, compared to the rest of the Aurelians, she was clean and smelled of roses.

Lord Aurelian drew a small cup of water from the last of the previous day's supplies, and took a sip. He offered her the rest of the cup.

'No, thank you. You have it. We'll get more at dawn. I must say, you have all been bearing up remarkably well down here.'

'It's far better than the conditions we endured under the Royal Palace in Ooste,' he said. 'That was an awful experience. Lady Doria was caring for Elspeth at the time, but Daniel's mother and I were chained to the wall of a dungeon. At least here we have no shackles.' He smiled. 'And Kagan comes down most days; occasionally he even drops off some brandy or other treat for us.'

'Kagan comes to visit?'

'Yes. That young chap is rather conflicted. Daniel is convinced that there remains a lot of good in him, but I'm not so sure. He's certainly never made any moves to have us freed. Ultimately, I believe him to be just as scared of Simon as everyone else. What's more, he is in love with Amalia, which certainly counts against his judgement.'

'Maybe he sees something in her that no one else sees.'

'Or perhaps he just wishes it so.' His face fell. 'My dearest Emily, there is something we should have told you as soon as you arrived, but it seemed cruel, and I, at least, wanted you to have a couple of days that you could spend with Elspeth without too much worry hanging over your head.'

'If it's about the executions, then I already know.'

'I see.' He sighed. 'Simon was merely waiting until you were captured. Your arrival here has brought us sorrow as well as joy. Not for myself, you understand; I do not fear death, but little Elspeth...' He put a hand to his eyes. 'It's too terrible to even consider.'

The kitchen door opened, and Lady Aurelian tip-toed in.

She frowned. 'Why are you both up in the middle of the night? Your talking awoke me.'

'Is Elspeth still asleep?'

'Yes, and my Daniel could sleep through a dragon attack. Nevertheless, shouldn't you both be resting?'

'It's too warm to sleep,' said Emily.

'You get used to it.'

Emily shared a smile with Lord Aurelian.

'So,' Lady Aurelian went on, 'what were you discussing?'

'Kagan,' said Lord Aurelian.

'That fool?' said his wife. 'Do you think he'll visit today?'

'I doubt it, dear. Now that Simon has moved into Maeladh, I don't think we'll be seeing much more of Kagan down here.'

'He'll have forgotten all about us, now that he has Maxwell back. I wonder if he and Amalia are upstairs, pretending to be part of a normal family. Drinking wine and laughing while the City burns. They make me sick.'

'Then don't think about them, dear.'

'Easier said than done, husband. Trapped down here, I have very little else to occupy my mind.'

'I think about the villa in the Sunward Range,' he said. 'I remember the vines, and the flowers growing along the borders by the front entrance, and the sound of the Reapers working to bring the harvest in. And the laughter of the workers' children as they played in the back yard, under the branches of the three oaks that my grandfather planted. Daniel used to play with them when he was young; do you remember when he fell out of the tree and twisted his ankle? He couldn't run for a month.'

'Stop it,' said Lady Aurelian, her voice quavering. 'I can't bear to think of such things.'

He put a hand on his wife's shoulder. 'We shall live to see and hear these things again. Simon will never see us despair; he will never break us.'

A loud pounding came from the front door of the apartment, and the three Aurelians froze.

Lord Aurelian collected himself, then strode to the kitchen door and opened it. Daniel was sitting up on the couch, and Elspeth had awoken, and was crying quietly in her cot. The front door swung open, and Naxor appeared.

Emily stood.

'What do you want?' said Daniel, also getting to his feet.

'Dear gods,' Naxor said; 'it stinks in here. I thought Rosers were the most hygienic of all the tribes, but I was clearly wrong. Prepare yourselves – Simon is on his way.'

Emily walked with Daniel's parents into the small sitting room, and Daniel lit a couple of candles.

'Why is he coming here?' said Emily.

Naxor shrugged. 'I guess you'll find out soon enough.'

'How does it feel to be a traitor?' said Lady Aurelian.

'It feels fine; thank you for asking. Not many people ask how I feel, so I appreciate it. How does it feel to be a condemned prisoner?'

'At least my conscience is clean.'

'Oh, I wish I had one of those. On the other hand, they sound like a frightful nuisance; always getting in the way of obtaining what one wants.' He held a hand to his ear. 'I do believe I can hear our lord and master approaching. Be on your best behaviour, you rascally Aurelians.'

Emily went and stood by the cot. She leaned down and picked up Elspeth, holding her to her chest as the child started to cry louder. Daniel joined them, standing between Emily and the door.

Simon walked in, decked out in his green and gold armour. He beamed at them.

'Good morning, Aurelians,' he said, his voice booming. 'I'm glad you're all up.' He crinkled his nose. 'Naxor, he said, 'is it better that they reek and look shabby, or should they be clean and well-dressed for their executions?'

'That, your Grace, would depend on the effect you wish to achieve. Do you wish the fine people of Tara to be disgusted by their former rulers, or would you prefer them to harbour thoughts of dignity regarding them?'

'Well, I would very much like to put on a great spectacle, one that will linger in the mind; ideally, one that would be passed down by the mortals from generation to generation.'

'In that case, your Grace, I would recommend fitting them out in the finest clothes in the palace. Daniel and Emily should be dressed in a simulacrum of their royal robes, complete with fake crowns. That would certainly stick in the minds of the audience. I understand that all of the highest dignitaries of Tara have been invited? The Merchants' Guild, the Council; every aristocrat in fact?'

'You make a fine sycophant, Naxor,' said Simon. 'If only you weren't such a deceitful weasel.'

'Whereas,' said Lady Aurelian, 'you make rather a lacklustre tyrant. Is there a point to this visit?'

Simon's faced turned red with rage, and he clenched his fists; then he paused, and smiled.

'Oh my,' he said. 'I had anticipated being spoken to like that, especially by you. In some ways, it makes a refreshing change to the usual grovelling and abject terror I tend to inspire. I will enjoy eviscerating you, Lady Aurelian. But, in answer to your question, I am here to take you out of this fetid apartment. I have decreed that you shall all be executed, by my hand, in person, at dawn tomorrow – just over one day from now. As this coming dawn will herald your last day alive, I wanted to see that you enjoyed it.' He turned to Emily. 'And, might I say how lovely it is that you decided to join us, Queen Emily? To imagine that you actually believed that Amalia would help you; with that level of stupidity, it's amazing I didn't catch you before now.'

He turned. 'Follow me.'

Naxor strode out after him, and Emily glanced at the others. None of them spoke, but Emily could see the resolute defiance in their eyes. She walked towards the door, Elspeth clutched in her arms. She had quietened since being picked up, and Emily was glad that Simon hadn't singled the child out. She reached the door to the apartment, then realised that the militia who had been there when she had arrived were gone. Instead, two greenhides were standing in the corridor, their talons and teeth glistening in the lamplight. They stared at Emily and the child, but made no move.

'They won't touch you,' said Simon, glancing back at her. 'Not unless I tell them to.'

Emily covered Elspeth's eyes as she crept between the two greenhides, her heart pounding.

Simon laughed. 'If you're scared of them, just wait until you see Matilda.'

The other Aurelians followed Emily out of the room, and the greenhides began to shadow them as they walked along the corridor.

'Where are we going?' said Daniel.

'The roof,' said Simon, as he turned left down another passageway; 'the long way round. I have something to show you first.'

They walked for a few minutes, traversing the hallways of the basement, until they reached a dank, stone-lined hall, deep underground.

'These are the dungeons of Maeladh,' said Simon, stopping. 'I don't have many prisoners at the moment.'

'Are you placing us in here?' said Lord Aurelian.

'Of course not,' said Simon; 'you are the renowned Aurelians! Do you think me so beastly that I'd clap you in irons for your last day alive? Not at all. Come.'

They walked into the dimly-lit hall, the greenhides following a dozen paces behind them. Simon paused at the barred door of the first cell.

'In here is poor old Salvor,' said Simon. 'I went too far with this one, and, in my rage, I destroyed his mind. I would allow him to roam the palace, but he would be a danger to himself.'

Emily peered between the bars. Salvor was dressed in rags, and was sitting on the floor, an absent expression on his face.

'Salvor was a good man,' she said. 'Why did you do this to him?'

'I told you; I didn't intend this outcome. Sometimes I forget just how powerful I can be. He isn't suffering. He isn't... anything. His mind is a void. Was he dear to you? What a shame. Oh well.'

Emily stared at Naxor, but the demigod wouldn't meet her eyes.

Simon moved onto the next cell, and the others followed. Emily looked through the bars, and saw a small dragon inside the cell, bound with chains, its face muzzled in an iron mask.

'What a fine little beast,' said Simon. 'One of Darksky's brood. With her child chained up, the dragon will do anything I ask of her. She has yet to find the renegade who has been attacking the City, but she will, in time. And before you ask, yes; it's suffering. Its mind is filled with misery. Killing it would be a mercy, but then how would I control Darksky?'

The Aurelians stared through the bars at the dragon, then Simon moved on to the next cell.

'Now,' he said, 'can you guess who is in here?'

'Silva?' said Emily.

Simon laughed. 'A fine guess, false Queen, but no. I have granted Silva the freedom to roam the palace, as she is harmless. Her powers might come in useful, if she were to ever change her allegiance, which I doubt. Still, let's give her some time to come around. In a few decades, she might well be willing to see sense. Have another guess.'

'Kelsey Holdfast?' said Daniel.

Simon squinted at him. 'Are you that stupid? Do you think I would place the mightiest mortal I have ever met in a damp dungeon? Kelsey Holdfast has true royal blood in her veins, unlike you, false King. She is worth a hundred of you. Guess again. I'll give you a clue. She isn't a mortal.'

'Lady Doria?' said Emily.

'Wrong. I tired of her; she was such a miserable wretch that she started to disgust me. She's around here somewhere; like Silva, I have allowed her the freedom of the palace. I'm going to have to show you. Come on.'

They walked in front of the barred door, and Emily looked into the cell. A woman was lying on the filthy ground, clutching a wound in her stomach, her fine clothes covered in blood. Emily gazed at her pain-stricken face, and gasped.

'That's right,' said Simon, grinning. 'Your enemy and rival. Does it warm your heart to see the former God-Queen suffer so?'

'No,' said Emily.

'You're no fun at all,' said Simon. 'I sense your sympathy for her, even after she had you locked up.'

Amalia opened her eyes, and Emily met her gaze for a moment.

'She was conspiring to have me killed,' said Simon, 'after all I have done for her. I gave her a palace, and riches, and yet she betrayed me. Tomorrow at dawn, she will be joining you on the gallows, so that the Rosers will get to see two queens die in front of them.'

'Where's Maxwell?' said Emily.

'He's safe, for now, with his father. Kagan also tried to betray me, but he's a mere mortal; his mind was swayed by Amalia, and so I have decided to show him some leniency. His son could be a useful ally in years to come, and I need someone to care for the boy. See, I can be merciful, when the mood suits.'

'You have achieved the impossible,' said Lady Aurelian. 'You have made me pity the God-Queen.'

Simon laughed. 'Wait until you watch me kill her on the gallows,' he said. 'Do you know my biggest problem? Deciding which of you is to die last. It was going to be Emily, but you are starting to change my mind, Lady Aurelian. Perhaps it should be you who gets to see the others die first.'

'You are nothing but a coward and a bully,' said Lord Aurelian. 'A child in a school playground who has happened upon the biggest stick, and who thinks that elevates him to greatness.'

'You know,' Simon said, 'Edmond, the blessed Second Ascendant, used to say similar things to me. Belinda also; she once called me a mindless thug; can you believe that? They have more blood on their consciences than I, yet because I like to kill with my own hands, they denigrated me.'

'In that case,' said Lord Aurelian, 'why don't you go and talk to them? Your fight seems to be with those on Implacatus; perhaps it is time you went there.'

Simon eyed him, then turned away, and began striding along the dank corridor. Emily held Amalia's gaze for another moment, then followed him. Simon led them up a flight of stairs, then they crossed to the eastern flank of the palace, and ascended to a higher level. They passed shuttered windows, then climbed a third set of stairs, which took them up onto the roof. To their right, the sky was brightening, while the lights of Tara lay spread out before them. Militia soldiers were clustered in groups all over the different corners of the roof, standing or sitting next to a large number of huge ballistae, while, down in the palace gardens, dozens of greenhides were roaming.

'If the renegade dragon attacks,' said Simon, 'then she and Jade will be in for a little surprise. I actually hope they attack; they caught me by surprise last time, but that will not happen again. I have gathered over a hundred ballistae from Ooste, Pella and the Bulwark, and five dozen catapults – enough to bring down any flying lizard. My fondest hope is that I capture Jade alive, so that she can die on the gallows with you at dawn tomorrow, but I doubt that she will be so accommodating.' He smiled at the Aurelians. 'The reason I'm showing you this is to quell any thoughts you may have that you might be rescued.'

'You are doing it to torment us,' said Lady Aurelian.

'No,' he said. He pointed down into Tara. 'But, if you turn your attention to Prince's Square, you will see the gallows I have erected for tomorrow's festivities. I'm showing you that to torment you.'

Emily glanced down, and saw the open plaza in the town below them. She remembered the platform from when she had been walking through the streets with Cardova, and she could see the ring of militia guards surrounding it.

'I shall have hundreds of seats laid out in front of the gallows, so that every rich Roser can witness your destruction,' said Simon, as he rubbed his hands together. 'It's going to be quite the occasion. I'm very skilled with a knife; my hands are as steady as any surgeon. Aren't they, Naxor?'

The demigod glanced up. 'Indeed, your Grace.'

Simon frowned. 'That was hardly the effusive flattery that I was hoping for. Has the sight of your brother in the dungeons dampened your ardour? Forget poor old Salvor; his mind is so addled that he doesn't even remember you. I'll allow you to put him out of his misery, if you like.'

'You told us he wasn't suffering,' said Emily.

'Did I? I might have been lying. How about it, Naxor? Would you take a sword to your brother's neck to relieve him of his pain? I can sense your mind flinch from the notion. Very well, let's leave him to rot in the dungeons. What about your sister Doria? Do you feel pity for her too? My dear Naxor, you cannot have it both ways – you cannot be a lying, treacherous weasel, and yet feel such empathy for your doomed siblings at the same time.'

Naxor lowered his gaze.

'What's that over there?' said Lord Aurelian, pointing to iceward.

They turned, and Emily saw a glow on the horizon. Simon frowned.

'It's not coming from Pella,' said Lord Aurelian, 'so it cannot be the daily execution pyres.'

'It looks as though it's coming from the vicinity of Dalrig,' said Lady Aurelian.

'Shut up,' growled Simon. 'I think this little tour is at an end.'

'It's the dragon, isn't it?' said Daniel. 'Jade is attacking Dalrig.'

Simon swung his arm, and caught Daniel with a blow across his face, sending him sprawling onto the roof. Emily hugged Elspeth to her chest and crouched next to him.

Simon stared in the direction of Gloamer territory for a moment.

'Naxor,' he said. 'Scout Dalrig for me.'

'But, your Grace,' said the demigod, 'haven't you already...'

'Do it!'

Naxor's eyes glazed over, then he glanced at Simon. 'I see three dragons, your Grace, circling above Greylin. The harbour area is in flames.'

'Yes, and inside the palace? Look there.'

'I... I can't, your Grace. Something is blocking my powers.'

Simon grabbed Naxor by the throat. 'How is this possible? I placed that witch on Implacatus!'

Naxor tried to speak, but only a choked gasp left his lips.

'Jade cannot use a Quadrant,' Simon went on; 'unless someone taught her. Did you teach her?'

'No, your Grace,' he whispered, his eyes bulging.

Simon released him from his grip, and the demigod fell to the ground. The Ascendant walked to the edge of the roof, staring out towards Dalrig, as the sun rose behind them, bathing the palace in light. Emily turned back to Daniel. Her husband was unconscious, with blood streaking from his nose.

'So be it,' said Simon. 'The Holdfast witch must have returned. Perhaps I underestimated her. Naxor, remain on the roof, and keep watch. Jade's usual pattern is to attack once and then retreat, but with the Holdfast girl alongside her and a Quadrant in her grasp, she might have raised her expectations. Inform me immediately if they approach Tara. Oh, and summon Darksky; I have a feeling we may need her soon.'

'Yes, your Grace,' said Naxor, struggling back to his feet.

Simon pointed at Daniel, and he opened his eyes, groaning.

'Get up,' said the Ascendant. 'I had planned to take you all to breakfast, but events in Dalrig have quashed my appetite. Follow me.'

Lord Aurelian helped his son to his feet, and they trudged after Simon as he crossed the roof.

'Jade has Kelsey with her,' Emily whispered to her husband, as they walked. 'And they have the Quadrant.'

Daniel met her glance, and nodded.

'Not to mention three dragons,' said Lord Aurelian in a low voice. 'Hope yet remains.'

Simon turned. 'Hope? Don't let false hopes ruin your last day alive. I am an Ascendant – there could be a hundred dragons, and a dozen Holdfasts, and I would still prevail.'

Lady Aurelian smiled. 'Then tell me, why do you look scared?'

'Scared? The only thing I fear is being trapped in this City for all eternity. A halfwit demigod and a freak mortal hardly worry me.'

'You're not as good at lying as you think you are,' said Emily.

Simon stared at her, and Elspeth started to cry.

'Shut that child up,' said the Ascendant.

'She's hungry and frightened,' said Emily. 'You mentioned breakfast?'

'You are the only one who isn't scared of me, false Queen. The others do a good job of pretending to be brave, but in you, I see no fear.' He moved closer to her. 'If we had more time, I would enjoy breaking you. Perhaps I should take Elspeth for the rest of the day?'

Emily said nothing.

'Give me the child, false Queen.'

'No.'

He pulled back his fist, and drove it into her face. Pain flashed through her skull, and her vision went black. She felt herself fall, then slipped into unconsciousness.

She opened her eyes, gasping for breath.

'You're all right,' said Daniel.

She glanced around. They were back in the basement apartment, and she was lying on the couch. Lady Aurelian was sitting at the table weeping, while Daniel's father was standing next to his son.

She sat up. 'Where's Elspeth?'

Daniel lowered his eyes. 'Simon has her. He ripped her from your arms after he hit you, then he got the greenhides to bring us back here.'

'No,' said Emily, putting her head in her hands.

'He won't kill her,' said Naxor, who was lingering by the door.

Emily glared at him. 'What's he doing here?'

'The dragons are on their way,' said Naxor; 'I wasn't needed on the roof any more. Elspeth's safe. Simon has given her to Kagan to look after; he's saving her for the executions tomorrow. He only took her away to make you more afraid.'

'Get out, Naxor,' she said.

'I can't,' he said. 'Simon has ordered me to stay here, to ensure that you don't escape if, you know, the dragons break through the outer defences.'

Daniel stood, and faced the demigod. 'Whatever happens, Naxor, you won't survive this. If Simon doesn't kill you, then one of us shall. I hope it's me.'

'After all you've done, Naxor,' said Emily, 'how do you live with yourself?'

'I bend with the wind,' he said. 'I'll admit that Simon's rule hasn't turned out exactly as I'd hoped it would, but what can you do? It could just as easily have been me in that dungeon, instead of my brother and grandmother.' He rearranged his shirt. 'I'm already starting to sweat down here in this fetid basement.' He smirked. 'Still, with three dragons on the way, I imagine it's about to get a lot warmer.'

CHAPTER 26

INSENSITIVE

Dalrig, Auldan, The City – 22nd Mikalis 3423

Kelsey leaned back against the low wall on the roof of Greylin Palace, watching the dragons circle overhead.

'Remember,' said Caelius, crouching beside her; 'don't say anything stupid or mocking to Jade when she comes up those stairs.'

Kelsey frowned. 'I wasn't going to.'

'That girl's had a rough time.'

'She's nine centuries old, Caelius.'

'My point remains.'

'I know; I get it. Did you hear the sound her finger made when she pulled it out of his eye socket? Like a weird squelch. I thought the old bastard's eyeball was going to appear on the end of her fingernail.'

Caelius sighed. 'That's exactly the sort of thing I'm talking about. Please do not say that in front of Jade.'

'She's winding you up, father,' said Van.

Flavus coughed gently, and Kelsey turned to see Jade and Rosie emerge from the stair turret. The others on the roof all got to their feet, and Van waved up to the dragons. Jade stumbled over to them, seeming almost oblivious to her surroundings. Rosie was guiding her with an arm, and Kelsey could plainly see that both had been crying.

'My sincerest condolences, ma'am,' said Flavus, bowing his head.

'Aye,' said Kelsey; 'that couldn't have been pleasant.'

Jade stared at her.

'We have the option of returning to the mountains,' said Caelius. 'It can be hard to concentrate after such... events.'

'No,' said Jade. 'We're going to Tara. We're finishing this.'

Caelius nodded. 'As you wish, ma'am.'

The dragons descended onto the smouldering roof of the palace. Dawnflame lowered her head down to Jade, and sniffed her.

'I smell grief. What happened?'

Jade opened her mouth, but nothing came out.

'She killed her father,' said Rosie. 'Her sister was... already dead.'

'This news causes me mixed emotions,' said Dawnflame. 'You have risen yet higher in my esteem, Jade, and yet I also pity you. Shall we raze the palace?'

'Yes,' said Jade, her eyes burning.

They clambered up onto the three dragons, and Kelsey strapped herself into Frostback's harness, next to Van. They soared into the air, then the three dragons positioned themselves above the palace. They angled their heads downwards, opened their jaws, and a great rush of fire flooded out from them, hitting the roof of the palace. Frostback flew over the closest street, and aimed at the great entranceway to Greylin. Her flames crashed through the doors in seconds, and smoke belched out of the opening.

'About bloody time,' said Kelsey.

Van eyed her. 'Have your feelings toward Jade changed any?'

'Maybe. What she did took guts, but I never took her for a coward. She's unhinged, but she's not a coward.'

'I like her.'

'What? You told me that she creeped you out.'

'Yes, but that was way back when she was trying to seduce me. She's not like that any more.'

'Gods don't change.'

'But she has. Give her a chance, Kelsey.'

'I am. What do you think I've been doing? I'm trying to be patient with her, but she clearly despises me.'

The three dragons circled the palace, but there were no windows to attack, and they had to be content with flooding the flanks of the walls with flames. They rose up from the burning palace, and turned towards Tara. The town was out of sight, hidden behind the cliffs of the Shield Hills that stretched from Dalrig to Ooste. They ascended to an altitude that was beyond the range of the ballistae on the walls of Dalrig, and soared along the line of hills, reaching the outskirts of Ooste in a couple of minutes.

'Someone's using vision on us,' said Kelsey.

'How?' said Van. 'Aren't we invisible to vision powers?'

Kelsey pointed down at the ground. 'We are, but the shadows we're casting aren't. It's Naxor, I think. They know we're coming.'

'Should we inform the others?' said Frostback.

'Yes, that would be wise,' said Van.

They flew on, soaring high over Ooste, then Frostback reared up in front of the others, circling. She descended, and Dawnflame and Half-claw followed. Frostback reached the sunward tip of the Shield Hills, where the cliffs next to Ooste fell into the waters of the bay, and landed on the summit of a high ridge.

'Is there a problem?' said Dawnflame. 'Why have we stopped?'

'My rider has sensed vision powers coming from Maeladh Palace. We have to assume that we have been seen.'

'That matters not,' said Dawnflame. 'The plan should proceed as we agreed.'

'What about the Ascendant?' said Rosie. 'Was it him? Can you sense him?'

'I think it was Naxor,' said Kelsey. 'It wasn't Simon; I can't sense him at all. That doesn't mean he's not in Tara – he might not be using any powers at the moment.'

'I saw something too,' said Halfclaw. 'In Pella. Van, it was that tall officer friend of yours. I can't recall his name – he was there, rooting around by the ruins of Cuidrach Palace.'

'Who, Cardova?' said Van.

'Yes,' said Halfclaw.

'You saw Lucius Cardova from this distance?' said Vadhi. 'How is that possible?'

Caelius laughed. 'A dragon could see a mouse scurrying along a dark alleyway in Pella from here, Vadhi. They could probably hear its heartbeat too.'

'That is correct,' said Dawnflame.

'It was definitely Lucius?' said Kelsey. 'Was the Queen with him? Or Silva?'

'He was alone,' said Halfclaw. 'The front of the palace, where the executions take place, is heavily guarded, but he was at the rear of Cuidrach, skulking through the ruins of the throne room.'

'Is he Banner?' said Caelius. 'His name sounds Banner.'

'He was in the Black Crown,' said Van.

'Oh. One of those. Still, if he's a professional, then let's leave him to carry on doing whatever he's doing. I agree with Dawnflame's analysis of the situation. We had to expect that the flames over Dalrig would attract some attention. I say we press on, but hold in a tighter formation than last time, so that Kelsey can protect us from Amalia's death powers.'

Frostback gazed over the entrance to the bay at Tara. 'There are ballistae on the roof, and greenhides in the palace grounds.'

'Then we fly low,' said Dawnflame, 'and go along the ridge where the big houses lie. There is an entrance to the palace there, beyond a large courtyard.'

'I remember that,' said Van. 'When Montieth was holding the King and Queen hostage, we used it as a staging post.' He glanced at Kelsey. 'It's where you landed after Yendra was killed.'

Kelsey nodded, then turned to Jade, who was staring out over the bay in the direction of Maeladh. She wanted to say something to the demigod, to prove that she wasn't hostile, but couldn't find the right words. The dragons took off again, and plunged down the cliffside to the waters of the bay. They flew a yard above the glistening surface, clustered together, with Dawnflame in the lead. The colossal statue of Prince Michael loomed closer, and they passed by it and climbed up the slopes of the hills. Below them, the vast mansions of Princeps Row rushed past, and the dragons weaved their way between them, keeping as low as possible.

'Still no sign of Simon,' said Kelsey.

The first ballista bolts sped through the air towards them as they crossed the gates of the palace grounds, and Frostback veered away, opening her jaws at the same time. Dawnflame headed straight for the palace roof, heedless of the danger, spraying fire at the ballistae. Frostback turned to the greenhides in the courtyard, sending flames at them. A bolt flew past her head, and Kelsey felt the dragon flinch a little. Dawnflame swept back and bathed the rest of the iceward-facing roof in flames, and the shooting ceased. Halfclaw joined the silver dragon over the courtyard and, between them, they incinerated the dozen greenhides that had been there.

'Shall I drop you here, rider?' said Frostback.

'Aye,' said Kelsey.

The silver dragon descended, and landed amid the smoking remains of the greenhides. Kelsey unbuckled the straps, and climbed down to the ground, Van seconds behind her. They began running towards the entrance to the palace, as Frostback took off and Halfclaw started to descend. When they were halfway across the courtyard, a huge rock flew over their heads, and smashed into the ground, missing Halfclaw by a foot. More enormous boulders flew over, and Halfclaw reared back up into the sky to avoid the barrage, the three passengers clinging onto his harness.

'They must have catapults on the other side of the palace,' said Van.

The barrage intensified, then more ballista bolts whistled through the air, and the three dragons were driven back to Princeps Row.

'Come on!' cried Van, grabbing Kelsey's arm. 'We can't stay out here in the open.'

They ran under the shelter of the large, arched entranceway, as boulders continued to smash down into the courtyard.

'The dragons will have to find another way,' Van said. 'They won't be landing here again unless they can destroy those catapults.'

A group of greenhides appeared round the eastern corner of the palace, keeping close to the wall. They were racing forwards, towards Van and Kelsey.

'Shit,' he said. 'Right; in we go.'

He pulled on the door, but it was locked, so he stood back and kicked it open. They ran inside, and Van shoved the door closed behind them, before they took off down a hallway. They reached a corner, and Van slid to a halt, turning. The greenhides had reached the entrance to the palace, but were still outside, doing nothing.

'Hopefully, that means that they've been ordered to stay outside,' said Van. 'I don't think even Ascendants can give them very complicated instructions.'

'Thank Pyre for that,' said Kelsey. 'So, this is Maeladh, eh? It's nicer than Greylin.'

'I think Amalia has better taste in interior design.'

Kelsey frowned. 'Wait, is that...?' She blinked. 'Silva. I just sensed Silva, trying to use her powers. She'll know I'm in the palace; she was always good at judging when I'm around.'

'Which way?'

She pointed left.

'Let's risk it. She might be able to help.'

'Unless she's with Simon.'

'Can you sense him too?'

'No, but that doesn't mean he's not here.'

'He would have used his powers by now; he would have used them the moment the palace came under attack. However, if we can get Amalia, then this will still count as a very successful day.'

They set off, their boots clacking along the marble floors.

'One wee thing to mention,' said Kelsey. 'When we see Silva, don't tell her anything about Belinda, alright? If she knows that Belinda is on Implacatus, and then finds out that you have a Quadrant behind your breastplate, then, she might... Well, I don't know. It's not worth the risk.'

'Silva wouldn't betray us.'

'I don't know if she'd see it as a betrayal. She wants to be reunited with Belinda, that's all I'm saying. I'm not sure how far she'd go to achieve that.'

Van raised a hand for quiet, then peered round a corner.

'I heard voices,' he said in a whisper, as he unslung the crossbow from his shoulder. 'There's an open door ahead; I'll go in front.'

He crept off, and Kelsey followed. They got closer to the doorway, and Kelsey relaxed, hearing Silva's voice, and then the sound of a child crying.

Van reached the door. 'Silva?'

Silva strode from the entrance, her eyes going straight to Kelsey. 'I thought it might be you, Miss Holdfast.' She glanced up and down the corridor. 'You'd better come in.'

Van and Kelsey walked into a large room. A man and a woman were there, sitting while two infant children played on the rug in front of them. The man stood.

'Kagan. Doria,' said Silva. 'This is Kelsey Holdfast, and Major-General Van Logos. I think our opportunity may have arrived.'

Kagan's mouth fell open. 'Kelsey Holdfast? Is Simon... have you...?'

'Is Simon here?' said Van 'Is he in the palace?'

'He moved in two days ago,' said Silva, 'and took up residence in the sunward wing. We heard the sound of rocks smashing onto the court-yard. Have you brought dragons?'

'Yes, but those rocks have driven them away for now,' said Van. He noticed the window, and strode over to it. 'The catapults have ceased loosing, but I can't see the dragons.'

'Have you come to rescue us?' said Doria.

Kelsey squinted at her. 'Kagan, I've heard of, but you are?'

'It's Lady Doria,' said Silva.

Kelsey shrugged.

'One of Naxor's sisters. The reason that you've never met her is that she lived in the Royal Palace in Ooste.'

'Naxor's sister?' said Kelsey. 'Unlucky for you.'

Doria shrugged.

'Don't worry,' said Kelsey; 'one of my brothers is an arsehole as well.'

'You didn't answer my question,' she said.

'We're here to kill Amalia,' said Kelsey. 'And Simon, if he's here.'

Kagan narrowed his eyes. 'Don't even think about touching Amalia.'

Kelsey laughed. 'That's right; you're her boyfriend. I forgot. Pyre's nipples, I remember it all now.'

'Simon has wounded Amalia and placed her in the dungeons,' said Silva.

'Aye? That's even funnier. Why?'

'Because we were going to kill Simon,' said Kagan. 'Naxor betrayed us.'

'I can see Dawnflame circling above,' said Van from the window. He turned to the others. 'There's no time to pack anything. Put some shoes on, Doria, you're leaving. Kagan, you take Maxwell, and Doria can take Elspeth.'

'What?' said Doria, staring at him. 'But Simon... the greenhides...'

'The dragons will clear the greenhides, and there's been no sign of Simon. Are you sure he's here?'

'He's here,' said Silva. 'I could sense his location within the palace, right up until Kelsey arrived.'

'Then, let's be quick,' said Van.

'I'm not leaving without Amalia,' said Kagan.

Kelsey frowned down at the two children. 'Hang on. If Maxwell is here, and Cardova is in Pella, then where's Emily?'

'Simon has her, along with the rest of the Aurelians,' said Silva. 'They're all in Maeladh.'

'Shoes on, Doria,' snapped Van. 'Now. And Kagan, pick up Maxwell like I asked. We're moving.'

Doria reached for her sandals, but Kagan remained where he was.

'You can't order me around,' he said. 'You're Banner aren't you? I watched you surrender in Pella. Take Doria and the children to safety; I'm going to get Amalia.'

'No,' said Van, walking back from the window. 'You're taking the children. Kelsey and I will release the Aurelians, and we'll pick up Amalia on the way.'

'Will we?' said Kelsey.

'Yes,' said Van. 'If she tried to kill Simon, then she has become the enemy of our enemy. Maybe Emily was right; maybe she's not all bad.'

Doria stood, then leaned over and picked up Elspeth.

'I'll stay,' said Silva. 'You shall require someone to guide you through the palace. I know the way to the dungeons.'

'Thank you, Silva,' said Van. He picked up Maxwell, and pushed him into Kagan's arms. 'Protect the children,' he said. 'That's your job. This way.'

Van walked from the room, and the others began to follow him, Kagan scowling.

'I don't like this,' he said.

'Let me guess – Shinstran?' said Kelsey.

Kagan frowned at her. 'What?'

'You're Shinstran, aye? How did you get out of going to Jezra like everyone else from Lostwell?'

'Bribery.'

'I don't understand,' said Doria. 'Why aren't soldiers here? Or green-hides? Simon must know we're trying to escape.'

'His vision doesn't work close to me,' said Kelsey. 'He can't see us.'

'But he will guess that you are here,' said Silva. 'He will have sensed the general vicinity of where his powers cannot penetrate, and will deduce that you are close to its centre.'

'Hence the need to be quick,' said Van.

They reached the entrance doors that led outside to the courtyard, and they peered through the small windows to either side.

'The greenhides are still there,' said Doria.

'Wait for it,' said Van.

Kelsey pointed upwards. 'Here they come.'

She watched as three dragons dived from the sky. They soared downwards, then a great burst of fire from Dawnflame erupted into the courtyard. Several greenhides were struck by the flames, and were incinerated in an instant, then Halfclaw swooped down. He collected a greenhide in his forelimbs and ripped it in two.

Van shoved the doors open.

'Run to the gates,' he said to Kagan and Doria. 'Then keep going, straight ahead. The third mansion on the left is the home of the Aurelians; go round the back and break in, discreetly, then wait there. The house should be empty.' He glanced back outside, then gestured with a hand. 'Go.'

Doria took off across the courtyard and, after a moment's hesitation, Kagan ran after her. The last of the greenhides between the entrance and the palace gates were dead, and Dawnflame was slowly descending. Doria was a few yards from the gates, when more huge boulders smashed down into the courtyard. She cried out, but kept going, Kagan right on her heels. Halfclaw was a dozen yards above them, trying to ascend, when he was struck by one of the boulders. It hit his side, just behind the left forelimb. He let out a cry of pain, but managed to clear the gates, his wings bearing him away from the palace grounds, the three passengers still strapped to his shoulders. Dawnflame and Frostback retreated again, pulling back from the palace as the barrage thickened. Kelsey caught a glimpse of Jade on Dawnflame's back, staring down as the dragon evaded the missiles.

Doria and Kagan reached the gates, and squeezed between the tall bars, clutching onto the children. They broke into a run, and fled down Princeps Row.

'We'll have to get out another way,' said Van. 'If I know Dawnflame at all, she will take this as a signal to start burning the palace.' He frowned. 'And we're on our own. There's no way the others will be able to land. Silva, please direct us to the dungeons.'

She nodded, and they turned from the doors. They set off, heading away from the rooms where Silva and the others had been staying.

'Halfclaw looked hurt,' said Kelsey.

'Jade will heal him,' said Van. 'Silva, what state are the Aurelians in?'

'I don't know. I haven't seen them.'

'I thought you said you'd been to the dungeons.'

'The Aurelians aren't in the dungeons.'

'Eh? Then, where are they?'

'I'm not entirely sure. Kagan said they were in a basement apartment; servants' quarters by the sound of it. He knew the way.'

Van groaned. 'Why did you not think to mention this before I sent him off with the children?'

'The children are the priority,' she said. 'Amalia also knows where the Aurelians are. Once we have rescued her from the dungeons, she can tell us.'

They came to a flight of stairs and descended at a half-run, Kelsey conscious of the racket their shoes were making on the marble steps.

'Where is everyone?' she said.

'The palace is almost deserted,' said Silva. 'There are just a few servants and guards around.'

They descended another flight of stairs, and Silva raised a hand for silence as they entered a dimly-lit hallway.

'Two soldiers are usually guarding the cells,' she whispered. 'One of them has the keys.'

Van nodded. 'Stay here,' he said to Kelsey, then he crept away, his crossbow ready.

Kelsey glanced at Silva as they waited. The demigod was helping them, but she had no idea that Van was carrying a Quadrant. She tried to shake her suspicions from her mind; she had disliked Silva at first, when they had met in the Falls of Iron, but the demigod had never actually done anything to harm her, and had even helped to rescue her from the Ascendants in Yoneath, but the doubts remained. She jumped as she heard a loud thump, followed by the sound of boots running. There was another thump, then a crash; and then silence.

Van reappeared round the corner, a set of keys in his left hand. He nodded, and they followed him, passing the body of a Roser soldier. The other was stretched across the stone floor a few yards away, a crossbow bolt lodged in his back. They entered a hall where cells lined three walls. Most were empty, but Silva led them to one on the left. Kelsey peered through the bars, recognising Amalia immediately. The former God-Queen was lying on the floor of the cell, her robes smeared in blood. Her eyes were closed, but Kelsey could see her chest rise and fall.

Silva gestured to Van, who stepped forwards, the keys in his hand.

'She's been dosed with anti-salve,' said Silva. 'I was too, but it has worn off.'

'That wound looks bad,' said Kelsey.

'It is.'

'So, if we just left her here, she might die?'

'She indubitably would, Kelsey. However, the executions are scheduled for tomorrow at dawn; she would likely survive long enough to be taken to the gallows.'

Van found the right key, and opened the barred door. Silva hurried inside, and crouched down by Amalia. She inspected the wound in the god's stomach, and frowned.

'I didn't anticipate this,' she said glancing up. 'I hadn't realised that her wounds were so severe. Her self-healing is not functioning.'

Van crouched down next to her, and placed the crossbow on the ground. He reached into a pocket and withdrew a small vial.

'What's that?' said Kelsey.

'I picked up one of the vials of concentrated salve from Montieth's laboratory.'

'You're kidding, right? You picked up salve, and didn't tell me? I should have guessed.'

Van pulled the stopper from the vial. 'This is why I didn't tell you; I knew you'd doubt my intentions. I took it in case anyone got injured.'

He lifted Amalia's head a little, and placed the open vial under her nose. She inhaled a thin wisp of the vapours, and then began to shake. Van pulled the vial away, replacing the stopper, then he and Silva held onto Amalia's limbs as she convulsed on the floor of the cell. The wound in her abdomen closed, and she opened her eyes with a choked gasp.

She stared at Silva, then noticed Van and Kelsey.

Van handed Kelsey the vial. 'You keep the rest.'

'There was another vial,' she said. 'Do you have it?'

'No. I only picked up one.'

She stared at him.

'Where's Maxwell?' Amalia said, her voice a throaty whisper.

'He's safe,' said Silva. 'Kagan has taken him out of the palace, thanks to Van and the dragons. They're hiding in the Aurelian's old mansion. They have Elspeth too.'

'They?'

'Yes. Doria is also there.'

Amalia sat up. 'Simon?'

'We haven't seen him.'

Her eyes went to Kelsey. 'Holdfast,' she said.

'You're welcome,' said Kelsey.

'Are you fully healed?' said Van.

She touched his arm with a finger. 'Yes.'

'Be very careful,' said Kelsey, narrowing her eyes.

'Do you think I am about to kill my rescuers?' said Amalia. She took a long breath, then got to her feet. 'Are we escaping?'

'Not yet,' said Van, picking up the crossbow and rising to his feet. 'We're getting the Aurelians first. Silva said that you know where they are being held.'

Amalia smiled. 'I see. This is the reason you have released me? I thought for a small moment that you had done it out of pity for me. But no. I am the means to your end.'

'We're still waiting for a thank you,' said Kelsey.

Amalia stared at her. 'I will show you how to get to the apartment where the Aurelians are residing, but then I am leaving. If Kagan and Maxwell are safe, then I'm going to join them.'

'That sounds fine to me,' said Kelsey. 'Count yourself lucky that we didn't just finish you off.'

'Aren't you supposed to be on Implacatus? How did you return?'

'Never mind that,' said Van. 'Show us the way.'

They left the cell. In the next one along was a small dragon, the size of a horse, wrapped in chains.

'Poor thing,' said Kelsey. 'We should release it.'

'A baby dragon would be easy prey for the greenhides,' said Amalia. 'It's safer where it is.' She strode to the next cell, and gazed through the bars.

Kelsey and the others followed her.

'Salvor,' said Van, lifting the keys from a pocket. 'We'll get him out.'

'No,' said Amalia, her eyes tight. 'It's too late for my grandson; Simon has destroyed his mind.'

'You can heal him, though, aye?' said Kelsey.

Amalia shook her head. 'There is only one thing I can do. Open the door.'

Van nodded, and unlocked the barred gate. Amalia entered the cell, and crouched by the sitting form of Salvor.

'Wait,' said Kelsey. 'Are you going to heal him?'

'Don't you listen, Holdfast? Salvor is beyond any healing. His existence is nothing but pain and torment. Salve would be useless, as there is nothing wrong with his body. Simon said it was an accident, but he's lying, as he always does. Salvor refused to bow before him, and so the Ascendant punished him, as an example to the rest of us. While we all submitted, only Salvor had the will to say no. He was brave, too brave; the best of Khora's children, and this was his reward; a living death.'

She placed a hand onto Salvor's arm. 'You can rest now, grandson; the nightmare is over. Be at peace.'

Salvor's eyes closed, and he fell back. Amalia caught him, and lowered him to the floor of the cell, keeping her face turned from the others. She wiped her eyes, and sat in silence next to the body. A tear rolled down Silva's cheek as she stared at Amalia.

'You killed him?' said Kelsey.

Amalia stood. 'He was already more than halfway there. It was the only mercy I could bestow.'

'He was your grandson.'

She turned to Kelsey, anger flaring in her bloodshot eyes.

'It is done,' said Silva. 'Amalia, please – the Aurelians.'

'You are lucky indeed that Silva is here,' said Amalia; 'for I would do nothing for you, Holdfast. For twelve hundred years, Salvor has served this City and its people with more integrity than you will ever possess. I have one other grandson who still lives; I will not be as merciful with him. If we see Naxor, you will leave him to me.'

She strode out of the cell, and the others followed. Kelsey shoved the vial of salve into a pocket, and they went after Amalia, leaving the dungeons. They entered a series of narrow corridors, lit by the occasional lamp, then Amalia slowed.

'Remain here,' she said. 'I will deal with the greenhides outside the apartment, but to do so, the Holdfast girl must stay back. I judge the rooms to be a hundred yards away. I will return soon.'

She walked off without another word, and disappeared round a corner.

'That's the last we'll see of her,' said Kelsey. 'Are we just going to let her go?'

'She'll be back,' said Silva. 'Have a little faith, Kelsey.'

'Faith? In Amalia? Are you joking? She's every bit as treacherous as Naxor.'

'Then trust me, and my own judgement.'

Kelsey glared at the demigod.

'I sense you doubt me,' said Silva. 'Why? What cause I have given you for this mistrust?'

'Belinda's on Implacatus.'

Silva's face paled. 'What?'

'She's getting married to Edmond,' said Kelsey.

'I... No. That can't be right; she hated Edmond.'

Kelsey shrugged. 'Not that much, obviously.'

Silva grabbed Kelsey's hands. 'Did you see her? How did she look?'

'She was in somewhere called Cumulus; I didn't see her.'

'Dear gods; this is terrible. She must have been forced into agreeing this. My poor Queen. Edmond finally has her, after all these long years.'

Van glared at Kelsey, as the demigod started to weep.

Amalia re-appeared from around the corner. She eyed Silva. 'What did you do, Holdfast?'

'Belinda is being held on Implacatus,' sobbed Silva. 'She is being forced to marry Edmond.'

'And the Holdfast girl chose this moment to tell you? That doesn't surprise me. First things first, Silva. Let's get today over with, and then I'm sure Kelsey would be delighted to let you borrow my Quadrant, for I assume that is how she was able to return here.' She smiled at Kelsey. 'The two greenhides that were guarding the Aurelians are dead – I struck them down, but did not enter the apartment. I have no wish to face Emily at this moment, or ever again, if I can help it.'

'Thank you,' said Van.

'I will leave you now, and find Kagan and Maxwell. My part in this is over. Silva, you can come with me, if you like.'

Silva glanced up through her tears. 'No. I pledged loyalty to the Aurelians. I will help them.'

Amalia gave Kelsey a look of raw contempt. 'You don't deserve to have Silva's help. I sincerely pray that I never have the misfortune of seeing you again, Miss Holdfast. However, the City is a small place, so I advise that you stay out of my way.'

She turned, and strode away, leaving the others to watch her leave.

'Let us press on,' said Silva, wiping her eyes.

'Sorry,' muttered Kelsey.

'For what – telling me the truth? It is far better that I know. I had hoped that my beloved Queen had travelled to your world with Corthie, but my deepest fears made me think that she might have died on Lostwell. At least I now know that Belinda lives.' Her eyes tightened a little. 'We can discuss the Quadrant at a future date.'

Van led the way, his crossbow out, and they followed the passageway that Amalia had gone down. At the end, the monstrous bodies of two greenhides were almost blocking a doorway, green blood seeping from their eyes. Van stepped over the corpses, and placed a hand on the door. It swung open, revealing a small hallway, with another doorway. Silva and Kelsey joined him, and they entered the apartment.

Van opened the other door, and Kelsey saw a small, crowded living-room.

Emily's eyes flashed up at them. 'Look out!' she cried.

A gauntleted hand reached from behind the door, and gripped Van's arm. He was hurled into the room, sent flying through the air, where he collided with a table, sending plates and dishes crashing to the floor.

'Greetings, Miss Holdfast,' beamed Simon, reaching for her next.

His hand gripped her round the throat, and he dragged her into the room, then forced her to her knees.

'Silva too, eh?' Simon said. 'Get in here, demigod, and fall to your knees before me, or I will strangle the life out of this witch.'

Silva raised her hands and entered the room, then she got to her knees. Around them, Kelsey could see the adult Aurelians. Emily and Daniel were on a couch, while Daniel's parents were watching from the kitchen door, their features frozen with horror. Next to them, Van was lying, unconscious on the floor.

'You are exceedingly hard to pin down, Holdfast,' said Simon, 'so I thought to myself – why go searching? Why not wait, and let you come to me? Do you smell the smoke? The vile dragons are starting to burn the palace. I could have easily killed them by now, but you were the prize I was after; you, Holdfast.' He tightened his grip, and she choked for air. 'Now that you are mine once again, I will never let you go.'

He dragged her over to Van's body, and crouched by him. He reached into Van's armour, and his eyes lit with delight as he withdrew the Quadrant.

'You fools!' he laughed. 'You brought it with you?'

He traced his finger over it, and the air shimmered. A moment later, everyone who had been inside the apartment appeared in Maeladh's great feasting hall. The walls were lined with greenhides and militia soldiers, and in the corner stood a young greenhide queen, towering over the others.

Simon threw Kelsey to the floor, then placed a foot on her back to keep her there. He looked at the Aurelians. 'Do you feel the heat? Do you smell the smoke? Maeladh will soon be engulfed in flames, but fear not – I will kill the dragons, and then I will kill you.' He grinned. 'The gallows are ready and waiting; I think we might bring the executions forward a little.'

He nodded to the militia soldiers. 'Fetch Naxor and the wagons. Maeladh has served its purpose; let it burn.'

CHAPTER 27

PRINCEPS ROW

Tara, Auldan, The City – 22nd Mikalis 3423

Maxwell was crying in Kagan's arms as he sprinted down Princeps Row. Behind him, he could hear the boulders continue to smash into the courtyard area by the entrance to the palace. Doria was a few paces ahead of him, while the enormous mansions of the Roser aristocracy loomed on either side, their ground floors hidden by trees and thick hedgerows. Kagan counted the driveways to their left, and they skidded to a halt at the third one along.

They gazed through the open entrance at the huge mansion. To Kagan's eyes, it was large as any of the palaces in Old Alea.

'Come on,' said Doria, her feet crunching on the gravel driveway as she walked past the trees.

Kagan glanced over his shoulder, and saw a few curtains twitch on the upper floors of the house opposite, then he followed Doria. They walked round the right hand flank of the mansion. All of the window shutters were closed, and the building sat in silence.

'Excuse me,' said a voice behind them.

They turned, and saw an older man approaching, dressed in fine robes.

'This is private property,' he said; 'you have no right to be here.'

'This is Lady Doria,' said Kagan, 'a member of the Royal Family.'

'The former Royal Family,' said the older man, frowning at them.

'Nevertheless, she has a right to be here,' said Kagan. 'I assume that you have seen the dragons attacking Maeladh? Lord Simon instructed us to come here, so that the children are safe. If you wish to make a complaint, then I'm sure the Ascendant would be happy to hear you out.'

The older man pursed his lip, his eyes tight, then he nodded. 'Very well. Make sure you damage nothing, boy.' He bowed to Doria. 'My lady.'

They watched as he turned and strode back down the driveway.

'Old bastard,' muttered Kagan. 'The City is in flames, and he's worried about us entering an empty house?'

They came to a side door, and Kagan tried the handle.

'Locked,' he said.

'Of course it is,' said Doria. 'Kick it down.'

He handed Maxwell to her, then took a run at the door. His shoulder hit the sturdy frame, and he bounced off it. He grimaced, rubbing his shoulder. He raised a boot, and began kicking the door, but it stood firm.

Growing impatient, he scanned the ground, then picked up a rock. He threw it at the small window to the door's left, and the glass shattered. He reached inside, careful not to lacerate his arm, then found the bolts with his fingers. He slid them free, and the door swung open.

'The Aurelians can bill me for the window,' he said.

They entered a tiled hallway, the air cool and still. Ahead was a large kitchen, and they walked into it.

'This is for one family?' he said. 'You could feed an army from this kitchen.'

There was a highchair by a table, and Doria placed Elspeth into it, then began to check the cupboards.

'There's no food,' she said. 'No one's lived here in months.'

'Maxwell's hungry.'

'So is Elspeth, but what can we do?'

She walked to a large sink, and turned on a tap. Water gushed out, brown at first, but it cleared after a few moments. 'At least we have something to drink.' She turned off the tap and picked up Elspeth. 'Let's explore. There might be a view of the palace from the upper storey.'

They wandered through the enormous house, passing a beautifully furnished dining room, and several sitting-rooms, many with tall windows and packed bookshelves. They ascended to the top floor, and entered a grand bedroom.

'This faces sunward,' said Doria.

She opened the large shutters, and daylight spilled into the room.

'The dragons are back.'

Kagan joined her by the window, his arms growing tired from holding a disgruntled Maxwell. Outside, the roof of the palace was visible beyond the mansions that stood in the way. Three dragons were circling in the sky above Maeladh, then one dived, sending a blast of fire onto the palace. The defences responded, and the air filled with ballista bolts and boulders. The dragon swerved to avoid them, and unleashed more fire. Smoke belched upwards as the dragon veered away.

'That one is much bigger than the other two,' said Doria.

'Why are they burning the palace? Don't they know that the Aurelians and the Holdfast girl are still inside?'

'They're dragons, Kagan; there's no point in trying to divine their motives.' She sighed and sat on the bed. 'At least we're safe here. And the children too. Try to be still, Elspeth.'

Kagan continued to stare at the palace as the largest dragon continued her attack. The other two were darting back and forth in support, but the lead dragon was taking most of the risks, swooping so low that the ballista bolts were practically grazing her flanks. The silver dragon dived down, out of sight, and the hail of rocks ceased.

'I think they got some of the catapults,' he said. 'Dear gods, the palace is starting to burn properly now.' He tore his eyes away. 'And Amalia is still inside.'

'Silva and Kelsey will free her.'

'Will they? You heard the Holdfast girl – they came here to kill Amalia, not save her.'

He walked to another wall, and opened the window shutter that faced east. Across the bay, he could see Pella in the distance. Smoke was rising from the town, but not from the area where the executions usually took place.

'Pella's burning too. The dragons must have passed over there. Why would they burn Pella?'

Doria lay back on the bed. 'I don't care.'

A huge burst of flame came from Maeladh, and Kagan turned back to the sunward-facing window. The dragons were still swooping, but one was tiring, the dragon that Kagan had seen being hit by a flying rock as they were escaping. A scream pierced the air, and the largest dragon plummeted twenty yards, then stabilised, a bolt protruding from her right flank.

'The big one's been hit,' he said. 'That's it; I'm going back.'

Doria glanced at him. 'Why?'

'To get Amalia. I can't just stand here while Maeladh is razed to the ground.'

Doria propped herself up on an elbow. 'You actually love her, do you?'

'Of course I do.'

'Really? After all she's done? I had presumed that you were, you know, forced into being her consort. I hadn't imagined that you were in love with her.'

'Well, I am. Are you happy to stay here with Maxwell and Elspeth while I go?'

'You will die if you go, Kagan. Simon will get you if the dragons don't. Or the greenhides; take your pick.'

Kagan held up Maxwell. 'Stay here with Doria. I'll fetch mummy.'

He placed the child on the bed next to Doria and Elspeth. 'I won't be long.'

'Van is a proper soldier,' said Doria. 'Leave it to him and Kelsey.'

'No. They've failed. They should be out by now; instead, the stupid dragons have trapped them inside. I might not be a soldier, but I survived the slums of Alea Tanton, and I'm not going to abandon Amalia.'

He kissed Maxwell on the forehead, then left the room. He bounded down the stairs, and hurried from the mansion. He broke into a run as soon as he reached the gravel driveway, and sprinted back onto Princeps Row and up the gentle incline towards the palace. Above, only the silver dragon was still circling; the other two were gone from sight. The silver dragon was diving down, setting fire to the far corners of the palace, as if in a blind rage, and as Kagan approached the iron gates, he could see that greenhides had re-occupied the courtyard. They were shrieking in fear from the rising flames engulfing the palace, but Simon's power was preventing them from fleeing.

Kagan paused at the gates. The courtyard was in a mess. Boulders were lying scattered among the broken flagstones, with piles of smouldering greenhides among them. He counted six living greenhides between him and the side entrance to the palace, and wondered what he had been thinking. There was no way through. He would be ripped to shreds within seconds if he entered the courtyard. He gripped the bars of the gates in frustration.

The silver dragon swooped again, dodging the ballista bolts from the remaining batteries. Far fewer were being loosed than before, and no more giant rocks were hurtling through the air, but the dragon still had to weave and swerve to remain uninjured. She doubled back to the courtyard, and incinerated three of the standing greenhides, and the others ran in terror. Kagan squeezed through the bars as the dragon soared off, then a scream ripped through his ears, and he saw the silver dragon fall, a bolt embedded into her underside, between her fore-limbs. She plunged from the sky, her wings beating, and managed to pull up just before crashing into the burning palace. She limped on, unsteady, and disappeared from view over the edge of the ridge to the west.

The greenhides reappeared in the courtyard, and charged at Kagan. He retreated back to the gate, but they were gaining on him, their talons clacking off the flagstones. He heard one right behind him, and closed his eyes, then a shriek filled the air.

No blow came.

Kagan opened his eyes and turned. The three greenhides were lying a yard from him, their bodies sprawled across the ground. Kagan glanced up. Amalia was striding across the courtyard towards him, a hand raised as she looked to each side.

'Amalia,' he said.

'What are you doing out here?' she said. 'You're supposed to be in the Aurelian mansion with Maxwell.'

'Doria has him and Elspeth,' he said. 'I came back for you.'

She stared at him. 'You could have been killed.'

'Was I supposed to just leave you in a burning palace? You are everything to me, Amalia.'

She smiled, and put a hand to his face. 'What did I do to deserve you, Kagan?'

They kissed, standing amid the bloody corpses and the ruins of the courtyard, while the flames rose from Maeladh, filling the sky with smoke.

'I love you,' she said. 'Now, let's get out of here.'

They squeezed through the bars of the gate, and walked down Princeps Row. More curtains twitched, but the gazes from the windows were directed at the inferno engulfing the palace. They turned up the driveway to the Aurelian mansion, and walked in.

Doria was in the kitchen, with both children in high chairs. She was drinking from a glass of water when she saw Amalia enter. She froze.

'Doria,' said Amalia.

'Grandmother.'

'Don't give me that look; you have nothing to fear from me. I have some sad news. Your brother Salvor is dead.'

Doria cast her gaze down. 'Simon did something to his mind.'

'I know, but he isn't suffering any more. I'm sorry.'

'You're sorry? That would be a first. Tell me, did you feel sorry for me when Simon threw me into his harem? I don't recall any sympathy or help coming from you.'

'I was too afraid to act, granddaughter; too fearful of what Simon might do to Maxwell. I'm sorry for that too. I have not been a good grandmother, or mother, and you are one of the very few left from what was once a large family. Simon has nearly ended us all.' She walked over to where Maxwell was sitting and kissed him. 'I will try to be better, Doria.'

'It's a bit late, don't you think? Jade and the dragons have been driven off, and Simon is still inside the palace.'

Amalia frowned. 'The dragons have gone?'

'All three were injured,' said Kagan. 'The silver one might be dead.'

'And Jade?'

'I saw a few people up on the shoulders of two of the dragons,' he said. 'One of them might have been Jade, I suppose.'

Amalia sat by the kitchen table. 'All we can do is wait. If Kelsey Holdfast does what she's supposed to do, then Simon will soon be dead. And, if she fails... then, we're all back to where we were before, only with nowhere to live. Simon will execute me, and that will be that.'

'There has to be another way,' said Kagan. 'Why don't we run for it?'

'And go where? Van gave me some salve, and my powers are back, as you saw in the courtyard. I am like a beacon to Simon, and even Doria's self-healing powers will be detectable to him if he searches hard enough. If he survives Kelsey, then he will come looking for us as soon as he realises we are not where we should be.'

Raised voices rang out, coming from Princeps Row, and they glanced at each other.

'Doria,' said Amalia, standing; 'stay here. Kagan, come with me.'

They left the kitchen and walked to the front of the house. The shutters were all closed, so Amalia peered through the slats.

'Roser militia,' she said, 'with wagons.'

Kagan joined her at the shutters. 'What are they doing?'

'It appears that they are loading the residents of Princeps Row onto the backs of those wagons. If I had vision powers, I'd find out the truth, but if I had to guess, I'd say that Simon has ordered this. This means that he is still alive.'

'Get your hands off me!' cried an old man, as he was led to a wagon. 'Don't you know who I am?'

'Shut up,' said a soldier. 'Orders are orders.'

'Where are you taking us?'

'Prince's Square,' said the soldier. 'Lord Simon is organising a spectacle.'

'In the midst of the worst fire to hit Maeladh in centuries? Madness.'

The old man was pushed into the wagon, and Amalia glanced at Kagan.

'He's going ahead with the executions,' she said. 'That settles it. It's over; Simon has won.'

'Not if we act,' said Kagan. 'He doesn't know where we are. Sure, he'll discover that we're missing; he probably already knows that you aren't in the dungeons any more, but that gives us an opportunity.'

'To do what – get ourselves killed?'

'You are a powerful goddess, Amalia; the most powerful in the City before Simon turned up. This is your City; take it back. We can kill him.'

'If three dragons, Jade, and Kelsey Holdfast cannot do it, then what hope do we have? You know how strong Simon is. He could kill us in a second.'

'Not if Kelsey's there. Would he kill her?'

They quietened as the wagons rolled further down the street. A few soldiers glanced over at the Aurelian mansion, but they turned away, and followed the wagons.

'See?' said Kagan. 'Simon doesn't know that we're here.'

'You're not thinking, Kagan. Say that we achieve the impossible, and kill Simon – what happens next? I will be clapped in chains and led back to a dungeon. Either that, or I'll be forced to slaughter the entire Aurelian family, along with all of their supporters, including Jade, Kelsey and the dragons. I cannot do it any more. Today, I had to end the life of Salvor, and it nearly broke me. You know that I didn't wish to become the God-Queen again; that hasn't changed. I certainly don't want to rule if it means I have to soak Tara in blood.' She bowed her head. 'I'd rather die.'

'So, we're going to sit here, while the Aurelians are tortured to death in front of the Rosers? They don't deserve to die like that. Emily sacrificed herself to give us Maxwell; does that mean nothing to you?'

Amalia closed her eyes. 'Emily is a better queen than I ever was. There, I've said it.'

Kagan took her hand. 'All the more reason to try to save her. If it ends in our deaths, then so be it. I would rather die fighting than watch you be strung up on the gallows. Which would you prefer? You know that Simon will kill you. Why not fight?'

'Because if we fight, then Simon will kill Maxwell. I can accept execution, if it means that you and Maxwell would be spared.'

'We could hide the children first. We could send them to Jezra on a boat, or up to Icehaven, with Doria. The Circuit is huge – Simon wouldn't find the children there. You've still got gang contacts there, yes?'

'You're suggesting we hand our child, and Emily's baby daughter, over to an Evader gang? To be raised in the slums of the Circuit?'

'I was raised in a slum. Believe me, there was a lot more love there than I've found in Tara. Doria could take money, and find a family who have no children of their own.'

'Only if you go with them.'

'No. I'm not leaving your side again.'

'Then my answer is no, Kagan.'

They walked back to the kitchen.

'What's happening outside?' said Doria.

'The militia are taking the occupants of the street down to Prince's Square for the execution of the Aurelians,' said Amalia. 'It appears that Kelsey Holdfast has lost.'

'Do we need to leave?'

'No, Doria; we're safe here. The militia passed this house by.'

Doria exhaled in relief. 'Now what?'

'That's what Kagan and I have been discussing. Do you know anyone in Jezra?'

'No.'

'The Circuit?'

Doria shook her head. 'Why would I know anyone in the Circuit?'

'Ooste? Surely you must know people in Ooste?'

'A few Reaper guards, I guess; and the staff at the Royal Academy. I used to sometimes visit Mona, before... you know.'

Kagan frowned. 'I thought you said that your answer was no?'

'I'm working on the basis that you leave with Doria, Kagan.'

'That's not going to happen.'

'Are you sending us away, grandmother?' said Doria.

Amalia stood. 'Let's get cleaned up. We'll raid the Aurelians' closets for clothes, for us and the children. If we are walking from here, we will need to look the part, and the blood covering the front of my dress might be a little conspicuous.' She glanced at the window clock. 'We have thirty minutes; be quick.'

Kagan found a wardrobe full of Daniel's things and, as he was roughly the same build as the King, he washed, then changed into a fresh set of clothes. Doria put on something that he assumed belonged to Emily, while Amalia emerged from Lady Aurelian's rooms looking elegant and aristocratic. There were no clothes for little boys in the mansion, but Doria had found some meant for Elspeth that almost fitted Maxwell, and the two children looked neat and presentable as they gathered again in the kitchen.

There was a pram by the side entrance, and they squeezed both infants in, and laid a light blanket over their legs.

'If anyone stops us,' said Amalia, 'we'll say that we're walking to Prince's Square to watch the spectacle.'

'Where are we going?' said Doria.

'The harbour. I am sending you to Ooste, granddaughter. Hide in the Royal Academy. If Simon emerges triumphant from this day, then I am trusting you to protect the children, in whatever way you can. Do I have your agreement?'

'What are you going to do?'

'I'm not exactly sure, but it will likely result in my death, probably in front of a baying crowd. Kagan is coming with you. You can pretend to be a mortal, married couple with two infants. Kagan is a good man, he will look after you.'

Doria glanced at him, but Kagan said nothing. It was pointless arguing with Amalia about it – he knew what he had to do, whether she agreed or not.

They slipped out of the mansion by the side door. Doria was pushing the pram, while Kagan and Amalia strolled behind her. Princeps Row was deserted, the huge houses sitting empty and quiet. They turned to the left, heading away from the flames that were ripping through Maeladh Palace, and walked down the gentle slope. Amalia led them along a narrow lane to the right, between two mansions, and they came to a long flight of steps that ran down into Tara. Kagan gripped the front of the pram, and between him and Doria, they lifted it down the steps, all the way to the bottom of the cliff. Fine townhouses lined the wide streets, but no one was out, and the town felt as if it had been abandoned.

'Which way is Prince's Square from here?' said Kagan.

'Directly ahead of us,' said Amalia, 'and the harbour is beyond. Let's take a slightly more circuitous route.'

She gestured to Doria, and they set off to their left, following the avenue of grand houses. The trees were in full bloom, and the blossom was drifting across the worn cobblestones. Kagan began to hear sounds to his right, the low rumble of a crowd in the distance, but they caught no sight of Prince's Square. Ahead of them, the statue of Prince Michael was towering over the town, and Amalia glanced up and blew a kiss in its direction.

Doria frowned.

'Michael was never your favourite, was he?' said Amalia.

'He was a bully and a beast,' said Doria. 'He would have forced me to marry one of my cousins, probably Collo. When Yendra killed him, I pretended to mourn.'

Amalia looked deflated.

'If anything,' Doria went on, 'Marcus was even worse. Just looking at him made me want to vomit.'

'Enough, Doria; you've made your point. Did I make mistakes? Yes. Do you have to cast them up to me continually? No.'

'It wasn't just your protégés who did terrible things, grandmother; you were just as bad. I remember when you put Mona into a restrainer mask – for nothing.'

'She had been conspiring against me with Aila, dear child. You know, I think I liked you better when you cried all the time. You seem to have found some spirit at long last; you would never have spoken to me like this in the past.'

'You would never have allowed me to speak like this, grandmother. You've changed too; perhaps the most.' She pointed at Kagan. 'And to think – a mortal did this to you. A mortal man. Thank you, Kagan, for turning my grandmother into someone who resembles a human.'

'This is a family row,' he said. 'I'm not getting involved.'

'If you marry her, you'll be my grandfather, even though you are nine hundred years younger than me.'

'Why didn't we get married?' said Kagan.

'I wanted to,' said Amalia; 'I still do, but our plans were ruined the day Naxor appeared at our house in Port Sanders. If we survive this, it should be the first thing we do.'

They paused, as a large crowd passed by at a junction, all heading in the direction of Prince's Square. Down the road to their left, someone was standing upon an upturned crate, calling out to anyone on the street.

'Come and see Lord Simon's spectacle!' he cried. 'Free drinks; free refreshments. Come and see the fallen Aurelian tyrants die! Come to the spectacle!'

Kagan narrowed his eyes. He glanced back up the cliffside towards

Maeladh. It was still sending thick flames and smoke into the sky, but there was no sign of any dragons. He turned to the crowd. A few were chatting loudly, and joking with their friends, but many were glancing up at the burning palace in silence, their expressions apprehensive, or even fearful.

'If this were Pella,' said Amalia quietly, 'the Reapers would be rioting at such news. Not so in Tara.'

'They might be rioting in Pella now,' Kagan said. 'I saw a lot of smoke coming from there, and not from the location of the executions.'

Amalia raised an eyebrow. 'Really? Good. I'm glad someone is resisting.'

They crossed the road when it was clear, and carried on towards the harbour. The sun was lowering to their right, and the warmth of the day was starting to cool a little. They reached the long piers that stretched out into the bay, and walked along the promenade. Few ships were in the harbour. Over to the right of the main docks was a row of abandoned vessels, unfit to sail, but unable to be repaired due to the lack of wood. The small fishing boats were still plentiful, and lined three entire piers.

Amalia tapped a pocket. 'I might have lifted a purse of gold I found in the Aurelians' mansion, but as it is going to help keep Elspeth safe, I'm sure they won't mind. Let's find the captain of a fishing boat who would like to earn a little extra today.'

They approached one of the piers, where groups of sailors and fishermen were clustered, talking and working in the afternoon sunshine.

'Good day,' said Amalia to the first group they came across. 'Who can take my sister, her husband, and their two children across the bay to Ooste? I'll pay gold.'

One of the sailors inclined his head slightly, an inbuilt Roser reaction to her aristocratic accent.

'Are you not going to the spectacle, ma'am?'

'I most certainly am, but my sister and her family have business in Ooste that needs to be attended to.'

'I'm leaving in five minutes,' said another sailor, thumbing over his shoulder at a small fishing vessel. 'Two adults and a pram will be a squeeze, but we'll manage. How much are you offering, ma'am?'

'What's the going rate? Two sovereigns?'

'Three,' he said, shrugging. 'The pram costs extra.'

'Deal,' said Amalia. She counted out three gold coins from the purse, then handed the rest to Doria. She gave the three coins to the sailor, and he bowed his head.

'Thank you, ma'am.' He turned to Kagan and Doria. 'This way; if you'd like to board?'

Amalia walked along with them, and stopped at the gangway, as two of the crew lowered the pram into the boat. Doria stepped down onto the deck without a word, but Kagan turned, his eyes piercing Amalia.

'Now that the time has arrived,' she said, 'I feel quite nervous. Scared, a little. Not of dying, but of losing you and Maxwell.'

'I can't leave you,' he said. 'The boat can go without me.'

'No, Kagan. If you go to the square, you will die. Maxwell needs a father.'

'He needs a mother too.'

'You don't understand. Simon might not even bother coming to look for you; you're a mere mortal in his eyes; and Doria means nothing to him. There's a good chance that he'll ignore, or forget about you. That will never happen to me. Simon will never stop looking for me. Therefore, to save you, I must kill him, or be killed.'

'I know what you're saying; I understand the cost. If you die, Amalia, then I don't want to live. I would rather die by your side than leave you to walk alone to your death.'

Amalia kissed him.

The captain of the boat coughed. 'We're ready to leave, sir. If you wouldn't mind?'

'Go,' said Amalia.

'No,' he said. 'Where you go, I go.'

'Not this time, Kagan,' she said. 'I hope you'll forgive me.'

She raised her hand, and he felt a sharp pain resonate through his body, and his knees almost buckled. The pain ceased, but the feeling of weakness remained. Amalia steered him towards the boat. A sailor took his arm and helped him down, and he sat heavily by the side of the vessel, his legs growing so weak that he was unable to move them. He tried to speak, to cry out in protest, but his voice wasn't working either. He stared up at Amalia.

'Is he alright?' said a sailor, frowning at him.

'He gets seasick,' said Amalia, from the pier. 'He'll be fine when he gets to dry land. Goodbye, Doria and Elspeth, and goodbye, Kagan and Maxwell. With any luck, I shall see you soon. Have a safe journey. I'm going now, because I don't want you to see me cry.'

She turned and strode away, while the sailors cast off the ropes attaching the boat to the pier. The vessel's only sail was raised, and a breeze from sunward drew them out into the main harbour basin, where the clear waters were glistening in the gentle swell.

Kagan stared back at Amalia, his eyes following her as she walked along the promenade, before she disappeared into the crowds who were making their way towards Prince's Square.

CHAPTER 28

THE EXILES

Tara, Auldan, The City – 22nd Mikalis 3423

Jade clung onto the folds of Dawnflame's shoulders as the dragon twisted through the air. The ballista bolt had struck her in the right flank, a few yards from where Jade and Rosie were located. The demigod could feel Dawnflame's agony through the scales, and she sent her powers into the dragon, easing the pain.

Dawnflame stabilised, and she veered away from the burning palace, heading out towards the Straits.

'I must land,' she said.

'The cliffs at Ooste are only a mile away,' said Rosie.

'Can you make it that far?' said Jade.

Blood was streaking out of the wound as Dawnflame banked towards Ooste. Jade glanced back in the direction of Tara. Smoke was filling the air above the palace, and she could see Frostback continuing to attack, but there was no sign of Halfclaw.

'What are we going to do?' said Rosie, her eyes wide. 'Van and Kelsey are still in there.'

Jade said nothing, her thoughts focussed on relieving the searing pain the injury was causing Dawnflame. Without her powers, the dragon would have crashed into the palace, or fallen into the waters of the sea. Her wings were sagging as they rushed across the neck of the bay, and the left tip hit the water, sending a glistening line of spray into the air. She rose at the base of the cliffs, and for a moment Jade thought she was going to hit the sheer rocks, but she made it to the top of the ridge, then collapsed onto the ground in exhaustion. Jade kept her hands on Dawnflame's shoulders, dampening the agony.

'We'll have to get the bolt out,' she said to Rosie. 'Will you help me?'

Rosie nodded. 'I've never seen so many catapults and ballistae before in my life,' she said, 'not even on the Great Walls. They were definitely expecting us.'

'The bolt,' grunted Dawnflame; 'please.'

Yes; sorry,' cried Rosie, as she clambered down the dragon's flank.

'I'm going to have to let go for a moment or two,' said Jade. 'We'll be as quick as we can.'

'Do as you must,' said Dawnflame.

Jade pulled her hands from the dragon's back and slid down to the ground. Dawnflame closed her eyes, taking the pain. Jade joined Rosie on the solid ground of the ridge, where she was staring at the bolt.

'It's in deep,' she said.

'Grab it,' said Jade. 'Both hands. But don't pull; not yet.'

They positioned themselves by the dragon's flank, and reached up, each of them taking a hold of the bolt's long steel shaft. Jade put her foot up against the side of the purple dragon, then nodded to Rosie. They heaved on the bolt, pulling it out a few inches, and Dawnflame roared in pain.

'Again,' said Jade.

Dragon blood spattered them as they strained, ripping the bolt out another foot.

'Just the barbed end to go,' said Jade. 'Again.'

She closed her eyes, and pulled on the bolt with all her strength. The sharp point came away from the dragon's flank, and Rosie and Jade toppled backwards, the front of their clothes covered in blood. Jade wiped her hands on her green dress, then pressed her fingers to the side of the dragon. She had already lost a lot of blood, and Jade closed the wound up first, then sent in her powers to heal the internal injuries. She felt herself weaken as she gave the dragon a good portion of the reserves that she had ripped from her father. The memory of that soured her thoughts as her knees buckled. Rosie helped support her, and Jade sat down heavily on the rocky ridge, her hands shaking.

'Dragons are so damn big,' she gasped. 'I could have healed twenty humans with the power I just gave her.'

Rosie glanced at the dragon's closed eyes. 'Was it enough?'

Jade nodded. 'I think so.'

The dragon lay motionless for a few long minutes, and Jade turned to watch what was happening over Tara. The smoke and flames were filling the sky in that direction, and she caught a glimpse of Frostback diving as she weaved through the barrage of missiles.

'Where's Halfclaw?' said Rosie.

'He got hit with a boulder,' said Jade. 'If he was here, I'd heal him too.'

'Should we have gone back to the mountains?'

'How could we have known that all this was waiting for us?'

'If only we knew what was happening inside the palace. Kelsey and Van might have killed Amalia and rescued any prisoners by now, or... or, they might both be dead.'

'Simon is there.'

'Do you know that for sure?'

'No, but he must be. He has no Quadrant, so where else could he be? He's brought every ballista in the City together to defend the palace.'

Rosie glanced around. 'Auldan is in flames – Dalrig, Tara; even Pella is burning; look.'

Jade turned to the east, and saw smoke rising from several places over Pella and its outer suburbs. She frowned.

Dawnflame let out a long groan, and opened her eyes. She turned to Jade. 'Once again, demigod, I am in your debt.'

'We are friends,' said Jade. 'There is no debt.'

The dragon tilted her head. 'You are gracious; thank you.' Her eyes scanned the horizon. 'What did I miss?'

'Frostback's still attacking,' said Rosie, pointing towards Tara.

'She is enraged,' said Dawnflame. 'Her rider is in the palace, with no easy way to get out. I fear she would do anything to get the Holdfast girl back. She may lose her mind if Kelsey dies. Come; we must help her.'

'Are you strong enough to fight?' said Rosie, as she and Jade stood.

'I am strong enough to fly,' said the dragon, 'but I feel the hand of exhaustion upon me. The bolt has sapped my strength. I will need to rest soon, or I will be too tired to avoid the missiles. Where is Halfclaw? I do not see him.'

'We don't know,' said Jade, as they climbed back up onto the dragon's shoulders.

Dawnflame launched herself off the side of the ridge, and Jade nearly fell off as the dragon plunged down to the surface of the water. She levelled out, and soared back across the bay. They passed the statue of Michael, and rose back up the steep slope of the ridge on the Taran side of the bay. They cleared the first mansions of Princeps Row, and Frostback came into sight. The young, silver dragon was swooping over the large courtyard where Kelsey and Van had entered the palace, then Dawnflame flinched as Frostback was hit. The ballista bolt sank deep into the chest of the silver dragon, and she let out an awful scream, and plummeted from the sky. At the last moment, she managed to pull up, then she disappeared over the edge of the ridge to their right. Dawnflame raced after her, putting on a surge of speed that nearly threw Jade and Rosie from her shoulders. She flew over the side of the ridge, and dived after Frostback, who was hurtling down towards the rocks at the base of the cliffs, where the waves of the Warm Sea were crashing against the shore.

Dawnflame reached Frostback just as the silver dragon was about to hit the ragged rocks. With her forelimbs out, she grabbed onto Frostback, and their momentum carried them both down. Dawnflame managed to veer away from the rocks, and they crashed into the waters of the Warm Sea. Jade was thrown from Dawnflame's shoulders, and went under. She couldn't swim, and panicked, her arms and legs flailing around as water flooded her mouth and nose. Her face reached the surface, and she gasped for air, then she plunged down again, the strong current of the Straits dragging her back under the waves.

Something gripped her round the waist and lifted her clear of the sea. She threw up a stream of water from her mouth, her eyes stinging, as she rose into the air. To her right she saw Dawnflame, holding onto Frostback's limp body, her claws gripping the harness on the silver dragon's shoulders as she carried her clear of the Straits. Jade glanced up, to see Halfclaw's green body above her. In his left forelimb was Rosie, clutched within the dragon's grasp. Halfclaw was toiling, his injury from the boulder causing him to strain as he skimmed over the water. Dawnflame turned for the west, and the two dragons limped along. Jade touched Halfclaw, and gave him some of the power from her depleted reserves.

'Thank you, demigod,' he grunted, 'but save what power you have for Frostback; she needs it more than I.'

The dragons struggled across the Straits, and Jade saw the cliffs of the Western Bank approach. It had been a long time since she had been in Jezra, but she recalled the words that Vadhi had spoken, and hoped the mortal girl would be proved right. They reached the harbour of Jezra, and passed low over the ruins. Soldiers dressed in Blade uniforms were up on the high points, but there were no ballistae, and they gazed at the dragons as they flew overhead. Halfclaw made for the large, flat foundations of the ancient palace, as every face in the town glanced up at them. Exiles began to pour out onto the streets in their hundreds, then thousands, and huge crowds were gathering as Halfclaw hovered over the foundations. He set Rosie and Jade down onto the stone slabs, then landed next to them. Jade rushed to Rosie's side. The young woman was weak, but conscious, and Jade exhaled in relief. Close by, Dawnflame lowered Frostback to the ground, then almost crash-landed, her limbs folding under her.

Jade jumped to her feet. All around the high foundations, Exiles were watching. Some were cheering, while others were staring open-mouthed at the injuries the dragons had sustained. A company of around a hundred Blades in tight formation were forcing their way through the crowds, heading towards the ruins of the ancient palace.

Halfclaw turned her head to face Jade. 'Ignore the soldiers,' he said; 'attend to my beloved, I beg you, demigod.'

Jade ran over to where Frostback was lying. Dawnflame was sniffing the bolt.

'I shall pluck it out as soon as you are ready,' she said to Jade. 'Can you heal her?'

'I'll try,' said Jade. She glanced over her shoulder at the approaching Blades.

'Halfclaw and I will deal with them, Jade.'

The demigod nodded. 'Alright. Remove the bolt.'

Dawnflame clutched the steel shaft with a forelimb, and ripped it from Frostback's chest, sending blood gushing out after it. Jade placed both hands onto the silver dragon's flank and closed her eyes. She sensed the wound. It was deep, but the bolt had missed the dragon's heart, which was beating faintly. Her life force was slipping away with every second, and Jade didn't hesitate. She sent what she had, emptying her reserves into Frostback.

Drained, she staggered backwards into Rosie's arms, then oblivion took her.

The light was starting to dim when Jade opened her eyes. Above her, the three dragons were peering down into her face, while Rosie, Caelius, Flavus and Vadhi were crouching by her side.

Jade's eyes went to Frostback. The dragon looked exhausted, but alive.

'You had us all worried there for a while, ma'am,' said Caelius. 'How do you feel?'

Jade sat up. 'Fine. Tired. How long was I unconscious?'

'Two hours,' said Dawnflame. 'The agony of watching you was worse than the pain I felt from being injured.'

Frostback bowed her head to her. 'You have my eternal thanks, demigod.'

'Kelsey?'

'My rider is in the hands of the Ascendant; for now,' said the silver dragon.

'That is so,' said Halfclaw. 'I patrolled while you were sleeping, demigod. The Ascendant has prepared a place in Tara – a wooden platform, with a line of posts. We believe he is intending to execute his prisoners in front of a vast crowd of Rosers who have gathered in the plaza.'

'Give her a moment to recover,' said Dawnflame. 'All of you, give Jade some space. Demigod, do you require anything – food, water?'

'Something to eat,' she said. 'What happened to the Blades? Did you burn them?'

'Vadhi,' said Dawnflame; 'bring some food for Jade.' She turned back to the demigod. 'We didn't need to do anything. The people of Jezra rose up, and every Blade on the Western Bank is either dead or disarmed and in custody.'

Jade reached out her hands, and Caelius and Flavus helped her to her feet. She glanced between the bodies of the dragons. The Exiles were packing out the area around the ancient palace. Some caught sight of her, and began to cheer.

'What do they want?' she said.

'They want you to lead them, ma'am,' said Caelius. 'Say the word, and they will board every ship in the harbour and sail for Tara. Young Vadhi was right, they have been watching the skies every day since the Banner surrendered, praying for the return of the dragons.'

The young Torduan woman appeared, bearing a basket of food.

'Thanks,' said Jade. 'Could everyone go, except for Rosie and Dawnflame? I need a moment or two to think before I do anything else.'

The two Banner officers bowed to her, then retreated, while Halfclaw and Frostback ascended into the sky, then banked for the harbour. Jade picked up the basket, and walked into the cool shade of the cliffside. She sat, her back to the sheer wall of rock, and felt exhaustion ripple through every inch of her body.

'You don't look so great,' said Rosie, crouching next to her.

'I'm fine.'

'How are your powers?'

'They'll be back in a while. My self-healing's working, but I won't be able to heal, or kill, anyone for a while. Not unless you have any salve?'

Rosie shook her head. 'I should have taken some from Dalrig, but I was too... well, you know.'

Jade's thoughts went back to Amber. With the intensity of the fight over Tara gone, the memories of the basement under Greylin came flooding back. She closed her eyes, wishing she could crawl into a dark hole and sleep.

'Eat something,' said Dawnflame. 'It may help.'

'I hated Amber,' she said. 'I mean, I really hated her, with all of my strength. She was mean, and horrible, and...' She started to cry, and she cursed her weakness.

'It's alright,' said Rosie.

'No, it's not. I had chances to try to be friends with her. Even Kelsey Holdfast tried to push us together, but I refused. And you were right, when I visited her to demand an apology. How I wish I had listened to you. If I had gone there to genuinely try to reconcile, it might have worked, but I didn't, and she was just as mean as she always was. And... now it's too late. I will never see my sister again. This is all my fault.'

'None of this is your fault,' said Dawnflame, 'not as far as I can discern. Your family treated you unfairly, and it is regrettable that you will have no chance to put things right, but that is not your fault, Jade. Your father and sister bowed before Simon, whereas you chose the harder road – to fight.'

Great sobs wracked through Jade's chest. 'Even though I hated them,' she said, 'I always knew that they were there. Now, I have no one.'

'That's not true,' said Rosie. 'You have Dawnflame, and you have me.

393

Flavus is also very fond of you, and you have earned the respect of the others. You are not alone.'

Jade glanced at them through her tears. They didn't understand – how could they? Rosie would be gone in a few short decades, even if she survived the next day or so, and even dragons were mortal. In a few centuries, Dawnflame, Frostback and Halfclaw would also be dead, while she would linger on, alone. The old Jade would have pointed this out to them, but she knew it would cause them nothing but pain, so she remained silent.

Rosie held out an apple for her, and she took it. They were watching her closely, so she took a bite, despite having no appetite.

'Good,' said Dawnflame. 'Eat more. It will help you recover your strength, and you shall need it. This day is not yet over, Jade.'

Jade wiped her eyes, and tried to quell her grief. They needed her, she realised. Without Kelsey, her powers were their strongest asset. She took another bite, forcing the apple down.

'Perhaps we should retreat back to the mountains,' said Rosie.

'We cannot,' said Dawnflame. 'Frostback would boil over with rage if she even heard such a thing suggested. She will not leave her rider to die in Simon's clutches, even if it means her own death, and I will not abandon her. Halfclaw is her mate, and he will never leave her side. Therefore, we have but one option – despite our exhaustion, we must fight on.'

'Halfclaw told us he went patrolling,' said Jade. 'What else did he see?'

'Maeladh Palace still burns,' said Dawnflame. 'Simon was evacuating it when Halfclaw was overhead, and the remaining ballistae and catapults are being transported down into the town of Tara. He saw no sign of Van or Kelsey, but there were several covered wagons. Halfclaw thinks Simon saw him, but the Ascendant did not attack.'

'Then Kelsey is still alive,' said Jade.

'That's what Frostback believes. Halfclaw also saw a huge crowd of Rosers gathering by the large plaza, where the execution platform has been constructed. That shall be our new target.'

'What about Amalia? Any sign of my grandmother?'

'None,' said Dawnflame, 'but he did see a greenhide queen, one of those from the nest we attacked last winter. We must assume that the Ascendant placed it under his control before he captured the Holdfast girl.'

Jade nodded, then frowned, noticing something strapped to Dawnflame's shoulders. 'Is that a harness?'

'It is,' said the dragon. 'The Exiles had spare ones made up for Frostback and Halfclaw, and they adjusted one to fit me. I am aware that you were thrown from my back when I dived to rescue Frostback; I do not wish for that to occur again. I am ashamed – not because I am wearing it, but because I mocked the two young dragons for so long for choosing to do so. You will not fall from my shoulders again, demigod.'

Jade finished the apple, then took a drink of water that Rosie offered her. She was so tired that she longed for sleep, but tried not to show it. She had slept for far longer after healing Halfclaw next to the Great Walls, and her reserves were enough only to keep her own self-healing running.

'I won't be able to heal any of you again,' she said; 'not for a while.'

'We understand,' said the dragon. 'If Simon has the Holdfast girl, then your powers to deal out death would not work in any case. This day will be won or lost with flame and sword, not by god powers.'

'Sword? You mean the Brigades? Are they really willing to face Simon?'

'They long for a chance to fight, especially once they heard the news about the Banner.'

'What news?'

'Something else that Halfclaw saw,' said Rosie. 'Do you remember he told us that he'd seen one of Van's officer friends lurking about the palace? Well, when he flew over again, he could see smoke rising from several of the buildings to the back of Cuidrach, including the old barracks where the Royal Guard lived. Banner soldiers were streaming out of it. They've over-powered the Reaper militia on guard, and hundreds of them are storming through Pella, armed. The officer was leading them down the coastal road towards Tara, and now the Brigades want their turn. Do you think you're able to speak to them?'

'Why? What could I say?'

Rosie smiled. 'You're their new hero, Jade. They've heard all about your attacks on the forts and palaces. You sustained their hope while Jezra was occupied by the Blades.'

'Which is why they were so keen to help us,' said Dawnflame. 'The Exiles do not wish to go quietly; they thirst for blood and vengeance, and they long to have their Queen back. You are their champion, Jade. Speak to them.'

Jade glanced from the dragon to Rosie. The last thing she wanted to do was address a crowd. She had never been a good speaker, and wasn't sure she had ever managed to successfully inspire anyone. She had hidden herself away from the Blades while she had run the Bulwark, and had hardly ever spoken to the officers there.

'Alright,' she said; 'I'll do it.'

She pulled herself to her feet. Hundreds of Exiles were ringing the ruins of the ancient palace, and more were packing out every street leading to it. By the edge of the platform, she could see Flavus and Caelius, talking to a small group of Brigade officials. Jade walked over to them, and the gathered crowd roared once they had seen her, their arms in the air. Jade flushed, feeling sweat appear on her forehead.

Caelius and Flavus turned as she approached them.

'The Brigades await your orders, ma'am,' said Flavus, bowing; 'as do we.'

Jade felt thousands of eyes upon her. 'Will they accept my orders?'

Caelius laughed. 'Shall I ask them, ma'am?'

Jade nodded.

The veteran sergeant turned to face the crowd and raised his arms.

'Exiles of Lostwell,' his voice boomed out.

The crowd roared again, and Jade could see that Caelius was revelling in their attention. She frowned, wishing she had his confidence in front of so many.

'Lady Jade is here,' Caelius called out, to more cheers. 'The mighty dragon Dawnflame, and the noble Lady Jade, the conquerors of Ooste, and Dalrig, and the fortresses of the Great Wall, have come here, to Jezra. The vile Simon intends to murder our beloved King and Queen, and put Kelsey Holdfast to the sword.'

The crowd booed.

Dawnflame lowered her head. 'Soldier,' she said, 'it should be Jade speaking, not you.'

Caelius grinned. 'Sorry; I got a little carried away there.' He gestured to Jade. 'Please, ma'am.'

Jade suppressed a scowl, and stepped forward.

'I... I have...' she stammered, her face flushing.

Rosie took her hand. 'Don't worry; take your time.'

Jade swallowed, and tried again. 'I have not been good to mortals. I am a member of the Royal Family who oppressed the people of this City for millennia. My grandparents, my father, my aunts and uncles, and my cousins – out of them, only a tiny few ever cared for the welfare of the mortals who lived here, and I was not one of them.' She glanced at the crowd, who were standing in silence, watching her.

'For centuries,' she went on, 'I remained in Greylin Palace, never leaving its walls. I had no interest in how the people lived, and mocked those such as Yendra and Aila, who claimed to care for the mortals. I am a god, and I thought that made me better than all of you. I was wrong. I am no better, in fact, I am worse. All I can do now is try to make amends. Simon has no good in him. He will destroy everything and everyone we love. Yendra told me that you cannot control how you feel, and right now I am afraid. I am scared that Simon will kill my friends, and they are all I have. But Yendra also said that each of us is in control of our actions, that each of us has the power to do the right thing, regardless of the cost. I didn't listen to her enough when she was alive, but her words mean more to me now than they ever did.'

She bowed her head. 'The dragons are going back to Tara, to fight, and I am going with them. We might all die, but I'd rather die than live under Simon's rule.' She raised her eyes. 'I cannot promise you that we will be victorious, but I swear that we will never surrender to Simon.

We will fight him, and we will win, or die. I will not order you to do anything. You can remain here, and watch as the flames and smoke rise from Tara, or you can arm yourselves, go to the boats, and fight along-side us. Each of you must choose for yourself.'

The crowd stared up at her in silence, then someone shouted, 'The boats!' The crowd erupted, their cries ringing in Jade's ears. Along the streets that led to the ruined palace, the people began turning, and hurrying down towards the harbour.

Caelius slapped Jade on the back, then Dawnflame growled at him and he retreated a step.

'Good job, ma'am,' he said, eyeing the enormous dragon. 'That ought to do the trick.'

'Let us depart,' said Frostback. 'The Exiles will take an hour to reach Tara, even if they board the ships immediately. We need to be over Tara before then. Kelsey could be dying, even as we speak.'

'My son is there too,' said Caelius. 'A few days ago, I thought he was dead, and I have no intention of losing him again.'

Dawnflame glanced at Jade, and the demigod nodded her head.

'Rosie,' she said. 'I want you to stay here.'

'But, Jade,' said the young Blade. 'I can help.'

Jade looked into her eyes. 'You have already helped me, more than you can ever know. Stay, so I know that, no matter what happens, you are safe. Do this for me.'

'But...'

'You heard the commander, Private,' said Flavus. 'I am also staying; there will be no need for a mapmaker in the coming battle. We can watch from the harbour, together.'

'Thank you, Flavus,' said Jade. 'Look after her for me.'

Flavus bowed. 'It will be an honour to do so, ma'am. Good luck.'

'I'm coming,' said Caelius. 'I wouldn't miss this for the world.'

'I shall bear you, Van-father,' said Halfclaw.

Dawnflame raised her head and sniffed the air. 'It is time.'

Jade embraced Flavus, then Rosie, who was crying quietly. 'Come back,' she whispered.

Jade climbed up onto Dawnflame's shoulders, and strapped herself into the harness. All over the town, the Exiles were heading towards the harbour, filling the vessels that remained there.

'They are brave,' said Dawnflame. 'Many will die.'

'Everyone dies,' said Jade. 'Let's go.'

CHAPTER 29

THE SPECTACLE

T ara, Auldan, The City – 22nd Mikalis 3423

Emily knelt on the gravel path. Her wrists were bound behind her back, and a hood had been secured over her head. Close by, the muttered words of the Roser militia guarding her would occasionally rise in volume, as the fires spread throughout the palace grounds. Chaos seemed to be sweeping over Maeladh, and the sound of carts and wagons being loaded reverberated around Emily.

She kept her head bowed, listening for any signs of her husband or daughter amid the confusion of shouts and running militia. The wheels of a wagon crunched next to her as it rolled by, and her guards got into an argument with the driver over who had the right of way. It was getting heated when an officer barked out orders, and the wagon moved on. More wheels crunched by, closer, and Emily was hauled to her feet, her knees aching. She was lifted up, and pushed into a carriage, where she fell to the wooden floor. The hood was yanked from her head, and the carriage doors were slammed shut behind her.

Emily tried to get up, and bumped into someone's leg.

'Your Majesty?' said a voice.

She glanced up, her eyes growing used to the dim light of the carriage's interior.

'Van,' she said.

'I'd help you up,' he said, 'but...' He nodded down to where his own arms and wrists were bound.

She leaned forward, and managed to stumble up onto the bench opposite Van. They were the only two inside the carriage, and the windows had been shuttered from the outside. She peered through the slats, but could see only smoke and flames.

'Simon is evacuating the palace,' said Van.

She frowned at the bruises and cuts on his face.

'Don't worry about me,' he said.

'Who did that to you?'

'A few of the militia,' he replied. 'Simon told them to. I've had worse. How are you? Have you seen Kelsey?'

'I'm fine,' she said. 'I had a hood covering my head from the moment we left the apartment in the basement until now. I haven't seen anyone. Simon didn't kill Kelsey last time he caught her, so I think she'll be alright. You arrived with Lady Silva, didn't you? Naxor told us that she was with Elspeth; did you see her?'

Van nodded. 'We did.'

Emily stared at him. 'Well? Tell me. If Kelsey is alive, then Simon won't be able to read our minds; and if she isn't, then he'll read it out of your head anyway. I need to know.'

'Kelsey and I entered the palace via the iceward wing, and we found Elspeth and Maxwell first. We sent them away, with Kagan and Doria. We told them to go to the Aurelian mansion on Princeps Row, to keep the children safe. None of them are in the palace.'

'Praise Malik for that. Thank you, Van. At least they're away from the flames. Although, I don't trust Kagan, and I don't know Doria.'

'We had no option, your Majesty. We needed Silva to guide us through the palace.'

'I wasn't criticising; you did the right thing. I wonder when Simon will find out. We're on our way to Prince's Square, did you know? We're all going to the gallows. Simon has driven the dragons away; I overheard the militia talking about it. All three of them picked up injuries.'

'Don't despair, your Majesty.'

She met his glance. 'I'm not despairing. I don't intend to give up until I'm dead, Major-General. If we die, then we shall do so with our heads held high, defiant to the bitter end. I wish I knew where Lucius was.'

'Halfclaw spotted him in Pella.'

'Pella? What's he doing there? I told him to return to Hammer territory.'

The carriage door opened, and the light from the blazing fires dazzled Emily's eyes.

'Getting cosy, are we?' laughed Simon. 'Just wait until I tell the false King how his errant wife was snuggling up to the Commander of the Banner.'

The Ascendant climbed up into the carriage, then leaned back out and picked up someone who had been hooded and wrapped in chains. He lifted the body into the interior and laid it down onto the floor of the carriage, and Emily noticed that he had one end of the chains gripped in his left hand. He sat next to Van and put his feet onto the chained body, as the carriage door was closed.

They began to move, the ponies pulling the carriage towards the gates of the palace.

'Kelsey Holdfast makes an excellent footrest,' said Simon. 'Though, I had to gag her first. She has an impertinent tongue on her, and wouldn't shut up.' He jiggled an armoured boot on the still body. 'Isn't that right, you freak?' He glanced up at Emily. 'She was extremely rude to me while I took her to Yocasta to get more greenhides. So much so, that I was forced to slap her. I admit that I forgot that she has no self-healing powers, and I might have gone too far. Still, at least she's quiet, eh?'

Van stared at the figure on the floor of the carriage, then rage coloured his eyes, and he spat in Simon's face.

The Ascendant's features rippled with fury. He raised a gauntleted fist, and Emily was convinced that he was going to strike the Banner officer, but then he relaxed, and smiled.

'I know your little game, soldier,' he said, 'but it won't work. You will die on the gallows, next to Amalia and the Aurelians. Let's call it revenge for Felice.'

'You can call it whatever you like,' said Emily, 'but it doesn't disguise the fact that you are a coward and a tyrant. The entire City hates you. Take the Quadrant, collect the salve, and go. Trust me; it's the only way you'll survive this, Simon.'

The huge god laughed. 'What a night we have ahead of us! Torture, blood and death, all in front of an enormous crowd of the richest citizens of this pestilent City. I've been using my imagination to think up bizarre and cruel ways to end each of your lives; after all, the event has been billed as a spectacle, and we wouldn't want to disappoint the audience, would we?'

The carriage turned left onto the main road leading down the steep slope to the town, and Emily almost fell forwards. Simon pushed her back onto her seat.

He glanced at Van. 'Fifty days, yes?'

Van narrowed his eyes. 'What?'

Simon sighed. 'The old Banner regulations? They may have changed over the last few millennia, but Implacatus has always stuck to its traditions, in the same way that a drowning man will clutch onto any piece of flotsam to delay the inevitable. Fifty days was the length of time a Banner soldier has to remain in captivity before their contracts expire, yes? Unless their commanding officer, and the holders of the contract, die first? Is that right?'

'Yes.'

Simon rubbed his hands together. 'Excellent. In that case, I am glad I forgot to have the surviving two and a half thousand soldiers of the Banner executed. I had pinned my hopes on using the Blades as my army of vengeance but, let's be honest, they're keen, but they're not exactly what I would call professional; not like the Banners. They will serve me, won't they, Commander? Banner soldiers don't care who they work for, as long as they get paid.'

Van said nothing.

Simon frowned. 'It is most infuriating, not being able to read your thoughts. The Holdfast witch presents me with a dilemma. She is valuable, very valuable, and I have learned that I cannot let her out of my sight; but the price is high. I cannot use my death powers to bring the dragons down, and I cannot see what mischievous notions are swirling around in that skull of yours, soldier. I will endure it as a test of my patience. I assume it was you who rescued her from Serene?'

'Assume whatever you wish.'

'Come on,' said Simon; 'don't be like that. All I want to know is what happened while she was there. Did she unleash chaos? Were the gods aware of what was causing their powers to stop working? Did they panic? I wish I'd seen it. I intend to use the Holdfast witch as my secret weapon against the Ascendants, and I would prefer to know what they made of her.'

'Take Kelsey's hood off, and I'll tell you.'

'No. Instead, tell me, or I will cause her great pain.'

The carriage slowed to a halt. The side door opened, and Naxor appeared, standing on the cobbles, his expression clouded with worry.

Simon turned to him. 'Yes?'

'We have arrived at Prince's Square, your Grace,' said Naxor. 'All of the preparations are complete, and the crowd has been assembled. The extra greenhides you brought are surrounding the square, and the artillery has been positioned exactly as you requested. Thirty catapults and fifty ballistae survived the dragon onslaught, and I have placed scouts on the roofs on the nearest buildings.'

Simon narrowed his eyes. 'Yes. And?'

Naxor's forced smile failed him. 'There was no sign of Amalia in the dungeons, your Grace, and Lord Salvor, my brother, is dead. Also, Kagan and Lady Doria have fled the palace, taking the children with them. We did, however, manage to save the infant dragon from the flames...'

Naxor choked as Simon gripped him by the throat. 'Amalia escaped? And Elspeth Aurelian is missing? You utter imbecile!' He shook Naxor like a doll. There was a crack, and Naxor's head lolled to the side. Simon released him, and the unconscious demigod slumped to the cobbles. Simon turned to Van and Emily. 'Where are they?'

Emily kept her features even. Simon's frustration was obvious, and she felt a deep satisfaction that he was unable to see into her mind. She knew he was paranoid, even with his powers; without them, she could only guess at the turmoil churning his thoughts.

'You plan on torturing us to death,' she said. 'What threats do you think will make us talk? Activate the Quadrant and leave the City; this is your last chance.'

'You knew about this, didn't you, false Queen?' Simon said, his eyes swimming in fury.

Emily smiled. 'Wouldn't you like to know?'

Simon climbed down out of the carriage and kicked Naxor in the ribs. 'Get up. Take the commander and the false Queen to their posts.'

Emily glanced over the Ascendant's shoulder. They were in Prince's Square, parked next to the long, high platform that had been constructed. To their right, the sun was low in the sky, and the street-lamps had been lit. Emily's courage dipped a little as she saw Daniel and his parents being led across the platform. Greenhides were positioned behind each of the posts, and dozens more were encircling the gallows. Beyond, were seated hundreds of Rosers – some dressed in their finest outfits, others in their night-clothes. Most looked terrified, and a few children were crying.

Naxor got to his feet. He gestured to a group of Roser militia, who approached the carriage. Van crouched down by Kelsey, and whispered something to her that Emily didn't catch, then the militia reached in and dragged them from the carriage. The murmurings from the crowd rose a notch as Emily was marched in front of the lines of seats, a crossbow nudging her back.

'You will be next!' she called out to the crowd. 'Do you think Simon will stop with us? He hates the City, and everyone who lives in it. Fight him, before it is too late.'

She saw Lord Chamberlain in the front row. She had known his uncle, and knew the enmity the Chamberlains felt towards her family.

Even so, the current lord was staring at her with nothing but fear on his face, his knuckles white as he gripped the sides of the seat.

Emily and Van were led to a set of wooden steps, where the enormous greenhide queen was standing guard, her insect eyes scanning the crowd. As they climbed the steps, Emily stared at the row of posts. Each rose over seven feet above the level of the platform, and had iron rings attached to their tops. Shackles hung from the rings, connected by chains. At the far end of the line of eight posts, Lord Aurelian had already been secured to the shackles of his post. To his left, Lady Aurelian's arms were being lifted high by Roser militia, and the heavy shackles were pinned to her wrists. Emily was led to the fourth post in the row, an empty space to her right where she assumed Elspeth had been meant to go. Daniel was to her left, surrounded by guards wielding hammers and iron pins, and then Silva was next, followed by Van. The last post, on the far left, was also empty.

Naxor walked up to Emily, a gold-painted wooden crown in his hands. He gave her a half-shrug, then reached up and set it onto her head, fixing long pins through her hair to keep it in place.

'Your Majesty,' he said, performing a mock bow.

'I'm sorry about your brother,' she said. 'Salvor was a good man.'

Naxor swallowed. 'He was.'

'Would your actions make him proud, Naxor?'

The demigod's eyes seemed troubled for the briefest of moments, then he smirked. 'Dear old Salvor never did approve of some of my methods. Look where it got him.' He nodded to the guards. 'Shackle her.'

The ties binding her hands were cut, and her arms were raised. A guard clipped the shackles round each wrist, then another hammered in the securing pins, leaving Emily on her tiptoes, almost dangling from the chain.

Simon appeared to her left, where the greenhide queen was guarding the steps. He strode towards the middle of the platform, with Kelsey slung over his shoulder. He dropped her next to a low table, where an array of knives, pliers and other implements of torture had been laid out.

Simon lifted his arms and beamed at the crowd filling the square.

'People of Tara,' he called out. 'The sun is setting. The day has almost ended, and when the last of the light is extinguished, so too will end the line of the renegade Aurelians. Rejoice.' He frowned, and lowered his hands to his hips. 'I had a whole speech planned out. It was excellent; one of my best. However, there are two empty posts behind me, and that little fact has... well, it has put me off my stride, to be frank. So, rather than enthralling you all with a speech about the new dawn I shall bring to this benighted City, I will instead get right down to the torturing. I feel the need to shed some blood tonight.' He smiled again. 'Who should die first? Let's ask Naxor.'

The demigod blinked. 'Your Grace?'

'Name the first victim, Naxor,' said Simon; 'the crowd awaits your response.'

Naxor inclined his head, then turned to gaze at the row of prisoners. His eyes fell on Emily. 'The Queen, your Grace.'

'Don't be stupid,' said Simon. 'I told you that she is to be last.'

'Then, the King, your Grace.'

'You're utterly useless,' said Simon. 'We'll start with Silva, and work our way up; we don't start at the top, you fool.'

A scream arose from the crowd, and Emily looked up. Amid the dying light, the shadow of a dragon was flitting overhead. A few Roser civilians jumped to their feet, and tried to run, but the greenhides and militia were blocking every entrance to the square.

'Don't panic,' laughed Simon. 'It's only Darksky.' He beckoned towards the dragon, and she began to descend.

The greenhides in front of the platform cleared a space for the dark blue dragon, and she landed onto the flagstones. She turned her long neck, her eyes taking in the figures shackled to the posts, then stared at Simon.

'Your palace burns,' she said. 'Where is my child?'

'He's safe,' said Simon. 'We rescued him before the inferno caused by Dawnflame could hurt him. We also wounded your rival, along with the two younger dragons, but they will return; I am sure of it.'

'You have other problems, Ascendant,' said Darksky. 'The bay is filled with boats, bearing the Brigades from Jezra, and around a thousand Banner soldiers are marching towards Tara. They were entering its outer suburbs as I passed overhead.'

Simon's eyes narrowed. 'The Banner? Impossible.'

'Are you calling me a liar?'

'The survivors of the Banner are locked up in Pella.'

'Not any more, Ascendant. They are coming here. A tall soldier leads them.'

Simon glanced over towards the entrances to the square.

'May curses rain down upon Kelsey Holdfast,' he muttered. 'With my powers, I would able to kill them all.'

'I would be happy to rip the girl to pieces for you.'

'I need her. Without her abilities, my invasion of Implacatus would be fraught with risk. The greenhides will have to suffice; they will defend Tara from my enemies.' He reached into a pocket, and took out a small chunk of refined salve. 'Eat this,' he said to the dragon. 'It will restore your energy, and provide you with extra aggression.'

Darksky sniffed Simon's hand, then swallowed the chunk of salve. Her eyes bulged, and she flexed her long talons.

'Get back into the air,' Simon said, 'and keep watch for your renegade kin. Wait; I have a question. Look at the prisoners. Whom should I kill first?'

The dragon turned her head to regard the captives. Her eyes moved over each in turn.

'Naxor,' she said. 'He is not a prisoner, but he deserves to die for his treachery. As do you, Ascendant. I will do your bidding, but do not think for a moment that I wouldn't slay you if I had the chance.'

She extended her wings and launched herself into the air. At that moment, the sun dipped below the horizon, and the dragon was silhouetted against the evening sky. She circled once, then soared away.

Simon turned to Naxor.

'Pay no attention to the words of an embittered dragon, your Grace,' said the demigod. 'I am your loyal servant.'

'Of course you are, Naxor,' said Simon. 'Do you trust me?'

Naxor bowed. 'Indubitably, your Grace.'

Simon nodded to a group of militia. 'Secure Lord Naxor to the empty post between Lady Aurelian and the false Queen.'

The soldiers approached, some with crossbows, and others with hammers and iron pins.

'No; wait! Please, your Grace!' cried Naxor, as the militia dragged him over to the post. They pulled his arms upwards, and attached him to the shackles. Simon walked over to the table, and selected a long, barbed knife. He raised it high, to show the crowd, who were huddled together in silence.

'This is the point where you are supposed to clap and cheer,' said the Ascendant. 'Pathetic.'

He turned, and strode over to Naxor, winking at Emily as he passed her.

'False Queen,' said Simon, brandishing the knife; 'which part of Naxor's anatomy should I remove first?'

'Please,' sobbed Naxor, as tears spilled down his cheeks. 'I'll do anything, your Grace; please don't torture me. I am on your side – the only god of the City who has remained faithful to you.'

'Nonsense,' said Simon. 'Lady Lydia is somewhere in the crowd tonight. She detests me passionately, but she's always done whatever I have ordered her to do. Whereas, I lost my faith in you when you tried to keep the existence of the salve mine from me. Nothing you say can be believed, Naxor, so perhaps I should remedy that.'

He reached out and clenched Naxor's chin in his left hand, forcing the demigod's mouth open. Simon smiled, then drove the barbed point of the knife into Naxor's tongue. He began sawing, his hand moving back and forth as Naxor struggled and choked on his own blood. Simon shoved the knife into his belt, then turned, holding up Naxor's severed tongue for the crowd to see.

'We'll be hearing no more lies from Lord Naxor,' he said, laughing.

Emily kept her glance on the maimed demigod, unable to pull her eyes away. Blood was pouring from Naxor's mouth, and he was making strange choking noises as he hung limp from the chain. Simon threw the tongue to a greenhide, who snapped it up within its jaws.

'You disgusting beast,' said Daniel, his eyes filled with anger.

'Shut up,' said Emily.

Simon turned. He glanced at Emily, then walked to her left, where Daniel was shackled to his post.

'Your wife is wise,' said the Ascendant.

'I am not afraid of you,' said Daniel.

'Liar. You are afraid. I don't need any powers to know that.' He lifted the knife, and slashed the blade down Daniel's face, opening his cheek.

Daniel cried out, and several gasps came from the crowd.

Simon grinned. 'They seem to like you, false King. Well, more than they like Naxor. Still, that's rather a low bar to get over. Where is your daughter?'

Daniel kept his head level, despite the blood coming from the open wound on his face.

'I told myself that I wouldn't blind any of you,' said Simon, 'as I wanted you all to see the others suffer. But, as Elspeth has been spirited away, I am prepared to make an exception. One eye should do it.'

He raised the knife again, then paused, as a shadow passed overhead.

'Dragons!' cried a Roser soldier, pointing upwards.

Emily stared up at the sky. To their left, Halfclaw was soaring low over the rooftops, with a man strapped to the green dragon's harness. They were heading in the direction of the outer suburbs of the town, while Dawnflame and Frostback were diving down onto the square. A withering hail of ballista bolts filled the air. The smaller dragon weaved, then pulled away, but Dawnflame increased her speed, plunging down through the sky. A bolt ripped through her left wing, leaving a ragged hole. She opened her jaws, and Simon flinched, raising his hands above his head, then Darksky appeared from the shadows by the cliffs, hurtling over the town. She collided with Dawnflame above the open plaza, a mere twenty feet over the platform, and the two dragons grappled, their claws raking each other's flanks. Darksky's jaws opened, and she tore a chunk out of Dawnflame's shoulder. The storm of ballista bolts ceased as the enormous dragons battled above the square. Dawnflame powered her wings, and they tumbled through the air, locked together, with Jade clinging onto the harness of her dragon.

A great burst of flames rose up over the roofs of the town, lighting the sky. Simon turned from watching the dragons fight above them, his eyes scanning the horizon towards sunward, where the fires had appeared.

'Halfclaw is aiding the Banner soldiers,' said Lady Aurelian, her voice a whisper. 'Why isn't Simon sending the greenhides?'

'I'm not sure he can,' said Emily. 'With Kelsey here, maybe he's unable to issue new commands to them.'

More flames exploded to their right, and Frostback soared past, her jaws spraying fire down onto the militia soldiers by the western end of the square, incinerating a dozen. Simon raised a clenched fist, the rage on his face reflecting the red glow of the flames. Frostback banked, and returned, sending a blast of fire at the greenhide queen. The monstrous creature screamed in agony as the fire enveloped her, and she lashed out at the silver dragon, who turned away, and vanished into the clouds of rising smoke. The greenhide queen, her skin mottled with blisters and burns, roared out in frustration, then charged through the audience of seated Rosers, trampling them as she tried to get to Frostback. The crowd screamed, and the queen slashed out with her great talons, ripping through the nearest civilians in a wild panic. The other greenhides started to become agitated, their jaws clacking together, as Simon stared, powerless.

The Ascendant slung the Axe of Rand from his shoulder. He scanned the square, then Frostback rose from behind a row of buildings, and blasted him with fire. She hovered for a moment, her jaws wide open as she spewed flames at the god. Simon was thrown backwards off the platform as the flames surrounded him, and he let out a howl of pain. Overhead, Darksky and Dawnflame had disappeared, but the sounds of their continuing struggle were heard above the screams of the crowd. Frostback turned her head, and sent another stream of fire at the greenhides by the eastern entrance to the square. Six fell, rendered to smouldering ash, and the others scattered, stampeding through a company of Roser militia.

A detachment of around forty Banner soldiers charged into the square, sprinting through the gap created by Frostback. Emily's eyes widened.

'Lucius,' she whispered.

The tall soldier was the first to reach the platform, a Fated Blade in his right hand. He cut down a Roser militia soldier, then gestured to his detachment.

'Artificers!' he shouted. 'Cut the chains.'

A dozen soldiers charged forward, holding long-handled shears. They clambered up onto the platform as Cardova and a column of crossbow-wielding Banner soldiers covered them from the remaining greenhides, who were starting to panic. Lucius ran to the chained body lying by the front of the platform, and freed the shackles from Kelsey's arms. Frostback reared up again, but the ballistae began to loose, and she was forced into a retreat.

Emily's chain was cut, and she fell. Arms caught her, and two soldiers helped her to her feet.

'Your Majesty,' said one; 'come with us.'

She glanced around. The other prisoners were also being freed, amid the pandemonium erupting inside the square. The greenhides had lost all semblance of order, and were rampaging through the trapped audience, following the young queen. More flames were rising over the rooftops, and sounds of fighting reached Emily's ears. In front of the platform, Simon pushed himself upright, his stone armour smoking and charred. He picked up the Axe of Rand.

'Pull back!' cried Cardova. Van ran to his side and, together, they picked up Kelsey.

Simon leapt up onto the platform. He swung the axe two-handed, cutting a Banner soldier in half. Cardova pushed Van and Kelsey behind him, and lunged out with the dark-bladed sword. It went clean through the Ascendant's armour, below his chest. Simon grunted, his knees almost giving way, then he ripped the blade from Cardova's grasp and threw it to the ground, then punched the officer in the face. Cardova was sent flying backwards. He crashed into one of the posts, and lay still.

Daniel appeared by Emily's side, and Banner soldiers started to herd them away from Simon.

'No,' said Emily; 'we're not leaving Kelsey and Van. If we don't kill Simon now, we never will.'

'But, your Majesty,' said a sergeant, 'the rest of the Banner are still a few streets away. We must get you to safety.'

'Nowhere is safe,' she said; 'not while Simon lives. Form up around the prisoners, and shield them from the greenhides; we're not leaving this square.'

'But, Captain Cardova gave us express orders...'

'I am the Queen,' said Emily. 'We'll never get another chance to defeat Simon; you will obey me.'

The Banner sergeant saluted. 'Yes, your Majesty.'

The battling dragons came back into view overhead. The bodies of Darksky and Dawnflame were each covered in wounds, and they remained tightly grappled together. Simon crouched down, and picked up the sword from the soldier he had slain. He drew his arm back, then flung the blade upwards. It shot through the air, and struck Dawnflame between her forelimbs, driving in to the hilt. The dragon let out a scream that echoed through the square, her neck arched, and her eyes widened. Darksky disentangled herself from her, and Dawnflame turned, banking, then she plummeted to the ground, crashing into the roofs of a row of houses in the next street along from Prince's Square.

The Ascendant surveyed the chaos. The greenhide queen had abandoned her senses to unleash death upon the Roser aristocracy, and the ripped and torn corpses were carpeting the flagstones, amid the scattered seats. Most of the surviving Roser militia had fled, leaving the ordinary greenhides free to feast upon any civilian who came into their clutches.

Darksky descended, and hovered over Simon.

'You're welcome,' said the Ascendant.

'The Brigades are landing at the harbour,' said the wounded dragon. 'Their numbers outweigh those of your allies. Give me my child.'

'I shall, after you fulfil your oaths. Find the two younger dragons, and kill them.'

Darksky tilted her head, and soared away.

Simon turned to Van. The soldier was crouching by Kelsey, cutting the last of the chains that were binding her, while Cardova's body lay a few yards away.

'Loose!' cried Emily, and the soldiers of the detachment formed into a line. They aimed their crossbows at the Ascendant, peppering him with bolts. Simon waded into them, swinging the Axe of Rand, his charred stone armour deflecting every bolt that struck him. Emily stared, as Simon struck down the soldiers, each swing of the axe cleaving their bodies apart.

Van dragged Kelsey away, but Simon reached them, stepping over the corpses of the soldiers.

'She is mine, Banner soldier,' said the Ascendant.

Van's fingers gave up trying to unfasten Kelsey's hood. He picked up a sword, and ran at Simon, but the Ascendant was too quick for him. He swatted Van aside with the back of a gauntlet, breaking his jaw, then he lifted Kelsey by the arm and pulled her away. The roar of fighting from beyond the square increased, and more flames appeared, just yards from the sunward entrance to the plaza.

'Look what you have done!' Simon roared. His gaze fell on the Aurelians, who were surrounded by the last of the Banner detachment.

More cries came from the eastern side of the square, where the harbour was located. Simon glanced in that direction, then hung his head.

'Perhaps I was a fool,' he said. 'My ambitions soared when I learned of Kelsey Holdfast's ability to block powers; in my dreams, I imagined the havoc she would cause on Implacatus; the finest weapon I could ever possess, yet here I stand, undone by vile lizards and renegade Banner soldiers. My greenhides are useless, my dragon is wounded, and my human soldiers are weak cowards.' He dropped Kelsey to the planks of the platform, and placed a boot on her waist. He ripped the hood from her face, and Kelsey's eyes blinked. He yanked the gag clear of her mouth.

'In a minute or so,' he said, staring down at her, 'everyone in Tara will be dead, and the greenhides will be back under my control. The Banner and the Exiles of Jezra will be annihilated, by me, when I unleash the death powers that you have been blocking. The dragons will also die – all of them. I may kill every living thing upon this world, such is the rage within my heart.' He shook his head. 'Why didn't you join me? Together, we could have destroyed Edmond; we could have laid our enemies low; made heaps of them, you and I. Instead, I am forced to kill you.'

He raised the Axe of Rand above Kelsey's neck.

'Farewell, Holdfast witch.'

CHAPTER 30

UNDESERVING

Tara, Auldan, The City – 22nd Mikalis 3423

Kelsey stared up at Simon. The dark blade of the Axe of Rand was glimmering in the glow from the fires as he raised it over her head. She moved her jaw to speak, but her face was still hurting from when the Ascendant had struck her.

She spat out some blood. 'If you kill me, you will never take Implacatus.'

His eyes narrowed. 'If I don't kill you, I might not survive to see the sun rise tomorrow.'

A roof exploded twenty yards to their right as a ballista position was struck by Halfclaw. Simon glanced at the dragon as he soared past, then turned back to Kelsey.

'Wait!' cried a voice.

Kelsey glanced at the steps leading up to the platform. Amalia was striding towards them, accompanied by Lydia and Jade, who was trailing a few yards to the rear, her head bowed.

'The Holdfast witch has to die,' said Simon. 'Don't try to stop me.'

'I wouldn't dream of it, your Grace,' said Amalia. 'Miss Holdfast and I have never seen eye to eye, and I would not weep if you separated her head from her body. However, you informed me that she was an essential part of your plan, your Grace, and I have come to tell you that you don't need to kill her.'

Simon stared at the three women. 'The Banner and the Brigades are approaching, and there are still two dragons on the loose. What exactly are you proposing, Amalia?'

'Guarantee us our safety, your Grace,' said Amalia, stepping closer until she stood only two yards from Simon, 'and we shall kill your enemies for you. Jade and I will flood the streets with death, while you remain here, with the Holdfast girl. All we ask is that you forgive us our previous transgressions.'

Simon frowned. 'Do you expect me to believe you?' He pointed at Jade. 'This one, I will never forgive. Not ten minutes ago, she was flying upon the shoulders of the renegade dragon Dawnflame; and now you think I'm gullible enough to imagine that she would help me?'

Jade glared at Amalia. 'I told you he wouldn't believe us.'

'Hush, granddaughter,' said Amalia. 'The noble Tenth Ascendant knows that he needs our help. Without us, he will have to kill Kelsey; and without Kelsey, he will never defeat Edmond.' She glanced up, as Darksky soared after Halfclaw, with Frostback on her tail. The three dragons were banking in tight circles, their jaws snapping at each other. She smiled at Simon. 'Well, your Grace? Do you accept our offer of assistance?'

Simon glanced down at Kelsey, then back at Amalia.

'Do you have salve?' said Jade. 'That's the only reason I agreed to this. Dawnflame is dying. I will help you if you give me salve to save her.'

'And I have always been loyal to you, your Grace,' said Lydia.

'You see?' said Amalia. 'You can trust us.'

Simon lowered the Axe of Rand. 'I'll need you to prove it.'

Amalia leaned over, and picked up the Fated Blade that Cardova had been carrying.

'Of course, your Grace,' she said. She nodded to Lydia. 'Show the noble Ascendant our proof, if you would be so kind, granddaughter.'

Lydia swallowed, then reached into a pocket. She withdrew a vial of liquid, and, her hands shaking, she hurled it into Simon's face. At the same time, Amalia launched herself at the Ascendant, driving the sword blade down. It cut through the armour covering his left shoulder and bit into his flesh, as his face burned from contact with the thrown salve. Simon roared in agony, his hands dropping the Axe of Rand. He stumbled forward, his fists lashing out. He caught Amalia with a punch, sending her falling to the platform, the sword flying from her grasp. Lydia was shoved back, but Jade ducked under the blows, and dragged Kelsey clear.

'You wicked bitches,' cried Simon. He raised his hands and wiped his face. Most of the concentrated salve had hit his armour, but the skin on his lower face was bubbling and smoking, and blood was flowing from the wound in his shoulder.

Jade helped Kelsey wriggle free of the last of the chains, and they crawled back, as Simon took a step towards Amalia.

'Is that all you've got?' he screamed. 'Some salve and a sword? Not one of you has battle-vision, or even knows how to fight, and yet you challenge me?'

Amalia glanced up from the planks of the platform. 'It was worth a try.'

He picked up the Axe of Rand. 'I am going to kill everyone, starting with you, Amalia.'

A tremendous roar of triumph came from a dragon above them.

The former God-Queen stared up, looking beyond Simon, then she covered her head with her hands and crouched low. Simon frowned, then looked behind him, just as Darksky's body plummeted from the sky. The dragon crashed into the square, flattening the greenhide queen, and ploughing through the corpses of the mauled citizens. She struck Simon, her forelimbs smashing through the wooden planks of the platform, and her tail sweeping along the row of posts. Kelsey closed her eyes, feeling Jade's arm round her shoulder as they fell through the shattered remains of the platform. A cloud of dust rose up, and Kelsey went deaf for a moment, her ears ringing as she struck the flagstones of the square.

Kelsey groaned. It felt as though a mountain of broken beams and planks had landed on top of her. She opened her eyes, and saw Lydia and Jade pulling themselves from the remnants of the platform. Kelsey glanced in the other direction, and jumped as she saw the head of the dragon lying a foot from her. Its eyes were open, but lifeless. Kelsey stared at Darksky, then felt hands grip her shoulders. She looked up, and saw Jade dragging her from the heap of broken beams.

'Van?' she said.

'Lydia will heal the wounded,' said the demigod. 'We can't heal you, though, so you'll just have to put up with the pain.' She stared at the body of Darksky. 'Dawnflame tried to reason with her, but you can't argue with a mother whose child is a hostage.'

Kelsey got to her feet, her body aching in a hundred different places. 'Is Dawnflame dead?'

'No,' said Jade. 'Lydia healed her enough to save her life, but she's spent, exhausted. Like me.'

Kelsey glanced around. Lydia was kneeling by Emily and Daniel, healing their injuries, while Lord and Lady Aurelian stood by, close to Silva. Amalia was rooting through the scattered piles of debris a few yards away.

Jade noticed where Kelsey was looking. 'Lydia and my grandmother found me when Dawnflame crashed. I told them that their plan was stupid, but Amalia talked me into it.'

At the far end of the square, Frostback and Halfclaw were clearing the last of the greenhides. The beasts were flailing around, swiping their talons through the air as the two dragons sent bursts of flame down at them. Bodies were carpeting the flagstones of the plaza, and many of the buildings of Tara were on fire. Dust and smoke filled the air, and Kelsey coughed, her eyes watering.

'It was a stupid plan,' she said, 'but thanks for trying it. I'm sorry for being...'

Jade narrowed her eyes. 'What?'

'I'm sorry for being so horrible to you, Jade. I was... I was wrong about you.'

'You weren't the only one.'

'Kelsey!' cried a voice.

She turned, and saw Van and Cardova hurrying towards her amid the heaps of debris. Before they could reach her, the ground shifted under the body of the enormous dragon, sending Amalia toppling over. Planks and beams erupted into the air with a crash, and Simon appeared, hauling himself out of the ruins of the platform, his right hand gripping the Axe of Rand.

Emily Aurelian got to her feet. She strode forwards to where Kelsey and Jade were standing, and the Holdfast woman noticed that she was still wearing the painted wooden crown on her head.

'Ascendant,' Emily cried, pointing at Simon. 'You still have the Quadrant. Use it. Get out of my City.'

Simon stared at her. 'This isn't over, false Queen.'

'Yes, it is,' Emily said, her blonde hair blowing in the drifting smoke. 'You've lost, Simon. Thousands of armed Exiles are entering the square, along with a regiment of Banner soldiers. They obey me, not you.'

Simon brandished the axe in both hands. 'Let them come. I am the greatest warrior who has ever lived. I am a destroyer of armies, of worlds; the divine light that dwells within me can never be extinguished.'

Emily folded her arms across her chest. 'Now, Frostback.'

The silver dragon rose up behind Simon, and dealt the Ascendant a savage blow with a forelimb, the thick claws tearing through his armour and flesh. She opened her jaws, and closed them round his legs, and shook him. The Axe of Rand flew from his hands as his legs were crushed between the dragon's teeth. She threw him to the ground, and clamped him there with a forelimb, pressing her weight down upon his armoured chest.

Blood came from Simon's mouth, and he choked, his eyes bulging. He reached into his armour and pulled out the Quadrant. He raised his fingers, then Amalia appeared by his side. She brought down the Fated Blade, severing his left arm at the elbow, then kicked the Quadrant away.

'Too late for that, Simon,' she said. 'You had your chance.'

She glanced over to Emily, who approached. The Queen held out her hand, and Amalia passed her the Fated Blade.

Emily took the sword, and looked down into Simon's face.

'You should never have come here, Ascendant. This is not your world; it's ours.'

She aimed the blade down and, with both hands, drove it through the armour and into Simon's heart. The Ascendant screamed, his cries echoing round the bloodstained plaza.

'Take his head, Frostback,' said Emily.

The silver dragon lowered her neck and opened her jaws. She clamped them round the neck of the Ascendant and ripped his head off, the blood spraying the front of Emily's clothes, and streaking the wooden crown upon her brow. The dragon spat the head out, and it rolled to a stop by Kelsey's feet.

'That was for you, rider,' said Frostback.

Emily lips formed into a grim smile. 'Now, it's over.'

'Not quite,' said Amalia, leaning over and plucking the Quadrant from the fingers of Simon's severed hand.

'Put that down,' said Van, his eyes tight.

'Let her speak,' said Emily.

Amalia glanced around at the small crowd gathered by the ruins of the platform. A handful of Banner soldiers were with the Aurelians, while Frostback had moved to where Kelsey and Jade were standing. Her eyes narrowed as she watched Naxor being unshackled from his collapsed post, then her gaze fell on Silva.

'I'm going to Implacatus,' Amalia said. 'I will take Simon's body, and leave it there, as a sign for the Ascendants, warning them not to come here. Silva, do you wish to accompany me?'

Silva stepped forward. 'Yes. Take me with you.'

Amalia nodded.

'No,' said Kelsey. 'If they go, we'll never see them again, and they'll lead the other Ascendants here.'

Amalia smiled at her. 'In that case, you'd better come along.'

Her fingers reached for the Quadrant. Van lunged at her, then the air crackled around Kelsey, and she blinked. The square disappeared, replaced by the same bare room in Serene where Simon had taken her thirteen days before. The mangled and crushed body of the Ascendant was lying on the floor, his head a few yards away from where Silva and Amalia were standing.

'You crazy bitch,' said Kelsey. She charged over to Amalia and pointed a finger in her face. 'You're not doing this to me again! Take us back.'

Amalia laughed. 'Calm down. We're not staying, Miss Holdfast.' She turned to Silva. 'Good luck with finding Belinda, old friend, if I may call you that.'

'You may,' said Silva; 'for you are a friend, Amalia. Before you go, I want to say something to Kelsey.'

Amalia took a step back.

Kelsey frowned. 'Are you running away from the City, Silva? What about Emily?'

'I served Queen Emily and King Daniel to the best of my abilities, Kelsey,' she said. 'My true loyalty has always lain with my beloved Queen Belinda; you have known that from the very start. I will find her Majesty, and I shall discover the truth about Edmond and this marriage. Thank you for helping me. You are an exceptional young woman, Kelsey; try to remember that you don't have to be angry all the time. There are many in the City who love you; let them.' She smiled. 'You know, I remember when King Nathaniel told us about his plans to create mortals with powers. We all tried to dissuade him; we told him that no good would come from elevating mortals to the level of gods.'

Amalia raised an eyebrow. 'Perhaps you were right.'

'I used to think so,' said Silva. 'I was one of the most vociferous in voicing my opposition. As too was a goddess named Asher; she hated mortals, and refused to believe that it might be wise to bestow powers upon them.'

'Asher?' said Kelsey.

'Yes. She went with Queen Belinda and Lady Agatha to your world.'

'I know. She killed my father in front of me.'

Silva's gaze fell. 'I'm sorry.'

'Don't be. My mother killed her in revenge.'

'Your mother killed Asher?' Silva shook her head. 'Nathaniel may have made you, Kelsey, but I don't think he understood what he was unleashing upon the worlds when he created the powers possessed by the Holdfasts. What your family decides to do with that power could change the future of every world; it could bring empires to their knees, and overthrow gods.' She placed a hand onto Kelsey's shoulder. 'I hope you use that power wisely.'

She stepped away. 'I will go now. Someone will find the body of Simon before too long, and I wish to be far from here when that happens.'

She bowed her head to Amalia and Kelsey, then left through the room's only door. Kelsey chewed her lip, then turned to Amalia, who was standing next to Simon's body.

The former God-Queen reached out, and pulled the Fated Blade from the Ascendant's chest.

'Is that it?' said Kelsey. 'Are we going back to Tara?'

Amalia said nothing.

Kelsey swallowed. 'Are you going to leave me here?'

Amalia smiled. 'Should I? After all, you hate me; everyone hates me. Perhaps it should be I who stays. If I go back, they'll probably have me executed.'

'You would deserve it.'

'Why? Because I opened the gates in the Middle Walls?'

'Aye; among several other crimes.'

Amalia shuddered. 'I wish I were stronger. If I were, then I would be able to walk away.' She sighed. 'So be it.'

The air shimmered, and Kelsey found herself standing next to Amalia on the roof of a tall building. Kelsey glanced around.

'Are we on the roof of the Royal Academy in Ooste?'

'We are,' said Amalia. 'Stay here.'

She glided her fingers over the Quadrant, and disappeared, leaving Kelsey alone. The last of the day's light had gone, but fires were illuminating the sky. Flames were rising to the left, from the direction of Dalrig, while across the bay, Pella and Tara were both ablaze. To Kelsey's right, the blackened remains of the Royal Palace stood abandoned, its towers in ruins. The four ancient palaces of Auldan, she thought to herself; all gone. She leaned against the railings and, for the first time in a long time, she wished she had a cigarette.

The minutes passed, and Kelsey started to believe that Amalia wasn't coming back. Why would she? She had returned Kelsey to the City, and fled, rather than face justice for all that she had done. It was the rational thing to do. She wondered how long it would take to walk to Tara.

The air crackled, and a small group appeared by Kelsey on the roof of the academy.

'You look surprised,' said Amalia, clutching Maxwell to her chest. 'I believe you have met Kagan and Lady Doria? And I'm sure you will remember the children.'

'Are you going back to Tara?' said Kelsey.

'Yes,' said Amalia. 'I'm tired of hiding and running. This is my City too, for better or worse.'

'You helped kill Simon,' said Kagan; 'that's got to count for something.'

'Does one right strike off a thousand wrongs, Kagan?' she said. 'Give me Elspeth; you take Maxwell.'

Kagan and Amalia swapped children, then the former God-Queen took the Quadrant from her robes. She closed her eyes for a moment, then transported them all to Tara. The air crackled, and Kelsey appeared with the others by the ruins of the platform. Hundreds of Banner soldiers were occupying the square, and huge groups of armed Brigade Exiles were clearing the piles of greenhides and Roser civilians from the bloody flagstones.

Amalia led the others directly towards Emily and Daniel, who were surrounded by Banner soldiers. Emily caught sight of them, and ordered the soldiers to clear a path.

Amalia reached out, and passed Elspeth to her mother.

'As you once did for me, Emily; so I now do for you.'

Emily hugged Elspeth to her chest. 'Thank you.'

Daniel joined his wife, and they embraced. The King's parents walked over, and Amalia backed away as the reunited family gathered round their returned child.

Frostback nudged Kelsey, almost knocking her over.

'I wish people would stop taking you away from me,' said the silver dragon.

'Me too,' said Kelsey.

'My apologies,' said Amalia. 'I needed your rider to prevent us from being detected upon Implacatus.'

Van and Cardova strode towards them.

'Next time, Amalia,' said Van, 'warn us before you do something like that. I was having visions of Fordamere.'

'Next time?' said Cardova, gesturing to a group of soldiers. 'I doubt that there will be a next time, sir. Sergeant, place Lady Amalia and Lord Kagan under arrest. If she resists, shoot her.'

'I shall not resist, Captain,' said Amalia.

Dawnflame and Halfclaw soared over the square, then landed close to Frostback. Caelius clambered down from the harness on Halfclaw's shoulders, and hurried over to where Van and Kelsey were standing.

'Good to see you, my boy,' said the old veteran.

Van frowned. 'Try not to look so happy, father.'

'I can't help it, son; this has been one of the best days of my life.'

Dawnflame tilted her head towards Frostback. 'You slew Darksky,' she said; 'something I was unable to do.'

'I could not have defeated her,' said Frostback, 'had you not greatly weakened her first. The triumph belongs to us both, but her death breaks my heart. Darksky always loathed me, but I did not wish her dead.'

Dawnflame gazed at the prone body of the enormous slain dragon.

'She was my friend. I will now care for her children, as if they were my own. Where is the one that Simon was holding captive?'

'Naxor knows,' said Amalia, while armed soldiers surrounded her, 'but I don't imagine he will be speaking for a while, praise the gods.'

'We found an infant dragon in a cage-wagon, madam dragon,' said a Banner sergeant.

'Point him out to me, and I shall carry him back to the mountains,' said Dawnflame. She glanced around. 'Where is Jade?'

'Here,' said the demigod, appearing from behind a pile of rubble.

'Are you ready?' said the dragon.

'I am.'

'What are you doing?' said Kelsey.

Jade turned to the others. 'I'm going with Dawnflame. I'm glad we got rid of Simon, but I don't belong in the City; not any more. I want my little valley in the mountains, with all the flowers and trees, and my cats, and the dragons.'

Emily strode closer, with Elspeth still held to her chest. 'You're leaving us?'

'I am, your Majesty,' said Jade.

'That saddens me.'

'Thank you for saying that, but I know what most people think of me. Do you remember when I was in charge of the Bulwark? That's not the kind of person you need. I'm a bad fit for the City.'

'You saved the City, Jade; you and Dawnflame. When no one else was fighting, you persisted. You will always be welcome in my home. Visit, as often as you like.'

Jade nodded. 'I might do that.'

'We shall also return Quill and the other stranded Blades, Queen,' said Dawnflame, 'and we shall stop off at Jezra, to say goodbye to Rosie and Flavus. They have been worthy companions.'

'Tell them to cross over to the City,' said Emily.

'We will, your Majesty,' said Jade.

The demigod glanced at the faces of everyone gathered round her and Dawnflame, her eyes lingering on the sight of Amalia. They gave each other a brief nod, then Jade climbed up the harness onto Dawn-flame's shoulders, and the dragon extended her wings. She hovered over the square for a moment, then clutched a wagon in her powerful forelimbs and lifted it from the ground. She rose into the sky and soared away, heading west towards the Straits.

'I too wish to go to Jezra,' said Frostback.

'I need Kelsey here,' said Emily. She glanced at the Blade officers. 'Send a detachment up to Princeps Row and secure the Aurelian mansion. Lord and Lady Aurelian shall go with them, and we shall follow later. We'll make it our temporary palace, and run the City from there, at least until somewhere more suitable becomes available. Major-General Logos, with the annihilation of the Roser aristocracy, I imagine that a few other mansions on Princeps Row will now be vacant. Take one, and make it the new Banner headquarters. You and Kelsey can live there.' She eyed Frostback and Halfclaw. 'There is plenty of room for two dragons up on the cliffs overlooking Tara. Why don't you both take a look, and see if there's somewhere suitable? We can have workers improve any location you find.'

Frostback glanced at Kelsey, who nodded.

'Very well, Queen,' said the silver dragon. She nuzzled into Kelsey for a moment, then the two dragons ascended into the sky and disappeared into the clouds of smoke rising from Tara.

'Your Majesty,' said Caelius, bowing; 'what should I do? I do not wish to return to Implacatus – my son is here, and I have the feeling that there's a mountain of hard work ahead of us to get the City back into shape. May I be of service?'

'I saw you up on Halfclaw's harness during the battle,' said Emily. 'Who are you?'

'This is my father, your Majesty,' said Van.

'The name's Caelius,' he said. 'Forgive me, your Majesty; I'm an old Banner veteran and I need to work.'

'Then stay close by, Caelius; I have a long list of things that need doing.'

Caelius grinned. 'Thank you, your Majesty.'

'Your first job,' she said, 'is to have Lord Naxor hooded, shackled, and placed into the most secure prison that remains standing within the City. I never want to see him again as long as I live.'

Caelius saluted, then gestured to a squad of Banner soldiers. They followed him to where Naxor was sitting on a pile of debris, blood streaking his chin. They tied a hood over his head, and then they marched the demigod away.

'Should he not be executed, your Majesty?' said Cardova. 'He is a risk, even without a tongue.'

'Perhaps,' said Emily. 'Daniel and I will decide later.'

She turned to Amalia, Kagan and Doria.

'Lady Doria,' she said. 'Of all the grandchildren of the God-King and God-Queen, you are one I know the least. Yet today, you helped save my daughter. What can I do for you?'

'Just let me live in peace, your Majesty,' she said.

'We can manage that.' She glanced at Kagan. 'And what shall we do with you?'

'That depends,' said Kagan. 'What are you planning to do with Amalia? Where she goes, I go. If you kill her, then kill me too, only, spare Maxwell; he has done nothing wrong.'

'I will certainly spare Maxwell,' said Emily. 'The crimes of the mother do not pass on to the child, and I didn't carry the boy halfway across the City only to see him condemned. Tell me, Kagan; do you think Amalia deserves to live, after all she has done?'

'Yes.'

Van shook his head. 'Of course he's going to think that, your Majesty; he's besotted with her.'

'I'm in love with her,' said Kagan, 'if that's what you mean.' He glanced at the accusing faces around them. 'I know her better than anyone else here; I've seen her ruthlessness, but I've also seen her kindness. Did she open the gates in the Middle Walls? Yes – no one's disputing that. Did she also risk her life to save Kelsey Holdfast? Yes – you all saw her do it. She could have fled with the Quadrant, but she didn't. She came back, to face up to her past; to face you, Queen Emily.'

'That reminds me,' said Amalia. She reached into her robes and withdrew the Quadrant. 'This was mine for thousands of years, before Simon took it.' She extended her hand towards Emily, and passed it to her. 'It belongs with you now.' She glanced at Kagan. 'Thank you, my darling, for saying what you did; however, I fear your words carry little weight in the company in which we find ourselves.'

'They let that lying rat Naxor live.'

'Naxor's crimes are relatively insignificant compared to mine, Kagan. He assisted Simon, but so did Lydia, and she stands here among us, unencumbered by any chains or shackles.' She met Emily's glance. 'Thank you for sparing my idiot grandson. In the old days, I would have probably killed him myself for his endless betrayals, but as you can see, I have very few family members left. Out of thirty grandchildren, only Doria, Lydia, Naxor and Jade remain; and Aila, though she no longer resides here. You have achieved what you set out to accomplish – the gods of the City have been almost annihilated.'

Emily frowned. 'I did not set out to accomplish that, Amalia.'

'No? You executed Vana, Collo and Ikara for lesser crimes than you have just spared Naxor for committing.'

Emily nodded. 'I regret that.'

Amalia smiled. 'I regret opening the gates in the Middle Walls, but there you are. Naxor once told me that there was no room in this City for two queens, and he was right. You are a stubborn woman, Emily, and I feel it very unlikely that you would ever decide to bow before me.'

'I will never bow before you,' said Emily.

'As I suspected. Therefore, I am left with little choice.' She got down onto her knees in front of Emily, and bowed her head. 'I submit to you, my Queen. To you, I pledge my loyalty and service. I do not beg for my life, for I can guess what the response would be; but you must know something before I die. I was a good servant of this City, once. I destroyed untold numbers of the greenhides that Malik and I brought to this world, and founded the City in which we are all gathered. I built the three encircling walls, to keep out the Eternal Enemy, but then I tired of it all, and gave the running of the City to my children, and grandchildren. The Civil War ripped my family apart, and I grew cold, and heartless; I see that now. Kagan and Maxwell have brought me back to what I consider to be my true self, and I condemn the actions that almost destroyed Medio. I was wrong. I do not expect forgiveness, but you must know that I realise that I was wrong, and I'm sorry, your Majesty.'

'Do not listen to her,' said Lady Aurelian. 'Her words are poison.'

'I believe her,' said Kagan, 'and I don't care if I'm the only one.' He fell to his knees beside the former God-Queen, Maxwell clutched to his chest. 'Amalia says that she won't beg for her life, so I will do it for her. Please, your Majesties, spare her.'

'Daniel?' said Emily.

The King rose from where he had been watching the exchange. 'I do not believe that Amalia can be redeemed, but I will listen to what you and the others think.'

Emily eyed Doria and Lydia. 'I will not ask either of you. As Amalia's granddaughters, I do not wish to put you into an awkward position.'

'Thank you, your Majesty,' said Lydia bowing low.

'You are a survivor, Lydia,' said Emily, frowning. 'I can respect that. Go back to Port Sanders.'

'At once, your Majesty,' said the demigod. 'Doria, do you want to come with me? I have plenty of space in Tonetti Palace.'

'Why?' said Doria.

Lydia looked abashed for a moment. 'Because, you're my sister.'

Doria said nothing, her eyes on Lydia, then she nodded.

'Thanks for healing Van and Lucius,' said Kelsey.

'My pleasure,' said Lydia, before she turned and hurried away with Doria through the crowds of Brigade Exiles in the square.

Emily turned to Van. 'Major-General; your opinion regarding Amalia, if you please?'

'I don't know, your Majesty,' he said. 'Would we ever be able to trust her? Perhaps she should join Naxor in prison, while you take time to decide.'

Emily nodded. 'Kelsey?'

'You want my opinion?'

'Of course.'

Kelsey puffed out her cheeks. She glanced down at Amalia. 'After everything you've done to me personally,' she said, 'how does it feel to know that I have a say in what happens to you now?'

'It doesn't fill me with much hope, I confess,' said Amalia.

'What would you do,' said Kelsey, 'if we just let you go? I mean, what would you actually do with your time?'

'Ideally,' said Amalia, 'I would be allowed to live a peaceful and quiet life, in Tara or in Port Sanders, or maybe upon the little estate in the Sunward Range, with Kagan and Maxwell, naturally. I have no desire to rule again. I would live as Lady Sofia lived.'

'You'll be a rallying point, but,' said Kelsey. 'Every discontented mortal in the City would be trying to get you to rise up against the Aurelians.'

'They could try, but they wouldn't succeed.'

'That's irrelevant. You are a symbol. It doesn't matter what you want.'

'Is this your way of saying that you think I need to die?'

Kelsey stared at her for a long moment. Jade was different from the person she had been before, that was irrefutable, and with her transformation, Kelsey's theory about gods being incapable of change had been shattered. Still, she thought, Amalia was in a class of her own. She glanced at Maxwell, held tight in Kagan's embrace as he knelt in front of Emily and Daniel. The child looked up at her, and caught her gaze.

'Do you have an answer?' said Emily.

Kelsey nodded. 'Aye, Queenie. Let her live.'

'Why?'

'I'm not sure, exactly. Only, once she's gone, she's gone forever. Without her, Simon would have killed me, and then he would have been able to kill everyone else too. I think we should give her another chance.'

'Do you believe she can be redeemed?' said the King.

'I don't know, but I don't want to be the one who condemns her. My family has its own share of mass murderers; my Auntie Keira slaughtered hundreds of thousands of people, and both of my brothers have killed Pyre knows how many. My mother isn't exactly innocent, either. Do I think the Holdfasts are beyond redemption? No. I can't believe that.'

'We aren't discussing the Holdfasts,' said the King; 'this is about Amalia.'

Kelsey shrugged. 'You asked for my opinion, and I've given it. Let them go.'

Daniel glanced at Emily. 'You should have the final word. I will go along with your decision.'

Emily nodded. 'Amalia,' she said, 'you are not forgiven. Even if Daniel and I were to absolve you, we cannot presume that the thousands of citizens whose lives you destroyed would approve. All the same, I agree with Kelsey. You founded this City, our home, and I shall not be the one who has you put to death. Stand.'

Amalia got to her feet, and Kagan rose beside her.

'Go,' said Emily, 'and live in peace.'

Amalia bowed her head, her eyes welling. 'I don't understand.'

'There's nothing to understand. You are free to go. You can thank Kelsey, and Silva, for she always thought that there was hope for you, and I trust her judgement. I do ask one favour.'

'Yes?'

'Yes. Once the City has settled down, you will show me how to use the Quadrant.'

'I do not deserve your generosity, your Majesty. All those people in Medio that the greenhides killed after I opened the gates; every death was my fault. Do they not deserve justice?'

'They do, and that shall be the burden you will have to bear. Go.'

Amalia and Kagan glanced around. The Banner soldiers opened a path for them to take, and they walked away, Kagan carrying Maxwell.

Cardova whistled as they disappeared into the crowd. 'That was an extremely courageous decision, your Majesty.'

Emily smiled. 'By which you mean you think it was the wrong decision, Lucius.'

The Banner officer laughed. 'No comment. By the way, your Majesty; nice crown.'

'Thank you, Captain,' she said. 'I think I'll keep it.' She took Daniel's hand. 'Shall we walk up to Princeps Row, dearest?'

Daniel smiled. 'Let's.'

They moved off, a crowd of Banner soldiers marching alongside them. Cardova glanced at Van and Kelsey, who were the only ones left standing by the ruins of the platform and the body of Darksky.

'I'll bet you five sovereigns that Amalia is causing problems within a month,' said the captain.

'I'll take that bet,' said Kelsey.

'You heard her, sir,' said Lucius. 'She can't wriggle out of it now.'

'I wouldn't dream of it,' said Kelsey. 'Now, piss off, so I can speak to Van.'

Lucius laughed again, then strode off after the royal party.

Van turned to face her, and took her hands in his. 'When Amalia activated the Quadrant, and you vanished,' he said, 'all I could think about was what happened in Fordamere. I thought she'd abducted you again.'

'She did, temporarily.'

He glanced at the smoke rising from Tara, and at the Brigade workers clearing the bodies from the square.

'This is going to take forever to put right,' he said. 'The City is in chaos.'

'That can wait until tomorrow,' she said. 'Do you love me, Van?'

'You know I do. I've loved you since Lostwell.'

'Even though I'm a pain in the arse?'

'Oh, I'm pretty sure that I can be a pain in the ass too.'

'You're quite right; you are.'

He smiled. 'And yet you love me anyway?'

'I do. I'm an idiot.'

'No,' he said, his hand on the side of her face as he gazed into her eyes. 'You're not an idiot. You're a numpty.'

She closed her eyes and they kissed; and nothing else mattered.

EPILOGUE

Tara, Auldan, The City – 11th Izran 3423

'Stay a while longer,' said Van, his arms round her waist.

'I can't,' said Kelsey. 'Frostback is waiting for me, and Pyre alone knows how many people are outside wanting to speak to you.' She kissed him. 'I'll see you soon.'

He gave her a look that almost robbed her of her resolve, then relinquished his grip on her waist, and sat down in front of his desk. 'Don't work late tonight,' he said. 'I'll be counting the hours until we're alone again, and you're back in my arms.'

Her eyes lingered on him for a moment longer, then she left his office. It was at the rear of the huge mansion that had become not only the home of Van and Kelsey, but also the operational headquarters of the Banner of the Lostwell Exiles. The hallway outside the office was filled with officers and scouts, all waiting to see the Commander.

Cardova was standing closest to the door, and he nodded at Kelsey.

'From the look on your face, Miss Holdfast,' he said, 'I'm going to guess that the major-general is in a good mood this morning, which is just as well, considering that I have about a hundred urgent issues that he needs to attend to.'

'Don't work him too hard,' she said. 'What's the biggest problem?'

Cardova frowned. 'To be honest, it's probably his father. Caelius means well, but he's been enthusiastically interfering in areas beyond his remit, again. He certainly knows how to rub people up the wrong way; I've had a dozen complaints about him. Do you reckon you could speak to Van about it?'

'No chance,' said Kelsey, as she slipped past. 'Good luck, Lucius.'

She eased her way past the lines of queuing Banner personnel, and emerged through the grand front entrance of the mansion into the bright red sunshine. There were no clouds above, and the sun had warmed the air. She took a deep breath, catching the scent of the summer flowers growing along Princeps Row. Most of the mansions were lying empty, following the cull of the Taran nobility two months before, and those that were occupied were filled with officials working for the government of the City. The King and Queen were living in their old family home, from where they ruled. Outside the Aurelian mansion were lines of people from all over the City, and from every tribe, watched from a discreet distance by well-armed Banner soldiers. Anyone who needed a decision made had to travel to Tara, but the Aurelians had assured the citizens that this was a temporary expedient; builders were already swarming over the ruins of Cuidrach Palace in Pella, working day and night to restore the iceward wing to habitability. Their first act had been to remove the lines of execution posts, and grant those who had died there a dignified burial. Some bloodstains remained along the harbour promenade, reminders of the Ascendant's brief reign.

Kelsey turned towards the blackened remains of Maeladh Palace at the sunward end of Princeps Row. The fires there had raged for days, gutting the ancient structure. Kelsey glanced along the high fence that surrounded the palace. A few days after the fire had died down, she had seen Amalia, standing alone by the fence, gazing through the iron bars at the collapsed ruins of her old home. It had been the only time Kelsey had laid eyes on the former God-Queen since Simon's demise, but she had heard that she had married Kagan, and was living with him and Maxwell in a small villa in the countryside close to Port Sanders. The exact location was a secret, and Amalia had been sticking to her end of the bargain; so much so, that Cardova had been forced to hand over five sovereigns to Kelsey after a month of hearing not a whisper from her. He remained convinced that Amalia would cause trouble, but Kelsey disagreed. She didn't know why, but somehow she felt that Amalia had been telling the truth about wanting to live a quiet life.

She turned right at the gates of the palace, and began to head round its perimeter, towards the large caverns that pocked the cliffs of the ridge. The way was lined with holly bushes, and a large hedge concealed the mansion to her right. A young woman was walking past, wearing the uniform of the Brigades, one of the many thousands who were assisting the Aurelians in the re-establishment of their rule. The young woman glanced at Kelsey, then her eyes glazed over, and she nearly stumbled.

Kelsey paused, frowning. 'Are you alright?'

The young woman turned her face to her. 'Kelsey.'

'Um, aye? That's me. Do I know you?'

The woman laughed. 'I can't believe that this is working. For the last two years, I've watched you, but I've not been able to communicate or do anything to help.'

Kelsey backed away a step. 'What? You've been watching me? Who are you?'

'The Sextant is so complicated,' the young woman went on, as if she hadn't heard, 'but I've had a breakthrough, and I can now use it to push my dream vision powers into people's heads. Well, not your head, obviously; some things never change.'

Kelsey felt her heart race. 'Karalyn? Is that you in there?'

The young woman nodded. 'Aye. It's your sister, Kelsey. I'm in Colsbury Castle, but I'm speaking to you here, in the City. Corthie wasn't kidding; the sky really is red.'

'Corthie made it back?'

'Aye, and Aila too. She's had a baby. Anyway, listen.'

'Don't worry; you have my full attention.'

'Good.' The young woman's face turned serious. 'Something's happened.'

'Something bad, I assume?'

The woman nodded. 'Kelsey, I need your help.'

City of Salve - The Royal Family

The Gods	Title	Powers
Malik (deceased)	God-King of the City - Ooste	Vision
Amalia	Former God-Queen - Exiled	Death

The Children of the Gods

	Title	Powers
Michael (deceased)	ex-Prince of Tara, 1600-3096	Death, Battle
Montieth	Prince of Dalrig, b. 1932	Death
Isra (deceased)	ex-Prince of Pella, 2001-3078	Battle
Khora (deceased)	ex-Princess of Pella 2014-3419	Vision
Niomi (deceased)	ex-Princess of Icehaven, 2014-3089	Healer
Yendra	Cmdr of the Bulwark, b. 2133	Vision

Children of Prince Michael

	Title	Powers
Marcus (deceased)	Duke, Bulwark, 1944-3420	Battle
Mona	Chancellor, Ooste, b. 2014	Vision
Dania (deceased)	Lady of Tara, 2099-3096	Battle
Yordi (deceased)	Lady of Tara, 2153-3096	Death

Children of Prince Montieth

	Title	Powers
Amber	Lady of Dalrig, b. 2035	Death
Jade	Adjutant of the Circuit, b. 2511	Death

Children of Prince Isra

	Title	Powers
Irno (deceased)	Eldest son of Isra, 2017-3420	Battle
Berno (deceased)	'The Mortal', 2018-2097	None
Garno (deceased)	Warrior, 2241-3078	Battle
Lerno (deceased)	Warrior, 2247-3078	Battle

Vana	Lostwell Returnee, b. 2319	Location
Marno (deceased)	Warrior, 2321-3063	Battle
Collo	Courtier in Pella, b. 2328	None
Bonna (deceased)	Warrior, 2598-3078	Shape-Shifter
Aila	Has left the City, b. 2652	Shape-Shifter
Kano (deceased)	Adj. of the Bulwark, 2788-3420	Battle
Teno (deceased)	Warrior, 2870-3078	Battle

Children of Princess Khora

Salvor	Royal Advisor, b. 2201	Vision
Balian (deceased)	Warrior, 2299-3096	Battle
Lydia	Gov. of Port Sanders, b. 2304	Healer
Naxor	Lostwell Returnee, b. 2401	Vision
Ikara	Courtier in Pella, b. 2499	Battle
Doria	Royal Courtier, b. 2600	None

Children of Princess Niomi

Rand (deceased)	Warrior, 2123-3089	Battle
Yvona	Governor of Icehaven, b. 2175	Healer
Samara (deceased)	Lady of Icehaven, 2239-3089	Battle
Daran (deceased)	Lord of Icehaven, 2261-3063	Battle

Children of Princess Yendra

Kahlia (deceased)	Warrior, 2599-3096	Vision
Neara (deceased)	Warrior, 2601-3089	Battle
Yearna (deceased)	Lady of the Circuit, 2604-3096	Healer

THE NINE TRIBES OF THE CITY

The Nine Tribes of the City (in 3422, when *City Ascendant* takes place)

There are nine distinct tribes inhabiting the City. Three were in the area from the beginning, and the other six were created in two waves of expansion.

The Original Three Tribes – Auldan (pop. 300 000) Auldan is the oldest part of the City. United by the Union Walls (completed in 1040), it combined the three original tribes and their towns, along with the shared town of **Ooste**, which houses the Royal Palace.

1. **The Rosers** – (their town is **Tara**, est. Yr. 1.) The first tribe to reach the peninsula where the City is located. Began farming there in the sunward regions, until attacks from the Reapers forced them into building the first walled town. **Prince Michael** ruled until his death in 3096. **Queen Amalia** ruled until her expulsion in 3420.

2. **The Gloamers** – (their town is **Dalrig**, est. Yr. 40.) Arrived shortly after the Rosers, farming the iceward side of the peninsula. Like them, they fought with the Reapers, and built a walled town to stop their attacks. **Lady Amber** rules from Greylin Palace in Dalrig.

3. **The Reapers** – (their town is **Pella**, est. Yr. 70.) Hunter/Gatherer tribe that arrived after the more sedentary Rosers and Gloamers. Settled in the plains between the other two tribes. More numerous than either the Rosers or the Gloamers, but are looked down on as more rustic. **Prince Isra** ruled until 3078. **King Daniel and Queen Emily** ruled the City from Cuidrach Palace, with **Lord Salvor** as their advisor.

The Next Three Tribes – Medio (pop. 220 000) Originally called 'New Town', this part of the City was its first major expansion; and was settled from the completion of the Middle Walls (finished in 1697 and originally known as the Royal Walls). This portion of the City was devastated by the Greenhide incursion in 3420. The name 'Medio' derives from the old Evader word for 'Middle'.

1. **The Icewarders** – (their town is **Icehaven**, est. 1657.) Settlers from Dalrig originally founded a new colony at Icehaven to assist in the building of the Middle Walls, as the location was too cold and dark for the greenhides. After the wall's completion, many settlers stayed, and a new tribe was founded. Separated from Icehaven by mountains, a large number of Icewarders also inhabit the central lowlands bordering the Circuit. **Princess Niomi** ruled until her death in 3089. Her daughter, **Lady Yvona**, governs from Alkirk Palace in Icehaven.

2. **The Sanders** – (their town is **Port Sanders**, est. 1702.) When the Middle Walls were completed, a surplus population of Rosers and Reapers moved into the new area, and the tribe of the Sanders was founded, based around the port town on the Warm Sea. Related closely to the Rosers in terms of allegiance and culture. **Lady Lydia** governs from Tonetti Palace in Port Sanders.

3. **The Evaders** – (their town is the **Circuit**, est. 2133.) The only tribe ethnically unrelated to the others, the Evaders started out as refugees fleeing the greenhides, and they began arriving at the City c.1500. They were taken in, and then used to help build the Middle Walls. The other tribes of Auldan and Medio look down on them as illiterate savages. Former rulers include **Princess Yendra** and **Lady Ikara**.

The Final Three Tribes – The Bulwark (pop. 280 000) The Bulwark is the defensive buffer that protects the City from greenhide attack. Work commenced on the Great Walls after the decisive Battle of the Children of the Gods in 2247, when the greenhides were pushed back hundreds of miles. They were completed c.2300, and the new area of the City was settled. The Bulwark faced the worst destruction in the greenhide incursion of 3420.

1. **The Blades** – (est. 2300.) The military tribe of the City. The role of the Blades is to defend the Great Walls from the unceasing attacks by the Greenhides. Officials from the Blades also police and govern the other two tribes of the Bulwark. Their headquarters is the **Fortress of the Lifegiver**, the largest bastion on the Great Walls, where **Lady Jade** was the commander.

2. **The Hammers** – (est. 2300.) The industrial proletariat of the Bulwark. Prior to the establishment of the Aurelian monarchy, the Hammers were effectively slaves, forbidden to leave their tribal area, which produces much of the finished goods for the rest of the City.

3. **The Scythes** – (est. 2300.) The agricultural workers of the Bulwark, who produce all that the region requires. Prior to the establishment of the Aurelian monarchy, they were slaves in all but name. Eighty percent of Scythes were killed in the greenhide incursion.

NOTE ON THE CALENDAR

In this world there are two moons, a larger and a smaller (fragments of the same moon). The larger orbits in a way similar to Earth's moon, and the year is divided into seasons and months.

Due to the tidally-locked orbit around the sun, there are no solstices or equinoxes, but summer and winter exist due to the orbit being highly elliptical. There are two summers and two winters in the course of each solar revolution, so one 'year' (365 days) equates to half the time it takes for the planet to go round the sun (730 days). No Leap Days required.

New Year starts at with the arrival of the Spring (Freshmist) storms, on Thanalion Day

New Year's Day – **Thanalion Day** (approx. 1st March)
   -- **Freshmist** (snow storms, freezing fog, ice blizzards, high winds from iceward)
     - Malikon (March)
     - Amalan (April)
     -- **Summer** (hot, dry)
     - Mikalis (May)
     - Montalis (June)
     - Izran (July)
     - Koralis (August)
     -- **Sweetmist** (humid, stormy, high winds from sunward, very wet)
     - Namen (September)
     - Balian (October)
     -- **Winter** (cold, dry)
     - Marcalis (November)
     - Monan (December)

- Darian (January)
- Yordian (February)

Note – the old month of Yendran was renamed in honour of Princess Khora's slain son Lord Balian, following the execution of the traitor Princess Yendra.

AUTHOR'S NOTES

OCTOBER 2021

Thank you for reading City Ascendant, the last book of the "City Trilogy" – I hope you enjoyed it.

City Ascendant deals a lot with the concept of redemption, and I wanted to explore some questions in this area. Can people do things that are so evil they can never be forgiven? What if they genuinely regret their previous actions, and strive to make amends? These questions, and others like them, went round and round my head during the drafting and editing of City Ascendant. Not everyone might agree with the conclusion to the book but, in the end, I decided to let the characters speak for themselves.

Now, onward to Dragon Eyre!

RECEIVE A FREE MAGELANDS ETERNAL SIEGE BOOK

Building a relationship with my readers is very important to me.

Join my newsletter for information on new books and deals and you will also receive a Magelands Eternal Siege prequel novella that is currently EXCLUSIVE to my Reader's Group for FREE.

www.ChristopherMitchellBooks.com/join

ABOUT THE AUTHOR

Christopher Mitchell is the author of the Magelands epic fantasy series.

For more information:
www.christophermitchellbooks.com
info@christophermitchellbooks.com

Printed in Great Britain
by Amazon

42961558R00270